BLOODMIND

Liz Williams is the daughter of a stage magician and a gothic novelist, and currently lives in Somerset. She received a PhD in philosophy of science from Cambridge, and her subsequent career has ranged from reading tarot cards on the Palace Pier to teaching in central Asia. Her short stories have been published in *Asimov's, Interzone, The Third Alternative* and *Visionary Tongue*, and she is the co-editor of the recent anthology *Fabulous Brighton. Bloodmind* is her eighth novel.

Also by Liz Williams

The Ghost Sister

Empire of Bones

The Poison Master

Nine Layers of Sky

Banner of Souls

Darkland

The Snake Agent

LIZ WILLIAMS

BLOODMIND

TOR

First published 2007 by Tor

This edition published 2008 by Tor
an imprint of Pan Macmillan Ltd
Pan Macmillan, 20 New Wharf Road, London N1 9RR
Basingstoke and Oxford
Associated companies throughout the world
www.panmacmillan.com

ISBN 978-0-330-44206-0

1 3 5 7 9 8 6 4 2

A CIP catalogue record for this book is available from
the British Library.

Typeset by Intype Libra Ltd
Printed and bound in Great Britain
by Mackays of Chatham plc, Chatham, Kent

For Tanith, for inspiration

ACKNOWLEDGEMENTS

Heartfelt thanks go to:

My agent, Shawna McCarthy
My editors, Peter Lavery and Stef Bierwerth
My parents
My unfailingly patient writing group
– and finally, to Trevor for all his encouragement, good humour and for being here . . .

ONE

PLANET: MUSPELL (VALI)

The other women of the Skald had crept from the room, leaving me alone with Idhunn's body. The investigation team had been summoned and were on their way. Someone had opened one of the tall windows of the lamp room and the sea air streamed in, diminishing the reek of death.

I stood in the fading twilight and looked down at her: friend, mentor, Skald superior and the woman I credited with saving my life. And now she was nothing more than a mutilated bag of flesh in a slow seep of blood. For what seemed like a long time, I could not look away, but eventually I dragged my gaze up from the filleted corpse. I felt like the ghost of the Vali Hallsdottir I had been so little time ago: Skald assassin, just returned from a mission, home safe, or so I'd thought. But now I was no more than a glimpse in the curve of the lamp casing, face a white oval in the gathering shadows, the scars livid against my skin as though those long-ago claw-tracks had only just been made. The hollow of my empty eye-socket was a well of dark and my good eye looked wide and sightless. I put a hand to the breastplate of my borrowed alien armour and it felt as though my heartbeat was pounding a hole through the leather. The gleam of

Muspell's evening star shone over my shoulder and it struck me then that the thing on the floor at my feet had been named for that star, but the spirit that ruined corpse had housed would never again stand at the windows of the lamp room and look for its burn in the heavens. I dropped to my knees beside Idhunn, taking care not to disturb the pooling blood.

'Idhunn,' I whispered. I reached out a hand, but did not touch her. Instead, I held my palm a little distance above her body and, closing my good eye, I called upon the senses that on Muspell are known as the seith, as if I shut off my physical vision in order to look through my ruined eye, like those old tales from ancient Earth where the people of the huldra and the fey steal sight away, only to replace it with other gifts. My ancestors had brought those old tales with them across the star roads, but they were only stories, nothing more. My nightmares were real.

The impression of another person present was very strong. I felt that I could see a shrouded figure crouching over Idhunn's body, making the first of many delicate cuts in order to detach my friend's spine. I could even smell this other person: a pungent, musty odour like an old and bloody cupboard. But there was nothing more. A haze lay over the body, a deliberate masking. I rose, still with my eye closed, and walked to the door. The trail led no further. Whoever had committed this murder had taken pains to cover their tracks in the non-physical world, and if that was the case, then the likelihood was that they had also gone to the trouble to hide more tangible evidence, too. And that suggested one thing to me: *vitki*.

A cry came from beyond the windows of the lamp room: a thin shocked wail. For a moment, I thought it was a seabird calling, but then the seith kicked in once more, telling me it was a human sound. It had come from somewhere in the fortress below me.

I ran to the windows of the lamp room and looked out. The sky was stained red in the east, all crimson and flame, but Muspell's moon, Loki, was already well up and casting a pale light across the water.

In the light of the moon a ship was riding. As I stared at it, I felt myself grow cold. When I'd come into the Rock a scant hour ago, returning from out-world, nothing had shown on the navigational array of my little seawing. In order to make a swift return to the Rock, I'd avoided the main naval forces of the Reach, which were gearing up for war with Darkland; something this size would have shown up like a bonfire on the screens. Yet I'd seen nothing and no one at the Rock had mentioned it, even during the traumatic aftermath of Idhunn's murder.

And anyway, this was no ship of the Reach.

The thing was huge, perhaps a quarter of a mile from stern to prow. Not as big as the gigantic war-wings that I'd seen being constructed in the shipyards of Darkland, but big enough. Frigate on top, bristling with antennae and gun placements, blast-cannons all along the sides, but icebreaker below. I could see the long ram of the ship riding just under the water, catching the moonlight. It bore no insignia that I noticed, but as I watched, a spiral of wings, shadow on shadow, coiled up from behind one of the spiked masts and soared upward towards the moon. Then, in the blink of an eye, they were gone. I'd seen those birds before – Darkland ravens, not real birds at all, but representations of information, metaphorical constructs carrying data between the vitki. A vitki ship, then.

But in that, I was wrong.

I turned from the window and hastened for the door. Going down the steep spiral stairs, I ran into an old woman, hair streaming in disarray, another one with a face like a ghost's. Hlin Recksdottir, one of the Skald elders, clawed at my arm.

'The vitki – the vitki are here! Vali, I've given orders for everyone to arm themselves. We'll fight them if we have to.'

'Has that ship sent any communication?' I asked, but I wasn't really expecting it to be a social call. The vitki were old enemies and the Reach had already gone to war with them, with the whole of Darkland. The vitki ship would aim to take the Rock and the Skald, controlling the strategic shipping lanes that led through into the most developed part of the coast. I clenched my fists to stop my hands from shaking.

'Nothing.' Hlin's shocked face grew grim. 'We've asked them what they want – as if it wasn't obvious. I've put the data stores on a destruct timer.'

There were backups in the Skald keeps on the mainland, on the secret islands on which we maintained tiny outposts. I nodded my agreement. Leaving Hlin to follow, I bolted down the stairs to the main doors. Women raced around me: the Rock going into lockdown. As I reached the primary entrance, the blast-doors slammed shut, leaving us in a sudden, eerie silence. The guards were already at their posts, weapons raised. The rest of us in the hall – Hlin, myself, a handful of Skald members – stopped dead, waiting. I don't know what made me glance up into the dark arch of the ceiling, but I did so and against old cold stone I saw a single feather drifting down, caught in a shaft of light. Mesmerized, I watched it spiral to rest on the floor and as it touched the flagstones, it disappeared. I had a split-second glimpse of each pinion streaming out, turning into data: numbers, letters, co-ordinates, streaking across the floor and melting into the walls. Next moment, there was the creak and grind of hydraulics as the blast-doors started to go up. They had hacked the fortress.

I seized Hlin by the arm and pulled her behind a desk. I'd not even had time to grasp a proper weapon: all I had was the alien bow I'd brought back as a memento from Mondhile, a light, quick thing, lethally effective against a medieval foe but a useless antique against modern weaponry. Better that than nothing, though. I had three arrows in the shoulder pack: I notched one of them up and waited to fire.

My chance came in the next minute. The main doors blew open and behind the boil of light and fire I saw someone standing on the steps. I didn't wait. I drew back and loosed the arrow, just as one of the Skald guards opened fire with a much more effective handgun. But neither bow nor finelight made any appreciable difference. My arrow clattered harmlessly to the floor after hitting an invisible shield; the finelight bolt dissipated into a shower of sparks.

The person stepped forward. A black-and-silver uniform encased a tall female form. Her hands were gloved, but the dataflow of enhancements ran across the exposed skin of her face. Blue eyes sparked silver, set in a gaunt countenance. White birds, like albino crows, circled around her head. And again a single feather fell. The woman reached out and took it and her gloved hand closed over it. I thought I saw her smile.

She said, 'My name is Rhi Glyn Apt; I am a commander of the Morvern Morrighanu. Put your weapons down. You're out-numbered. There's a blast-cannon trained on the keep. We have your access codes.' A pause. 'I suggest you consider terms of surrender.'

It was useless to believe that I would tell them nothing. They may not have been vitki, but they were still from Darkland and they seemed to know all the tricks.

Glyn Apt had me taken to the lower regions of the keep: what had once been a dungeon in the older, and bloodier, days of the Reach, and was now used as a meditation chamber. It was windowless, built of thick, dovetailed slabs of stone, furnished only with a settle. The Morrighanu commander took the settle, and had me bonded to the wall. It wasn't torture, not quite, but she made it clear that there wasn't going to be a choice. First, she had me injected with a mnemonic over-ride, and then she wired up the map implant in my head to her own information system. To anyone who watched, it would have looked as though a white bird perched on my shoulder, plucking at the socket of my eye.

They wanted to know about Mondhile. They made me relive it, over and over again.

The tower. Gemaley's home, rising mottled from the rock, the stone lit by its own shifting light. Inside, a ruin containing a bloody heart: the energy well that motivated both Gemaley and the animal pack that lived there. My former lover Frey, prowling through the dungeons, luring me with weird vitki promises that I still didn't understand.

Then, my escape to a nearby town – an ordinary, not-yet-tech settlement, transformed by the bloodmind, the feral state into which the Mondhaith were prone to fall. Gemaley's beast pack had attacked then, just to see what would happen. I'd seen elderly grandmothers battling wild animals, and not always losing.

Human and animal. Animal and human.

Why were they asking me all these *questions*?

They made me go through it again, and then again.

I didn't even realize when they'd stopped, or understand that I was no longer in the interrogation chamber. At first I thought I was back in Gemaley's dungeon, but then it changed, shifted, to somewhere alien and smelling of musk, the Hierolath's chamber on Nhem where he had raped me before I'd killed him, and then – still bleak, still cold – the room I'd shared with my brother in Scaraskae and he was the one on top of me, in me and I shrieked as I'd never allowed myself to do in my parents' house, because he would tell them it was my fault—

The Hierolath was dead, and so were Frey and Gemaley. I did not know if my brother still lived and I told myself that I did not care. It should have made a difference.

But knowing, somewhere in back-brain, that Rhi Glyn Apt was witnessing all these events through the mirror of my mind, felt like violation all over again. I suppose some might say it could have been cathartic, but I didn't do catharsis very well: spiralling back to the same old nightmares was like trying to prove the past to myself. Trying to prove, and failing.

When the drugs wore off, and the white raven had sipped the last piece of autobiography from my mind, Glyn Apt came to stand before me. I managed to look her in the face. The valkyrie I had seen in Darkland's capital of Hetla had been perfect, a sculpted ice warrior. Beneath the chasing data, Glyn Apt was not so like that woman, more recognizably human: in her late forties, perhaps more, with pouches under her eyes and the beginning of lines around her mouth. She had not bothered with corrective surgery any more than I had; I could see the tracery of scars around her jaw. Accident or duel? I didn't know enough about the Morrighanu to be able to tell.

She said, 'You used to cut yourself.'

Without asking, she pulled back my shirt sleeve and revealed the myriad scars on my arm. An adolescent way of coping, and yet I'd kept my scars, just as she'd kept her own.

'I haven't done that in years,' I said, and hated the way the words mumbled out.

'No,' Glyn Apt replied. I saw silver spark behind her eyes: something transmitted? Something incoming? 'Now you get others to do it for you instead.' There was no mockery in her voice; she spoke as someone making a statement of fact. She turned my face to one side, not gently: I could feel the power of the servors in her glove. Turn up the ratio and she'd be able to rip off my head as easily as a fenris. Data streamed across her face like moonlight. As though she'd read my thoughts she said, 'Those scars on your face. They were made by an animal, your records say. You were put on an ingsgaldir initiation, for all that you are neither vitki nor of Darkland.'

'My ex-lover was vitki. Frey. You must know that by now. He put me through an initiation, with a fenris out on the ice. It would have been nice if he'd told me that it was initiation. At the time, I thought he was trying to kill me.'

Again, I thought Glyn Apt might have smiled.

'You'd have done better to seek out the Morrighanu than the vitki,' she said.

'You said it yourself,' I told her. 'I'm not from Darkland.'

But that night, when they'd set me free of the wall and put me in a cell, it was Darkland of which I dreamed.

I was once more standing on the headland overlooking the city of Hetla. It was night and Darkland's capital was under curfew. Only a few red lights flickered along the coast, denoting observation turrets and anti-aircraft installations, baleful scarlet eyes in the darkness. The only sounds, apart from the constant thunder of the spring sea, were the boom and crash of construction work across the fjord in the wing-yards. In my mind's eye I could still see those massive war-wings sitting in dry-dock, awaiting completion before being sent out across the ocean to the Reach, my home.

Then, above the sounds of preparation for war, I heard another noise: a thin, high singing, very sweet. And in my dream I remembered that when the equinoctial tides sweep across the seas of the north, the semi-sentient species known as the selk come down with the arctic melt water, and sing. This voice I now heard was beautiful and cold, and it paralysed me. I stood, suspended in the night, with the ocean ahead of me and the deep forest behind, and listened to the song of the selk as it curdled my blood to frost.

'Do you hear that?' a voice said at my elbow. I looked up, to see the vitki Thorn Eld. Friend of Frey's, or foe? I'd never really known, but I wasn't surprised to see him there. Eld had known all about me, after all, and when he'd interrogated me in Darkland he hadn't even had to give me any drugs to get the information. It had been as if Eld had been living in my head.

'Yes, I can hear it,' I said.

'When you killed Frey,' Eld remarked, his round face bland in Loki's light, 'you used a beast pack to do so. A proper ingsgaldir in the ancient sense, to link yourself with the world, with animal mind, with a gestalt. Do you think you can use the selk in the same way?'

'It's not even occurred to me,' I told him with perfect truth, but suddenly we were out on the ice, and the selk were surging up under my feet, shattering the floe, sending us down into cold dark and I was reaching out for Eld, to save him or to help myself, I did not know. But Eld was already gone and—

I woke, into freezing air, gasping for breath. It was a relief to find myself still in the cell, though the heating had evidently gone off. The knowledge of Idhunn's death came crashing in on me all over again.

Yet the selk-song went on. It was coming from beyond the cell, penetrating the chamber and lodging inside my head, echoing against the walls of my skull like the rush of blood when you hold a shell to your ear. I waited for a moment, but the song continued insistent and summoning.

A moment after that, Glyn Apt was there on the other side of the cell shield. The dataflow had been temporarily switched off and her face was unremarkable without it, pale and plain, with blunt features. Without the silver underlay of information, her eyes were a faded blue, like spring ice.

'Can you hear that?' she asked, just like Thorn Eld had asked me in my dream.

'It's not easy to miss.'

'It's coming from a group of the selk.'

'They're taking a risk, with a Morrighanu warship floating several hundred yards offshore,' I commented.

Glyn Apt frowned. I didn't know why she was choosing to confide in me on the subject. 'The Morrighanu have no quarrel with the selk. That's a vitki matter.'

'It's become a Darkland matter, and you're from Darkland. I saw those sheds outside Hetla.'

Glyn Apt gave a little nod. 'I noticed, from your interrogation. I repeat, it's nothing to do with us. We're a different sect from the vitki; you know that. Morvern isn't Hetla.'

'Why are you bothering to justify yourself to me?' I had no real idea what the connection was between vitki and Morrighanu, though the link with the valkyries, the female sect of the vitki, was much clearer. Though I'd heard that the Morrighanu were a sect of Darkland's far north, and that was after all where Morvern lay, I didn't know how all these Darkland security forces interrelated.

'Because the selk are asking for you,' Glyn Apt said.

She even let me out of the cell, but under heavy guard. It was in any case useless to try anything under the circumstances; I was weaponless and although the seith offered opportunities for disguise, it wouldn't have worked against people who were already versed in such matters. Glyn Apt took me up the stairs to the guard room and showed me the monitor that scanned the foot of the Rock on the western side.

Lights played along the barnacle-encrusted ledges, ready to illuminate any vessel that might be approaching the fortress. I saw nothing, except rock and wave and the great bulk of the Morrighanu warship, turning a little on the swell of the tide. Then – I was not sure if it was only the shadow of a wave, but it moved again and I saw that it was indeed a selk. It turned its blunt head to the camera as though it sensed me watching.

'Ask it what it wants,' Glyn Apt demanded.

I leaned forward and spoke softly into the monitor, tracking the speaker setting.

'Are you out there? Can you hear me? Can you understand me?'

I knew that the selk had their own language of Shelta, but it was only at certain times of the year that they possessed sufficient sentience to speak it. The tabula hummed as it translated my Gaelacht.

Silence. The song had stopped. I had just convinced myself that there was nothing out there after all when a voice like running water said, 'I hear you.'

'Is it you who sings? Why?'

'We have been looking for you. We came before, but you were not here. You saw our siblings, captured.'

Why hadn't the Skald told me that the selk had come looking? But then I realized that there had not been time, and Idhunn's death would have driven it out of everyone's mind. 'Those tanks outside Hetla? Yes, I saw them. I could do nothing to help them.'

I didn't like sounding so defensive, when it was nothing more than the truth. I think I expected some kind of protest from the selk, some criticism, but it said nothing. And I was surprised that Glyn Apt had brought me out here to speak with them at all, rather than blasting the selk out of the water. But perhaps it was true that the Morrighanu had a different relationship with them to the vitki.

'Tell it to come closer,' Glyn Apt hissed.

'Why? What are you planning to do?'

She gave me a glance of contempt. 'Nothing. If I'd intended them any harm, I'd have done it by now.'

'Come into the light,' I called, and the selk did so, gliding with surprising swiftness and ease over the rocks. Seen through the monitor, it was larger and sleeker than the purely animal sealstock that thronged these northern waters. Its complex, flanged nose and the gills that collared its throat glistened with seawater. Its eyes were obsidian and alien and sad.

'What do you understand, about my kind?' it continued.

I hesitated. 'I know that the selk were engineered, genetically, by my ancestors.' It's one thing to know that most of the non-human life on one's homeworld has been created and altered, an unholy mash of genes, but it seemed an awkward thing to be discussing this with one of the results. It made me think of Mondhile, where humans had been altered instead.

'You understand that we are now close to the time when our self-awareness will be lost, until the waters begin to grow cold once more? When sentience is gone from us, we will not be able to help our captured kin.'

'And you're asking me – the Skald – for help?' I thought of Idhunn's ruined body in the Rock's medical ward, of the vacuum of power she had left behind her, now filled by the Morrighanu, and of the oncoming war. At the moment, the Skald was not in the strongest position to help anyone.

'I am asking anyone who might listen. Most of your kind see us as beasts, nothing more.'

And that was true enough. It was illegal to hunt the selk,

at least in the Reach, and during their periods of sentience it carried a murder charge. But even in the Reach I had seen what I was certain had been selk fur, on the collars and coats of the pinch-faced wealthy, in plain view on the streets of Tiree.

'Your kin are imprisoned in Darkland,' I explained to the selk now. 'And you must know that we not only have no jurisdiction there – at all – but that we are also on the brink of war and this fortress has been captured.' I did not look at Glyn Apt, and she said nothing.

The selk shifted uneasily against the wet shadows of the rocks. 'We know this. Why else were our kin taken?'

It took a moment for this to sink in. 'You mean the selk in those tanks are undergoing some kind of preparation for the Darkland war effort?'

'So we believe.'

'Do you know what it is? What the vitki are trying to do with them?' That was Glyn Apt, surprising me. But perhaps it shouldn't have been so startling that the Morrighanu weren't informed about vitki plans, given the nature of Darkland and its sectarian in-fighting.

'Or what they were being used for,' I murmured. I thought I might know the answer to that. Glyn Apt ignored me.

'We do not. But ourselves and the kind you call the vitki have a long history, like the deeps beneath the ice, cold and black and little seen. Once, there was war between us.'

'War?' I knew nothing about this and this time I couldn't keep the surprise from my voice. Beside me, Glyn Apt shifted as if restless. But the selk itself spoke in so musical a tone that I was sure there were cadences, nuances, that were missed by my limited human hearing. 'When was this?'

'A thousand thousand seasons ago.'

This was not a great deal of help: the selk calculated time differently to humans and there was little point in asking it to translate into our years if the tabula could not do so.

'Who won the war?' I moved on, picturing the icefields running red with the blood of the selk. Apart from a brief period in their long bleak history, the vitki had always been in possession of technology; the selk had not.

'We won. But not without great loss.'

'You won a war, against men with machines?'

In the dim window of the monitor, the selk's face contorted strangely, the ruffles of the gills rippling as though a strong wind blew across it. Perhaps the selk smiled. I could not tell.

'The outcome of a battle may depend on the place of its fighting. They followed us onto the icefields, at the start of the spring thaw. They thought we were few, and failing. But our kind, The People, sang to the ice and in the spring it is brittle and treacherous. It gave way beneath our enemies. They thought the made-skins they wore would save them, but there were more of The People under the ice, many more, and the enemy were attacked as soon as they were in the sea. The cold killed as many as we did. They did not make that mistake again. They kept to their land of black glass cliffs and great mosses, we to the poles and these islands, where—' the selk paused, with unexpected tact, '—our losses *are* fewer.'

'But if the selk and the vitki were to encounter one another again, on ground more congenial to the vitki—' something was nagging at the back of my mind, '—do you think it likely that your kind would lose?' Considering those great war-wings I myself thought it more than likely: in fact, a certainty. But the selk hesitated before saying, slowly, 'I do not know.'

'Tell me this. Do your kind possess weapons?' *The People sang to the spring ice*. That suggested some kind of innate sonic capability. But the selk answered, with only a hint of irony in its musical voice, 'Why? Your kind see us as no more than beasts, and soon, so we will be.'

Not going to tell me, then. I could not blame it. I thought again of the furs worn by the rich of Tiree. And the selk was right. When they entered their animal awareness, they would have no memory of their captured kin, so it did not matter what weaponry they might own.

'Look,' I said. 'These are difficult times. I can't promise you anything.'

'This was no more than I expected,' the selk replied, dipping its head, whether in acknowledgement, disappointment or respect, I did not know. 'I will come again, on the next tide. Will you meet me?'

'She'll be here,' Glyn Apt said, surprising me again. For sure I'd still be a prisoner, but Glyn Apt's willingness to let me talk to the selk was unexpected. It still didn't make sense to me.

The selk slid rapidly to the edge of the rocks and was gone into silver water. The guards moved swiftly forward as if unleashed and I was taken back into the fortress. Before they put me in the cell, I caught a last glance at a monitor, out to sea past the warship. I do not know what I was looking for – a wake, perhaps, of something swimming? But there was nothing there, only the great drowning moon on the horizon's edge, and the cold and endless waves.

TWO

They say I am a weapon.

I surprised them, I think, by the nature of the killing, but why should one hold back, when one is good at something? After that, they asked me if I knew why I had these abilities.

'You tell me,' I said. 'You brought me here, after all.'

I hoped to startle them. They did not think I knew this, or so I believed. But they just smiled, the old woman and the old man. They said, 'Do you remember life, when you were a girl?'

'I remember the heat,' I told them. *The burn of the day outside the cavern walls, in the sinks and crevices, sun baking off sand into a greenglass sky*. I didn't like the heat but the other women did, and could not understand why I crept from it. But then, I was different in many ways.

'Nothing more than that?' That was the old woman, very sly.

'I remember the men coming, and my sister crying.'

'Do you remember your mother's death?' That was the old man, avid for pain, and it was my turn to smile.

'Should I have done?'

'Did you not love her?'

'Should I have done?' I said again, remembering my

mother clutching and grasping at the bars of the cage, her eyes as white and mad as moonlight.

The old woman and the old man did not answer that, and they left me alone to go my own way, back into the forest. They did not bother to attempt a memory 'ride. They'd tried that before and I'd called on the world beyond, summoning figures from the shadows of my head. Warriors with animal faces, intestines hanging through the rents in their armour, beasts with wicked, knowing red eyes. All the figures from my dreams that had comforted me as a child. I had sent one of my interrogators mad, the old woman told me later with a kind of pride.

'You are a weapon,' she had said, after the events in Morvern. That was all, and there was no talk of reward. Why be rewarded, after all, for that which you love?

THREE

PLANET: NHEM (HUNAN)

My children haunted the bell tower. I didn't see them every day, just sometimes, and usually it was a sign of storms. Perhaps the violent air conjured them up, drew their spirits down from the north. They looked just as they had when I'd escaped: First Joy with his small stern face, Boy-Next-Time's buttoned-up mouth and anxious eyes, Luck-Still-to-Come no more than a little thing. It's likely that the girls were put to death when my going was discovered, but I don't know for sure.

I didn't dream about First Joy as often as the girls: it was as though he ignored me in my dreams just as he'd ignored me in life, following House Father around like a hound. But Boy-Next-Time and Luck-Still-to-Come were never far away, just out of sight or round a corner, watching everything I did.

They were different, in my dreams. I know perfectly well now that my daughters had no more awareness than I: they were little animals, nothing more. Yet in my dreams, we spoke together and they told me everything about their day – the beetle they'd seen in the garden, with its shiny green back; the bird in the leaves; the flying machine that had streaked across the sky and frightened them so that they ran indoors.

We didn't speak of House Father in these dreams, and yet of course in that life he'd been the centre of the household. We crept around, always trying to please. The girls used to bring him presents from the garden but he never saw them as gifts, just as something the hound might bring in.

In the early days, he'd pull me away from my duties to go inside me, almost absent-minded, and I remember hating and not understanding it. I never got used to it. It is a joy now, not to be touched by anyone. He didn't touch the girls, but that was because they were too young: it would change when their blood came, as I now knew too well. I hadn't understood it in my own Father, either, and I suppose that was where the hating came from. But it was the way of things. We couldn't complain, for we didn't have words. Now, I like to think that I'd have killed him if he'd laid a finger on my daughters, but this is just a dream. I'd have shut my eyes instead. I've never heard of a woman killing a grown man, not even after the change. House Father, for instance: so big, such a strong man. I don't say that admiringly. When he hit me, my head rang for hours.

So it was not surprising, in a way, that he made no appearance in my dreams. I had cut him out of them, and it was just me and the girls, speaking of things that mattered.

If they were alive now, they would be a man and two women, not these little ghosts. At one time I thought that the guilt might fade, and that made it even worse, driving it deeper and deeper into me until it spilled plentifully out like harvest. Then I realized that the guilt was never going to go away, and strangely, that made me feel better: the vicious wheel stopped and I could settle down to simply feeling bad. People like Seliye tried to console me.

'You didn't know what you were doing. You didn't understand. How could you have done? You had no choice, none of us did,' – on and on in her grating voice, all of it true, all of it useless. For *now* I knew, *now* I had knowledge.

I'd disobeyed House Father.

I'd fled from Iznar.

I'd abandoned my children and so now they haunted the bell tower, like the efreets that rose up to catch the insects that come after storms. I saw their faces glancing around the corners of doors, a running form out of the corner of my eye, a whisper in the night. I couldn't go and find them. I would die. But if they had been free, would they, I wonder, have tried to find me? First Joy would not have done, I am sure: he was House Father's son. In the dreams, I remember the men making their noises in the corner, my head going up when I heard the grunt of my name, or a recognizable command. To First Joy, I was the moving lump that gave him food and made his bed, slowly – I remember that – tucking the corners of the blanket down in the way I had been trained.

But the girls – when the women of the colony talked of such things, we treated it as a mystery, as powerful as the mystery of who built this ruined city. We'd had no speech, before, and yet I'd understood my daughters and they'd understood me. Slowness, stupidity, language's lack, and we still knew what each of us thought. If we could do that still – the women say, in the language that now seems to separate us rather than bring us closer. If we could do that still, and keep what we have gained. But it seems that there's always and ever a price. Their haunting is the price I pay – their haunting, and the smell of roots and earth that comes over me every time I think about Iznar.

But I'm like a ghost myself. We all are. We can't exist. We are not real, we have no place and no substance. We are a nightmare in the minds of men, who have yet allowed us to remain here, something that doesn't make sense.

But the colony looks real enough, when I look out of the window of the bell tower, across the yellow-brown roofs and steaming earth to the black line of the sea. The men of the north will not come to the sea; they fear it, so our spies have said, but I don't know why. True, its waters burn if the skin is held in them too long, but the women of this colony have become used to it, our skin hardening even further, our hands like tools as we burrow in the hot sand for the shellfish and the shore scorpions.

I know exactly how many of us there are, down to the last incomer. Four hundred women today, while yesterday there were four hundred and one, and the day before that, four hundred and three. The fever took its toll; we buried twenty in all, outside the city walls.

Not a great number of women, but enough. Last year, I note from my records for this same month, there were three hundred and eighty. Our numbers fall and rise, rise and fall, like the pull of the little moons. But we won't go on to the world's end. We are here on borrow-time, and I do not understand why we are here at all.

Sometimes I wander through the temple, up to the bell tower. We call it a temple, but we've really no idea whether this is what it was. More borrowing, of the home of someone long dead; someone who wasn't even human. The women – myself included – like to think of it as a temple, to something like the Hierolath, but female, because this comforts us. But maybe the figures it depicts weren't Hierolaths at all. Maybe they weren't even female. We just don't know, and so we change them to fit our dreams, since there's no longer any chance that they might disturb us by being real.

I visit them once or twice a day, going from my own quarters up the long, winding flights of stairs. It's a bird's eye view from up here, the city spread out below, like a map. Up here, the air still smells of salt, but here the smell is faint, almost refreshing, and there's a stiff breeze even on the hottest days. No wonder they built their city here on these rocks. There are sudden, surprising views of city and sea, glimpses where you least expect them.

Everything is an odd size, however. The halls and corridors are much too big, and much too thin. I think of our female Hierolaths as being very tall and flat. There's nothing to show their true size in the wall drawings, which are in the very highest room, just before the bell tower.

This room is open. The roof rests on columns, of a dark red stone marbled with green, and the stone floor is always a little dusted with sand where the wind blows through. The skeleton-winged efreets of the desert gather in the eaves, chittering and rustling, and when you look up in the evening, you see a rash of red eyes. But during the day, it's quiet and still.

From here, you can stop to look at the wall drawings, or go up to the bell tower. The wall drawings are worth looking at. They must be very old – we don't know how old, since we know so little about these lost people, but despite the wind and the sand, they are still bright in the more sheltered places. It's easy to see figures and faces: a tall, slender people. They have huge eyes, golden skins, complicated slits where a nose and mouth should be, shining cowls which cover their heads, like the head-coverings we had to wear in Iznar. Or maybe they are a form of hair. Their hands are more like huge petalled flowers than human fingers, and their arms come from too low in the body. They wear simple things: long slit robes, flowing capes, small perched hats (which suggests hair rather than cowls). It's hard to say what they are doing. They stand in groups. None of them holds anything. Looking at these women – these creatures – I feel a sharp tingling of shame, and then pride. Perhaps that's why I like this place so much: it shows what women can do, the kind of beauty they create. And then it's back to that central question: are they female at all?

The younger women have no such doubts. They are worshipping, they like to say. They love these supposed female-Hierolaths, and they hold rituals here on holy days that bear no relation, as far as any of us can remember, to the holy days of the men's cities, of Iznar and Chem and Bachassar. All of our legends are made up, no more than a few decades old, the same age as our colony. Do something twice here, and it's a tradition. They need something to believe in, and so do I.

On, then, to the bell tower, leaving the goddesses in their green and grey robes behind, leaving the lilies among which they walk, the wetland scenes which must have had some meaning then, and now are lost beneath the dust and the encroaching desert. Was this why they died or went away? Did everything simply dry up and die out? Did they die of the heat and their plants with them? Their world lives on in my dreams, when the colony is arranged on a series of canals, flowering with lotuses like the ones in the men's pools to the north, rushed with reeds.

On to the bell tower, and up.

From the bell tower, which has only one rusted bell hanging on a hook, you can see *oh so far*. All the way to the Middle Mountains, the yellow-banded barrier of the Great Desert. The men's words are so practical, so lacking in imagination. The Great this, the High that. Middle and Lower and Upper. Soldiers' words. We've made our own tongue over the last fifty seasons, but we've borrowed a lot all the same, words seeping up into our newly conscious minds, heard for years and barely understood, or not at all, until the day when the mist lifts and understanding slowly comes.

Our colony is called Tesk, the Edge, in the men's language.

The edge of the world, the edge of the land, the edge of our lives as we cling to this thin strip, this ruined city that is nothing to do with us at all.

From the bell tower, it's obvious just how much of an edge this is. *There* is the black sea, *there* is the gold-and-ochre of the desert beyond. *There* are the mountains, purple with shadows in the evening light, beautiful and far. *There,* tumbling down beneath my feet, are the crumbling sandy tiles of the high chamber and then the city itself. All our little lives beneath my feet, like beetles. Is that how the men think? I hope I'll never know.

I wait, here in the bell tower, until twilight rolls down from the mountains and the bowl of the sky above my head glows with light, and then fades. Below me, the lights start to come on, smouldering at first. Sea-burn lamps, from the weed gathered from the shore, stinking of the sea. A few candles, rarer, made from the casings and the shit of the wax grubs that are found in the cool places between the rocks. Light is rare here, but we don't mind the dark. Those lamps won't burn for long, as people do the last few night tasks, then go to bed. I wait until the efreets spiral up from the temple chamber in a great dark cloud, flit shrieking past my head on their stretched bone wings, hunting insects. I wait until the air grows cool, and then I go back down through the hushed temple, with that unhuman golden gaze upon my back, to my own small room, and there I sleep.

FOUR

Planet: Muspell (Vali)

When I next woke, it was to see Glyn Apt watching me from the other side of the cell field. The data stream was back and her birds were whirling around her head in a snowy cloud.

'I wanted to talk to you,' Glyn Apt said, politely enough but with an undertone that suggested it was an order, 'about the selk.'

'I've told you all I know,' I said. I thought she was referring to the ones in Hetla.

'I'm more interested in your theories,' the Morrighanu said. 'About the selk, and about what the vitki are doing with them.'

I laughed. 'You might almost persuade me that you care. I'm more interested in your own plans for the Rock. How about a trade?'

It was Glyn Apt's turn to laugh. 'I've already strip-mined your brain, Skald girl. Not much of a choice, is it?'

'You've raided my memories. I'm not sure you can get me to spill my thoughts so easily.' Bravado, it's true. The seith field can protect you from only so much and I'd already had the seith ripped from me. Not during the rape on Nhem – I'd killed a man with it there. But later, during Gemaley's attack on me, the seith had been no help at all: the Mondhaith girl had torn it into shreds and tatters. Perhaps Frey had taught her vitki tricks. And perhaps not.

'You killed my leader,' I said. 'Why should I help you any more than I have to?'

Glyn Apt's pointed black eyebrows went up. 'Is that what you think?'

I stared at her. 'Who else?'

'We gained access to this fortress when you were down in the hallway, not before. We've killed only one member of the Skald and she went down fighting. I can prove it to you, if you like. But we didn't kill Idhunn Regnesdottir.'

'Then who the hell did?'

'Tell me what you think about the selk,' Glyn Apt repeated, 'and I'll tell you what I think about Idhunn's murder. How about *that* for a trade?'

'Very well,' I said after a pause. 'I believe that what the vitki are doing to the selk in those tanks is directly related to the war effort.'

'How?'

'To isolate the switch within their genes that causes their sentience to be seasonally switched off, and create a virus which mimics it, to infect those of us of the Reach. To render us unsentient.' If she was closer than she claimed to the vitki, then this wouldn't be news. And if that was the case, then she must be aware that I already knew. If Glyn Apt didn't know – well, that might be knowledge she could use, and which might make her better disposed towards me. Some hope.

There was a long silence. I could not read Glyn Apt's expression. After a while, she said, 'I read your report to your leader – that was what Frey was doing on Mondhile, wasn't he?'

'Yes. He hadn't got very far, luckily for us. I wasn't long behind him. The people there undergo periods where they are unsentient, like the selk. They look human, but sometimes their self-awareness, their consciousness, falls away and they're just human-shaped animals, basically. They call it the Bloodmind. And the Nhemish men do a similar sort of thing, too, to their women. Makes them no better than breeding-cattle.'

Glyn Apt, still unreadable, nodded.

I went on, 'Release a geno-virus, wait for a while, then walk in and enslave us. The Nhemish women might be docile enough. But the Mondhaith weren't – not in this state, Glyn Apt. They turned into predators.' I shivered, thinking of that town turned to nightmare, in which I had become trapped. 'But they were engineered for that, and so, presumably, were the selk, unless it was some kind of side effect. If the vitki could create a geno-virus that would make the rest of us no more than half-alive, to be used as slaves – I can see where their research is going. I'd have said that makes these experiments a critical part of their war effort. And we don't know how far they've come.'

Glyn Apt shifted position.

'Let's assume that Frey went to Mondhile to try and find an answer to this issue of sentience. Say he was sent there as part of the war effort. Yet the vitki I spoke to – Thorn Eld

– he wanted Frey dead. Why so, if Frey was doing the vitki's own work?'

'Perhaps he wasn't,' the Morrighanu said, after a moment. 'Perhaps he was working for himself, against the rest.'

We stared at one another, frustrated, in what felt like a sudden, odd alliance. 'We might never know,' Glyn Apt added. 'The politics of your own Skald are bad enough. Imagine how much back-stabbing goes on in the Darkland sects.'

I sighed. Coming from Glyn Apt, that amounted almost to a girlish confession. If the Morrighanu commander had been telling the truth, the thought of sitting here while Idhunn's killer roamed free was chafing at me. 'And what about the selk that came here?'

'*I'll* go and speak with the selk, if it returns,' Glyn Apt said. She spoke grudgingly, as if she was sparing me some social burden. 'I will tell it that we're in no position to assist others. And now, I have to go.'

'You said you'd tell me your thoughts about Idhunn's murder.'

'Did I?' The Morrighanu commander gave a thin smile. 'Maybe later.'

And later for the selk, too. But the selk were to prove more insistent than either of us knew.

FIVE

Planet: Mondhile (Sedra)

It was on one of the coldest days of the year that I left the clan house forever. I'd insisted on taking the parting ceremony the night before, with the moon Elowen hanging over the eaves of the house and the frost crackling and snapping like a live thing as I walked across the courtyard. I said goodbye to all of them in turn: from the next oldest man to the youngest girl, only recently returned to the world. She turned her face away: she hadn't yet felt the pull back. Some of them miss it and never adjust, but she wasn't one of those. To her, the outside meant beasts and nothingness, hunger and cold and constant danger, without words to describe it all. She could not understand yet why I had to go and why I wouldn't be coming home again.

'It's the way things are done,' I told her. 'Winter's coming. Too many mouths to feed. What, would you have me die in my bed? As though I was cursed with sickness, a weak old thing? You wouldn't want that for me, would you?'

But she just stared into the fire and wouldn't answer. The others took it well, of course.

'So,' Rhane said. 'You're off, then?'

'Off and not coming back.'

'Well, that's as it should be.' She gave an approving nod. I'd always got on well with her. I remembered her birth, her mother gritting her teeth against the pain and not making a sound, as befits a huntress. I remembered, too, the day we'd put the infant out onto the hillside and left her to fend for herself for the next thirteen years. And the day she'd returned, stumbling in out of the howl of the wind, a fierce small thing. Now, Rhane was one of the best huntresses of the clan, still fierce, still small, still doing what had to be done. Just like me.

'When are you off out, then? In the morning?'

'I'll go at dawn. It's been good to me, this clan, this family, you. I'll miss you all.' I said it reluctantly. I don't like sentiment, all those southern poets' ways.

'I know. We'll miss you, too.' Rhane gave me a slanted glance. 'It won't be the same without you telling me what to do, old woman.'

'Or without you ignoring my advice, chit of a girl.' We laughed, and then I said goodnight.

I didn't sleep well. Too many feelings, whisking round the chamber like birds, and none of them settling. I was glad when the thin light started to creep through the paper pane and I could honour my decision and get up. I wasn't planning to take anything with me; it was a pleasure not to have to pack, like going on migration. I told myself that this was all it was: just another migration, my fourth, although this time it was to Eresthahan, to the nowhere-land of the dead. But I'd been there before, before my birth, before the one before that.

I did not take weapons, and in that respect it was nothing like a migration. Even when you're in the bloodmind, it still helps to be armed. Instinct will carry you a long way, further than claws or teeth. But this time, my death would come to meet me and take the form it was destined to take, perhaps at the mouth of visen or altru or wild mur. Or perhaps it would be the cold – I confess, I was rather hoping for that. They say it's a quiet death, though I've never been one for peace and quiet. I wasn't afraid of pain, but I didn't court it, either. I'd no wish to go down fighting. Who are you proving yourself to? It's your death; no one will know how you died, nor care. Perhaps it's part of the men's mysteries, though, some old tradition. Perhaps you're supposed to end up in some particularly appealing part of Eresthahan, with dancing girls and a lot of drink. I'd just be happy when it was over and done with, but I admit, too, that part of me was looking forward to the chance for this one last trip. I hadn't been out in the winter world for years – it hadn't been my time to die, before, and why court lung fever or worse? But now the time had finally come, no more excuses. I was off.

The fire had burned down in the grate overnight and the hall was cold, smelling of ashes. I did not look back. I closed the doors behind me, with the shock of morning air in my lungs and the scent of blood coming from the murs' stable. They'd brought the mur off the mountain pastures only a week ago, and already the snow had crept halfway down the slopes. The mountains blazed in the new light, all glacier gold. I walked slowly to the end of the clan house and the moat twitched and tingled to let me through. I wonder sometimes whether the moats know when we are leaving for the last time, earth-consciousness, whether in their own way they bid farewell. But it's probably just a fancy, nothing more. I stepped over the invisible line of the moat and felt the world shift a little. Then on, across the bridge that crosses the roaring waters of the Sarn, down the stepped streets to the town wall, with the morning town silent around me. We rise late in winter, go to bed early, are glad of the rest.

The walls, and then the town gates. I pushed the gates open, felt again that twitch and snap, of the town moat this time. Then I was pushing the gates shut behind me and walking up through the thorn path that leads to the pastures, the hunting grounds. By now, the golden light had spread to the bottom of the snowfield, though the narrow valley and the torrent were still in shadow.

I knew where I was going. Some people don't. They just wander about, following this line or that line, listening to the energies and patterns below the earth just as they've always done, depending on their particular speciality. My sister had been water-sensitive, but though we came from the same litter, I didn't share that. I was drawn to metal: I could smell it in the earth like the dinner cooking. I'd taken a lot of people to the metal lines, and they'd mined them, too. The town was famous for it: bracelets and cuffs, earrings made out of the darksilver substance. I never used to wear it – it interfered too much, in what I was seeking. But now, the time of my dying, it did not matter and I wore a ring of it in my ear and one on my finger. Vanity perhaps, in a woman so old, long past any attraction to men or her own sex, and yet it felt good to wear it, after so much denial. In my youth I'd been considered a beauty, but that doesn't matter when you grow old. I still had a sharp enough wit and a readiness to laugh and that makes men look past the face. Make them laugh enough and you'll keep them, whilst beauty fades and grows quiet. But this wasn't a time for wit or beauty. I was alone, the town silent behind me, the mountains ahead. I turned my back to my home and went on.

By noon, I had already reached the foothills of the Otrade. It was slow going, with the tracks obscured by snow and the rocks slippery with ice, but I was in no hurry. I took it step by step, until I reached a stone outcrop, jutting high above the valley, and then I stopped and finally looked back.

By now, my breath was wheezing in my chest and it hurt. I didn't know whether this was a premonition of the sickness that would, eventually, kill me, or simply a sign of age.

The satahrach had not been clear about the nature of my death, saying simply that he had looked into my lungs with the aid of the fire and that they were diseased, gone beyond any help his herbs might give me. But I already knew the truth myself. I'd woken too often in the night, my breath rasping, my throat tightening as though a hand had closed around it, the nightmare sense of something huge and heavy crouching at the end of the bed. I dimly remembered being a very small child, and feeling the same sensation, although since we retain so little of our childhoods, I thought I might be making this up. I remembered more than most, after all. Whatever the case, I didn't speak of this to anyone except the satahrach. I did not want the clan's pity nor its care. No *fuss*. Someone in the family always fusses and nothing annoys me more. So I endured the night terrors as best I could, took the herbs that the satahrach gave me, and gradually, as they failed to work, accepted that the time of my death was at hand. And now I was here, in the high cold hills, looking forward to it, because I would be with *her* again.

SIX

Planet: Muspell (Vali)

Inside the cell, I had time to think, but my thoughts circled like the white birds around Glyn Apt's head. The image of Idhunn's body was never far away: it was as though I could glimpse it out of the corner of my eye, a bloody jumble. *Who killed you, Idhunn?* I asked her spirit. Was it the Morrighanu? It must have been; I just did not believe Glyn Apt. Why slaughter her so violently? To paralyse us, to shock us, send the hive that was the Rock into chaos and mayhem while all the time that great warship was riding up, hidden under its stealth capacities, making ready for its crew to stroll in and club us down like sealstock pups. Idhunn's death came as one more blow, one more tragic bead on the necklace that was my life.

Mondhile. Nhem.

I could not decide which had been worse. On Nhem, I'd killed the Hierolath. I'd used the seith, while he was raping me. An extreme measure for a female assassin, but I thought I could handle it, take control of the situation, own it. And then Mondhile, and torture at the hands of Frey and the Mondhaith girl Gemaley.

But I'd been raped before, by my own brother, and

survived. And I *had* handled the events of Nhem and Mondhile, taken control of them, owned that pain as all the counsellors taught me. *Survived*. Hadn't I? But in this dungeon dark, I wasn't sure of anything any more and the nightmares were back and swarming. I felt myself shutting down, withdrawing until I was nothing more than a little seed of awareness. Was this how it was for the selk, for the Mondhaith, for the women of Nhem? Just a spark in the darkness of unsentience? Maybe it would be better if I could stay this way, I remember thinking.

Eventually, I dozed, but did not sleep. For a moment, though, I thought I was dreaming when I heard the sound. The selk were singing again. Their song echoed around the walls of the cell, and through the hollows of my head. I put my hands to my ears, but could not shut it out. It went on and on, penetrating, seeping through the cracks and *shattering*.

I was engulfed in a rush of cold sea air. Loki's light poured through the sudden gap in the wall with the glitter of the warship. The hulking form of a selk was crouching in the gap.

'You must hurry. There is no time,' it called me.

I agreed. No more time for nightmares – regardless of what the selk wanted or were planning, I had to act. I threw myself through the gap and down the rocky outcrop on which the Skald's fortress stood. Shouts sounded from high on the walls and something hummed past me, splintering rock and pulverizing seaweed into a stinking, pulpy mass.

The selk were waiting at the base of the rocks. One of them pushed the back of my knees. I stumbled forward.

'Where are we going?'

'Quickly. You will see.'

They guided me out onto the rocks. Behind me, the fortress had started to hum with voices, like a hive indeed. I could hear someone shouting: I thought it might be Glyn Apt. Then the sound of weapons fire, but surprisingly not aimed in my direction: could it be my own Skald, fighting?

'Hallsdottir!' That was Glyn Apt. Making my unsteady way over the sharp slabs of rock, I glanced back. The Morrighanu was standing in the ragged hole made by the selk's sonics, a gun in both hands and sighted on me. Ahead, the warship had started to move, swinging round to train its port guns on the selk. Something singing and hot struck the rock not far from my feet, sending black wet splinters hissing into the sea. If I went in, it wouldn't take me long to freeze. Another bolt, and the selk beside me cried out. At first I thought it had been hit, but then I saw that something was rising from the water.

Glyn Apt snapped an exclamation that I did not catch. I was concentrating on the gleaming wing, coming up in a stream of sea with Loki's light burning off its sides. The hatch was opening. I jumped, slipping a little on the rocks, nearly fell, grasped the edges of the hatch and threw myself inside.

Outside, the selk were splashing into the sea and safety. The wing's navigational array was already firing up, lit with unknown co-ordinates. The hatch closed behind me; though

I was alone I was passenger, it seemed, not pilot. It took seconds for the wing to power up. I looked through the wet window of the hatch to see Glyn Apt running along the rocks, leaping sure-footed, weapon up and firing. On the other side, there was a sunlit burst of fire from the blastcannon of the warship, sending seawater spattering over the wing like a sudden storm shower. But the Morrighanu forces came too late. The wing was speeding off, taking me with it, under the warship's guns and far out into the western sea.

SEVEN

Planet: Nhem (Hunan)

Make that four hundred and one.

The new woman came in over the ridge this morning, not long after dawn. The gate guard was the first one to catch sight of her and she called me. I was already awake – I didn't sleep for long on those nights that were hot and stifling even when it rained. The heat reminded me of Iznar; the odour of old earth hung around me, the smell of roots, the closeness of a dark cellar.

So I hurried down from the height, through the quiet, steaming streets to the gate. The walk left me breathless. Aches and pains that had not been so present when I was a younger woman were making themselves felt. I leaned against the warming stone of the guard gate for a moment to catch my breath. Pride perhaps, but even in the colony, I didn't want to show too much weakness.

The guard was a woman who was vaguely familiar to me, a squat girl, with stumps where some of her fingers should have been. But she was bright enough: I could see the glimpse of it in her face, and you learn to recognize that sort of thing here.

She said, 'High Counsellor, you're here.' She looked

relieved; her own responsibility lessened by my arrival. 'I think there's another one coming.'

'You think?'

'I'm not sure. I saw something up on the ridge. It was too tall for a carne and it moved in the wrong way.'

I took her binoculars – more men's tech, stolen and precious – and peered through them. Up on the heights of the mountains, the light lay heavy and slanted with the sun's rise. Beyond the gate, the earth was already smouldering. But up in the mountains it looked pale and bleached and cold – an illusion, I knew, for the summits were baked bare by the long summer, the earth cracked and arid. Everything was in retreat: water, beasts, plants, sinking down into the earth and crevices of rock until the first of the day-rains. If someone had made it across, at this time of year, it was a miracle.

And yet, in the next few minutes, I saw that a miracle had happened. The guard had been right to call me: there was someone there. Impossible to tell whether it was male or female from this distance, but I chose to believe it was a woman.

She was stumbling as she walked, weaving from side to side. Illness, lack of water, fatigue, abuse, or perhaps all of these. I knew we were going to have to go out there and bring her in, and it might already be too late. Not many of them made it as far as the colony: those who did spoke of the corpses, mummified in the dry air, all of them gazing south as if the north was still something to turn your back on, even in death.

I should not have offered to go myself. The walk down

here had given me warning and I expected to pay for it later, with a night of wheezing and cramps in the chest. But that same old pride bit back now, making me say, 'Fetch the land-car and Seliye. I'll go with you.'

It took a few minutes for Seliye, roused from sleep, to come down the stairs. After what she'd been through, she could have had a room in the central buildings – I'd offered her a chamber in the tower – but she preferred to stay here, facing north, watching and waiting. We all knew who for; knew, too, that the daughter she waited for would never come. But Seliye still held tight to hope, lived quietly and watchful in the guardhouse, was often the first one out whenever a new person was spotted.

'Hunan?' she said when she saw me. 'You're up early.'

'I had good reason to be.'

She raised an eyebrow, dark against the darkness of her skin, and I realized that the guard had woken her, not told her.

'There's another,' I said.

Seliye grew very still, like a lizard.

'Where?'

'Up on the ridge. She made it over. We saw her fall. We need to hurry.'

'You're sure it's a woman?'

We stared at one another. I did not need to reply.

She gave a curt nod. 'We'll need water, a med kit,' she said. She was speaking more to herself than to me, I thought. But then she gave me a sharp kind of look, the sort that told me she had taken in far more than I'd thought.

'You're coming with us, Hunan? Are you well enough?'

'I'll manage.'

She nodded. 'It's up to you.' But I could see from her face that she disapproved.

At that time of the morning, the compound was quiet. Whirls of dust spun around the land-car as we started it up, the roar of the old engine loud in the morning silence. The land-car wouldn't last much longer, it was already in its last days, and we had nothing with which to replace it. Someone had stolen it from Iznar, and I was amazed that it had made it this far and that the thief had been able to drive it. She'd been trained on a road from a mine, she said; back and forth, back and forth. She'd learned.

We'd have to keep the land-car going, and yet, we couldn't. It was one of the things I didn't want to think about, but I had to. Pushing the colony along, moment to moment, not giving in or going under. But how to live, when you know that everything around you is failing, including your own body? You endure, I suppose. You can't do anything else.

We went through the guard gate, the engine starting to whine as the land-car hit the first rise to the ridge. Behind the walls of the colony, the ground went up sharply and it wasn't long before you were in the mountains themselves, the range that the men apparently call Char Fen, the Death of Earth.

Out here, the morning sun was already a blast of heat off the white-and-ochre rocks. The sand was criss-crossed with snake tracks, the thin windings that showed a deadly presence.

'Watch your feet when you get down,' I said, unnecessarily. Seliye had already seen the tracks. She nodded. I knew we were both wondering whether the carrion hunters had got to the woman first. The sky was free of birds, but that might mean only that the bigger predators had crept out from the rocks to eat her, keeping the birds away. As the landcar swung around, bumping over the stones, I looked back.

The colony lay sharp against the black sea. The bell tower rose above it all, clear in the morning light, with the efreets circling the bell tower's spike. I felt a little stronger: when the efreets came home to roost, shrieking and hissing, that's when my day really began.

And now the colony was falling behind us, lost behind arches and spires of rock. The wind had carved the stone into odd shapes out here. It was almost like a kind of art, as though the people who made it had gone into hiding, shy about their creations. Maybe once, women could be artists: maybe the artists who had created the wall-paintings of the colony were women. Now, we made do with wind and stone.

'Where is she?' Seliye whispered. I saw her knot her fingers in the ritual gesture for luck, a gesture only a few years old, already hallowed. 'Where *is* she?'

'I can't see her.' Neither of us wanted to say it, that a carne had already got to her. They smelled blood quickly in the mountains, where food was so scarce. If they lived further north, then no women would make it here at all. But Seliye gave a stifled shout. 'There!'

She had crumpled and fallen, but she was alone. No carnes, no sign of snakes. The land-car wheeled up in a sweeping stop, showing the driver's joy, but it was too soon to tell whether or not she was alive.

'Take it easy,' I said sharply.

But Seliye was already down from the car and running across, sand puffing up from her sandal heels. In the early days, we'd been more careful, fearing traps. It was stupid when I thought about it. The men could come at any time, send a squadron down, kill us all. We expected it, erected makeshift defences behind the high earth wall of the colony, wooden spikes on the ground, defensive ditches – pathetic, because if they came, it was likely to be from above, and we had no guns, and no means to make them, although we'd scoured the colony for weapons and found none. The goddesses must have been peace-loving. Mustn't they?

But the men did not come. At least, not yet.

And now here was another woman, another sister, lying unmoving on the bare baked earth with Seliye running, and myself hobbling – after my walk to the gatehouse – towards her.

As I drew nearer, I heard Seliye give another shout, this time fully voiced.

'Hunan!' But I had already seen the woman stir.

•

All those journeys back from the mountains stick in my mind, the journeys I had made as High Counsellor, though it was never a title I'd have given myself. I could give you details of every one. Morning or evening, day or night, summer or the short coastal winter, any season when the storms come and the mountains bloom . . . all the journeys. But I remember the time we brought Khainet back more clearly than all the rest, although she did not have her name until later.

I'd never seen anyone like her. I suppose to an outsider, all the women of Edge – all the women of Iznar – must look a little similar. We are short, we are dark-haired, at least in youth, and brown-skinned, we have black eyes. We are the colour of the rich northern earth that they bring down for the gardens of Iznar. But Khainet was different. She was like a man; tall and pale, with hair that was the colour of the sand under the noonday sun: a blazing white. When we pulled back her eyelids to check her condition, they were a man's blue.

Seliye took a step back when she saw this.

'*Is* she a man, do you think?'

I laughed. 'A man with breasts?' Nor was there any telltale lump at her groin, though I would not check further. But I think it crossed both our minds that she might be some sort of spy, a man made to look like a woman, if such a notion were not too strange. Surely the men would not allow it, unless it was some kind of punishment.

And her hands were badly scarred: the skin pink and shiny, twisted across the knuckles. A lot of us have scars.

We carried her into the vehicle and the memory of that, too, is very clear. Bumping down the mountain, calling to the driver in an agony of anxiety to go more slowly, drive with more care, in case we jolted something loose in her head and she died. She had a head wound. Later, she said she didn't remember how she had come by it, but I thought she must have fallen. There was a deep gash running down the side of her face, the blood matting her hair to the skin. The long hair suggested either that she had been travelling for a long time, or that she came from a part of the north where the women's heads were not shaved. It had taken my own hair a year to grow out, and now, even though it too was white, and coarse like animal hair, I still could not bear to cut it.

I wish now that I could say I'd a feeling of disaster. But there was nothing. As we jolted in through the city gate, the high walls rising on either side and the gate swinging shut with that creak that always meant sanctuary to me, I just wanted the new woman to wake, and smile, and know that she was among friends.

EIGHT

Planet: Muspell (Vali)

It was a long ride across the sea. I had control over the immediate functions of the wing, but not over navigation: the settings were fixed and when I tried to access them, a notice informed me that they were hidden. The warmth of the wing could protect me only so far, and after a while, strapped into the pilot's chair yet with no real function (let alone any idea of where we were actually going), I grew stiff and cold. The rushing sound of the water was hypnotic, sending me into a light trance. But I examined the nav-array and there seemed to be no way of communicating with the selk, who must be far behind now.

I remembered Thorn Eld, smiling at me on the foreshore under the black-glass cliffs of Darkland; the things I had seen in that dreamscape forest outside Hetla. Travelling through the forest, with its hallucinogenic conifers and the ashy floor, redolent of ancient fires, I would have believed anything. It was no surprise that everyone in the Reach was so superstitious, given the nature of Muspell, and yet I doubt I could have lived anywhere else for long.

Eventually I shut my eyes and entered into the liminal state provided by the seith, trying to keep out the chill. But

I found my thoughts turning inexorably to the mess that I had left behind me on the Rock, to Idhunn and the selk.

Now that I thought back, I realized how little I really knew about Idhunn. She had given me a sketch of her upbringing and I knew that she came originally from a place called Whitland, a small, remote island that was part of a chain called the Wraiths. They had gained their name because the region was so often shrouded in mist, a consequence of the differing currents that swirled around the north-western parts of the Reach. Not even the most hidebound northerners expressed a great deal of enthusiasm for that part of the world. I think it explained why Idhunn had spent all that time in the lamp room: that high tower from which one could see so much of the seas and the weather. But I knew very little about her family, or what had brought her from those misty islands to the Rock. It was as though she had always been a member of the Skald, as unchanging as the fortress that housed it, and of course this was not true. I remember being surprised to discover that she had become a Skald member only twenty years before, when she must have been in her mid forties at least. She had never spoken of her relationships, or children – I did not even know whether she preferred women or men, though some intuition told me that it was probably the former. The closest friendships she had possessed within the Skald were, as far as I knew, with Hlin and myself. Perhaps she had confided more in Hlin, since they were after all closer in age. I could not help wondering what had brought her to the Skald in the first place. People entered the Skald for all sorts of reasons: personal conviction, a desire to follow a more spiritual path, although the Skald was not a religious order as such. And then there were the casualties – myself among them.

Now, my friendship with Idhunn seemed somehow false, as though she knew everything of me and I knew little more of her than the shell she chose to present to the world. But then I told myself I was being unreasonable. Wrapped up in my own problems, as I had been for most of the past seven years, I did not think I had even bothered to ask Idhunn very much about her personal life and she tended not to take part in the gossiping sessions that some of the other women indulged in. The realization washed over me in a hot wave of guilt. I should have tried to find out more, and now it was too late. She had saved my life and probably my sanity and now I could never repay her. I knew that this was often the way, when someone dies unexpectedly and you thought you still had years together ahead, but that knowledge did not make it any easier. And then I reminded myself that I could repay her, even if I couldn't get the truth out of Glyn Apt.

I could find her killer.

Several hours later, the wing reached the northern icefield, leaving the islands of the Reach far behind me. By the time I neared the edges of the ice, it was growing light. The wing soared under the lunar crescent of Loki, hanging pale and prim in a greening sky. It seemed strange to know that I was on the farthest limits of the Reach, away from thoughts of war and occupation.

As soon as we came to a halt, a set of instructions crept

onto the navigational array. When dawn came, I was to leave the wing at the edges of the ice, its stabilizers set onto remote. It would remain here, barring accident, until my return. The icefield would be deserted, except perhaps for the occasional party of hunters, but I thought that was unlikely given the circumstances. The Reach would be calling all able-bodied citizens into the armed forces: conscription was compulsory. Besides, anyone with any sense would *want* to fight. The Reach wasn't a paradise but remembering the narcoleptic look in the eyes of the citizens of Hetla, almost anything else was worth fighting for.

According to the instructions, I was supposed to meet the selk a little distance along the coast, at a place where the ice was breaking up into a series of floes. The channels would be too narrow to navigate the wing through them and it would be difficult to traverse on foot. There was a lightweight canoe packed inside the wing itself.

I wanted to stay in the relative safety of the wing for as long as possible, and put off the moment when I would have to venture out into the icefield. Memories of my last visit to Darkland were jostling close, and the seith could only limit their power, not banish it. But it seemed that I was to have no choice. I waited for dawn, and once more, I dreamed.

I was back on the ice. The fenris was standing over me, eyes golden-hot. My blood was staining the snow to a delicate pink and I stared down at the rose-and-pale as though it was something from a fairy story. My torn face burned, but the beast did not stop: it devoured me, tearing me piece by piece. I could see my own eye, staring back at me, and from its bed of snow, it winked.

I woke from my nightmare, heart hammering, and hit my head on the low ceiling of the wing as I came upright. This was not that day, the day on which the old Vali had died and a new one begun to be born, though I did not then know that. This was not the day on which Frey had sent me out on my own bloody ingsgaldir, the initiatory journey of the vitki. My ingsgaldir had failed. Had I been vitki, I would not have survived, and I only did so because a brave woman distrusted Frey and followed me, to shoot the fenris as it bent for the kill. She had been only a little late, and I had kept the scars. I did not remember being brought away from the ice and sometimes, as now, it seemed to me that I had never left it; that part of me still remained on the icefield, my missing eye in the beak of a black bird perched high on an icy crag, my blood still staining the snow, my bones whitening with frost until they cracked, to release what was left of my spirit after Frey had done with it.

There's a legend in the north that a woman stalks the icefield, half witch and half spirit. She carries a skinning knife made out of starlight and when she catches you, she uses that knife to pare you down to the bone, stripping your flesh away, ridding you of all excess, but that excess is your body itself. She frees your spirit, whether you wish it or not. I felt as though I'd met her, that day of my ingsgaldir.

But this was not that day. I kept telling myself that as I suited up in the cramped confines of the wing, wrestled the canoe from its tightly packed cocoon form, and left the wing behind me. It had started to snow; the sides of the wing were spattered with the first fat flakes from those anvil cloud-heads. Across the curving expanse of the hull, they looked like wet meteor strikes and I repressed a sudden shiver. All I needed now was to start spooking myself, so I set up the canoe and paddled out over the bitter water beneath the lightening northern sky.

I did not want to be late, so I left in good time, but the cold was biting, even through the protective layers of the slickskin. And I found that I was as scared of the darkness, just like a child. I chided myself: the dark should be no threat to a northerner, one who lives so many days without any real sight of the sun. I told myself, too, that this brittle, fractured crust through which I was making my slow way would be unable to support the weight of anything lighter than a seabird, let alone an animal the size of a fenris. But I found myself looking over my own shoulder all the same, quick nervous glances that revealed only black cracks of water, the white glimmer of ice under Loki's light, the fading stars. I do not know what I expected to see. My own ghost, perhaps. I felt insubstantial, unreal. If Frey had left a spirit behind him, and I hoped he had not, it would not be here. He had died on another world, torn to shreds by other wild animals, gone in a bloody instant. He was not here. He never would be here again. Once I had remembered this, I stopped looking back and stared ahead to the dawn sky.

There was a grey thread just above the horizon, spreading upward like frost. I found that I was hungering for dawn and the spring light, and soon enough it came. The edge of Muspell's sun Grainne touched the horizon's line and the quick flare sent a thousand suns into my sight. I ducked, blinked, and when I could see again the sun was rising. Ahead of me was the long, sharp point of the ice, a cliff a hundred feet high, jutting out into the paved mass through which I was threading the canoe. The slabs of ice glimmered in the light and at first I thought they were a mirage. The realization sent shivers through me, close to uncontrollable, as though all of it had been some huge cruel joke and Frey would be there, the trickster waiting. But then the sea heaved and the selk surged up out of the water, heads bobbing.

'You have come.'

'I have. Are we safe?'

Stupid question. The last time I'd been up here, someone had to drag me out of a beast's mouth and carry my bleeding body to safety. The ice didn't hold very positive memories.

'Who does this wing belong to?' I added when the selk did not reply.

'One who wishes you well.'

I knew of no one who wished me well, except the Skald, and this wasn't a craft from the Rock. So why did I keep thinking of the vitki Thorn Eld?

'Will you take me where I need to go?'

'We will. It is still long and long. You cannot paddle your craft so far. Do you have a rope?'

'Yes, but—'

Three of the selk swam around the prow of the canoe. 'Attach it,' one of them said. I did as they told me, then, following further instruction, looped the rope around the neck of the nearest.

'I'm afraid of hurting you,' I told it.

'You will not; you are light enough.'

It did not give me any more time to protest. We were off, shooting through the cracks and channels to the clearer water with a speed that frankly alarmed me. I did not want to risk the canoe overturning, spilling me into the killing chill of the sea. But the canoe remained stable as we whipped along and soon we were out into the glassy calm of the edges of the ocean. If the rest of the selk followed, I did not see them, but once I glanced down into the depths and thought I saw myriad bodies, twisting and turning with salmon-speed.

The day swiftly lightened. I watched as the edge of the icefield flew by, a long undulation of solidity like a white serpent, broken by immense cracks into which the canoe could easily have become lost. The sight filled me with an old, atavistic dread: genetic memories perhaps of ancient Earth. It was said to have been melting icecaps and changing currents that had led to the drowning of the world, forcing my own ancestors to flee outward. They had found Muspell: I did not think it was a bad exchange. And yet something in me still mourned old Earth, a world I had never known, a place I would never visit, never call home.

Towards noon, the selk began to glide closer into the icy shore, bringing me up the course of a narrow inlet that was, indeed, one of these cracks. I had to fight down the panic as the blue gleam of the walls started to close in. I felt as though I was drowning in a breath of cold, the water closing over my head to filter out the sunlight. Soon, the ice walls grew even closer together until there was only a twisting chimney above me. The selk's head shot out of the shadowy water.

'You must climb, now.'

'Why?' I asked. The fear started to creep, choking, up my throat. 'What's up there?'

'One who will help you.'

Carefully, I stood up. The canoe rocked and the selk helped to settle it. I climbed up the old-fashioned way, striking the metal handholds into the wall, clinging on with the canoe's ice axe, clawing my way to the summit of the chimney with the surface scraping against the slickskin. I came out into the afternoon sun like something being born, a child of ice.

I was expecting to see another selk, but instead a bone-white sledge stood on the high shelf of the icefield, and a hunched figure upon it. It wore a cloak made from the pelt of snow lynx: pallid and dappled with tips of black. The air around it was filled with the ghosts of birds: dark shadow wings beating around its head. I took a step back and narrowly missed falling down the chimney. *Vitki.*

Unhurried, the figure turned and the spirit-birds disappeared. I met cold grey eyes in a round, unremarkable face.

'Hello, Vali,' said Thorn Eld.

NINE

Planet: Mondhile (Sedra)

They say you're not supposed to remember. Only snatches and fragments, of the life-that-was in the middle of the life-that-is-now. Childhood is not something to be recalled: no real awareness, no language, only the feral game of kill-be-killed. And so many don't make it back from the world. Their families wait, consult the books that tell us how many moons the child has had, when they might stand on a town wall to watch a new person come out of the rainy dark or the burning day, and no one ever comes. But when some of them do come back across the moat – that's when your life begins. That's when you're given your name and your voice, when you begin haltingly to speak and have opinions, when you are no longer animal – at least, for most of the time.

You're not supposed to remember, but I did. Not all of it, true, but I remember *her*, and running with her, for months and maybe years, looking after one another. My sister, who never had a name because she never came home. The one who must have died, out there in the wild world.

But she did not die. She was stolen, and I meant to find out who took her.

Again, *not supposed.* Yet I remember the day it happened. The year must have been just on the turn, because there was still a summer haze over the land. She and I had been up in the Otrade, very high, along the glacier's back, trekking down onto the area that's known as Moon Moor. It was a bleak place – I'd only been there once since then, and that was to a different part, for it's deep in the mountains and there's no real reason to go there: this was as part of a warband, and we'd got lost. The landmarks had changed with the seasons, the snows creeping down and obliterating everything in their white wall. But when I was a child, it was a known place: *lai* upon *lai* of scrub and scree, with sinkholes in which a child could shelter and rings of stones, too regular not to have been man-made, in which we hunted the small creatures and the ground birds. I remember seeing the moor as a good place, not safe, but then nowhere was safe. I liked the soft black soil, the low-growing plants with their aromatic scent, which always seemed more intense at night to attract the huge moths.

Yet it was from here that she was taken.

Just as summer was turning away, with a sudden sharp chill in the air at night, so the day was turning. It was twilight; the air gentle and blue, with the first stars and the first moths coming out together. We had been living in a burrow, not far from one of the stone rings, having chased out the family of little predators that lived in it. Their musk still stank out the burrow, but we were not yet of an age to care about such things. We probably stank enough ourselves. Neither did we care whether it was day or night. So on the night that my sister was taken, we were not hiding deep in the burrow, but out on Moon Moor, among the stones. I can't remember what we were doing: playing, perhaps, as young animals do, at games of chase. Or maybe we were listening to what the moor had to tell us: it spoke to us, in voices of water and earth, of stone and metal and the wind-blasted scrub, until we were dazed with its stories and its information. Others had been there, animal and human. Warbands had marched across it, or fallen: its earth was soaked with their blood and their voices rose from Eresthahan, the land of the dead, and spoke to me, relating the manner of their deaths. I was not afraid of the dead. They were thin ghosts, nothing more, blown by the night wind, gone when morning came. And sometimes the voices of the moor and the dead, the voices of stars and moons, overwhelmed me like a tide until all I could do was hide my face in the thorny branches of the scrub and wait for it to go away.

We were part of Moon Moor. So when the thing appeared that stole my sister, it came as a rupture in the world itself.

At first we saw it as a light in the sky, very high up. I remember my sister's panicked face and then the thing growing, glowing over the stones, accompanied by a roar. It landed not far away on the moor: an insect that changed its shape to reveal three people. At the time, as far as I can recall, I saw them only as other predators, and perhaps I was not wrong. They were not human, but ghosts: with no sense of the connection to the world that I had, not even as much as the voices from Eresthahan, insubstantial as they drifted across the face of the moor. Later, when I became grown and self-aware, I saw them more clearly in my mind's eye. They were tall and had pale hair and white faces, and they wore green armour that shone in the light from their carrier beetle, a light that was itself a kind of watery iridescence. They must have been some kind of spirit or demon, for many are said to haunt Moon Moor. But they were also female.

One of them spoke in a hard harsh voice. Even if she had spoken in Khalti, I wouldn't have understood her then. Two of the ghosts ran after us. My sister ran in one direction and I in another, dodging between the towering blocks of the stones. Our pursuers were too large to fit into the burrow.

The ghost who chased me was quick. I darted into the scrub, but she was at my heels and her hand closed on my hair. I stumbled and she dragged me backwards. It hurt, but I was used to pain. My hair caught on the thorns and it slowed her down enough for me to be able to twist round in her grip and sink my teeth into the ball of her hand. Her blood tasted wrong: metallic, true, but rank and somehow old. Perhaps the blood of ghosts rots in their veins and does not renew itself. I don't know. It hurt her, though, for she shouted out and struck me. But my teeth were still embedded deep in her flesh and I would not let go. She punched me in the side of the head and I tore part of her hand away as I fell. She was shouting and grunting, blood pouring from the wound I'd made, and I took to my heels and ran as fast as I could. The burrow was not far away and I threw myself into it and waited.

Nothing more to tell. The ghost did not come and drag me out, and she'd have had a hard job of it if she'd tried.

But my sister did not come, either. I waited, and grew cold. I thought I heard her screaming, but it was a thin, distant sound like a night bird and I could not be sure. I did not dare crawl out of the burrow and look, in case the ghost was waiting. I have never blamed myself for this. Children are as they are: fiercely selfish, or they would not survive. They live in bloodmind, they are a different kind of creature from ourselves, and there is no use in applying the same standards. So I do not blame, but I do regret.

I never saw her again. Next morning, I searched the whole moor, first making sure that the insect had flown away. There was no sign that it had ever been there, except for some long black marks and flattened scrub, and spots of blood where I had savaged the ghost. I licked them but they had dried, and the rotten taste was even stronger. There was nothing else, and I know I searched hard. They had flown away and stolen her with them, or eaten her so entirely that nothing was left. I kept a watch all the same, knowing of the night birds who spit out a mass of bones and hair in a little ball. I think I half expected to find one of these little balls, all that was left of my sister, but I never did. Moon Moor was restored to peace and the uneasy balance of the things that lived there, and in time I forgot I'd had a sister, though there was always the feeling that something was missing and sometimes I would check my hands and feet, to make sure that they were still there. It was not until I returned to the clan house and became self-aware that I remembered, and even then people tried to persuade me that none of this had happened, for memories of childhood are rarely real. But I remembered, and I knew, and when the warband took me back to Moon Moor I went out one night and looked for her still, but there was nothing there.

TEN

Planet: Muspell (Vali)

'It's you,' I heard myself say.

'It's me,' Eld agreed, mildly. He stood, chafing bare hands against the cold. I wondered why he was not wearing gloves, but then he flicked a finger and the slickskin slid down to cover his hands in a shiny black coating. 'That's better. It might be spring in the Reach and in Hetla, but it's certainly cold enough here, isn't it?'

I gave an involuntary smile. Myself on the path of a murderer, fleeing an enemy invasion, our nations at war, and here were Thorn Eld and I chatting about the weather.

'Are you here to bring me in?' I asked Eld.

'Do you mean into custody? No. I'm here to take you to Morvern, at the request of the selk.'

I must have gaped at him, for he made a little gesture towards the sled. 'It'll be a lot quicker than a coastal voyage and we won't be detected, either, believe me. I've taken good care to see to that.'

'You're helping me? Why? And why Morvern? I've just escaped from the Morrighanu.'

'I'm aware of that. We need to get moving. Yes, I am helping you, but I won't tell you why just yet. In case you take this for more vitki gamesmanship, let me note that it's simply that it's hard to talk on the sled and the explanation can wait until later. I'm afraid,' and here he gave a small, ironic motion that could almost have been a bow, 'that you are going to have to trust me.'

'I can't do that,' I said.

'Please don't do anything foolish,' Eld said. He nudged the lynx-fur cloak aside, revealing the black muzzle of a weapon. 'Or I'll have to insist.'

From below, a thin voice called, 'He is here at our will. He is telling the truth.'

And the vitki were versed in mind control techniques. I glanced down the chimney, to see the sad gaze of the selk. 'Go with him.'

'All right.' What else was I going to do, apart from stand here arguing? I'd go, but that didn't mean I had to trust. I walked reluctantly around to the other side of the sled and sat down on one of the ridged seats. The minute I did so, a slippery band shot out of the sides of the sled and confined my hands and waist. I turned a furious glance to Eld, who was holding out placating palms. 'This is only for a little while, Vali.' He paused. 'I'm sorry. But I don't want you bolting.'

'Why would I—' and then four fenris stalked out from behind a pinnacle of ice. Their eyes were yellow, their mouths scarlet, and their coats were as white as the snow, turning them into ghost-beasts, all gold and red and pale. My throat grew dry; I felt myself turn to bone and snow, as though the spirit witch of the north had found me and brought her skinning knife down.

'These are the sled team,' Eld explained, but I could not speak. I watched as the fenris padded to the front of the sled and stood patiently in the traces, one behind the other. They were close enough for me to smell their rank odour. As they passed, each one gave me an incurious glance from sun-coloured eyes. They had been bred from wolf stock originally, but they were much larger and there were other genes in there, too: the feline ancestry that had flattened their faces and tufted their ears, the long switching tails, and something else, something *knowing*, behind those hot yellow eyes. The vitki had crossed humans with beasts, a thousand years ago. The original colonists of Mondhile were said to have done the same thing. The fenris brought back too many memories.

I watched, aghast, as Eld harnessed the beasts to the sled, and when I finally found my voice, it was stolen by the wind as he spoke a word to the team and we were hurtling across the icefield.

I don't remember a great deal about the journey. I was too afraid, and the slickskin and snow goggles robbed me of much of my sight. Eld either said nothing, or could not be heard, and eventually I found it easiest not to look at what was pulling the sled, but to concentrate instead on a point between the dappled fur of Eld's shoulder blades. Occasionally the birds returned, gliding in shadow across the sunlit ice to perch on Eld's shoulder and whisper in his ear. Vitki fancy had formed them into the shapes of Odin's ravens, just as Glyn Apt had been kept informed by her own white birds. But out here, on the ice, technology fell away to become no more than superstition.

I don't know how long we travelled. The day went by in a cold blur, the fenris no more than great drifting shapes at the front of the sled. At one point I looked down and saw that the bonds that had held me had disappeared. Eld had clearly come to the conclusion that I was no longer likely to flee. He was right: I had no intention of throwing myself from the speeding sled, no matter what might be pulling it. I was very aware of the edges of the seith: flinched back, drawn tightly against my body, away from the humming electricity field that was how Eld's own seith felt to me. If I had ever had any illusions about the power of the vitki, then this would have dissipated them, but there was one thing for which I was thankful. Eld felt nothing like Frey. Eventually I closed my eye and concentrated on maintaining my own seith: going down into the imaginary dark that was the source of it, envisaging black sparkling light, mined from space and stars, from the deep earth itself beneath the ice, rising to protect me and encase me. The world fell away and I was enclosed.

When I looked out again, I realized that the sled had come to a halt. Eld was unhooking the fenris team and I tensed, gripping the edges of the sled, but they did not look at me and made no move. I reminded myself that before Frey had died, I had controlled a pack of animals that matched these beasts in both ferocity and intent. Still, the visen of Mondhile had been alien, unfamiliar to me, and the connection we had established had therefore, paradoxically, come more easily. With the fenris, there were just too many memories.

Eld glanced over his shoulder and saw me watching.

'You vanished there for a while, Vali.' It was said with a smile. I did not trust myself to give an explanation, but simply nodded.

'You would have made an excellent vitki. But of course I've told you that before.' He spoke with his usual mildness, but I could not help remembering that the last time he had complimented me on my abilities, the compliment had been accompanied by the words 'breeding program'. And that brought back Nhem. Wherever I turned, the past was there, lying in wait for me. The day suddenly seemed a little colder yet. I did not answer, but forced myself to climb down from the sled and walk over to him. I was very aware of the presence of the beasts: they radiated their own particular aura, a predation held barely in check, as if I stood too close to a sun. I drew up the black sparkle of the seith and shut them out.

'Where are we, Eld? Where are we going?'

He raised a slickskinned hand and pointed. Across a narrow channel, sailing with the icebergs of spring thaw, lay a line of coast, high cliffs gleaming with ice.

'That,' said Eld, 'is Morvern.'

'Where the Morrighanu come from.'

'Just so.'

'They've taken the Rock. You intimated that you're aware of that.'

'Of course,' Eld said, with a touch of impatience. 'Why else do you think I went to so much trouble to get you out?'

'Both Morrighanu and vitki are from Darkland. I was assuming you're on the same side.'

A bark of laughter, like a fenris' cry. 'You said it yourself. Both Morrighanu and vitki are from Darkland. I'll explain later, Vali. As far as I can.'

Twilight was falling when we crossed the channel. I was concerned that there might be spy-wings along the coast, but Eld assured me that Morvern was a law unto itself even in this time of war and the coast would, literally, be clear. He left the sled where it was and released the fenris team. I did not see where they went, but was glad to have them gone. Even the broken pavement of the ice seemed safe in comparison to their presence.

'We'll have to go across on foot,' Eld said, pointing to bobbing ice and racing water, so cold that it ran green-clear through the cracks. I said nothing, but the expression on my face must have told him everything he needed to know. He gave a slight smile.

'Believe it or not, I know what I'm doing. The selk have been better scouts than any human or device could ever be. I worked out the route with them when I came this way and it's keyed into my map implant. All you have to do is follow me and you'll be all right.'

All you have to do is trust me. My paranoia was beginning to work overtime.

'Very well,' I said, not without effort. 'Lead the way.'

Ultimately, it did not take long to cross the channel, but at the time it seemed like several days. It was easier to connect my seith to Eld's, though I did not like doing so as I was not sure what I might be betraying. But the man seemed to know everything about me as it was, just as the Morrighanu now did, and I liked that even less. It was as though an invisible line stretched between us, towing me along as we stepped or jumped from slab to slab. A surprising quantity of the ice was steady, seemingly stone-solid even though I could see through it to the twisting water beneath, but some of the slabs rocked and heaved as we set foot on them. Eld and I danced and balanced our way across the middle part of the channel and as we did so I wondered just how much the configuration of the ice had changed since he last came this way. It must only have been a little time ago, but things change quickly in the northern spring. Then, through the green race of water, I saw three round heads emerge, blink, sink once more and knew that the selk were keeping an eye on us. I could have done with the knowledge of their presence earlier, but it was good to know that they were there.

And then at last we were standing on a snowy shore, looking back across the channel. I could feel the difference in the air, as though the land itself had turned and was watching me. We had reached Darkland.

ELEVEN

How to explain it? When I kill, I feel a great love and sympathy for my prey. It's as though I can see their souls going down into the dark and that darkness is a mother's womb, no place to be feared. It is clean and pure, especially when done outside in the snow of the forest, and I make sure that they suffer no pain. I bring the illusions to them, drawing visions from the earth and from their own blood. Sometimes, I like to think, I give them what they most wish to see and then I am doing them a great service, am I not, in freeing them from the slavery of the flesh?

Besides, everyone dies.

TWELVE

Planet: Nham (Hunan)

We gave her the new name when she was well enough. She herself chose to be called Khainet, an invented name, as all must be. We held the ceremony up in the bell tower, about ten days after Seliye and I had brought her down from the mountains. She did not have much speech at that point, naturally, none of the rescued women did, but she was learning fast and she picked up my name and Seliye's very quickly. The words for 'water' and 'hot' were soon to follow, then 'food' and 'light' and 'want'. Once she had regained consciousness, Seliye and I spoke in front of her for hours, using simple terms, repeating whole conversations. We were used to this – we'd had a lot of practice. I could see the patterns settling into her mind, as she silently mouthed the words after us, as the men's language that she'd heard all her life gradually started to make sense. It was a good thing to see, as satisfying as the grinding of grain. If we were to teach a small child, how quickly would she learn? We'd often discussed this, but we had no experience of it: we thought that the learning process might be even faster, but maybe it was just that these grown women were making up for lost time.

But no one pregnant had ever made the journey from the north. Not made the journey and lived, that is to say.

And now Khainet was standing on the platform at the far side of the bell tower, flanked by the goddesses on the wall. I saw her gaze drift towards them, wondering, as if afraid to believe. We had told her how we saw them, but I did not know what *she* thought. Her white hair streamed down her back; I had never seen anyone so beautiful.

Seliye stepped forward and spoke in a strong voice.

'*Khainet*. Do you take this name?'

'Yes.'

'What does it mean?'

A lost look from the newly named and I said quickly, 'It means whatever you wish it to mean. It is your word.' Who knows where she got it from? Perhaps it was a word in the men's tongue. But now it would be a word in ours.

Her voice faltered at first, but then a breeze stirred our hair, a hot draft from the ochre sands, and she said, 'It means – it means the mountain wind.'

'All right,' Seliye said. She reached out and took Khainet's hand. 'From now on, from this day, the word "khainet" means just that. We have a new word!'

And the women made soft sounds of approval, a hissing whisper. But I could see that Khainet was starting to falter. We had brought her up here in the early evening, that favourite time when the shadows were long, but as that wind had proved, it was still hot, the air between the gusts baking our lungs. A look passed between Seliye and myself and together we led Khainet down the steps of the bell tower to her chamber below, not far from my own. Later, she could choose a place of her own, if she wished. She looked back over her shoulder at the silent goddesses as we left, that same disbelieving glance, and it made me sad, but it also made me smile.

The day after that, we went to the shore. On the way down the steps, Khainet had given a longing look towards the black sea, and I noticed it.

'Do you want to go?'

She turned to me at once, eagerness clear in the bright blue eyes. 'Is it possible? Is it safe?'

I'd laughed. 'Nothing's ever really safe here, Khainet. But it's safe enough.'

I took her down on foot, with one of the off-duty gate guards who fancied a trip herself. It was mid-afternoon, with the ancient bricks breathing heat. I'd brought a scarf for her, to keep the dust from her hair and face. We don't like to cover our faces here in the colony; it's too much of a reminder, and I thought she might baulk at it, flinch. A lot of the women did, before they grew resigned to its practicality. But Khainet took the scarf without a word and wrapped her pale hair in its sky-blue folds.

'Where do you get the – the *stuff* from?'

'The thread, you mean?' She was examining the weave, twisting it between her scarred fingers.

'The thread,' she repeated after me, softly.

'It comes from the efreet nests. They spin it from mucus

– the fluid in their beaks – and wind it around twigs. If you soak the nests, once the young have flown, you get skeins of this substance. We dye it with plants. This blue, for example. It's a little brown lichen that grows in cracks.'

'And how do you know? That it will make blue?'

I laughed. 'We just did it until we got it right. We've been here a long time – enough time to make a great many mistakes.'

'I want to learn.'

'I'll ask the women in the workshop. I don't see why not. There's always room for another pair of hands.'

She grimaced, suddenly, and for a moment I thought it was because she felt ill, but then she said, 'Food. I don't want to cook.'

'You don't like cooking?'

She scowled. 'No.' She held up her scarred hands. 'This – this was oil. Hot.'

'You had an accident while cooking?'

'No. Not accident.'

'I see.' We walked in silence for a while, then I said, 'Look. You can see the shore.'

We had left the colony wall a little way behind and were now heading down the bumpy track that separated it from the cliffs. Once, perhaps, the city had stood directly on the shore, but now the waves lapped a safe distance from the walls. From this vantage point, the ochre walls were a contrast to the black rocks: transparent in places, with swirls and spirals inside them. When I was in a certain mood, I would half-close my eyes and imagine that there were creatures trapped in the rocks, peering out, faces gaping in horror. But there were no faces, only marks.

Khainet still moved slowly, like an old woman; stiff from walking across the mountains. But now her true age was apparent: she was only around her late twenties. I can't remember noticing beauty when I was in Iznar, though my daughters' faces made me light up inside, so perhaps that was it. But there was a subtle arch to the bridge of Khainet's nose, an arch, too, to her brows and cheekbones. It made me uneasy. I told myself that perhaps I was jealous: so ordinary myself, I disliked beauty in others. Why should this be, when we put so little stock on appearance here, just glad to be alive?

We walked together across the black rocks, down to the beach. The sand, too, was black, gritty at the poisonous edges of the water, but soft as fur further up the shore. The wonder was back in Khainet's face. She bent and scooped up a handful of it, letting it sift through her fingers.

'It falls like hair,' she said.

'It's very soft,' I agreed. 'But don't touch it beyond the tide line.' I pointed to the glitter in the sand. 'Beyond that, it's sharp enough to cut your hands.'

She nodded. 'I won't.' A pause. 'It's so – different. I never knew the sea was there.'

Did I want to show off my knowledge a little, or instruct? I said, 'There are lakes along the northern coast, they say – not poisonous water, but water you can swim in.'

'Swim?'

I decided to explain it to her. She was frowning. 'How do you know about the north?'

So I tried to explain that, too, about the handful of women who had come here from beyond even Iznar, but I don't think Khainet believed me. She gave a little smile, as if to say that she could see through my game of trying to tease her, and walked along the sand to the tide line. A graceful walk, I thought, and was back to wondering again.

I walked more slowly than she did. I caught up with her at the tide line.

'It's so quiet,' she said. There was nothing but the breeze, the skittering cries of the efreets that lived in the cliffs – different to those of the bell tower, with long curved wings and beaks like tubes – and the soft hiss of the sea on the shore.

'It's a quiet place,' I agreed.

'Not like the other.'

I didn't ask her which other. I simply waited.

It's common for memory to come back in shards and fragments, to be pieced together like a broken pot. The pot will never be the same: it may look similar, but it won't hold water any more, there are too many leaks and holes. We mend pots from a glue made from resin – it dries thick and lumpy, it's impossible to spread it thinly, and you can see all the joins and fractures. Our minds are like that, too; you can tell where and how we were broken. And the glue is formed from the stories that we tell, to fill in the gaps. Sometimes I think that all memory is nothing but a story. Sometimes I wonder whether any of it was ever real.

The wind was rising a little, sending swirls of sand across the shore. Khainet began braiding her hair to keep the sand out of it. She did it deftly, with quick movements of her scarred fingers, and it was a joy to watch. So I told her this.

'I never had enough hair to do that,' I said. 'This is as long as it's ever been.'

She gave a faint smile. 'It's one of the first things I can remember. Someone teaching me to braid my hair.'

'A woman?' I asked. 'Your mother?'

Khainet shook her head. 'I don't know. I suppose so. But I can't—' She hesitated. 'I remember seeing a woman in a cage, and knowing that she was my mother.'

'In a cage?' Perhaps the woman had transgressed and been confined as a punishment.

'Yes. She snarled at me when I went near. She was tall, like me, and she had hair like mine – long and white, but it was tangled. She had long nails and teeth, and pale eyes.'

'She sounds unusual.'

'When she saw me, she threw herself at the bars and grabbed them. I was very frightened. My sister picked me up and carried me out of the room.'

'Your sister?'

'She looked like me, too. And she was very fierce. She used to hiss and spit at the other women.'

'Which other women?' It sounded as though Khainet had been brought up in one of the group complexes. We'd pieced it together: the men closest to the Hierolath kept the biggest number of women.

Khainet frowned. 'There were a lot of them. They – spoke.'

It was my turn to frown. 'They spoke?' I echoed.

'All the time. But I never understood what they said. They were kind to me, but I remember – rooms. Pale green rooms, with metal in them. I kept going to sleep in them.'

This all sounded very strange to me. 'Are you sure it wasn't a dream?' I asked.

'I don't know. Maybe it was. I must have been very young. But then the men came.'

'You didn't have a House Father?' That couldn't be. But Khainet was insistent.

'I didn't see any men. I didn't know what they were, until they came. My sister came running into the room and she was scowling. She picked me up and carried me into a cupboard and then she shut the door. It was dark and I was afraid of her, so I didn't make any noise, but when the door opened again there was a man standing there. I remember thinking that he looked like me: his skin was pale and so was his hair. He shouted at me and so I closed my eyes again. Then he hit me. When I woke up, I was in a man's house and I stayed there until I was moved.' She shrugged. She did not want to remember those parts of it, I could tell, and who could blame her?

Then she said, 'Always *noise*. He used to shout. And then the children . . . all of us packed into one little house.'

I thought she must be talking about her House Father, but then she explained, 'They were all boys. I only remember my other mother a little bit. Not the one in the cage. The new one.'

'What happened to her?'

Khainet blinked, as if trying to remember. 'I don't – I can only see bits. She ruined some food. She was clumsy and I understood things she didn't. I don't know why.' The words were coming more easily now, I noticed. 'I remember her dropping the pot. He came in and he shouted. Next thing I remember, she was lying on the floor. She wouldn't move. Two of the boys carried her out; they were laughing and joking. I did the cooking after that. Then he sent me away before the boys could use me.'

'Where did he send you?' I felt cold, despite the warm wind from the sea, and for a moment the wind smelled of earth.

'To a house of use. I don't know why,' she echoed.

I know, I thought, as I stared at her beautiful face, but I said nothing. For the upper echelons of the Most Holy, when they grew tired of the dull meat at home. She added, 'I remember a lot about that. But I don't want to.'

I couldn't hold back the question I'd been longing to ask: the same question as always. 'What changed you?'

She took a long time answering, but that's normal. It still takes me time, when I talk about it.

'I don't know. I remember standing by a window. It was in the morning, I think, because the sun was climbing up. I saw the green domes – the Most Holy, Seliye tells me they call it – and I thought how beautiful they were, but they also terrified me. Then I looked down at my hands and I saw them as mine. After that, it happened slowly, maybe over one month. When the men spoke at me, I started to understand a few words. I spent a lot of time staring in the—' she frowned, '—the mirror, as though I was trying to recognize myself. And then I was down in the main hall, waiting for a man, and I saw a girl. She came in with another man and he made her wait. It was very hot. When he went to the desk she pushed her head covering back and her eyes met my eyes. I knew she was looking at me as a person and I was looking at one too. Then the man came back and she was a thing again.' Khainet paused and slid a sandalled foot along the black sand, back and forth. The straps of those sandals were worn and scuffed, fraying almost to the point of snapping. 'That night, a bird came. At first I thought it was just sitting on the window sill, but it didn't fly away when I went to it. It spoke to me. I don't know how, but it spoke. It flew around me and gave me a picture in my head: of the streets and the gate. It told me to go to the gate when the crescent moon rose.'

'Other people tell similar stories,' I said. 'It was the same for me.'

She looked doubtful.

'I didn't know how I'd go, but I did. They weren't expecting me to do anything like that. I just slipped out before dark and followed the picture, and then I hid in the shadows by the gate. And it opened.'

'But you saw no one.'

'No. How did you know?'

'Because no one ever does.' That had been the same for me, too. 'And then you ran.'

'I knew I had to get out of the city, but you know, Hunan, I didn't really understand why. All I knew was the men's world, and my place.' She paused again, scuffing the sand. 'I never looked back once I'd started running. I hid in the rocks. Once I was out of the city, the pictures were new ones. They showed me where to go. They showed the colony.' She reached out and grasped my hand. 'You sent the bird, didn't you, Hunan? You sent the pictures. You showed me the way to go, how to come here.'

Her face was lit with gratitude and I sighed as I told her that no, I had sent neither bird nor maps, that the colony does not have the resources for such things, and that we did not know who sent them. We had no idea.

THIRTEEN

Planet: Muspell (Vali)

Eld and I came off the ice close to midnight. The moon hung in the south, floating just above the sea, and we used it to head towards the forest of Morvern.

I knew little about this part of Darkland, but then, no one knew much, except the Morrighanu, and perhaps the vitki. It had been the first part of the continent to be settled, by renegade scientists outcast from the Reach. Frey had come from Morvern, and that alone was enough to make the land feel cold to me, more alien than even another world, the air crackling with hostile intent.

The monotony of the journey was beginning to slow me down, though I took careful note of all and any markers, like the tracker I had once been and, indeed, still was. I was grateful for the afternoon's sleep, or trance, whatever it had been. A couple of hours passed, during which neither Eld nor I spoke, but finally we reached a lip of slippery rock. Below, a cliff plunged away into a great dark expanse. I could smell snow, and trees, and something beyond that that spoke of spring, like a promise. It smelled similar to the forests of the Reach, and I began to feel just a little easier. A false comfort, I knew.

'Morvern,' Eld said, pointing. 'This is the start of Sull Forest.'

'And where, Eld, do you propose that we stay the night?'

Eyes gleaming in the moon's light, Thorn looked at me as though I were mad. 'Why, in a hostel, of course.' Then he turned and disappeared. I stared stupidly for a moment, then saw the crack in the rock down which he had gone. When I investigated it, I found a series of worn steps cut into the cliff. Eld was already some distance down them; I followed, as quickly as I could.

I'd naturally assumed that he was being sarcastic, but when we came to the end of the steps, with my calves vibrating like harp strings from the long climb down, I realized that the joke at my expense was a minor one. I could see a bank of trees, but above them, the arch of gables. There was a settlement at the foot of the cliff. No lights were showing: perhaps a curfew had been imposed, or maybe they had simply all gone to bed.

'Eld?' I nudged him. 'Is this safe? To be seen?'

'Safe for me.'

'And what does that mean, precisely?' My own voice was as cold as the ice above us.

'It means that you, my dear, will *not* be seen. And I will be disguised.' As I watched him suspiciously, the moon seemed to drift behind a cloud and when I could see once more, someone else stood in front of me. Even in the faint illumination from Loki, I could see this, but I could not have said how Eld was different, even though I studied him feature by feature.

'Just raise your seith as you did on the sled,' Eld explained. 'It'll be enough. My ravens will do the rest.'

I did as he suggested. I was glad that he seemed to have such faith in my abilities; I wasn't sure that I shared it. Just before we headed into the trees I looked up at the sky. Loki hung among the spring stars, the Ship and the Corona. There were no clouds to be seen, only the silent flutter of black wings.

Eld did not have to counsel me to keep my mouth shut. I followed his unfamiliar figure like a shadow, through the doors of a building among the trees. All was quiet, apart from the occasional cry of a hunting bird and the occasional slop of snowmelt from roofs or trees. I did not even see how he opened the door, but shortly we were standing in a hallway that could have been anywhere in the Reach: carved panels with quaint hunting scenes, an overstuffed couch. The very familiarity of it was unsettling. There was a grille in the panelling across the hall. Eld spoke to someone whom I could not see and started to negotiate rates. My attention wandered. The place was dingy and smelled of mould and damp. A girl sidled down the stairs and through the door, keeping her face averted from us. I started, but the seith held, together with whatever protection had been afforded by Eld's information system, and she showed no sign of having seen me. As she slipped out, I saw that one side of her face was a mottled mass of bruises. I could almost taste her hopelessness on the air, lingering like sad perfume in her wake.

Eld took a small piece of metal from a hook on the wall.

After a moment, I recognized it as an old-fashioned key. I had only seen one once before, in a theme restaurant in Tiree. It made me wonder just how far Morvern might be behind the times . . .

I followed Eld up a narrow flight of stairs to a landing. Eld glanced at the key, and it was then that I belatedly realized we would be sharing a room. I was reluctant to be left on my own in this vitki haunt, but equally uncertain about the prospect of sleeping in the same place as Thorn Eld behind a locked door. The same thought had evidently struck Eld himself, for he looked a question back at me.

'It doesn't bother me,' I said in an undertone. I did not want to show the vitki that his presence unnerved me. I had the satisfaction of seeing Eld look mildly surprised.

'If it doesn't bother you, it doesn't bother me. Of course, you know that you're entirely safe with me?'

'Thanks for making that clear,' I said, and was surprised to find myself slightly put out. I was that unappealing, was I? But of course, he had seen the full extent of my facial injuries and one could hardly blame him for failing to find me attractive. A whisper within told me that this was why I'd chosen to keep the scars. But I paid no attention to the voice and besides, it didn't matter even if it was true. I had no interest in Eld, I told the voice. No interest at all.

The room was as dank as the lobby, with twin beds and a slight gap between. Eld bade me goodnight, removed his coat and boots and lay down on a bed with his back to me, where he fell into a silent, motionless sleep. It was, I suppose, foolish to hope that he might have proved human enough to mutter or snore, but the more sensible part of me reminded myself to be thankful for this. I lay staring into the dimness, fancying that I could see the flicker and beat of ravens' wings in the shadows, carrying knowledge to and fro. We were in Morvern, in Darkland, a nation with whom my people were at war: I could not afford to forget who Thorn Eld was, nor what. Thousands of years ago, perhaps he and I would have been magician and witch, shaman and seer. These days, we were simply people who had been trained in normal human abilities, nothing more than that – or so I kept telling myself. But in spite of the long day and my fatigue, it took me a while to fall into sleep, all the same.

FOURTEEN

Planet: Mondhile (Sedra)

As I have said, I remembered the terrain from my days in the warband. Then, we had travelled to Moon Moor at the start of winter, with the frost thin on the ground and crackling in the thorn bushes and the glaciers bright against the high white sky. We moved in single file, on the backs of war murs, bred for hard fighting. In those days there had been many skirmishes across the north; now, they were fewer. A succession of difficult winters, and long ones, had put paid to any wish to continue fighting – that and the deaths in war of some of the more intractable clan leaders. That never hurts.

I had been towards the back of the warband. There was no call for a metal-speaker up front: the useful people there were those who could discern the easiest way across tricky terrain, avoiding the marshy places where a mur could stumble, or the patches of sand where a mur might sink. But I had other talents, of use all the way along the line.

We filed across the scrub, with the murs' breath and our own blowing out in clouds into the chilly air. Even in thick leather gloves, my hands were cold. I did not remember being so cold as a child, but now I marvelled that I hadn't frozen. Everyone was bundled up in leather armour and furs, or thick woollen capes, apart from the feir warriors, who seemed to feel the cold as little as children themselves. They walked bare-armed and bare-headed, without weapons. They're close to the bloodmind, those folk. They spend as much time in it as out of it – not all the time, like the mad wandering people, for they are tied to clans, but it's a close thing. We did not have to be warned to avoid them: they were as dangerous as half-tamed mur, snapping and snarling at the slightest intrusion into their vicinity. I watched them as we rode: a group of tall men and several women, with long tangled hair. Their claws and teeth were longer than the average, too. I wondered what it must be like, to live in the bloodmind so much of the time, a quasi-childhood, lacking anything other than the traces of self-awareness, not to be able to name your own name, or your clan, conscious only of threat and the opportunity for battle. I'd been in it myself only once since childhood: the result of a masque, when the bloodmind's focus turned from savagery to sex. I remembered a bit about that, too, and I grinned as I rode.

Moon Moor stretches for perhaps thirty *lai* along the edge of the mountains, before the scrub turns to the bare earth of the foothills. It takes a day to cross on mur-back, longer if the mist comes down from the mountains. We were perhaps a third of the way across when the attack came.

They were a band of northern clans: wild people, rumoured to live on lines of dark energy and eat human flesh. When I rode with our warband, I believed this, but later, when I had lived a little, I thought that they probably believed the same about us. They rode swift mur, the coats mottled black and white to blend in with the northern forests. Even against this thorny scrub, they were well disguised due to the sprinkling of snow, and they were as fast as ghosts.

And they had dreamcallers with them. We found that out soon enough, but I felt them before I saw them. Their dreams prickled at the edges of mine and I threw a wall of shivering illusions into the air, but they were stronger than I was. I sent out a silent call to our other dreamcallers, further up the line, but it was too late: I'd been snapped. One moment I was facing a brake of scrub, sharp with thorns and frost, and the next, I was in a wasteland of the dead. Everyone around me was dead: corpses torn to pieces and the air thick with the smoke from the funeral pyres. I started to choke on it, even as a small cool voice at the back of my mind told me that it wasn't real. The mountain wall drifted into view through the smoke: we were still on Moon Moor. I turned with a flush of hope. I wanted to know if I could find my sister. But one of the corpses sat up and spoke to me, its jaw clicking back into place as it did so. It was another woman, a warrior like me, with the curve of pregnancy just visible beneath her battle dress. I could see the litter squirming within, as though she had become transparent.

'You shouldn't be here,' the dead warrior said. 'You're still alive.'

'I can conjure dreams. I'm lost in someone else's. Where is this supposed to be? Is this Eresthahan?'

'The land of the dead? Of course not. This is Moon Moor. Past and future meet here. By the way, someone's trying to kill you.'

She opened her mouth wide and the dreamcaller's song came pouring from it like the smoke from the pyres, visible and glittering against the charnel air. I'd got a hold on it now, a mesh. I could see the warrior behind her, sword upraised, real, and I raised the big bow with its notched arrow and shot him in the gut before he could come any closer. He dropped, screaming, and the sound cleared my head. The battlefield of the past vanished, along with the pregnant warrior, and I was back on Moon Moor with my own warband.

I took out another girl with an arrow, but the enemy dreamcallers hadn't finished yet. I could see them up on the high ground, protected behind a wall of bowmen. They stood in their ritual postures, mimicking the flight of birds, calling illusions up out of the frosty air. Puffs of the hallucinogenic dust that they used to enhance their natural abilities came from their mouths as they incanted, and the bowmen in front of them, their own warband, wore elaborate face masks attached to their helmets, in order to avoid the effects. We didn't use that sort of shit; it rotted your brain in the end. I had to get to them, because they were causing such havoc among the warband: people staggering to and fro, getting cut down as easily as winter-fat waterfowl, not even noticing their own dying in the mists of conjured visions. I ran towards the dreamcallers, zigzagging across the moor. There were wider tunnels underneath that ridge: I remembered them from childhood. We hadn't used them much, because they were big enough for predators to follow us in and we had preferred the narrow, child-hiding tunnels. But they led out to the back of the ridge, a hive-comb of passageways. If I could slink up behind the enemy dreamcallers and cast an illusion of my own . . .

As I drew nearer, the invading visions started to creep back. I breathed shallowly, pulling my collar over my face, but the pregnant warrior was pacing beside me now. Her ruined face was amused.

'It doesn't matter, you know,' she said. 'Everyone dies.'

'But it isn't my time. Our clan satahrach looked at the stars, did a tide-reading. I'm not supposed to die now.'

One eyebrow, the one not buried in clotted blood, arched. 'You believe all that?'

'I won't doubt the satahrach. She knows what she's talking about.'

But the warrior only grinned, her shattered jaw flapping, and I ran on, dodging under the bowmen's gaze. I couldn't see their eyes behind the elaborate metal masks, but I could hear their laboured breath. An arrow sang past my ear and buried itself in a shower of black earth, but I was through the bushes that shrouded the tunnels' mouth and into cool darkness.

The sounds of the skirmish were immediately cut off. I had no time to bask in the lovely quiet, but pushed on through overhanging roots and out-juts of stone. Old curls and coils in the rock betrayed the presence of things that were long dead and they spoke to me, of ancient rolling seas, life that was nothing like the lives of the *now*. I wanted to listen to their voices, until the memories of the screams of warriors and mur no longer echoed in my ears, but I did not stop. Onward, following the smell of air through this cradle of earth, seeking the other side. I was too intent on the back of the ridge, of reaching it. I should have watched my footing instead, for when the earth gave way beneath me in a slip and shower, I felt only a quiver of surprise before I fell.

I shouldn't have been able to see light, and my first thought was that the enemy dreamcallers had reached me and trapped me in illusion again. But this wasn't the battleground of Eresthahan, with the sun breaking through smouldering clouds. This was a soft, blue, dim light, like the light you see on fungi in the depths of winter, picking up the light of the snow and reflecting it back at twilight. But this place did not smell like the forest. I'd never smelled anything like it before: it was too clean, and at the same time, moist.

I checked for injuries and found few. I'd twisted my ankle, but it wasn't broken or even sprained and I was able to clamber to my feet and walk without much pain. A few minutes later and I'd forgotten that the ankle even existed. Away from the rupture that had brought me here, the earth above my head was packed and solid, as though it had been moulded. I had to get back to the warband, but the hole through which I had fallen was too high up and there was no way to climb up to it. Maybe there was another way out.

The light was coming from a short distance ahead, and I followed it, half expecting to come out into fresh air. But further down the passage, the earlier clean scent changed – this air was not fresh at all: it smelled dead, if air can die. A moment of walking and then the passage was opening out into a network of chambers: I could see them extending into the distance, but then movement attracted my attention and I saw that I was facing my own reflection.

I confess to studying it with some interest. I'd never seen myself full length before: a tall, thin woman dressed in layers of black, her hair caught back in the severe warriors' knot, looped to one side so that I could more easily pluck an arrow from the shoulder quiver. And I saw for the first time, without the burnish of metal or the shiver of water to get in the way, that I really was beautiful, just as they said. I noted this with surprise, not satisfaction. No time for vanity now, however. I had to find out where I was.

The chamber was round, and led into another round chamber. It gleamed, faintly, and it wasn't made of stone, nor metal, either. I could not tell what it was made from. It must be durable, to last so long under the earth, even though it had picked up a sheen of moisture that beaded itself over the curving walls and ceiling. I couldn't tell where the light was coming from. There was no sign of any furniture: all the chambers were empty. I went from one to another and found that there were ten of them. All of them had a depression in the floor, bowl-shaped like the marks on the rocks of the seashore. I marked each chamber with a little smear of my blood, taken from one of the scrapes I'd sustained in the skirmish. I didn't trust these round rooms. I wanted to be able to get out again.

In the tenth room, I was turning to leave when there was a flicker of movement. I stood still, expecting to see my own reflection, but it wasn't myself that I had glimpsed. Something was rising from the depression in the floor, floating in a column of light. I nearly ran but I made myself stand still and watch.

It was a child. But it didn't look quite like the children of the clan, or the litter to which I myself had given birth. Its face was too narrow and elongated, more like an animal's muzzle. As I stared, however, the muzzle withdrew, back into its face, and now it looked human. It was naked, but showed no sign of a sex: the place between its small legs was bare and smooth. There was something repulsive about this, something unreal. It grew, stretching, the limbs extending, until it was almost my own height. The peaceful face changed too, becoming adult, but the muzzle was back again and now the limbs were changing, bending back upon impossible joints, until the creature stood on all fours like a mur. The face was something like a mur's, too; the long sharp skull and sharper teeth. Then human once more. The satahrach of my clan had once told me that mur and human shared a common ancestry, that the riding beasts had a language of their own which they would not speak before humans, although some people seemed able to understand it. I had never believed this, though certainly the mur seemed cleverer than other animals and more malevolent, too. But now, looking at this shifting, changing, sexless thing, I wondered what it meant and whether the satahrach had been right after all.

The thing was growing old, withering down into bent age. I remember watching the process with revulsion, knowing that I'd come to that as well, if I lived through the warband. And then it died, but it collapsed in upon itself, neither human nor animal, only something small and skeletal and strange. Its face remained peaceful until the last and then the thing was gone, along with the light. I waited for an uneasy moment, but the chamber was still and quiet. I did not understand what I had seen. I turned and followed the clues of my own blood, out of the chamber and back to the starting place. From there, I took the other side of the passage, which led into further caves and – at last! – a place where the earth had crumbled away in stages.

It took me an hour to clamber up the wall to the second hole. I hauled myself over the lip of the tunnel, expecting a waiting group of enemy soldiers, but there was just another passage beneath the rock, with fresh air blowing through it. As I hastened along the passage, bending double in some places, I saw and heard no one. The passage was shattering in its silence. I kept thinking about what lay beneath my feet, preoccupied and wondering, and when I finally glimpsed a change in the light and stepped cautiously out on the further side of the ridge, I found that it was dusk and I was quite alone.

This was all wrong. When I had gone in under the ridge, it had been much earlier. I was certain that I hadn't been knocked out: a little dazed, maybe, but not unconscious. Nor had I spent much time exploring the chambers, and yet here I was, a whole day later with the ghaiths rising in a cloud over the remains on the battlefield, carrion birds squabbling and battling over scraps of human flesh. There was no sign of dreamcallers or warriors, only an emblem stabbed at an angle into the black earth of Moon Moor.

I had to search for the warband. At first I was afraid they'd all been killed, but a quick examination of the corpses revealed an almost equal number of enemy and my own folk. I tracked them across the moor, following blood and mur-prints and boot-prints and broken scrub. They'd gone fast but not, I thought, fleeing.

I eventually caught up with them just as dark was falling over the moor, the moons already rising in a blue-stained sky and catching the clouds in a web of light. They were camped up in a knoll of rock, celebrating an unexpected victory: the enemy leader's mask had failed and he had become subject to his own dreamcallers' illusions, running amok and killing some of his own band. My people had fallen upon them in the confusion and they had fled. The warband had followed them for a distance, but they had vanished into the foothills, following tracks known only to themselves. It would make a good story for the winter fires; I wished I'd witnessed it. My clan leader said he'd never seen anything funnier and everyone was sorry I'd missed it.

I told them what had happened to my own self, the truth of it, with no small shame. But I did not tell them about the round gleaming room, nor the thing I had seen. I wasn't sure if it only had been a dreamcaller's conjuring, or that they would think me mad. I was a dreamcaller myself, after all, even if I wasn't a very strong one. They teased me enough as it was.

I slept badly that night, dreaming it all over again, and waking stiff in the morning to find the dawn coming up over Moon Moor and the warband ready to move on.

FIFTEEN

I am a weapon, or so the old woman had told me. But I am more than that. I am a creator.

I don't know what made me come up with the idea of the lodge. Maybe one of the visions whispered it to me out of the darkness and the flying shadows, or maybe it was simply that I was growing up and wanted a place of my own. After all, I'd never had one: first the place of heat, then the caves where we'd hidden, and then the journey to Muspell. Then I'd lived with the others, with the women's clans in their brochs. But now, Sull had proven something to me; my coming-of-age, if you like, my own personal ingsgaldir. I could work alone, I needed no one. But I wanted a house.

So I found one. It was in the deep forest, but oddly, not in Morvern. Instead, it was not far from Hetla: in a region so close to civilization that no one bothered going there. A small lodge, in a clearing in the forest.

There were people living in it, of course. I didn't want to inhabit a ruin. But soon I had the place to myself, and I settled down for a month or so to get the lodge into shape. I enjoyed decorating. I went out on little expeditions to get what I needed and soon the place was looking like it had in my mind's eye. The bones chimed when the wind blew and the sound made me feel sad and filled with longing, as though for somewhere that I'd never been.

I still think of it. I'll go back there one day, when I've done what I need to do, or perhaps it would be more realistic to re-create it somewhere else. Maybe then, it will be time to settle down.

SIXTEEN

Planet: Muspell (Vali)

I don't know what woke me. I came up out of sleep, or thought I had, with a strong, unquenchable conviction that there was someone in the room besides Eld and myself. I could be dreaming, I thought, but it seemed too real: the musty smell of old blankets and the distant hum of a generator somewhere didn't feel dream-like to me. Willing myself to lie still, I sent out the senses of the seith and encountered nothing, but the feeling lingered on. Eld still lay in an unmoving huddle.

I pictured someone tracking our thoughts, sensing our trail – this was paranoia, but I could not seem to shake the idea away. I lay there in a kind of half-waking doze, imagining something coming closer and closer yet.

And then someone *was* there, but I felt quite calm about it. I looked up into black blank eyes. The person – I could not have said whether it was male or female – gazed down on me with compassion as their hands moved, busy with something that I could not see, but functioning with a discernibly brisk efficiency. It would not take long, I thought. The person – it was a woman, I knew now – regretted some of what she had to do, but we both understood that it was necessary. It must have been the same with Idhunn – something deep inside me shrieked that this was Idhunn's murderer, the person I'd vowed to find in such grandiose vengeance, and soon, she would be my murderer too. But, strangely, I couldn't manage to feel upset at the idea. In a little while, I would be dead, and she would go on her way. I wondered, with detached curiosity, whether she had plans for Eld as well, or whether he would simply wake to find me there on the bed, filleted as Idhunn had been. I could even find a little trace of amusement in the notion—

—and the room exploded. The person was gone, hurled away from me. I heard a crash as something struck the wall and then everything was bursting with light. I shielded my eyes but it did no good: I could not see a thing. And then there was nothing, and after that, hot swimming dark.

When I came round, Eld was sitting on the opposite bed, wrapped in his lynx-fur coat, hands resting lightly on his knees and his gaze turned inward in the manner of someone examining a newsfeed. The air was thick with wings; feathers showered around him like autumn leaves and disappeared.

'Eld?' My voice sounded as small and frail as that of a mouse.

'Vali?' He did not look at me. 'You're awake. How are you feeling?'

I felt as though I should have been fragile and bruised, as though someone had spent a lot of time and effort in kicking me as I lay helpless, but the sensation was more psychic than physical.

'Battered,' I said, honesty overcoming pride.

Eld gave a small grim nod. 'I'm not surprised.'

'What the hell happened?'

'Seems Idhunn's assassin has found us.'

I sat up straight on the bed and this time he did look at me. I did not like what I read in his face, or in his eyes.

'Thorn, what's going on?' Glyn Apt had said she'd tell me, and so had Eld, but neither had kept to their promises, not that I expected them to. It simply infuriated me to think that they knew, and I and the Skald did not. Idhunn's bloody ghost seemed to stand before me for a moment, in unspeaking reproach, and behind her I thought that I glimpsed the Mondhaith girl, Gemaley. There were silver stars clasping the ends of Gemaley's braids; her face was frozen and blue, her lips gleaming with ice as she smiled. She didn't mind being dead, it seemed to me. She barely noticed the difference. I blinked, and both of them were gone.

'Eld?' I prompted. I expected a degree of prevarication, but not what the vitki subsequently said. 'You did a good job, with Frey. Was it hard to kill him?'

I thought for a moment before answering. 'Hard to get to the point of killing him. But not hard to kill, no. Do you mean that in an emotional sense, or a practical one?'

'Both.'

'I longed for his death. And he died.'

'How did you do it, exactly? We picked up from your

report to the Rock that you'd killed him, but you didn't say how you'd done it. Did you shoot him?'

'I set a pack of wild animals on him.'

That captured Eld's interest. He swung around, the pale eyes wide. 'Wild animals? That has a certain brutal elegance, especially considering what he did to you. It was supposed to be your ingsgaldir, your journey of initiation, wasn't it, when the fenris attacked you? But it went wrong.'

'He wanted me to realize that I could control other life-forms – animals, and other people. He told me that I had Darkland blood.'

'Did he tell you what I told you? That you could have been vitki? That you were special?'

'Yes. I didn't believe him and I cared less.' I spoke quietly, to show that this was truth and not bravado. Eld gave a slow nod.

'I see. Frey was always very concerned about status, about hierarchy, even though he pretended not to be. I thought it would be his downfall in the end.'

'You don't believe that the vitki are special? Superhuman? I thought that was the whole point of your sect.' I did not see the aim of this discussion. The bruised sensation was beginning to fade, a little.

'It was, and to most of us, it still is. But some of us see beyond that, and I am one of them.'

I rose and walked slowly to stand a little distance away from him. The window was a sea of night, boughs tossing in a rising wind. I could see the tip of the moon, hanging like a weapon in the branches. 'Does that mean that you don't agree with the war?'

Eld laughed. 'They can go to war if they wish. People's ambitions are very small these days. I don't care about the Reach, Vali. Darkland can subdue it, or negotiate with it, or destroy it, or sail away and leave it alone for all I care. I have other goals.'

'You said you know who the quarry is. Idhunn's murderer. You said she was here. Where is she now?' I rose to face him, backing him against the window. 'What is she? Tell me, Eld.'

'You've met her, Vali. I could feel her on you, around you, the last time we met. Here, in Darkland, near Hetla on the shore. A little piece of her presence, fluttering around you like a moth.'

I thought back. Ashy woods, with trees that erupted into sudden blaze as the resin caught in the heat of Darkland's fleeting summer. A forest like a gathering of cloud, captured mist above the thundering sea. A woman in a house in the forest depths, sitting in a room full of bones with a skull in her lap, staring at me, unblinking.

'That cabin,' I said. 'In the forest. It's her.'

'I told you that you knew her,' he said.

'But who is she?'

'She isn't a vitki. She's Morrighanu. I don't know what else she is.'

'What's her name?'

'Her name is Skadi. But they called her Skinning Knife, when they first found her in the forest. That was over ten years ago now. She had no papers, no documents, no clothes – she was living on her own and no one knows how she survived. Occasionally you find children who are feral – on the world you visited, Mondhile, that seems to be the norm. On more – human – worlds, you sometimes find children who are cared for by animals. But in the case of this woman, nothing would go near her. She was maybe twenty or thereabouts, and she took down two of the men who tried to catch her. Eventually they brought her back to Hetla and she was studied in an institute. No one ever found out who she was. They gave her a name but she wouldn't use it even after she learned to speak, and she learned damn fast. Feral children usually don't do very well once they're returned to civilization. This one did. This one did very well for herself.'

'They called her "Shadow",' I said, for that was what her name meant in one of the old Earth tongues. The goddess Skadi: the winter warrior, whose symbol is the snow itself. I could see why they'd given her the name. I thought of the spirit woman with her skinning knife. 'You said she isn't a vitki but she is Morrighanu.'

'Yes, she never joined the vitki. Although that's not entirely true. She initially became a valkyrie. She had considerable innate ability. Usually there's an argument with some of the upper echelons if we try to take outsiders in: valkyrie and vitki keep to their own. Not with this one. Everyone wanted the kudos of having her in their sect. She killed like an animal kills – quickly, with no remorse.' He paused. 'She was said to enjoy it as well as being good at it, and that always gives one a cachet in certain quarters.'

'And now she's working for Darkland,' I said, 'and may have murdered my mentor, though I don't know why.' Glyn Apt *had* lied to me, no surprises there. 'In that case, why are you trying to find her? And how did she find us? Was she ordered to kill Idhunn?'

'I am trying to track her down,' Eld gave a small ironic snort of laughter, 'because she isn't working for Darkland any more. At least, not for the central Parliament of the security forces – any more than Frey was. As for why she killed Idhunn, I've no idea.'

You do not have to be versed in the seith to sense the webs tangling around you, part of a greater, unglimpsed weave. In that dingy room the air seemed to thicken.

'So if she wasn't working for you, who was she working for?'

'I don't know.'

I frowned. 'But Frey was working for himself?'

'I don't know that, either. Tell me, Vali, what do you know about Nhem?'

That surprised me. 'Nhem? It's one of those extreme religious worlds. Founded by a fleet of cultists who'd captured a group of women and taken them along for breeding stock. There's a disparity between the actual races – the women are small and dark, the men are tall and light-skinned, a classic form of discrimination on old Earth. And the women are bred to be non-sentient, but some of them have reverted and banded together. They approached the Skald and hired me for a mission.'

'To assassinate the leader. Which you did. At no small

personal cost, I think.' The pale gaze was seeing too much now, boring into me, and I turned my face away. 'You were raped, after all.'

'And then I killed him.'

I could almost taste the question Eld was too sensitive, or perhaps too cunning, to ask. *Who was he standing in for, Vali? Which part of the past were you trying to avenge?*

'It was worth it, if they can use it,' I said curtly. 'Besides, I'd been raped before.' There was a little silence, filling the hollow of my words.

'Nhem always struck me as a very . . . black-and-white world. The men are cruel and ruthless, the women are victims.'

'Perhaps.' Eld was too clever to make trite observations, or to expect me to agree with them. I'd suffered at the hands of men: first my brother, then Frey, then the Hierolath. After Frey, I'd sworn off men, wanted nothing more to do with them. But I'd killed two out of three; my brother was long gone. And after all of them, the last person who had sexually assaulted me had been a girl: Gemaley. A young man had helped me, risked his life, and since then I'd teamed up with Eld. Well, in a manner of speaking. Nothing is simple.

Eld, watching me closely, went on, 'Not many shades of grey, on Nhem. But genetic engineering is a sloppy process; they must have realized that. It was bound to breed sports, not to last.'

'Switching sentience on and off,' I said, 'That's the common pattern – on Nhem, on Mondhile, here.'

'Do you know why you were hired to assassinate the

Hierolath? After all, the infrastructure of Nhem doesn't depend on one man.'

'We were told that it would destabilize things enough to let the free women create some changes. I don't know what they were planning, though.' I'd had my doubts at the time. 'Do you, Thorn? What does this have to do with Skinning Knife?'

'I don't know. Maybe nothing. But you're not the only one to have seith senses, Vali. I do, too. And something keeps prodding at me.' He paused. 'Frey's visit to Nhem with you wasn't his first visit.'

'I can see him getting on with the Nhemish like a house on fire. All those claims of male superiority.'

Eld's mouth quirked. 'He tried to give *you* an ingsgaldir.'

'Yes, but without bloody asking first! It's the same mentality, Eld, and you know it. Either they strip women of their identities by engineering them, or they apply psychological abuse that has the same effect. After Frey, I barely knew who I was. It's a difference in sophistication, that's all.' And Eld had tried much the same thing. More vitki mind games.

And last night, when *she* had bent over me, and made my death seem so perfectly reasonable. Vitki tricks and secrets . . . 'Where is Skinning Knife now?'

'You should have some understanding by now of how we operate. The vitki and the Morrighanu both are well versed in disguise, deception, sleight of eye. We use skills that we've been honing for the past thousand years.' He gave a brief smile that, after a moment, I realized had been intended to be reassuring. 'I don't think she came here to kill you, Vali, though I'm sure that's what you thought at the time. She came as a warning of what she is capable of doing. As soon as she saw me, she was out of here and in case you think I defended you, then think again. I did nothing, Vali. I could not. I sat here paralysed until several minutes after she had disappeared into the forest dark. And that terrifies me.'

I stared at him. I had not thought him to be the kind of man who would be terrified at anything. When we had met in Hetla, when he had brought me in for questioning, he had seemed all-powerful, knowing my head and my heart, completely in control. And now, as I stared into the cold grey eyes and saw the fear that he was no longer hiding, I understood that I had once again made the same mistake. I had invested him with powers and with an authority over me to which he was not entitled. It was unconscious, but potent nonetheless. It was exactly the same mistake I had made with Frey.

I rose to my feet and walked once more to the window. It took a moment of effort to look out into the forest, as though Skinning Knife herself might drop from the trees like some great silent bat. I felt myself shiver. Frey had been human. Eld was human, and so was Skinning Knife. On old Earth, my seith abilities would have seemed like magic. We were not, I told myself, dealing with anything beyond nature, simply someone versed in a variety of techniques, and the ruthlessness or insanity required to implement them in murder. I had put Frey to his death. I would track her down and I would serve this woman as she had served Idhunn. Before me in the moonlight, the forest seemed to glare and swim. I turned back to meet Eld's gaze.

'Tell me then,' I said. 'Where do we begin?'

SEVENTEEN

Planet: Nhem (Hunan)

The next few days were spent trying to bring in the meagre harvest before the rains came. Some of us had been farm-wives in our past lives, and knew instinctively what to do: they had it easier than us city women, I sometimes felt, for the farm-wives were the ones who had experienced more freedom. Though they all spoke of the hardships of land-working – something all of us knew by now – they also spoke of being left alone in the hot fields, the silences, the wind rushing through the grain, the pleasure of just *being*. I could understand that. It was why I liked the bell tower so much: there were no voices. The goddesses were quiet. The dust made only the faintest rustling as it skittered across the floor, and the high skirling of the efreets soon faded into the background. No one shouting, incomprehensibly or half-understood. No one making demands. The only thing that made demands on us now was the land itself; harvests don't wait.

Khainet came to join me in the gardens. We'd built these over a number of years, in the lee of the wall. The gardens were shady, but also got enough sun for the crops to flourish: gnarled fruit grew there, and a variety of tough, seeded grain that we made into porridge and bread. It was monotonous, but no one much minded. When Khainet found me, I was picking the long orange fruits we called *saq* and piling them into a basket. The sun had touched them a little too much and they were already starting to turn to mush; this evening, they would be sliced and layered in earthenware jars, or dried on the roofs for the short winter. Beyond the bulk of the wall, the clouds were massing and the air had the metal smell of approaching thunder.

Khainet took one of the *saq* from the basket and studied it as though she had never seen it before. Perhaps she hadn't, although they were common enough in some of the eastern districts around Iznar.

'If you eat that, you'll regret it,' I told her. 'They're bitter unless they're dried first.'

She put it back in the basket. 'Do they grow here naturally? Or did someone bring them?'

'We found a small grove of them inside the city. We've been cultivating them ever since. Birds drop things sometimes and they grow. But some of the women brought seeds in their clothing, or in scraps of food, and we've grown those, too.'

She nodded. 'I wondered where the food on the table came from.'

'It's a struggle, all the time. I'm sure you can see why. This isn't fertile country.'

'How did they manage, then? The – goddesses? Did they eat air?'

I smiled. 'We don't know. Maybe the land was more

fertile then. Maybe there was a blight, and that's why the city is ruined and abandoned now.'

'Where did they go, then? Why aren't any of them here now?'

'I've no idea.'

'I'd like to have seen them,' Khainet said, and I nodded as if in agreement, but privately I wondered whether it was best after all that the goddesses had gone, so that we could make them into whatever we wanted them to be.

Khainet wanted to help and so I let her carry some of the baskets through into the dark-store, where other women would prepare the fruit later. Years ago, I'd have done the carrying myself: I was a strong woman then, bred for it. But now the twists had come to my joints and I left the carrying to the younger women, like Khainet.

She took five baskets in, and I had to show her how to carry the first one, balancing it on her shoulder rather than hauling it along two-handed. It was clear that this kind of work didn't come naturally to her, and that bore out the truth of her story. It wasn't that I distrusted her, but our memories have been so ruined, and sometimes are nothing more than a smashed puzzle. You can get very confused as you pick through the fragments.

Khainet got the hang of the lifting, though, and I watched as she swayed down the narrow path between the bean rows, with the heavy basket cocked on her shoulder. After that first trip, when I'd made sure that she knew what she was doing, I took my eyes off her and went back to paying attention to the fruit. It was some time after she'd taken the last basket away that I noticed she hadn't come back.

I called her name. No answer. I hobbled along to the store, fearing the worst, and I was right. She was crumpled on the floor, with the basket beside her: she hadn't dropped it, but must have fainted just as she set it down. One hand had flopped into it, as if reaching for a fruit.

I felt for her pulse. She was breathing raggedly and her colour was bad: her skin looked like white dust. I tried rousing her, then forcing a little water down her throat, but she did not respond. I pushed a folded sack beneath her head, turned her on her side and went for help as fast as I could. By the time I reached the first row of homes – not far from the gardens, but in the full blaze of the sun away from the wall – I was panting and the buildings were turning from dark to light and back again. I was aware of hands taking me by the arm, leading me into the shade.

'Hunan! What's wrong?'

My sight was still too blurred to see her, but I recognized the voice. She'd come to us a decade ago. Her name was Tare. I tried to tell her what had happened, calmly and quietly, but I ended up blurting it out and not making much sense, either.

'Don't worry,' Tare said, and she *was* calm and quiet. 'I'll send someone to see to her.'

'I have to go back. I—'

'You stay here. Get your breath back first.'

She didn't give me a chance to argue. A moment later, she was gone into the warren of the house and I heard her calling out to somebody. It occurred to me that I had no idea who lived here: years back, I'd have been able to say exactly who lived with whom, even who loved whom, and I didn't know whether it was that the colony had grown beyond my ability to remember, or whether I was simply losing my grip. I leaned back against the rough grain of the couch and closed my eyes. I didn't mean to sleep.

In Iznar, we were allowed out by ourselves, but only to the marketplace by the city gate. As children, we were trained how to dress over and over again by our Fathers, while our mothers stood dumbly by. The sack-like thing we wore in the confines of the households had to be covered by another gown that we slipped over it, a wide, shapeless thing made of flounces. I don't know who made them, although years later one of the incoming women told me that they were issued by the Hierolath's people. It was obvious, looking back, that they kept to a standard pattern: as concealing as possible, with a head covering that was supposed to go over the face. Since we all looked more or less the same anyway, however, that rule was not so rigorously enforced as the actual covering of the head: failure to do so in the street would result in a beating from one of the militias and delivery back to house confinement. I never understood why my wrist ached and burned when I was a small child, nor the nature of the ceremony I underwent when I was delivered by my Father into House Father's custody along with a number of jars of household fuel, an old electric fan, and two pigs. It involved cutting the top of my wrist, then a tugging and pulling while I tried not to cry, then a bandage. Now, I think they were putting in something that held the details of where I lived, since I did not have enough words to tell anyone that.

The market, then, was the only place where we could go on our own. House Father would issue me with a piece of paper, which I was somehow given to understand was magical: if I handed it to the marketing manager, he would give me what I needed and I would carry it home, trotting like a dog, laden with baskets. Later, when Luck-Still-to-Come and Boy-Next-Time were older, I took them with me and they carried things, too.

But there was one day when we went somewhere other than the market. If I'd had awareness, it would have surprised me greatly, because the household routine had barely altered from its few patterns ever since I'd gone to House Father's house. As it was, House Father shooed myself and the girls into our gowns and out of the door before we had time to blink, then took First Joy by the hand and led him down the road. Meekly, we followed. We had no idea where we were going and we did not make a sound.

It was very hot. The cracked tarmac of the road surface had blistered into peeling puddles and they smelled pungent. Above us, the sky was bleached of colour by the heat. Iznar smelled and looked as it always did: low buildings, many of them falling down and separated by wide areas of weeds, filled with the smell of vehicle fumes, cooking oil, dust . . . And there were many more people than was usual even for market day: men and women, the women all gowned, just like ourselves. There was an odd feeling in the air – something tense and excited. I did not understand it, of course, but it affected me, making my skin itch beneath the flounces of the gown.

We trudged on through the afternoon heat, past the road that led to the marketplace. The girls tugged at my hand, expecting to take that road, but House Father, with First Joy close at his heels, was marching past. Mute and puzzled, we followed the men.

There was another gate. It was much bigger than the gate near the market, high and arched, topped with a dome made of a pale green stone. I thought it was beautiful. I couldn't stop staring at it, to such an extent that when House Father turned and saw me, he gave an impatient curse and struck the side of my head. It was a light blow, for which I was grateful, but I did not want another one and so I scurried on.

In the centre of the square that lay before the great gate was a strange thing: a tall turret, with a chain hanging from it. Crowds milled before it, not just men and their womenfolk, but traders selling food and baskets of things that, later, I understood to be religious symbols. House Father bought a basket of cracked corn for himself and First Joy. There was nothing for us, and I could see that Boy-Next-Time, who was greedy, wanted some, so I slapped her before she could howl. House Father would have hit her harder and I did not want that.

All of a sudden, however, the crowd fell silent. Everyone turned to the thing at the centre of the square as if they knew what was about to happen. We did not. We just stared. Beneath the green dome, the gates began to creak open: an awful sound of metal on metal. It reminded me of the forge down the road, which scared me – the showers of sparks, the terrible clanking and hissing noises – so that I always crossed over the road on market day and did not have to walk past it. I clasped my daughters' hands more tightly and took a step back.

They were the Hierolath's militia. They were bringing a woman through the gate, dragging her as if she was asleep. Now, I realize she had been stunned. A man stepped up to the base of the turret and started saying something in a loud voice, which naturally I did not understand. Every so often there would be cries and shouts from the men in the crowd. I stole a look at House Father and he was staring raptly at the man on the stage, his mouth slightly agape.

The militiamen hauled the woman like a sack of roots up to the stage. She was starting to wake up now. She looked wildly around her and she did not have control of her mouth: she was dribbling, saliva pouring in skeins down her chin. The ranting man on the stage grabbed the end of the chain and it came rattling down to hit the stone flags of the square with a crash. The woman flinched when she heard it and so did I. Very quickly, the militiamen attached the end of the chain to a ring round the woman's ankle. The man on the stage touched something set into the turret that I could not see – a winch, perhaps. The chain again rattled up, taking the woman with it. She was screaming. I looked up and saw her outlined against the burn of the sky, jerking and twisting from the chain that held her leg. A white bird fluttered up from somewhere and flew around her head, close enough that its wings brushed her twitching head. It made me hot and sick to look at the bird, though I did not know why. When they saw it, many of the men cried out as if they, too, were afraid.

More words from the man on the stage. Boy-Next-Time, Luck-Still-to-Come and I all stared in anticipation. The chain was released. The bird disappeared. The woman crashed to the floor and her head struck the flagstones. It burst like a melon dropped out of a window. Blood and something grey, like sponge, spilled out across the flagstones. The weight of the chain fell across her unmoving body.

The men all gave a great sigh, as if they spoke with a single voice. The women were silent. After that, we went home, but I looked back just as we were about to leave the square and saw that a swarm of hornets had settled on the body of the woman and were busy stripping it down to bone. The militiamen were going back through the gate, and I could not see the man who had been on the stage at all. No one was paying any attention to what was happening to the woman's body.

I dreamed about it that night, and for many nights to come. I still dream about it, and on the day when Khainet fainted, it came back with such force that I felt as though I'd lived through it all over again.

I woke to the stuffy heat of Tare's house, with the shadows falling long across the floor. Nothing stirred. I got to my feet. The heat sickness had faded and I felt clear-headed and light, too much so, as though I'd been detached from my body and was floating. It felt so strange that I almost nipped my arm with my nails, to make sure that I wasn't still dreaming.

I went out into the street, just in time to see Tare hurrying along it.

'Oh!' she said when she saw me. 'You're up. I didn't want to wake you.'

'I'm all right. How is Khainet?'

'She fainted. We took her to one of the houses and put her to bed. She'll be fine.'

'It must have been the heat,' I said, but the thought made me uneasy. Khainet hadn't long come out of the desert, and she'd been ill enough when she first arrived: what if I'd worked her too hard? Or what if she was still ill, with something we hadn't seen? We had no real medical knowledge, although we were learning. None of us had been doctors in the past: all the medics were men, of course. We relied on a few herbal painkillers and stomach remedies, but when someone got seriously ill, we couldn't save them or cure them. All we could really do was watch helplessly as they got better or died. If Khainet were among the latter – I remembered that beautiful face and graceful walk. If I'd seen my daughters grow up, I'd have liked them to look like that, though I knew full well they would have been just like me. Khainet's hair was the only odd thing; it fascinated me, but although it was long, it was too much like a man's in colour.

Tare took me to see her, but she was sleeping. She looked smaller already, as if she had shrunk, and the guilt for making her work washed over me like a wave, even though she'd insisted on helping. Together, Tare and I left her and walked back up through the town in what was now the evening cool. The clouds were still building up: big anvil thunderheads above the walls, lining the bell tower with indigo and flashes of golden light as the sun broke through.

'Storm on the way,' said Tare.

I nodded. I hated these coastal storms: building up all day until they filled your skull with pressure, then bursting once darkness had fallen to send hissing rains against the walls of the bell tower and thunder rolling overhead like a drum. It had been bad enough in the north. The girls had been calm enough, oddly, but my son had hated thunder, and, I realized now, hated me for seeing his fear. I felt a cold prick of shock at the thought.

It was almost dark now. I wanted to get in before the storm broke, and for Tare to be back at home. I wished that I'd stayed with Khainet, but she was safe enough where she was. I still felt responsible and once inside, even with the four walls of my chamber around me, I couldn't sleep.

The storm came an hour later, with the first downpour of rain. Lightning, a livid pink, lit up the chamber, casting the shadows into nightmare figures. I decided to forget about sleep: this storm would last until dawn. I got up again and made tea. The act of steeping herbs in the hot water was soothing, almost a meditation, but then there was a crash so loud that I wondered whether the bell tower had been struck. The walls shuddered and the tea slopped in its clay cup. It turned out to be the worst of it, though. After that, the storm rolled away a little, and shortly after that, there was a knock on the door.

My immediate thought was for Khainet. She had died. And when I saw Seliye standing on the step I knew that this was what she had come to tell me. So when she spoke, it took me a minute to understand her.

'There's a boat out there,' she said. 'With women on it.'

All the way to the shore wall, through that lashing rain, I thought she must be wrong. There was no boat. Or there was, but it was crewed by men. I asked Seliye over and over again if she was sure, until she became irritated with me and snapped that I would just have to see for myself.

Word had spread fast, in spite of the storm. There was a crowd on the shore wall, sheltering under sacks. Everyone was wringing wet, all the same, but they did not seem to mind. They were chattering and laughing as though it were a holiday.

'They see it as a sign,' Seliye said. 'First Khainet and her naming, and now this.'

'As a sign of what?' I asked.

She looked as me as though I'd spoken treachery. 'Of hope, of course.'

But I was not so sure. I could see the boat now – a little thing, a white oval with a ragged sail. But I stared at the raging sea, split with long lines of spray, and could not see how anything might survive it. Far out towards the horizon, I couldn't even tell what was sea and what was stormy sky.

'Seliye,' I whispered. 'They're not going to make it to shore.'

We had never considered the possibility that anyone might ever arrive by boat, not over that toxic sea. Years ago, one of the women had gone mad: her name had been Melay, I remembered. She had run screaming through the colony, shouting out that we were all devils and the men were right to take our tongues and our minds. Then she had run up to the rocks and thrown herself off into the high tide. The sight of her falling, limbs outflung, her graceless shrieking dive, imprinted itself on my memory like a burn scar. Now, the scar had flared up again and I saw her still. Her body had washed up a day later, eaten down by the sea until she was nothing more than a huddle of bone and rag. We had no boats, to go out and help this one, no grapples or ropes long enough to bring it in. All we could do, as so often, was watch and be helpless.

But the boat was still coming closer to the shore. We could see the crew: three women, half naked, clinging to the spars and paddling furiously. And to my amazement, they were bringing in the boat. As soon as they saw this, some of the women ran shouting down the steps on the outer side of the wall to the rocks.

'Be careful!' Seliye called. 'Don't get too close to the spray!'

It would be hard to avoid, I thought, and the women were running towards the edge of the rock. One of the women on the boat stood up unsteadily and threw what looked like a chain. A miss, another miss, our hearts in our mouths and then the women on the shore caught it. More had poured down to join them now, and they hauled the boat onto the rocks. The women tumbled from it without looking back, clutching a bag.

Like Khainet, they did not look like us. They were taller, still very dark, but with round faces that resembled one another. I wondered if they were sisters. There was no sign that they had been burned by the sea: they couldn't have been in it for long enough, and that was a mercy.

Shouting and celebrating, the crowd took them to the nearest house complex, Tare's home, and into shelter. Seliye threw everyone out except myself and the house complex's mothers. We all stood staring at one another in sudden quiet and yellow lamplight.

'You're welcome here,' I told them, the formal greeting, even though I knew they would not yet have language. But to my surprise the tallest woman – almost as tall as a man – spoke. It was guttural and strange, and I could not understand her. Seliye's face was a mask of shock.

'They can *speak*,' she said.

Another language. And so, maybe, another colony, somewhere. We weren't alone. There were others.

I glanced up and Khainet was standing in the doorway, clutching a robe around her. She was staring at the strangers, and I could not tell what was in her face.

EIGHTEEN

PLANET: MUSPELL (VALI)

Eld and I left the hostel the next morning. We saw no one and took care to go out by a back entrance that took us directly into the forest. I approved of such caution, but all the same, there seemed little point. Skinning Knife knew we were after her, knew where we were, could walk through a locked door as easily as a blade through air – I had to steer myself away from such thoughts, for they served no purpose except to increase my paranoia, already running at record level.

All the same, I asked Eld where we were heading. I didn't even know any more whether we were hunters or hunted and when I voiced that thought he gave me a sideways look and did not reply. The silence hung heavy in the air between us for a few minutes. Then Thorn said, 'You have to understand. It does not matter whether we pursue or are pursued, as long as we find her.'

'She's already found us first, Eld. What if you were wrong, and it was indeed murder she had in mind?'

'She likes to play, Vali. I've seen it in her before.' He paused and looked up into the cloud-grey trees, dripping with snowmelt. The air sang with cold. 'A cat with mice. It's a characteristic of both vitki and valkyrie, probably of Morrighanu as well. You do not understand it, I think. You are perhaps a more efficient killer.'

'If I am efficient, Eld, it is because I don't take any pleasure in killing. I see it as a necessity, nothing more.'

Eld gave his little smile. 'You are not attached to it. That's a good quality, Vali, and one that I believe I share.'

I wondered whether that was true. In him, or in me. Frey had enjoyed killing, and so had his Mondhaith girl. Gemaley was dead, drowned, but I kept thinking of her: tall, lovely, the ice-blue eyes and star-clasped hair, the sharp teeth and sharper smile. A demon princess. Gemaley's primary interest had been in hurting people. I suppose everyone should have a hobby.

Beside me Eld shivered, suddenly, so that the moisture on the lynx pelt flew in all directions.

'You haven't told me where we're going.'

'That's because I don't know.'

'Ah. So we are standing in the middle of a forest, in enemy territory, because . . .?'

'She'll have left traces.'

'Are you sure? I've seen nothing.' Since we had started making our way through the trees, I had been searching the air, sending out the seith for her, even though I feared what I might find. Apart from our time on Nhem, I had been able to track Frey as easily as if he had left his scent glowing upon the air, but Sull Forest felt dead to me. No birds sang; nothing rustled in the undergrowth. Perhaps it was a result of the devastation that the forest had apparently endured elsewhere, and perhaps not. I looked at moss, at lichen, at the slabs of bracket fungus that layered the tree trunks, checking for wind direction and the fall of infrequent sunlight. I looked at the ground, too, ashy with leaf fall, but there were no small footprints patterning it, no sign of animal life.

'She will have left something,' Eld said with grim confidence, and marched on into the gloom of the trees. Towards noon, we discovered just what she had left.

From above, the forest would have appeared impenetrable, but Eld led me sure-footed through the trees. Either he had some vitki means of tracking, or was using a more reliable map implant than the one I possessed. I kept a watchful eye on the sun, marking the twists and turns that we were taking: if anything happened to Eld, I did not want to be lost in the middle of Sull with an assassin out for my blood. I'd learned not to rely on my map implant. Technology, pitted against the harshness of worlds, is never all that reliable no matter what we want to pretend.

It was not just Skadi who was worrying me, nor concerns about the progress of the war, which were never far from my mind, but also the thought of what else might be lurking in these woods. Despite the lack of animal tracks, I was sure that there was bound to be something in the deep forest, perhaps further from human habitation. Fenris, sabre-toothed lynx, dire-wolf, aurochs – although the trees would have discouraged the latter. Like those of Mondhile, the ancestors of both Eld and myself had taken to engineering fauna imported from Earth with a lamentable degree of enthusiasm: reconstructing all those northern species that had perished amid Earth's climate changes and woeful record of pollution. No doubt they had considered Muspell's forests and ranges to be the ideal wildlife arena, and though I sympathized with the ideal, reality left much to be desired in these hostile, dripping woods. Moreover, no one in the Reach really knew what indigenous life Darkland might possess: I remembered the thing I had once seen in a tree outside Hetla, half-human, half-*other*, dying in a burst of flame as the tree exploded. I had no idea what it might have been. My far-back ancestors would have spoken of huldra or fey. This thing had been alien in some sense of the word: maybe genetically engineered like the Mondhaith or simply indigenous. Our ancestors were supposed not to have colonized worlds with their own sentient life, but accidents happened. And more than accidents, too. Intention.

With all these thoughts running through my mind I was well on my way to spooking myself even before Eld discovered the body.

We were crossing a stream, a narrow race of melt water through the tree roots, when I heard him exclaim. Balancing on a mossy rock in mid-torrent, I looked downstream to see him crouching over something in the water. The rocks made regular, if uneven, stepping stones and I went cautiously down to join him. He looked up at me, face white in the shadow of the trees, the lynx fur bedraggled where it was trailing, unheeded by Eld, in the water. A swirl of scarlet was welling up from the clear bottom of the channel.

I took a step back and nearly fell into the torrent. I could feel it in the air now, as though a rent had been torn through the air, a gateway into death. The place sang with the echoes of recent violence. Whoever lay at the bottom of the stream had been killed, brutally.

I looked over Eld's shoulder into the water. Someone lay there, face down, but the stream was clear enough for me to see the long lesion where the spine had been, the flesh fluttering in the water-flow like the tentacles of an anemone. Here was a man, killed in the same manner as Idhunn.

Eld was eloquently silent. I drew the seith around me, merging myself with the rush of the water and the slow presence of the stones. To anyone who might be watching, I would not be invisible, exactly, but hard to see. Their gaze would glide over me, seeing me merely as part of the landscape. I would be of so little interest as to be unnoticeable. It was hard to do, in the wake of this atmosphere of violent death, and I doubted whether it would fool Skinning Knife, but it made me feel better. Eld watched without comment.

'Do you feel her here?' I asked.

He shook his head. 'Not any more, but I confess I can't be sure. Help me bring him up, Vali.'

Even through slickskin gloves, the water chilled me to the bone. Together we pulled and tugged at the filleted corpse, which had either become wedged, or had been deliberately secured, amongst the rocks on the stream bed. With Eld taking the head, and myself the feet, we managed to bring the body over to the opposite bank and set him down on a carpet of curling fern shoots. Eld rolled him over, revealing a young man with long dark hair, now matted into a sodden mass. His jaw was wedged open in rictus, a soundless shout. Sea-blue eyes stared up at us. Eld and I stood looking down at him, noting the patched slickskin, the knives at his belt. She had not bothered with his weapons and they had not been enough to save him. A hunter, clearly, probably a local. I wondered whether he had crossed her in some way, or whether he had simply been unfortunate enough to be the first one she met who would serve as a demonstration model, a gory clue to be thrown carelessly in our path. Somehow, I had no doubt that we had been meant to find him.

Then the man blinked. Both Eld and I leaped backwards and clutched at one another. It must have looked comical, had anyone been watching. The locked jaws released, clattered together with a click.

'Better look harder,' the corpse said, in a soft and mocking woman's voice. I barely heard it through the clamour of questions in my own head: *he cannot be alive, can he? His backbone is gone, this is madness, am I really seeing this?* – a tumult of atavistic, superstitious horror that was broken only when Eld gave a muffled curse and dropped to his knees by the body. He reached into the opening mouth and swiftly extracted a small gleaming pellet.

'Holographic recording. He's dead as dead can be, Vali.'

I pretended that I was kneeling by his side, as opposed to sinking into the ferns with relief.

'She's teasing,' Eld said softly in turn.

Rapidly, we searched the man's pockets but found no

trace of identification. Eld rolled him over and parted the mass of hair at the back of what remained of the corpse's neck.

'What are you looking for?'

'Identification coding. Everyone in Darkland whom the state can reach has a code embedded in the skin.' He brushed the hair up to reveal an area of thick grazing, already bled pale and puffy by the action of the stream. 'Nothing. I wonder whether she's mutilated him to hide the code, or the fact that he hasn't got one?'

'You said: anyone the state can reach. Presumably that wouldn't mean the forest clans?' We were a long way from Hetla, and my experience with the Morrighanu had taught me that Darkland was filled with different sects. And if Skinning Knife *was* Morrighanu anyway . . .

'No, it wouldn't. They're an unknown quantity.'

'Do you know what she does with the spines?'

'Trophies, perhaps. Or maybe not. She collected the bones of previous victims but I don't know whether that's still the case.'

'If this was the Reach,' I said, 'we'd bury him with as much honour as we could.'

'But this is not the Reach. This is Morvern, where bodies are put in the branches of the blaze trees, or sent out to sea, or left for the beasts,' Eld said. And so we learned what we could from the corpse and walked away, leaving the dead among the first fronds of spring.

*

I could feel her on the air, now: a clotting trace of rage. It was intermittent, a sensation which came and went, sometimes curling insidiously over my skin when I was least expecting it, sometimes casting a shadow over my senses like a rush of dismay. It reminded me of Gemaley, but it was much stronger and more assured: Gemaley if she had been older, trained, more subtle. *Angrier*. This made me nervous; it felt too much like my own fury, the rage I'd lived with after my brother, after Frey. The rage I pretended I didn't have, that I'd tried to cut out of my skin, carving its runes in my own flesh and blood. It made me feel a connection with Skinning Knife and I didn't want that. How much had dead Gemaley reminded me of myself, hurting because she could? I was a career assassin, she was an isolated psychopath. We were not the same, nothing like.

I wondered whether Skadi had left such a trail on purpose, if she might be luring us in with gleeful patience. Eld had suggested, and I had felt, that she was mad. Still, it was impossible to second-guess the insane, without following them too far into the dark. And I did not like feeling so trapped. Eld and I could leave Sull, return to our respective nations, hide out, but she would still find us if she chose.

We made a rudimentary camp in the middle of a small grove of trees. The ground here was bare of ash and snow: we were moving steadily south into Morvern, away from the ice, and the snow was growing patchier.

'How long does summer last here?' I asked Eld, as we sat around a small glow-pack.

'Not long. The same as the northern parts of the Reach in

these latitudes, but Morvern has always had a reputation for being colder than elsewhere. In Hetla, the snow is almost gone now.' He held out his palms to the glow-pack, the faint light flickering across his face. He looked unreal in the half-light, and harmless: a slightly soft middle-aged man. I was having to remind myself more and more often that he was vitki, that I shouldn't let my guard drop. *My enemy's enemy is my friend.* An old and bitter saying, and I wondered in this case how true it really was.

'What about you, Thorn Eld?' I asked him, curious. 'You know all about me and I know nothing of you. What's your life like, in Hetla?'

Eld gave me an indulgent smile. 'The same as any vitki's. I have a small apartment in security headquarters, the fortress. My work takes up most of my time. I live quietly, outside it. You are too subtle, Vali, to think that the vitki spend all their free time in torture and espionage simply because of the love of it, but I have met people who think this. I do what needs to be done. That's all.'

'And so if you're not spending all your free time torturing dissidents, what do you do?'

'Listen to music, read, study history, play chess. Very dull really.'

'Are you married?'

'No, I never have been. Vitki tend not to form permanent attachments. The natural partners are the valkyrie – a lot of the younger men go from one to another, and vice versa. But they can be a little . . . demanding.'

'I can imagine. The valkyrie are enhanced, aren't they?

The one I once saw in your office had some kind of visual implants.'

'They're heavily enhanced, the more so as one goes up the ranks. The upper echelons are really barely human any more and have no wish to be. Ultimate strength, ultimate fighting capability, no time for emotional weakness – they draw on mythology. Like the Morrighanu.'

'In mythology they were also celestial bar girls.' I had a hard time imagining a modern valkyrie with a pitcher of beer and her hair in braids.

Eld laughed. 'I know that, but I've never dared mention it. They pay a price for what they undergo. Some societies have a far greater technological efficiency than we do. The modifications one can undergo on Muspell are not always that . . . effective. The body rejects, starts to break down. A lot of the valkyrie have immune problems.' He paused. 'It makes them tetchy.'

'And this woman – Skadi, Skinning Knife? What enhancements did she have?'

'She had none at all. That's what worries me. She claimed not to need them, claimed innate genetic superiority – and believe me, among the valkyrie, that's a claim that can get you challenged or dead. But they left her well alone. Perhaps they sensed that it was true.'

'She's psychotic. But what else is she?'

'Of course she's psychotic. But to the valkyrie, that's an advantage. Like the Morrighanu, they practise disciplines that aren't all that far removed from those of your Skald, but which rely to a greater extent on personal suffering as a tool for self-discipline. They go through extremes of self-denial, mortification, pain.' That explained Glyn Apt's ill humour, I thought.

We fell silent. After a while, Eld said, 'If you want to sleep, I'll sit first watch.'

I did not want to say: *I'm too afraid to fall asleep,* like a child in the dark. I thought, *I have the seith,* but the seith had not protected me from her last time, and it hadn't protected me from Gemaley. It was erratic, tied too closely into my emotions. Maybe that was why the valkyrie tried not to have any.

I thought of waking again to find Skinning Knife standing over me as I lay, passive and helpless. I had not minded that she had been about to subject me to terrible death and I wondered whether the man we had found in the stream had also slid indifferently down into the dark, convinced of the rightness of it all. This seemed to me to be the most dreadful thing about her: that she could kill you and you would not mind.

As if he had read my thoughts, Eld said, 'Use what powers you have. Now that we know what she can do, I will remain vigilant.'

'And if she overpowers you?'

'She will not,' Eld reassured me out of the dark. In the light of the glow-pack, I glimpsed the beat of wings and strangely, this made me believe.

When I woke again, Loki was high above me and Eld was touching my shoulder.

'What is it?' I came awake immediately, as if doused with snowmelt.

'There's someone out there.' Eld's voice was a breath in my ear; even so close as he was, I barely heard him.

'It is her?' I hated myself for sounding so fearful, but Eld ignored it. I rose to my feet, listening.

'I am fairly sure that it's not,' Eld said. 'See what you can feel.'

Shadows. I sent out the seith, probing cautiously into the darkness. It was like putting a hand through a hole in the cellar wall, expecting the bite at any moment. But the bite did not come. I could feel traces in the night, a strange, half-hesitant expectancy, as if someone out there was waiting for something to happen. Power, and pain, and loss – all of these things were waiting.

'I don't think it's an animal,' I murmured to Eld. 'I think it's human.'

There was a soft laugh behind us. Eld and I span round. Someone was standing at the entrance to the grove. Eld brought the glow-pack up, along with his weapon.

'You won't have to shoot,' a voice said. Female, and not young. The wavering light played across the figure of an old woman, wrapped in a mass of skins and pelts from which a seamed face peered.

'And who the hell,' said Eld, with an uncharacteristic quiet fury that I thought was born of fear, 'are you?'

'A herder, once. I live here, now. I know you're looking for someone, a shadow-woman. A killer. She passed this way, as she did last spring and then again in the winter. They know her, in Sull, after the massacre. But no one goes near her.' The Gaelacht of this part of Darkland was different to that of the Reach, although I had a tabula with me. But this woman spoke clearly, in a strong voice and I had no difficulty in understanding her accent. I would not have expected this, from the remoteness of Morvern. And what 'massacre'?

'Then where is she now?' Eld spoke with urgency.

'The place where she always goes. Her home.'

I felt Eld become still and tensed by my side, like a hunting dog. 'And where might that be?'

'In the heights. The oldest place of all Morvern.'

'Can you take us there?'

The woman snorted, in an *are-you-joking?* manner. 'Why would I?'

'Well then, can you tell us where it is?'

'You can follow her yourself, vitki. Tell your ravens that it is in the crags of the far northern icefield, close to where the blight has crept. It is hidden, high in the rocks, in the volcano known as Therm. Tell your ravens to look for the heat traces, seeping through the rocks above it. You'll find her there.'

'How do you know that?'

'I told you. It is her home. Or as close as she seems to get to one.'

'And how do you know this?'

'They would not go near her, even when she first came here, a grown girl. Her foster mothers lived there.'

'Her *foster* mothers?'

'What, you thought the fenris raised her? Perhaps they would have been kinder kin.'

'Are any of her foster mothers still alive?'

'Oh no. The forest clan that the last one ravaged killed her, when they finally tracked her down. It was the talk of Morvern, but of course no one would speak to an outsider of it.'

'Yet you are doing so now.'

'I can see what you are. You are vitki, and her enemy – I can feel it on you. I also want her gone. This one is worse than the foster mothers, much worse. The forest clans have had their fill; they are preoccupied with fighting the fenris and the other beasts that have been driven north out of blighted Sull. But make no mistake, they want her gone, and so do I.'

'All right,' Eld said warily. 'We'll do as you suggest.' I glanced at him, and when I glanced back again, the old woman was gone. Eld and I, keeping close together, made a quick search, but she was nowhere to be found: it was as though she had been snatched up into the trees.

'Therm,' Eld said bitterly, when we were once more sitting over the glow-pack trying to warm our numb hands. 'If there's a worse bit of Morvern, I don't know of it.'

'Could she have been lying? And what was that about a massacre?'

'Very possibly. And there was a massacre here, a couple of years ago, but I don't know anything more about it. I thought it was some clan thing. Anyway, I'm reluctant to go off on a wild goose chase on the word of a fucking Norn.'

Eld sounded more harried, and more human, than I had ever heard him. The vitki polish was beginning to wear thin.

'So am I. I'm reluctant to *be* here, Eld. My nation's at war; I should be back there.' But Skadi was Idhunn's murderer. That gave me a reason to go after her, but I still wasn't sure about Eld's own reasons.

'But you're not back there, are you? And there's no way of getting back.'

I sighed. 'But we do have a choice, don't we? Follow her advice or follow our own wits.'

'The trouble is,' Eld said gloomily, 'that the two might very well prove to be one and the same.'

By this time, the sky was glowing green with the light of approaching dawn.

'You ought to get some sleep,' I said to Eld.

'I don't need it.'

'You'll need to sleep some time, surely? You didn't get much last night.'

Eld rose abruptly and started packing up our scattering of possessions. What was I, I thought, his wife?

'It's all right,' he insisted. 'We are depending on one another's fitness, mental and otherwise. It's right for you to be concerned about mine. But I assure you, we're trained in sleep deprivation. I've certainly had enough practice in it.'

And with that, we set off. By unspoken consent, we were heading in the direction of Therm. It was still cold, with a bite and snap to the air, but I could smell spring on the wind and also, sometimes, the sea. I checked the map implant for the configuration of Morvern, but it was incomplete. When I mentioned this to Eld, he said, 'Morvern is also called the Unknown Land, even in the rest of Darkland. There are legends of ships approaching charted bays, only to find impenetrable cliffs; hunters realizing to their doom that the land has shifted and changed around them.'

'Are the legends true?'

Eld hesitated. 'I would like to say that they are not.'

Certainly, I would not have been surprised to find that the forest was prone to shape-shifting. The grey needles of the trees drifted above us, merging with the rise of snow-clouds that massed far to the north. It was late in the afternoon when we saw our first fire.

Fortunately, Eld and I were not close to the tree when it went up. It exploded in a hissing cascade of sparks, sending burning cones shooting out through the snowy branches like fireworks. Eld pulled me back as a blazing cone landed at our feet and smouldered to ash in the snow, releasing its cargo of hot seeds, which sizzled down through the snow to the earth beneath. The rest of the tree was soon consumed, branches withering to black twists in the intense heat, needles transforming into a welded grey mass, soft as wool hung on wire. Eld and I hurried on.

'What makes them burn?' The air was still bitter, snow still patching the ground. I could see how wood might spontaneously ignite in hot desert climes, but not here.

'Legends say,' Eld explained, with an arch look, 'that these trees are linked to the fires of Hellheim and sometimes those fires blaze up within them and take their spirits down to the underworld. But that's just a story. In fact, the fires are caused by some kind of internal photosynthetic reaction that is triggered by light and not heat – now that the days are getting longer, the trees are starting to respond. The seeds are activated by heat.'

'So we'll see more of this?'

'Almost certainly.'

Not reassuring, I thought. I could see one of us easily being felled by a burning branch: the trees might look frail from a distance, but among them, you could see how substantial they were. The tree had gone up without warning; had barely registered in the seith before it was ablaze. And there was no way of avoiding them. We would just have to be extra careful, and hope.

As we gradually trekked further south, the snow that covered the ground began to merge into ash, until we were ploughing through ankle-deep grey drifts. It was softer than snow, but clung to my boots so that I began to develop bears' feet, shaggy with ash. Perhaps, I thought hopefully, it would at least serve to muffle my footsteps, assuming anyone was listening. I could still sense Skinning Knife, a thin, eerie presence hanging on the air, faint as the scent of the sea. But I began to feel a little easier, knowing that the trees through which we walked had already blazed up to release their seed load. Surely, I thought, they would not do so twice . . .

We camped in another grove that night, one filled with the stench of fire, and I took the first watch. No one came out of the shadows to visit us this time, neither ally nor enemy. Eld sank into immediate sleep and remained unmoving until I woke him in time for his own shift. I did not expect to sleep, but when I next awoke, it was morning.

NINETEEN

Planet: Mondhile (Sedra)

The mountains for which I had always longed hung in the air beyond the moor, the foothills invisible in a sea of mist, the glacier summits floating like islands. Now, with memories of my time in the warband still echoing in my head, I set off in the direction of Moon Moor.

And it wasn't just the mountains that were calling me. I wanted to see that strange underground place again. I wanted to find out if I'd just imagined it, under the enemy dreamcallers' thrall, or whether it had been real – and if so, what it was. There were all manner of weird things in the north – ruined towers, ancient abandoned fortresses. But I'd never heard of anything like the underground chamber, with that shifting half-beast half-human figure, and I'd never heard of anything like the insect that had descended onto Moon Moor and stolen my sister, either. The Moor held mysteries and I was at the end of my life now, not far from dying. I didn't think I had anything left to lose.

By the time I reached the old earth road that led to the Moor, it had started to snow. I'd taken warm clothes with me: the same thick cloak and stout gloves that I'd worn in the warband all those years ago. No point in getting rid of them if they were still good. The cloak was a little bloodstained, but I didn't mind that, though I couldn't remember now whether it had been my blood or someone else's. So much war, resulting in nothing. But we'd all had a good enough time, even the dead, so I suppose that was what counted. There weren't many of the warband left these days: most of them had died in other battles, or from fever, or had gone out into the world when their death drew near, just as I was doing. I counted myself lucky to have made it this far. So I pulled the stained cloak a little closer and trudged on through the snow.

It was only a light fall, this early in the winter, just enough to dust the scrub. The mountains were lost in it, but towards late afternoon, the clouds rolled back to reveal those floating peaks, still very far away. I looked back to where the sun was settling in a red smear over the coast, staining the snow with a bloody light. I started looking around me for shelter, reading the lines of the land, and finding it in a heap of rocks like a cairn, piled high above the path. The lack of a knife bothered me as I climbed the low rise of the slope: if this was a beast's lair, visen, altru, perhaps even wild mur, or if a child was hiding out here, I'd be in trouble. But so be it, I had to remind myself. This was what I was here for: to meet my death, no matter what form it took.

But not today. There was no sign of any animal up at the cairn, no spoor, or footprint, or telltale smell. Altru stink: it's something in the glands under their tails, and they say that people in the south keep tame altru and make perfumes of it. Still, I wouldn't fancy smearing myself with something out of an animal's arse. They're a funny lot down there, though. If you keep yourself clean, what do you need perfumes for?

At the back of the cairn, facing the mountains, was a pile of rock with a hole in it, a good place to spend the night. I gathered ferns, dry and crackling now with the cold, dusted off the snow and made a bed. A few minutes after that, I had a fire lit. Then I found a heppet burrow, sat in front of it in silence for a while, and started drumming on the earth with my fingers. You have to get the pressure right, or they won't fall for it. But I'd had a lot of practice over the years and soon enough the heppet stuck its head out of its burrow for a look, and that was when I collared it. It didn't have time to be surprised. I broke its neck and skinned it with my claws, leaving the skin for those nightbirds that eat fur. The rest of the heppet went on a makeshift spit over the fire and it made a good supper, once I'd found some late herbs to go with it. I thought of eating it raw, but my teeth weren't as good as they'd once been. Then I buried the bones and lay down, though it was a while before I slept. The clouds were still hanging over the mountain wall but directly overhead the sky was clear enough to see the winter stars: the Island, and Visen, and Cold Castle. I traced them all, and thought of my sister. I felt very close to her then, as though she was just around the corner of the rock, waiting for me. And then I slept. But I do not remember what I dreamed.

The snowfall had taken the edge off the air, but during the night another wall of freezing air rolled down from the mountains and touched the land with its breath. When I woke, the embers of the fire were grey and the edges of my cloak were stiff with frost. I got to my feet, with a bit of difficulty. Growing old is just the way of things but I've never stopped resenting the way it traps and ambushes you, so that what you never used to think about is now a constant pre-occupation. Maybe dying in battle is better after all.

And maybe not. The land was silent, locked in snow halfway down the slopes and frost below that, magnificent under a sharp blue sky. The mountains were very clear this morning: seeming so close that I felt I could reach out and touch them, run a fingernail down the ridge of a glacier and scrape out snow. And at the base of the frosty hills lay a black line, very well defined and rolling like a snake. That, maybe fifteen *lai* away from where I stood, was Moon Moor. Well named, for the moon Embar was hanging above it, its chewed face transparent enough to show the sky behind. The ghosts that lived on Embar would be sleeping now, although someone had once told me that it is always night on the moons, with no real sky.

I broke a thin rim of ice on a nearby pond, more a shallow puddle at the bottom of the cairn, and washed as best I could. There's no excuse to go dirty to your death. Then I wrapped myself in the cloak again, ate some of the heppet and made a small parcel of the rest, and scuffed over the ashes of the fire. I did not want to leave tracks behind me, just in case – a legacy of warband days. It would have been a small luxury not to have bothered, I suppose, but old habits die hard. Then I set off, towards Moon Moor.

I'd hoped to keep the moor in sight all the way, though I don't really know why this seemed so important to me. Perhaps I thought it might vanish, shimmer into mirage if I took my eyes off it. But the best path led me down into a dip, following a crashing stream, through groves of satinspine and cruthe. The black bark was peeling into strips now, and a few red leaves still hung from the branches like banners. But most of them were gone, and the summer vegetation – the ferns and dream-plants – had rotted too, sinking down into the earth for their winter sleep. I'd heard – another family story – that the plants appeared in Erestha-han, growing out of the sky in the land of the dead as though it lay beneath our feet instead of the place-between. But the thought made me smile, all the same. I even looked up, to see if roots and coiled shoots were hanging down from the clouds, but the sky was empty, bright and bare even of the promise of snow. I must be growing senile, I thought, and I walked briskly on. Towards noon the woods thinned out and I took a beast track up through the trees to a ridge. I was at the edge of the Lakeland country now: pools and ponds were strung like a skein of beads below the ridge, all the way to the edge of Moon Moor. I dropped down to them once, to pick up a bird whose feet had been frozen into the ice. A kindness to kill it, and I did so. That took care of my night meal, and then I made my way back up to the ridge and on. As the glaciers started to shine in the sun's dying light, I reached the edges of the moor, in sight of the place where the warband had been ambushed.

It had been long ago. Maybe forty years, or more: I'd been a young woman then. Good days. I liked to think that I could still see the scorch marks on the scrub, still smell the smoky, dream-laden air. But now the moor was peaceful and overgrown, the ridge far smaller than I remembered it, lost in growing bushes. Yet I could still feel the dead beneath the earth, their bones pulling and tugging at me like the tide, and I could hear their faint angry voices as they lamented their death. Their spirits had perhaps not gone to Erestha-han, but had become part of the substance of the moor, just as the pregnant warrior with the shattered jaw had done. I remembered her well, her fierce broken grin, her exultation in the latest killing. Maybe my own dreamcalling had summoned her up but I hoped I would meet her again, that she would be the one to greet me at my death and take me down to hell. She reminded me of me.

I pushed my way between the bushes, looking for the entrance to the cave. Nothing. There was no sign of any opening, not even a hole small enough for a heppet. When I had finished scrabbling, and emerged scratched from the thorny scrub, the sun was low on the horizon and I knew that I had to find somewhere to make a shelter for the night. In the end, it was the back of the ridge itself, the spine of rocks. I lit a fire and cooked the bird, wondering whether it had been a dream only, or whether there really was another world beneath my feet.

*

And then the dream came back. I woke, or thought I had, and it was night. The moon Elowen hung in a sword's curve where the sun had been, and Embar was still at its height, sailing the summit of the sky. The darkness was dusted with stars and the cold roared into my throat when I sat up and took a breath.

At first I didn't know what had woken me up, and then I heard it. *Voices*. People were speaking, in hushed tones that occasionally rose like the sound of the sea. I thought for a moment that they'd seen me, were discussing me, but then I realized that the voices were coming from the other side of the ridge.

I might be old, but I could still move quietly. I crept up over the top of the ridge, relying on soldiers' tricks of stealthy movement. They came back quickly enough. When I reached the summit of the ridge and could look through the rocks, I did so.

There were four of them. They were standing in Elowen's light. They were human, at first sight, and then I saw that this was not true, not quite. They wore clothes – long tunics like robes, and boots made out of leather strapped with thongs, like the people who live in the deep forest. But I could see their faces quite clearly in the moons' light and their faces were all wrong. Not muzzles, but too long for human faces, with eyes that were either too big or too small. Their jaws looked mangled, as if their owners had met with an accident. They had patchy, mangy hair, and fingers that were little more than stubs. I had never seen anything like them before and I did not want to see them now. The teeth that I could glimpse through their mangled jaws were sharp. I could not understand them – it was no language that I'd ever heard – and they smelled rank, an abnormal smell, like sickness, which drifted through the clean scents of scrub and cold earth.

I did not fancy challenging them, or making them aware of my existence. But perhaps they were aware of it already; had been watching me from secret places as I made my way across the Moor. I didn't like that thought. And it raised the question of how long they had been here.

I began to draw back among the rocks, but as I did so, they vanished. It made me blink. They had simply gone, as if they were shadows. I did not want to investigate the place where they'd stood: that would wait for morning and daylight, which in any case was not now far away. I went back to the remains of my fire and huddled wakeful until dawn.

TWENTY

Planet: Muspell (Vali)

By mid-morning the trees were starting to grow thinner, and the ash that coated the ground was now banked in great drifts against the curves of the land. Eld frowned when he saw this, but said nothing, and I remembered the woman in Hetla telling me of Sull Forest and its blight when I was in the capital on a previous journey. This, perhaps, was the real start of it and when we came out of the trees and found ourselves on a long, empty slope of hillside, with the blackened stumps of trees across the distant lee, I knew that I was right.

Eld stood unmoving for a long time, staring across the slope. At last he said, 'It's worse than I had imagined. Worse than I was shown.'

'You've seen images of this?'

He nodded. 'At the top levels of the vitki high command. And now I am finally telling you something that is not common knowledge.'

'Eld – what caused this destruction? That woman I met in Hetla said that it was the war effort. What did she mean?'

'The common people were not told, Vali. Everyone in Morvern knew about this, but only the vitki and the upper echelons of the valkyrie were informed. I don't know about the Morrighanu. The vitki knew, of course, because we caused it.' He glanced uneasily around him, as though the wind was listening. 'It was a weapon. Something new, something prototypical.'

'But this is a huge tract of land, Eld,' I said. I could see the wasted hillsides rolling as far as the horizon. A thought crept into my head and nestled there like a worm. 'This wasn't nuclear, was it?'

'You know that's illegal, planet-side,' Eld said, perfunctorily, as though paying lip service to some impossible ideal. 'But no, in fact it wasn't nuclear. It was something else, developed in a vitki lab.'

'Then what was it?'

'I don't know.'

I stared at him. 'What do you mean, you don't know?'

'No one knows except the people who engineered this thing, and activated it.' Eld grimaced, as if embarrassed. 'I told you about vitki arrogance, vitki short-sightedness. This is probably the best example of that.'

'"Probably"?'

Eld pointed to the distant wastes. 'The lab was over there, somewhere. The epicentre was at some point in that direction, according to the map implant.'

'It blew up?'

'It vanished. And it seems to have dragged the rest of the land with it, like water down a plughole.' Eld took a handful of his own cloak, pulling it taut and poking a finger in the centre of the stretched fur. 'Just like that.'

I looked down again at the ashy ground and now that he

had shown me this, I could see the long striations in the soil, running north to south.

'But of course, no one knows what they were working on, or what actually happened, because there's no one left. One minute the lab was transmitting data back to Hetla, the next – it was gone, blinked off the screen. And when my colleagues investigated, they found that it had taken a large chunk of Sull with it, as well.'

'But you said "vanished". Surely an explosion would have caused the same effect on a monitor?'

'It could have done, yes, but later the high command received raven reports which showed the lab at the time of the catastrophe. It simply blinked out of existence and a firestorm raged through the forest. Some ravens are partially satellite-generated, so the data stream remained constant. If there had been any recording devices actually here, they would have been incinerated.'

'And you really have no idea what they were working on?'

'No. I suspect that other people in the high command do, but the trouble with the vitki hierarchy is that it is highly cellular and compartmentalized. Our right hand doesn't know what our left hand is doing, and that's the way we prefer it.' Eld spoke sourly; I did not think it was a policy with which he agreed. 'And if someone knows, they're not telling.'

'What was a *vitki* lab even doing out here? I thought you said that Morvern is a law unto itself. The Morrighanu are a different sect. Why would it be safe to plant one of your operational facilities in the middle of what amounts to hostile territory?'

'It's not that simple. There are connections, negotiations, informal treaties. The existence of the lab would have been agreed with the Morrighanu, at least.'

'Do you have any idea whether it's even safe to walk through this region now? Might there be some kind of . . . taint, like radiation?'

'Vali, I have no idea. But if we are to get to Therm, then the swiftest way is through the blight itself.' Eld and I stared at one another for a moment. 'But it does have one advantage,' he added, with a smile. 'No one from Morvern is likely to come in here after us.'

'Very well,' I said at last. 'Then we'd better start walking.'

The only pity was that Eld was wrong.

It was only towards evening that I began to realize how extensive the blight had been. Sull stretched ahead and behind us, a wasteland of shattered tree stumps, black and glossy as if vitrified. When I tentatively touched one, it felt as hard as stone and was icy even through my glove. It reminded me of the cliffs that surrounded Darkland's shores. Eld watched me sidelong.

'Best left alone,' was all that he said.

The rest of Sull Forest had seemed barren enough, but this area looked absolutely lifeless, without even a wind stirring. The ash still covered the ground, but there were many places in which it had worn away and there was no earth beneath it, only something hard and, occasionally, polished, as if the whole region had been carefully paved. It was often slippery underfoot and I began to be grateful for the ash. When I reached out with the senses of the seith, I felt nothing: an absence of life, of presence, as though this land was no more than a stage set, an unreal shell, concealing nothing. And the air itself smelled strange, hollow, as sterile as a hospital wing.

Eld and I again made camp, again kept watch. Nothing came to disturb us, but I did not sleep well this time. And when it was my turn to take watch, I felt increasingly as though I was merely playing some kind of role, detached from the world. I did not want to tell Eld how much this alarmed me, but next morning I could tell that he, too, was spooked. I noticed that we were keeping close together, that he kept darting glances at me from those pale eyes as if to reassure himself that I was still there.

'How far is it to Therm from here?' I asked him, towards noon.

'About fifty miles. I'd estimate that we have another couple of days in the blight.'

'How are you doing for rations?'

'I have enough. Although I must say that I'm growing very tired of strip-food and pills.'

'So am I. If we could only hunt . . .'

'Ah, yes. I sometimes forget that you are a huntress, Vali.' I wasn't sure whether it was admiration or amusement that I glimpsed in those colourless eyes.

I chose to laugh. 'Used to be.'

'But still are in a way, of course. Only these days you hunt your fellow killers, rather than animals. You don't eat much meat, do you?'

'You know so much about me,' I said, trying to keep my tone light. 'I remember from our very first conversation in Hetla that you know that.' I did not like being understood. Frey had understood me, and had used it.

'You will have wondered why.'

'Well, yes.'

'You told me, Vali.'

'But I don't—' I broke off.

'You don't remember? That is what I mean by "subtle". These mind-reaping techniques used by the Morrighanu are not subtle. The valkyrie use similar ones. They are too much of a blunt instrument for my own preferences.'

'And what techniques do you use, Eld?' My voice sounded very quiet in the forest silence, and very cold, but I think we both knew there would be no follow-through.

'I had you taken into captivity, interrogated you myself, made a few memory adjustments, fed it back to you to check that you had no recollection of the process, and you still do not remember. Whereas I am prepared to say that you could cheerfully murder Glyn Apt for what she put you through on the Rock.'

'You've made your point,' I said.

'Yes, I think I have.' A statement of fact, no smugness or gloating. There was little point in engaging with him on this. He was vitki, I was Skald. That was the game that was played, I told myself. And the name of the game was violation.

Neither of us spoke further about it. I felt I'd lost yet another piece of the puzzle that was myself. As we trekked through the blight, I began to become aware of something else, too. The memory of the fenris' onslaught was itself becoming unreal, hollowed out and stripped of its previous emotional content, the fear and rage and trauma. Paradoxically, now that I was finally beginning to lose this fear, I clung to it, but it was no use. Memories of Frey, of the beast, of Mondhile and Nhem and the rape and torture I had undergone on those worlds, Frey's death – all of it was ebbing from me like some slow tide, leaving me empty and clean. Perhaps it was an effect of the journey, of the land itself, or even of Eld, but whatever it might be, I did not find myself grateful for it. I felt that it was stealing my soul away.

Surreptitiously, when I thought that Eld could not see, I rolled up one sleeve and checked that the old scars were still laddering my arm, the ghosts of pain. They were still there. They anchored me.

That night, camped among the ruined trees, I sensed that someone was there. Without saying anything to Eld, I sent the seith senses out again, cautiously opened my eye and glanced around me, careful to remain still as if in sleep. Eld sat no more than a few feet away from me, hunched under the lynx-skin cloak. I could tell that he was awake. I could see and hear nothing – but someone was there, I was sure of it.

Then the person next to me rose and cast off the cloak and it wasn't Eld at all. It was a woman, someone I'd never seen before, with a beaky, intense face. Eld was lying a short distance away, face down and motionless. I scrambled to my feet. The beaky-faced woman whistled and the sound tore at my ears. Glyn Apt came at me out of the darkness in a rushing crouch. She struck out, caught me a glancing blow on the side of the head that, had it connected properly, would probably have knocked me unconscious. I kicked her in the midriff, but she was already dancing backwards out of the way. She whirled, twisted, and a moment later was high in the air above me, leaping upward to grasp a branch and swing herself forward. I was too slow. We both fell in a tangle on the floor.

'You,' Glyn Apt said, quite conversationally, 'are coming with me.' The forest was suddenly flooded with light, eclipsing the faint glow of the moon and casting us into a monochrome tableau. A wing was gliding down out of the heavens: a black-and-silver craft, with the outlines of birds etched along its hull. The Morrighanu were flooding the rocks, and half-stunned, I was picked up, slung over a woman's shoulder and taken on board.

This time, I was conscious all the way there, tightly bound to a stretcher as the wing lifted up from the forest. I do not know whether I was angry at being taken by the Morrighanu, or relieved at being out of Sull – out of the trees, anyway. At least, I thought, where we were going would be likely to have a roof, no wild animals, and some form of heating and food – even if they tortured me.

The interior of the wing was dim, and I could not see anyone very clearly from where I had been placed. I could not see Eld at all and the thought that they might have left him behind or, worse, killed him, was not a pleasing one. And I couldn't help wondering when I'd become so attached to someone who was, after all, a vitki.

I kept my ears open, but heard nothing of use, though I thought I detected the word 'Skald'. The Morrighanu were no longer speaking Gaelacht, but one of the tongues of Morvern with which I was unfamiliar, and Rhi Glyn Apt had taken care to detach the tabula from my belt when I was brought on board. It was impossible to tell where we might be heading. The wing encountered turbulence at one point, lurching and churning like a ship at sea. I heard the women cursing, and then the wing righted itself and we glided on. Before long, I felt the stabilizer jets go on and we drifted downward to settle to a halt in somewhere unknown.

It was snowing hard, that much I could tell. The blast of air as the doors of the wing slid open was bitter and I flinched. I heard Glyn Apt shout something and saw another stretcher being sent past, with a muffled form on it. I hoped the form was Eld and that he was still alive. Then it was my turn. I was carried down a ramp to a waiting vehicle and loaded unceremoniously inside. Rhi Glyn Apt followed me and sat on an opposite bench, pensively chewing a thumb.

'Where am I being taken?' I asked. I did not really expect an answer, but she said, civilly enough, 'Headquarters. Don't ask me where that is tonight.'

An odd way of phrasing it. Perhaps their HQ moved around. I tried to analyse the twists and turns taken by the vehicle: we seemed to be travelling over somewhere rough and then, from the care which the driver took, somewhere high, and wondered why we could not reach it by means of a wing. Shortly after that, the Morrighanu commander stood abruptly and said, 'Good. We're here.'

I was offloaded. By this time I was beginning to grow uncomfortable: stiff and aching, and with an urgent need to empty my bladder. Much to my relief I was freed from the stretcher and rolled onto gleaming black stone, with the steady drip of water in my ears. A breath of cold air ghosted over my face and I could hear whispering. I opened my mouth to speak but no sound emerged and I could not move; it felt like sleep paralysis, when one is awake and still dreaming, and held motionless by the still-shut motor function. Then I felt it slide from me and I was able to stand. A woman training a weapon on me motioned me towards a set of facilities. I was allowed to wash in a cold trickle of water, and issued with a set of black coveralls. Before I could put these on, I was thoroughly and intrusively searched, a process to which I submitted. I told myself that I had endured worse – it was better than the mind-probe to which Glyn Apt had previously subjected me – and there was little to be gained by making a fuss. Then the door was locked securely behind me.

The next day, I thought, would probably bring another

interrogation. I wanted to be alert for that, with the seith on full defence, and so after fruitlessly trying to turn off the light, I lay down on the pallet and closed my eye. I dozed, sinking into a half sleep and losing track of the time. But suddenly the seith was prickling me awake. I sat up, with an intense moment of disorientation before I realized where I was.

A raven was flying slowly around my head, dark wings beating through emptiness. When it saw me watching, its bright bird eye winked once, and its beak opened in a soundless caw. Thorn Eld's voice said, inside my mind, 'Where are you?'

'In a cell somewhere,' I murmured aloud. I did not think the ravens could be telepathic, though given that they were artefacts of the vitki, one never knew. 'I don't know which part of the building it is.'

'This is one of the Morrighanu's command structures. I don't know which one – I couldn't tell which way the wing was flying and anyway, I don't know them all.'

'Are you free, Eld?'

'No. They've put me in a cell as well, but it's obviously been designed for the more important captives.'

'I'm surprised they let you keep your ravens.'

I heard Eld laugh. 'They didn't. They took all the implants, except the one that is *very* securely hidden. I'm using that channel. I've already sent word to the vitki, but they have their hands full with the war. I wouldn't expect a sudden rescue mission.'

'What do you want me to do?'

'Stay where you are,' Eld said. 'Not that you have a lot of choice. They'll start questioning us tomorrow. They'll want to know how much we know about Skinning Knife, I'd imagine; and exactly what we're doing in Sull. I leave it to you as to what you tell them.'

'It will be little enough. Glyn Apt's already ransacked my mind once. She wanted to know about Frey, about Mondhile. Most of the Skald's practices are a matter of public record; there's not much point in interrogating me about those.'

'Interesting.' Eld sounded faintly surprised. 'I hadn't considered that the most secure defence might be public knowledge.'

'That's because you're a vitki.'

'True enough. I'll sign off now, Vali. I don't need to tell you to keep your senses open for an opportunity, whatever happens tomorrow. We don't want to waste time here. And I will do the same.'

'Don't worry,' I said. 'I have no intention of remaining as a guest of the Morrighanu.'

The raven made another slow, shadowy circuit and then vanished, as if swallowed by the air. And I slept.

TWENTY-ONE

Planet: Nhem (Hunan)

By dawn the storm had blown itself out to sea, leaving a froth of water along the coast and steaming puddles in the streets. The sky, too, looked clouded and muddy, as if the rain had stained it. Everything smelled of damp, clammy in the rising heat as the day drew on. I hadn't expected to sleep after the excitement of the night, but I was out as soon as I lay down: I didn't even remember falling asleep. Memories of the women on the ship filled my head as soon as I woke and I got up immediately. I couldn't be bothered to eat. I washed myself, threw on some clothes and the stouter of my two pairs of sandals, and went out into the wet streets, heading for Tare's house.

Everyone had heard about the new arrivals. The colony was bustling, filled with excitement and an eagerness that was as easily felt as the steam from the puddles. Tare came to greet me at the door, and I saw Khainet just behind her shoulder, peering out of the doorway like something lurking in a burrow. She drew back as soon as she saw me and I wondered whether she was angry about the previous day, or perhaps, in some way, ashamed.

'They're eating,' Tare said. She spoke in hushed tones, as

if she hadn't expected our visitors to do anything so normal. 'And they've been talking among themselves. I knew the words, some of them, but I still didn't understand what they were talking about.'

'Did you speak to them?'

Tare looked away. 'I didn't dare. I just put the food on the table and went away.'

'Tare, they're not the goddesses on the wall! They're women like ourselves.'

But she didn't look as though she believed me, and I'd always thought Tare to be one of the more sensible women in the colony. I'd deal with people's reactions later. 'Take me to them,' I said.

They were huddled around the table, gnawing bread and fruit and speaking in low voices, like conspirators. I closed the door behind me. In their borrowed clothes, with their hair combed, I began to see why Tare had been so impressed. They had a strange air about them, an authority, like men, and yet they were clearly female. They looked up when I came in.

'You were there last night,' one of the women addressed me. She was hard to distinguish from the others but perhaps she was a little older, and as the sleeve of her shirt slid back I saw that there was a blue mark on her wrist: three blue lines, circling the skin like a band.

'You're speaking our language,' I said.

The woman with the blue mark motioned to one of the others and her companion rose and pulled up a chair, gesturing to it as though this was their own home. 'Yes.' She did not explain further.

'How can that be? And where do you come from?' I asked, as I sat down.

'It's called Perchay. It's in the mountains – not the ones near here, but the ones in the far north, beyond Iznar.'

'I know Iznar,' I said.

'Yes, you come from there, don't you? Most of you, except the ones from Sahrait.'

I thought of Khainet's bird. 'Are you the ones who sent us here?' I asked, but the woman gave a small smile, which didn't seem to me to show much amusement.

'Not now. There's someone here I want to meet.'

'Who?' I felt upset. I'd been one of the colony's founders, after all, and I was the only one who was still alive. *We don't have leaders,* we liked to say, though they called me High Counsellor. But still.

'She's here in the house. A tall girl, pale-skinned, with light hair. She doesn't look like anyone else. Her hands are scarred. I've seen her. I tried to speak to the other woman, the older one, but she ran away.'

I frowned at that. 'There are a lot of people here. This is a house complex.'

It was the woman's turn to frown. 'You live communally? All together?'

'Most of us. But some of us are too . . . damaged. They live in the old walls, on their own. They don't have much to do with the rest of us, but we leave food and clothing for them.'

The woman nodded as though this was not news to her, or as though she wasn't interested. 'But the woman I want to see is not one of them.'

I knew exactly who she was talking about, of course. And I also felt that I should protect Khainet: they would not know her name, for her name was new. But protect her against what? Shouldn't I trust these women? We'd always welcomed incomers before: they were *women*, after all. But the women who had come here before had no power, they were afraid and confused, exhausted and ill, just as Khainet had been. And all of them had been alone: coming over the mountains, guided by visions that we liked to think were a gift from the goddesses.

And now these four, with the feel of men about them, their language that was the same as mine, technology that we'd never possessed. Was I afraid of them, or afraid of something else?

The woman with the mark on her wrist was watching me closely.

'You know who I'm talking about,' she said and the box hummed and whirred as if in agreement, apparently echoing her words.

'Before I let you talk to her,' I responded, grasping at the shreds of my control, 'I need to know who you are. Do you have names? Where are you from? Tell me now, not later. Later might never come.'

Two of the women exchanged glances, while the others sat with downcast heads as though keeping out of potential arguments. That told me a lot about their hierarchy. I tried to see if the second woman had a band around her wrist as well, but the long sleeve draped down and I wasn't able to check.

'All right,' the first woman said abruptly. 'I am Mayest and this is Hildre. This is Geneffa and this is Samuat.'

'I don't know what these names mean,' I said. 'I am called Hunan, which means "mountainwalker". I decided that when I took my name.'

Mayest looked confused. 'You took your name? Yes, I suppose you would have done. Our names don't have meanings. Our mothers gave them to us.'

It was my turn to stare. 'Your mothers gave you names? Not the House Father?'

'We don't have Fathers where we're from.' Mayest's face grew hard, as if about to change to stone.

'What?'

'Not all this world is like Iznar, like the places you know. Most of it, yes, but not all. And Iznar is changing. Please, Hunan. I know this is confusing and strange. You must understand that we are much more in touch with the cities and the men's world than you are.'

'But in that case, how can you "not have Fathers"?'

'It's . . . a technological thing. You wouldn't understand.' Mayest spoke with assurance, not even bothering to be condescending, and I felt a little lump of anger settle in my chest. I told myself to wait.

'Hunan – did you have children? Can you remember them?'

'Yes. Two daughters and a son. My son was called First Joy, and the girls were Boy-Next-Time and Luck-Still-to-Come.'

They were all staring at me now, with pity.

'And you don't speak ancient Iznari, do you, the men's naming language? You don't know what those names mean?' Again, that assurance. But she was right; I did not know, and I didn't like that. I didn't like feeling stupid all over again. In Edge, I knew as much as everyone else, usually more. And now I felt dull and slow. I felt as I had when I lived with House Father.

'They have meaning, too?'

'Then I'll tell you,' Mayest said, and she told me the meaning of my daughters' names, and the meaning of my son's.

After that, I was silent for a long time. Then I said, 'I thought they were just names. Just words.'

'No. The men give proper names to the boys in a big ceremony that the women, obviously, don't know anything about. And the naming of girls is a recent thing, only within the last seventy years even though the words are old – the result of a very liberal Hierolath. There was great protest at it, but the change was made. When you decided to let those old names pass, when you came here, and take on others, you were wiser than you knew.'

'But you,' I said, and I was angry now. There was no man to be angry at and so I turned it towards Mayest. 'You have proper names, given by mothers. Where are you from, Mayest? Why do you have these privileges?'

And so she told me.

The bell tower was stuffy and airless, but I went up there anyway, to seek out a breeze. Below me, the mud roofs of the colony were dry, and beyond the walls the roaring of the storm-churned sea had softened to its usual murmur. The colony should have looked the same, and yet everything had changed.

Now, I had somewhere to compare it to.

I turned my back on the colony and looked north. The mountains were almost lost in heat haze. Beyond that lay the desert, and then, hundreds of miles away, the sprawl of Iznar. I'd never really considered what might lie north of the city, apart from fields and irrigation ditches and then desert, and beyond that the lakes, but now I knew. Mayest's women had come in a flying machine that had hit the storm and turned itself into a boat. They had come from the north. For after the lakes were more mountains, and within them, caves. And in those caves lived another colony of women: much older, founded by a particular family, sisters who had been born self-aware and who had fled from Iznar years before and somehow made contact with other worlds. Made contact with women who had built places called laboratories and practised the things they had learned and created daughters who were all alike, daughters who, within the last year, had hired a woman from another planet to kill the

Hierolath of Iznar and set the city in a turmoil. I could scarcely believe that.

And all we'd done had been to run away, and eke out a living in someone else's long-dead city. I should have felt proud, Mayest had said. They were proud of me and what we had done here. So why did I feel so ashamed?

The anger came up in me then like a storm surge and I couldn't hold it back. It roared over me, just as the sea had roared when it tossed the women of the north against the coast, like House Father when he shouted at me, and First Joy shouting too, because his father did. I'd felt that anger then, but it was locked in the fear and I'd never let it out. Except, there was that smell of earth and roots again, the sound of something striking stone.

'Hunan?' a voice said. I turned to find Khainet standing hesitantly at the door of the bell tower. 'Tare told me you were here.'

'I wanted to think,' I said. After a pause, I added, 'Have you talked to the strangers?'

'No. Not yet. I wanted to see you first. The strangers – they scare me.' She knitted her fingers together and yet something flared in her eyes that did not look like fear to me. I smiled.

'Perhaps,' I said, and I did not mean to sound so bitter, 'they are just what women are meant to be.'

'Tare said they aren't like us. That they have . . . machines, which help them do things. That they didn't spend their childhoods without minds, but always had them.'

'Tare has been listening at doors.' But that wasn't fair. Maybe she'd found the courage to speak to Mayest.

'Hunan – what will happen to the colony, now? To Edge?' She came forward, into the sunlight, and she looked older than I'd thought: her skin showing lines around the eyes, the promise of more lines at her mouth. And I thought that she had touched the truth. The colony wouldn't survive this change, this new knowledge – couldn't and shouldn't. Either we would go there, or Mayest's group would come here, and whatever happened it would never be the same and already I missed that. I could feel my power settling around Mayest's head like a cloud of efreets.

I said, abruptly, to Khainet, 'Do you blame me, for yesterday?'

She grew hot with embarrassment, her face darkening. 'No! I was so ashamed of myself. I was weak.'

'You weren't weak. You've just been through a terrible ordeal.' *Your life is an ordeal.* But would Mayest and the others grasp that? Thick resentment flooded me, too, and I wasn't prepared to face that now. I went over to Khainet and put my hand on her shoulder. 'It's hot up here. You need to rest.'

'Are you going to make me see them?'

'Khainet, I can't make you do anything that you don't want to do. I'm not the . . . the Hierolath. I'm just the elder here, because I'm the oldest and I've been here the longest, that's all. If you want to talk to them, then that's fine. If you don't—' I paused. I wasn't quite sure what we'd do then. 'We'll find some way round it, I promise you.' I heard my words but they sounded hollow. I'd always been respected because I was the first one here, but now Mayest's knowledge made that seem a slight thing.

She still looked unhappy. 'I don't understand why they want to see *me*. I don't know anything. I don't remember more than anyone else.'

'Go and rest,' I repeated. 'I'll find out what they want.'

When I returned to Tare's house, I found Tare herself hovering in the hallway.

'They're still here,' she explained. She spoke in that hushed voice again, as if given a great honour.

'Good. Have you spoken with them?'

'Oh yes.' Her eyes widened. 'Mayest's been telling me all sorts of things, about how they live in the north. It sounds wonderful.'

'Does it.'

'Yes, Mayest says that they have weapons and machines of their own. That women can talk to people from other planets, and learn anything they want to learn.'

'That does sound wonderful,' I agreed.

'And Mayest says—'

'I'm sure it's all very interesting. But I need to talk to Mayest now myself.'

'Of course,' Tare replied, looking shocked that she might be keeping me away from this wonder.

The four women were sitting in a huddle by the window. Shadows of one another, all so similar. If it hadn't been for the blue marks and the clothes, I still wouldn't have been able to tell Mayest from the others. I wondered if the blue marks were how they identified themselves among their own kind, or whether they had other means of telling who was who.

'Hunan,' Mayest said, looking up as I came in. 'I was going to come to find you.'

'I wanted to ask you something,' I said, before she could continue. 'Something about the person you want to see.'

She nodded, as if she understood. 'You want to know why. Why do we want to talk to this woman, out of the hundreds who have made the journey? If I were you, I'd want to know that, too.'

'Did you follow her? Did you give her directions? If you did, then how is it that you know about us and yet no one from your colony has ever visited ours?' There was that resentment, back in my voice . . . *while we were struggling on, you were living in your safe caves with your free minds and your borrowed machines* . . . Unfair, maybe, and yet . . . And yet the biggest question of all. 'And the men of Iznar. Why haven't they come here? Why have they allowed us to live?'

The thought of House Father coming here – I'd stopped seeing him so much in my dreams, in recent years, but at first I'd seen him all the time, out of the corner of my eye, starting awake at night at the thought that he was in the room. He'd be an old man now. But when I looked into the shadows at the far end of the room, there was House Father, as young and angry as ever.

'They've let you get away with it,' – the second woman spoke unexpectedly. I'd become so used to Mayest being the spokeswoman that I blinked – 'because they can't allow themselves to believe that you exist. If they let themselves think that women had regained their identities and memories, that they'd become human beings instead of just breeding stock and slaves, just female animals, then the foundation on which their ideology is based becomes a lie. They persuaded themselves that women were no better than animals. And then, when that didn't quite work, they made sure that women weren't. They bred self-consciousness out of the female population, and then they could believe what they liked to their hearts' content. I could guarantee that ninety-nine percent of the male population of Iznar would refuse these days to credit that women had ever been genetically engineered. So you – and us – are anomalies, which cannot be allowed to enter their theories about how things are, because those theories cannot sustain us. So they pretend.' She spoke in a hot, angry rush. I understood that, though I didn't understand everything she had said and that made me feel stupid again.

'And that will be our saving and their downfall,' one of the other women – Hildre? – commented. She had a surprisingly deep voice, quite unlike the others.

'But why don't they just kill us? Then we really wouldn't exist.'

'They're afraid. They are afraid to come here, because they think it's a place of demons. And maybe they think, too, that because you are not supposed to exist, you are the stronger for it: that the sight of you will cause their reality to unravel and crack.'

'I find that hard to believe,' was all I could say.

'You're used to seeing men as all-powerful, and to you, when you lived among them, they were. But we've never lived among them, and to us, and to the rest of the galaxy, they're a bunch of superstitious barbarians who – from somewhere – have got the ability to tinker with DNA at a sophisticated level. We've been trying to find out where they got that knowledge from.'

'And do you know?'

'Not yet,' Mayest said, and there was the slightest flicker of her eyes, downward, to where lies are kept. 'But we're still trying.'

'And the woman you want to meet?'

'That woman is the key.'

'To what? To where this genetic knowledge comes from?'

'No,' Mayest said. 'To where it's *going*.'

TWENTY-TWO

PLANET: MUSPELL (VALI)

For a moment I convinced myself that it had been nothing more than a nightmare from that blighted land, but it was real. I was still in the dripping, black stone room. Cautiously, I raised my head and looked around me. No one was in sight. At one end of the room stood a tall, arched doorway. I got to my feet, my joints stiff and aching. I felt as though I had run a marathon and there was a buzzing in my head. But there was no accompanying headache and my vision seemed clear. The seith, still present, gave me an immense sense of oppression, as though we were deep underground, but it was more than that: there was a conscious weight of anguish and old sorrow. It reminded me strongly of Gemaley's tower on Mondhile, a mad, sad place that I had no desire ever to visit again. I walked swiftly to the arched doorway to see if there was a way out.

The doorway looked empty, but that meant little in this day of force fields and restraining capacitors. I took off my jacket and threw it through, and just as I'd expected, there was the crackling sizzle of energy.

I stepped back. The seith could help disguise me, could confuse my enemies, but it wouldn't enable me to walk through either stone wall or force field. I checked the cell carefully: no way out. Then, as I was examining the doorway, taking care not to activate the field, something flickered across the corner of my vision.

White wings, not black this time. And that meant Morrighanu.

Thinking back to the capture of the Rock, I remembered standing in the hallway and watching that single white feather drift down towards the flagstones. A key, encoded information to open the doors of the labyrinth that was the Rock. Eld's ravens, too, were information: many hugins and munins, thoughts and memories, data and details.

I thought it was time for some experimentation.

The map implant was the only piece of internal technology that I possessed. I didn't have the enhancements of the valkyrie – nor, from what I'd seen of Glyn Apt, the Morrighanu themselves. The map implant had served me on Mondhile: I'd been able to download information from it, into a sink of what had been described to me as dark energy. I still didn't know what that energy sink had really been: Mondhile was apparently riddled with ancient technology and the most likely explanation was that this had been a rogue piece of that. But the map implant wouldn't even serve me so well here: it was Skald tech, not Morrighanu. I didn't have their passwords and runic codes. But I did have the seith.

I sat back down on the bench and closed my eye. In one of the old tongues of Earth, one of the tongues of my ancestors, the practice of the seith was also known as 'seething'.

It had been a shamanic practice then, not the modern meditative, neurologically linked discipline that it was in my day. But it didn't matter how it was seen. What mattered was what it could do, and I'd never really even reached the limits of it yet. I sent out the seith, just as I'd been taught, just as I'd done a thousand times. I reached out and called to one of the white birds: I could see them, a flock of wings, with my mind's eye, just beyond the doorway.

They ignored me. But with the seith, I could see the data of which they were composed: skeins of numbers and letters, like the information that had flowed over the stones of the Rock and caused the fortress to fall, or that which flowed across Glyn Apt's face. But gradually a knowing red eye would turn in my direction and as if the birds saw me watching, they formed a tight, protective spiral.

Then, one of the birds – less cautious than the rest, just like a real creature – fluttered too close to the door. I think it was the lock of the door itself, the closing and opening mechanism, come to check itself in the light of this weird new presence.

Closer, I told it. *Closer*.

And it came, closer and closer yet, until suddenly its pinions brushed the edge of the force field and it disintegrated in a burst of unreal light. I heard the force field singe down and knew I might be free. I had absorbed the lock. I flicked a stray pebble through and, this time, nothing happened.

I stepped through the doorway unscathed and found myself in a corridor, the walls towering above my head. I wondered where Eld was being kept. I made my way down the corridor, expecting at any moment to hear alarms going off and heralding my capture. But the place remained silent, with only the constant drip of water as a backdrop. Running my hand along the wall was like touching the petrified trees in the blighted forest: the same unnatural hardness. And when I looked more closely in the dim light from sconces set high on the wall, I thought I could see an odd pattern within the wall's ebony surface: the fronds of ferns, branches, leaves – as though the wall itself was the remnant of some ancient forest. If we were underground, I wondered whether the corridor had been carved out of some prehistoric strata. The weight of age seemed to fall in upon me, making me reel. And then the whispering began.

It was definitely the murmur of voices. I crept along the corridor as quietly as I could, weaving the walls into the seith, trying to disguise my presence as best I may. I followed the whispering to its source: the end of the corridor. This led out onto a narrow gallery and I could see light beneath it.

Two figures stood below. As I looked, dodging behind one of the columns that formed the spine of the gallery, the closer figure moved into a pool of light. A black uniform; long, tightly bound black hair. I did not need to see the dataflow across her face, nor the white wings which clustered briefly about her head, to recognize her. It was Rhi Glyn Apt.

The second woman was wearing a similar uniform, but it was partially covered by a coat of pelts, rougher than Eld's luxurious fur and held together by a series of silver loops and leather thongs. It looked home-made, as though it had been cobbled together by its wearer – or stolen from someone more savage. I thought with a moment of regret of my Mondhaith bow. Without a weapon, I felt that I might as well have been naked. This woman's hair was as white as Glyn Apt's was black, falling down her back in a complex arrangement of braids. I had a dreadful feeling, quite suddenly, that when she turned around I would see that she had Gemaley's face, that I'd see the Mondhaith girl's blue drowned visage staring up at me. Perhaps the Morrighanu picked up a twitch in the seith, for she did turn round and look up then. But her skin was tanned, unlike Gemaley's pallor, and instead of chilly blue eyes she had the yellow eyes of a goat, with slitted pupils. She gave no sign of having seen me, and neither did Glyn Apt, but the sight made me move back.

'It should be done now,' Glyn Apt said to the other woman. 'See to it. I don't want another failure.'

Goat-girl touched her forehead, presumably in acquiescence. More hints of animal–human crossbreeding: I'd never seen or heard of anything like Goat-girl before. But maybe the eyes were just implants, some local affectation.

I did not like the sound of what Glyn Apt had said, and what I saw next, I liked even less. Goat-girl touched a strap set into the wall, tugging at it. The wall opened and out of a wide slit, a thing like a mortuary tray glided forth. A row of scalpels and other instruments stood in a holder along its side. On it, unconscious and stripped of his lynx-fur cloak, though not his slickskin, was Thorn Eld.

Was he dead? I couldn't tell. I wondered how soon it would be before the missing bird was discovered – and the missing prisoner. I didn't know how good a chance Eld and I had of getting out of here alive, nor just what the Morrighanu were planning to do with captured vitki and Skald. I didn't feel like waiting to find out, either.

Dropping over the rim of the gallery, I snatched up a scalpel and seized Goat-girl, placing the weapon at her throat. The Morrighanu gave an inhuman squeal of shock and struggled; she was strong, but I kicked her feet from under her and pricked her skin with the point of the scalpel. A drop of dark blood oozed out, slow as tar, and strong-smelling. Glyn Apt stared at me with pallid impassivity. I gestured to Eld.

'Let him go. Or I'll kill this one.'

Goat-girl opened her mouth and hissed at me, displaying very un-goatlike pointed teeth. 'Kill me, then,' she spat. 'See what that does for you.' I did not think she was bluffing. I made a swipe at my captive's throat, hoping to draw Glyn Apt off guard, but she did not move. The feint, however, bought enough time for the apparently unconscious Eld to surge up off the couch and clip the Morrighanu commander across the back of the neck. She turned just a little too late and folded like a falling sapling soundless to the floor. I put Goat-girl under as well and turned to face Eld.

'Any clearer ideas as to where we are?'

Eld's pale face was even whiter than usual. 'I still have no idea. This is one of the Morrighanu strongholds, but I don't know which one.'

'Then who are these people?' I gave Goat-girl a shove with the toe of my boot.

'Vali, I don't know. They look like something out of myth. I've never seen anything like them before.'

But I thought of the forest outside Hetla, the creature tied to a tree that then blazed up, taking the thing shrieking with it. There seemed to be a lot of odd things living in the forests of Darkland – including Skinning Knife.

'Whatever she is, we have to find a way out.'

I pocketed the scalpel. My weapons were gone and we would waste time in finding them. 'Come on, then,' I said. We slammed the heavy door of the laboratory behind us. I hoped it would seal the pair in before they had a chance to wake and sound the alarm, but I did not hold out a great deal of hope. Eld and I ran back up a flight of stairs to the gallery and then along the corridor, finding the arched doorway and the room where I had awoken. We went out again, and located another door. We went through into a corridor.

'Glyn Apt seems to be taking quite an interest in you,' Eld said.

'Not as much as she was taking in you. After all, you were the one on the slab.'

But Eld did not reply. By now we had reached a higher-ceilinged section of the corridor. A fine mesh was set into the wall and beyond it, a light was visible. A spiral stair led up into a wide chamber, made of the same black stone containing the ghosts of ferns. To my surprise it was also lined with windows. But they did not show the snowy wastes of Morvern, or the blight of Sull. They looked out onto stars.

I saw Loki hanging close, his craters and meteor scars clearly visible.

'That's got to be an illusion,' Eld said. I agreed.

A console stood in a basalt column at the far end of the room. When we came close, I saw that it contained nothing but a swirl of shadows. There had been no further sign of the white data birds and this worried me: surely my absence would have been noted by now. A moment later, I discovered I was right.

Goat-eyed Morrighanu troops poured out of the walls, shouldering their way through fronds of ferns that were suddenly real, as if the walls had melted and left us standing in a forest. Their slitted eyes glittered, their jaws gaped, and their hands were adorned with long, artificial talons. Behind them stalked a tall figure whom we'd last left lying on the floor of an interrogation chamber. Commander Glyn Apt did not look pleased.

TWENTY-THREE

Planet: Mondhile (Sedra)

I spent another day or so in the vicinity of Moon Moor, trying to find the underground place. But those mountains – the blue ice that crowned them, the way the light shadowed the snow, the pattern of high and distant rocks – were still calling to me, and I knew I wouldn't be able to resist. Winter was coming. I had to make for the mountains while I could.

I did not see the four strange people again and I was glad of it. But it did suggest that what I had seen, or thought I'd seen, beneath Moon Moor hadn't merely been the product of the dreamcallers' manipulations – unless those ancient dreams had somehow become preserved here, trapped by the lines of the land and held in the fabric of the moor; unless I was already mad.

I followed a snaking track up the mountain, made by wild mur. There was no sign of the animals, either, and I kept a sharp look-out. Whatever the way of things, I did not fancy meeting my death by being torn to pieces by a herd. But only the ravaged turf, a remnant of the passage of their clawed feet, remained. Soon, I had reached the first of the foothills, and kept going. The air bit into my lungs, wonderfully fresh and scented with the fragrance of the scrub, rising up from the Moor. At the top of the highest ridge before the mountain slopes, I stopped and looked back across the expanse of the Moor. There was the place where I had found the cave, clearly visible. I thought I saw something moving around it, a pale shape, but my eyesight wasn't what it used to be and though I squinted, I couldn't make out the shape. An animal, perhaps – but it looked too tall and that suggested one of the half-humans. I waited, but it had gone behind the ridge and did not emerge, and so I turned and went on.

But if I thought I had left the half-humans behind by going up into the mountains, I was mistaken.

It probably was a foolish thing to do. But then again, I had come out here to die, and let the world choose the manner of it. I had neither reason to complain, nor any reason to expect that I'd live through it.

I first knew something was wrong on the morning of the third day up in the mountains. After sleeping amongst the rocks and cairns as usual, I walked through most of the day for as far as I could before I grew too tired. On the evening of the second day, however, the weather turned warmer – an unseasonal day of sunlight, summer's borrow, as we say – and after a few hours of the sun on my face, the clouds drifted down and brought rain, not snow, in their wake. By that time, I was already camped for the night, secure, or so I thought, in the greatcoat, wrapped against the chill. I got only a little damp, and for someone raised on the coast and accustomed to storms, I didn't think anything of it.

In the morning, however, I woke to a thick mist. I decided not to push on, but I needed to light a fire. When I stood up to go in search of sticks or moss, assuming any had survived dry through the night, my head felt light and there was a faint singing in my ears, as though the wind was whistling through me. I sat down again, abruptly, with my back against a rock, and my sight dwindled to a small dark point. That was that for the next few hours. When I came round, the mist had rolled away, leaving a perfect, cloudless sky and a bitter chill. By this time, I was shaking and cold to the bone. I tried to stand, and couldn't get up. Some kind of bone fever, brought by the wet cold. My chest hurt with every breath. I huddled in the coat, staring at the mountains and thinking: *so, this is it*. I was not too sad at the way of it. Bone fevers are nasty but quick, and it would soon be over.

I don't know how long I lay there. I remember growing colder and colder, and then I was warm again – feverish by hot – and I knew this meant I was close to the end. I heard voices and I thought that they were the spirits of Erestha-han, who had come to bear me to the land of the dead. I hoped the pregnant warrior of Moon Moor was among them, and maybe my sister also.

But the voices faded in and out, and the darkness above me changed to a dull blue glow. I felt something cold and sharp touch my arm; there was a moment of intense clarity, and then blackness again.

And after that, I was awake. I was in a forest, but it wasn't like any forest I'd ever seen in the north. Instead of the crimson trunks and black leaves of satinspine, these trees were cloudy and grey, like smoke. There was the pungent smell of burning in my nose, but the air around me was cold, almost as chilly as the mountains in which I had lain down to die. I looked down at myself. I still wore the greatcoat, but my clothes were a lot cleaner than they had been over the last few days. My hands were still wrinkled, the veins roped across the thin skin of my knuckles, but there was no pain, no difficulty, in moving and I knew that this meant I was dreaming. Maybe this was hell, after all. But there was no one there to greet me. I stood still like a fool for a time, and then I thought that I might as well explore the place a little, see whether there was anyone else there. I started walking, forcing my way through undergrowth that was as thick and thorny as that of Moon Moor, but which shortly turned to powder as I made my way through it. I walked on ash, seeing bushes and trees that seemed intact until I touched them, whereupon they crumbled. The ash rose up in clouds, releasing heat, and coating my skin with its dust. I started to cough.

A clearing. In it stood a house – an odd-looking thing, with a low gabled roof, made out of logs. The door was open, and warily I went up to it. I couldn't feel any house defences sizzling under the earth, nor anything else, for that matter – no metal, or water, only endless stone under the coating of ash. This was a place without landlines, a land that had died. I stepped inside the house.

Now I knew that this probably was Eresthahan after all.

The blue glow, the voices – those had been my death, and now my spirit was walking in the land of the dead. Soon, no doubt, I would begin to grow younger, here in this hunting lodge.

I knew it to be a lodge because of the bones. They rattled along the ceiling, twisting in the breeze from the thin chains that held them. Some looked animal, though I couldn't have said what kind they were. But some were human – there was a pelvis, and over here, sitting on the desk, a skull. Not large, either – whoever used this place had been hunting children. That wasn't acceptable, but it happened – and maybe here in the land of the dead, it didn't matter anyway.

All the bones had been polished in the traditional manner, and some of them were tipped with metal to give an ornamental effect. It reminded me very much of a lodge I had seen in the satinspine forests north of Essedura, high along the coast. I'd spent a pleasant few days there years ago, in the company of two other huntresses from other settlements. So the place had a comforting air of familiarity, for all that it was filled with death.

It was well governed, too. There was a spit on the fire, and the ashes had been cleaned from the grate. Two cooking pots were placed by the side of the hearth. A table bore traces of herbs – again, ones that I did not know – and there was a low bed covered with animal pelts along one wall. Someone lived here, or at least had been staying for some time, and was clearly making a good job of it.

I'd have been quite happy to stay. If this was the land of the dead, I'd seen a lot worse. The lodge was clean, functional, and cared for. I found a chair, started to pull it up by the grate, with thoughts of heading back out to locate the wood store.

But something was tugging at me. Something insistent, buzzing, like an insect that had lodged inside my skull and was trying to battle its way out again.

'Leave me alone!' I said.

A voice replied, 'I think she's coming round.'

'Make sure her hands are secured. Are the bonds still holding?'

I didn't like the sound of that.

'It's all tight. It's old, but it still works. You saw that last year.' That voice sounded odd: furred and lisping, like the voices of the half-humans I'd seen on the Moor. But I could understand what this one was saying, though I couldn't see anything apart from a thick blackness. It felt as though they'd blindfolded me. I struggled a little, hearing an exclamation of alarm from my captors, but the bonds were indeed holding. Pity. All I could do then was to wait.

TWENTY-FOUR

PLANET: MUSPELL (VALI)

They'd already interrogated me once, so they didn't bother to do so again, except to check how I'd managed to break out of their cell. Glyn Apt tried to wring it from me, but this time fatigue and stress turned out to be my friends and I simply fainted during the mind 'ride. I remember feeling smug as I passed out.

Then, I didn't know how much later: *'Vali.'* Someone was whispering my name.

'Who's there?'

My voice caught in my throat, as though snagged on thorns.

'Vali, this is Eld.'

'Thorn,' I said, and it made me laugh.

'Vali, remember the Skald? Tell me about the Rock. Tell me what they make you do, in the early morning meditation sessions.'

'I don't go to those,' I said. I stared up at a black glass ceiling. We were in the same cell. 'It's for the acolytes.'

'All the same, tell me what they do. I'm curious.'

I looked across. He was sitting on the edge of one of the rough beds, leaning forward a little, once more in that fur-collared coat. There was nothing on his face, no pity, no amusement.

If there had been, I would not have told him what he wanted to know, running through the meditation, focusing first on the soles of the feet, then the ankles, then each part of the body in turn. It knitted me back together again, not whole, but enough to allow me to sit up.

Eld's face was still that bland, unreadable mask.

'How are you feeling now?' he asked.

I grimaced. 'Sick. Disoriented. It's to be expected.'

Eld nodded. 'As you say. It will pass.'

'I'm surprised to see you in here.' This was a one-person cell, clearly: a single cot, limited washing facilities. I'd been grateful that it hadn't been another stone dungeon, but perhaps they didn't trust me in that. But that they'd put Eld in here with me was odd.

'There's some kind of panic on,' Eld said. 'I don't know what's happening. They brought in some people – I didn't see them but they were making enough noise on a psychic level to wake an army.'

It puzzled me. 'Darklanders? Or my people?' *The war.* What the hell was happening back in the Reach? And I was here, not safe, in enemy territory, but still unable to do anything to help my home. I tried to stifle the guilt and failed.

'I don't know. Glyn Apt wasn't exactly forthcoming. I think they needed the cell space, so they put us together.'

I'd already communicated to Eld how I'd broken out of the previous cell, and I wanted to discuss options with him, but we were probably under surveillance. I strolled over to the doorway and closed my eye, hoping he'd understand what I was trying to do. Eld was silent, but when I opened my eye again, a black bird was in the room.

I looked a question. 'They didn't have time to look for my final implant,' Eld said. 'Their loss.' He gestured towards a socket on the wall. From most angles, it looked like nothing more than a lump of moss, an artful conceit, I thought, especially since the Morrighanu hadn't bothered to make it all that convincing. 'It's safe to talk. I've shortcircuited the camera.'

'But can you open the door?'

Eld laughed. 'Unfortunately . . .'

'I could try again.'

'They're probably wise to that by now. But Vali, one thing – you told me that you accessed one of their birds. That should mean that you still have its co-ordinates in your head. Can I try to contact it?'

I hesitated. 'I think it was just a door lock. And anyway, you're probably right. It will have changed by now.'

'But even though it might not open the door, it's still encoded information. We don't know what it will do until we try.'

'No, we don't know.'

'Will you let me try?'

'What exactly does that *involve*, Eld?'

So he showed me.

The last man who had touched me had been Ruan. He was Mondhaith, it's true, but really just a gentle boy with a feral side. I'd cared what happened to Ruan, but I hadn't loved him. Before that, it had been the Hierolath, and before that Frey, and before that, my brother. Best not to go to those places, best to stay away – or so I told myself, even though I knew that keeping away was not an option, for why in that case did I keep going back? Letting Eld into my head might have been another violation, but he'd already been there, he already knew me better than anyone else, except perhaps Idhunn, and she was dead. I told myself this, and I winced as he touched me, and he understood. Hands on either side of my ruined face, that was all, a brief and flickery touch, and then it was gone. Eld's mind brushed my mind and it was icy cold, with the promise of heat far within. I didn't want to look at the possibility of that furnace, either. I jerked my head back, but Eld had already seen what was to be seen. I looked up to see white wings. Eld said, 'Well, well, well.' He made a gesture. A raven swooped.

I felt the brush of feathers against my skin and then I was *inside*, Eld's raven breaking down barriers. The white bird was no more than a sketched ghost: they had stripped it of most of its encoding, but it was still showing the raven the way.

Snowstorm. Tendrils of ice licking my flesh, leaving paradoxical fire in their wake. Dimly, through the snow, distant lights: a homestead, perhaps, or the landing lights of a rescue craft. I struggled towards them, battling cold and the weakness of cold, but they danced away from me like marsh fire. I walked on, thinking that at any moment the fenris would come at me out of the storm and the dark, that the lights were its hot yellow eyes, laced with sunbright death. At that thought, I tried to turn away, cowering – knowing that my body was still in the cell and that Thorn Eld's wary hands were hovering around me, hoping to steady without touching. Eld had learned something of me, and did not want to breach any more barriers. That, by itself, almost made me cry.

Snowdark. I knew there was something I should be looking for, but I didn't know what it was. I moved towards the light, as the ancient myths tell you to do when you are at the moment of your death, but the light was information, cascading around me in skeins and torrents, data scrolling too fast for me to grasp its significance. I wondered whether this was what it must be like for Glyn Apt, perpetually in the heart of a data gale.

And someone was calling my name.

'Eld?' I said, or thought I heard myself say. But there was no reply from the man at my side, or if there was, I did not hear it.

Vali.

'Who are you?' I knew the voice, that was the strange thing.

Vali. I'm here. Walk towards me.

Very clear now. I did as the voice – it was a woman's – told me.

Vali!

'Oh, the gods of my mothers,' I said, because it was Idhunn.

She was standing in the middle of the streams of data, like someone who stands beneath a waterfall. The data poured down, dripping from her long white hair and over her hands, but she made no move to brush it aside. She looked much younger, and as I stepped closer I saw that she *was* younger: this was not Idhunn as I had known her, but a woman in her late twenties, close to my own age, and this Idhunn was herself composed of data. She wasn't real, but she'd been encoded.

At first I thought she was some kind of trap. But there was a weird rightness to her, as if this was her home and her place and one couldn't properly expect her to be anywhere else.

'Vali?' she said.

'It's me. How do you know who I am?'

'Ah,' she said. 'I've updated myself, on a regular basis.' She paused. 'But there hasn't been an update for a week. Am I still alive?'

I didn't want to lie to her, but I didn't want to tell her the truth, either. I made myself face it. 'I'm afraid not,' I said. 'You died, back on the Rock.'

'I did?' She frowned. 'How did *that* happen?'

'You were murdered.'

The frown deepened. 'By whom?'

'By a creation of the Morrighanu. A woman known as Skinning Knife.'

'Ah,' Idhunn said again. 'You know, I always thought that would lead to disaster in the end. I spoke about it to Rhi. She's the only one who's ever really believed me. All the others are too convinced of their own rightness. It's what drove me away in the end.'

'*You* belonged to the Morrighanu?'

'My mother did. I lied to you, to the Skald. I falsified records, when I came there. I had to; they wouldn't have taken me in, otherwise, and I had nowhere else to go. It was at another time of crisis: they didn't ask too many questions. People had defected and they wanted trained personnel to rebuild the organization. But I was born here, in Morvern. I joined the Morrighanu as a young woman, and fifteen years after that, I ran away.'

The first question from my lips was, 'Did Frey know?'

'No. At least, I don't believe so. He had dealings with the Skald; you know that. Maybe he knew and never said anything, because I was also in exile and he wanted us to believe that he was, too.'

'And Skadi? Skinning Knife?'

'I knew about the project. I wasn't directly involved, but my mother had been and she kept me informed. She shouldn't have done it, but mother was always an iconoclast. She thought someone outside her sept should have the information. Just in case.'

'Why should Skinning Knife have killed you? What do you know?'

'Here,' Idhunn said. She opened her mouth and spat something delicately into the palm of her hand, like a cat spitting. It was a single, glowing coal. 'Take this.'

'What is it?'

'Information. Everything I know about Skadi. You won't be able to access it immediately; you'll need Morrighanu tech for that. As for why she killed me – revenge, I should imagine. Revenge for being the creation of her creators, one of whom was my mother. They made her what she is and she never forgave them.'

'I thought she was supposed to be the ultimate warrior.'

'She is a weapon,' Idhunn said. 'She feels she needs to kill, otherwise she herself will die.'

'Is that true?'

'I doubt it. But it's what she believes, and that's what matters. Would you like to believe yourself to be such a being? With an in-built addiction?'

'Sounds to me like it's more of an excuse,' I said, but who was I to talk? I'd sliced up my own arms, before I became an assassin for hire. I reached out and took the coal from Idhunn's hand. And as I did so, her image wavered, blanking into snow, fading, and then gone.

It was only when I came out that I became aware that Eld had been riding alongside me. I felt us separate and that was much too close for comfort. Instinctively, I struck out. Eld caught my hand; we sat eye to glaring eye for a moment. Then he said, with that vitki mildness, 'Sorry. I needed information.'

I had to force myself to be polite. 'You'll ask me, if there's a next time.'

'Unlikely that there will be. In the next few minutes they'll cotton on to the fact that we've been inside their system – I imagine there's even more of a panic going on right now.'

'If they know it's us, can they do a mindwipe?' The thought of that filled me with weariness.

Eld looked smug. 'Not on me. I've buried my information too deep for that. Oh, and yours as well, by the way.' As he spoke, a raven perched on his shoulder, holding a glowing coal in its beak. It winked a jet-black eye at me and disappeared.

'Idhunn was Morrighanu,' I said, expecting Eld to nod – he knew everything else, after all. But instead I saw his eyes widen with the faintest of shocks.

'The leader of the Skald, from Darkland? That's – that's startling, to say the least.'

'You didn't know?'

Eld was frowning. 'We checked her out, obviously. All the details added up.'

I couldn't resist a smile. 'So it's not only the vitki who can cover their tracks, then?'

'Apparently not.' Eld looked sour. It was the most gratifying moment of my day. It lasted for perhaps a minute, until the door hissed open and Glyn Apt stormed in.

TWENTY-FIVE

How do you explain what makes something beautiful? I could tell you about crimson and pale, about hardness and flow. I could tell you about the softness of marrow at the bone's crack, about the raspberry seep of spinal fluid. The contrast of scarlet against the snow and the dark trees; old fairy tales that my new mothers told me, about red and white and black. About sorrowing and the thin sound of a spirit snatched by the wind, of how it makes me feel when I set something free, save it from its prison of flesh and its cage of the skull, release it into the sunset storm and taste the salt of its passage on my lips.

I could talk to you for hours of beauty, but I don't think you'd understand. No one else has, after all.

TWENTY-SIX

Planet: Nhem (Hunan)

I still didn't understand why Mayest considered Khainet to be so important. After telling me about some family trait that Khainet was supposed to possess, she became vague: said that they needed to run tests. I did not like the sound of this. I sat, up in the bell tower, then thought about things.

Khainet had regained her awareness of herself, true. But so had everyone else in the colony and I didn't think that her story had sounded very different from other people's. My own was similar.

I'd been down in the cellar where the root crops were kept. I liked it down there: it was dark and quiet and smelled of earth. Down there, I couldn't hear the voices of House Father or his friends. I did not put this in words: it was more the sense of *quiet/roots/earth/darkness/peace/safe* that came to me.

I had lit the dim lamp and was bending over the roots, stacking them in neat rows as I had been trained to do. And suddenly, there was the beat of wings around my head and a voice was shouting. I don't know what it said – it was loud and startling, echoing around the walls of the root cellar, and I jumped. The bird was whisking round my hair, wings filling my sight. I remembered the bird during the execution ceremony: it meant death and the stink of blood, a woman crumpling to the floor, her head shattered. My heart pounding, I knocked into the side of the box in which the roots were being stored. The box overturned, sending them rolling across the floor. I whipped round and struck out. I was aiming for the bird, but next moment, it was gone.

My son was sprawled on the floor. His face was white in the lamplight, and I remember noticing for the first time how different the colour of his skin was from mine. I stood over him, looking down. It felt as though the walls of the root cellar were closing, faster and faster, crashing over me in waves. I thought he said something: the word that meant 'mama'. There was blood running down his face.

The world had changed. Before, I mirrored it; now it mirrored me. I looked out of my own skull for the first time. There were no words, not yet. The old me was still there, wailing over her injured child, terrified of what I had done, horrified at the blood, loving First Joy, but there was also a person who stood in the root cellar, thinking in a clear sequence of images.

I have hurt a male.

I am in danger. House Father will kill me when he finds out.

I have to get out of here.

And I forced the weak, wailing, helpless person away and ran up the stairs of the root cellar, pushing back the training which told me that I should not move too quickly, should keep my head down at all times, should be quiet. My footsteps slapped on the floorboards and they sounded like my heart. When I reached the door, I looked into the main room and my daughter Luck-Still-to-Come was kneeling on the boards with a scrubbing brush. The scent of strong soap filled the room. Her face was screwed like a fist: she was concentrating. She did not look up, and I wrenched my gaze away. I pulled the folds of the slip-gown down over my head and went out into the burning day. Just another woman going about her errands, just another *thing*.

I knew the layout of my neighbourhood, but with this new understanding, everything looked different, seen through my fear and my need to survive. I knew where the gate was, because the household women weren't supposed to go near it, though the farm-wives came and went. I remembered my one trip through the gate to a farm: the green fields beyond, the sprinkler systems. I wanted to go there now, to see the trees and the river.

No one paid any attention to me as I made my way through the marketplace. I kept my head down, looked at my feet, and now, it was difficult. I felt as though there was something hanging over my head, bright as the sun, telling everyone that I had changed. Then the gate was there: huge slabs of packed earth, with a flash of green beyond. It was open, but guarded. I scurried through. The guards were talking to a farmer; they paid no attention to me. It was easy and there I was, out among the fields.

That was that. I just kept going and going. Sometimes the bird came to me and at first I ran, but later I grew used to it. It never hurt me – in fact, I could not even feel its feathers as they brushed against my face. I slept in the ditches and stole roots and leaves. Every time I did so, I learned more. I started applying words to things – words that I'd heard before, but never understood. 'Tree' and 'night' and 'sun' and 'wind'.

No one stopped me or spoke to me: I was just a woman. When I reached the end of the farmlands and there were no more fields, I hesitated for a moment, but fear drove me on. The desert was ahead and I went into it. I walked and walked, doing so at night because it was colder, and hiding in the rocks during the day. I sucked a pebble and once or twice, it rained. In the morning, the desert was a sea of flowers and I ate some of them, picking them as I walked. Sometimes my stomach hurt. I came to a riverbed that was almost dry and I followed it, sipping muddy water. I had no idea where I was going, only that it was *away*, and that this was a good thing. My daughters came to me, running through the rocks, and once I saw First Joy, standing on a high crag and staring at me. I was glad, because there was no sign of blood on him.

And then I came down from the rocks and there was the city. I was afraid at first, and waited to see what kind of men came in and out of it. But no one did and eventually I screwed up my courage and went in through the eastern gate. There was rainwater in stone tanks, and leaves growing along the cracks of the pavements. Later, I found the old fruit trees. I made a nest up in the bell tower, because it was high and safe and the figures on the wall were there. I talked to them, at night, making meaningless sounds. Six months after that, another woman came. And she had more words, and we put them together.

My story. Different from Khainet's, because by that time – some years before, in fact – the women who reached the city had started talking about voices in their heads, more maps and pictures, *instructions*. And unlike me, they found women to welcome them, although sometimes, deep in the night, I missed the peace of those early days, the silences.

And yet. Khainet had followed a familiar if mysterious pattern; how extraordinary could she be? I needed to speak to Mayest again, maybe persuade Khainet to talk with her in my presence. But I still didn't trust Mayest, and I still didn't know why.

It was late in the afternoon now, and the rain had completely burned away, leaving a slightly steamy heat. I went down through the winding streets to Tare's house complex, expecting to find Tare herself there, hanging about the four women. But the house complex appeared to be empty and quiet, with only a big insect zooming around in the kitchen, trapped and unable to find its way through the window spaces. I picked up a rag and flapped at it, and after a few minutes it shot through the window in a flash of blue-green and out into the day.

I cannot say, now, that I felt something was wrong. Looking back, it seems that there should have been something, some clue to what was to come, some message in the shafts of sunlight. But as I went up the stairs, looking for Mayest, there was no sign that anything was wrong.

I heard the breathing first. I was walking along the corridor that led to the guest chambers, relieved at being in this cool earthen place and out of the hot sunlight, even though the complex reminded me too much of the root cellar. But something was disturbing the quiet: rhythmic gasps that reminded me of House Father and those sudden dreadful flurries of sex.

I knew that some of the women slept together. I never had; I did not want to be touched after my life with House Father, and every night I was thankful that there was no one else to share my bed. But I had no objections to what the women did, if that was what they wanted. Perhaps Mayest's group were lovers, or contained lovers among them. I did not want to intrude – to be more honest, I did not want to see – and so I hung back for a moment, but there was something in the sound which was not pleasure, more as though the person was trying to draw in enough breath to survive.

I stepped through the door of the nearest guest chamber. Mayest was lying on the floor in a crumple, with one arm outflung. There was a seep of blood from the back of her head. Her eyes were open and staring. I thought at first that her face was white, and the room was darker. There was the smell of roots and earth, but only for a moment. Then it was gone.

Khainet was crouching over her, the source of that painful rasping breath. Her arms were wrapped around herself, clutching herself tight as though she might fly apart if she let go. But she was not rocking, and when she glanced up I saw a flash of something fierce in her face.

'What happened?' I barely recognized my own voice. My first thought was that Khainet had killed her, but I pushed it away, down to the cellar of my mind.

'She fell.' Her voice was loud and defensive. 'She slipped on the tiles and she hit her head.'

We stared at one another for a moment.

'Then that's what happened,' I heard myself say, as though I hadn't believed her, as if saying it would make it real. 'Where's everyone else?'

'Tare and the women went to the orchards for the last of the fruit. Tare wanted to get it done. They took the other three women with them, to show them the fields and how we do things here. I think Tare wanted Mayest to go with them, too, but Mayest stayed behind and she caught me in the hallway. She asked me to come and see her. I didn't know how to say no.'

I looked at Mayest's body and felt a sort of pity, because at the back of it lay waves and waves of root-smelling horror and I could not allow myself to feel that.

Khainet said, 'I don't want to stay here.'

'I understand.' I was blocking out everything except the need for flight, including what she had done. It was like that first knowledge of self-awareness, the overwhelming impulse to *get out*. Everything else that I was: elder of Edge, the responsible person, the one who sorted out problems – it was as though the thick rind of this had been pared away and left me nothing but a desperate skin. I was again the woman who had fled across the desert, nothing more.

But there was no other ruined city waiting for us, I was certain of that. Only Iznar, where I would not go, and the mountain colony where – if Khainet had really killed Mayest – we could not go. I would have to take Khainet into the mountains near the city, and hide her, then return. There was water there, and I would find a way of getting food to her. No one knew I had come here, to Tare's house. If we left now, by one of the wall passages, I could be back before nightfall and could pretend to be surprised at the death, which would be discovered by then. But they would think that Khainet had fled alone.

The other choice would be for her to stay here, and face the questions. If the woman she'd killed had been one of the colony, one of our own, I would have put her in bonds myself. But Mayest was different, Mayest was an outsider, and in some way that I did not yet understand, Mayest was a threat.

'Hunan?' Khainet spoke in a whisper. 'What are we going to do?'

We. If I had been unable to decide before, I'd made up my mind now.

'We're leaving,' I said.

I expected the household to return at any moment, and Mayest's companions with them. All we took with us – gathered in haste from Tare's kitchen – was food and water: the dried vegetable and fruit strips which the women had laid down for the winter, and strung gourds filled from the well bucket. Then we were out through the back of the house, into the winding streets where no one lived, the ruined hives that we had still not properly explored. Old wood creaked and groaned in a rising wind and I didn't like the sound of that; it meant another storm was on its way.

I saw Khainet look around her as we drew closer to the little-used eastern gate; recent events did not seem to have made her less curious. And I was curious, too. I wanted the truth about what had happened to Mayest, but something told me that Khainet would not give me that truth until we were both well away.

More ruins, their windows eyes onto black earthy rooms, like that place where I had once felt so safe.

As we neared the eastern gate, the streets grew narrower, so that someone in the windows of one house could have touched the fingers of someone in the house opposite. I'd never understood why the districts were so different. But I was glad of the change, because it meant that the streets now lay in shadow, and were cooler. Khainet was shivering, however, and I did not think it was a result of the changing temperature. I touched her shoulder, and she reached back without looking and clasped my hand in a grip that hurt. We were nearly at the gate. I kept listening out for shouts behind us, for Tare's household to have come home and raised the alarm, but the city was silent.

When we finally reached the eastern gate, there was no one there. The gate itself was massive: slabs of solid stone surrounded by earthen bricks that had long since caved in to block the entrance. An enemy could not have forced their way through it without heavy firepower. It reminded me of the massive gates of Iznar. Once more I seemed to see a screaming woman fall.

But there was a way out: a little tunnel winding through the wall. I didn't know what it had been, but suspected that it was part of the old irrigation system: it led down under the wall and there was a channel running through its smooth stone floor. It had small hinged valves that perhaps used to control the flow but which were now broken. Water still seeped through it, during the time of rains. Like now. I'd wondered before whether the valves had been shattered by the sudden force of too much water.

I gave Khainet a hand down the broken steps that led to the channel and then followed her myself. More earthen coolness, a damp breath from bricks that had long ago been smoothed into mud. It was not very far through the wall, and minutes later we were coming out into the sunlight. The edge of the desert lay before us, the rocks sharp and red in the early evening light, casting hard shadows. I glanced back up at the wall. No one. Khainet was already hastening into the limited shelter of the rocks and I was close behind her. The rocks were too sharp and scorching to walk on and we made our way between them instead, up through a deep gulley that gave a bit of shade. We climbed for a while, already drenched in sweat, and sharing one of the water gourds between us in silence. I wondered if Khainet regretted what she had done. I couldn't allow myself regret, not now, but it was hard. I looked back once and the colony lay far enough below us that I could see over the eastern wall.

The bell tower rose in its spire above the city, with the drift of efreets circling around it. Beyond the city, along the sea horizon, the storm clouds were building again and that made me nervous. I knew how fast the storms could come in and this, I'd learned from years at the desert's edge, was exactly the kind of place in which one might expect flash floods. But we had no choice, we had to stay in the gulley: the rock walls were too sheer to climb up. If a flood came, better hope we'd be drowned, rather than swept back down to be hammered against the mass of the eastern wall. We would be broken like twigs.

I didn't know this side of the city well, but Seliye and I had come up here once, exploring. We'd filled the tank with fruit oil and driven the land-car up the gulley, during one of the long dry seasons with the seedpods exploding and crackling in the heat and sending showers of seeds down into the gulley. We'd followed it up as far as a series of piled-up rocks – whether eaten by the wind or put there by the goddess folk, I did not know – and then the land flattened out into a level place, pockmarked with scratches and potholes. If we could make it as far as the level place before the rain came, we'd have a good chance of making it further up into the mountains. And we could refill the water gourds, too.

That was my hope. But as the evening wore on, it became clear to me that the storm was coming in too fast. Above the gulley, the sky was dark green, and the first crack of lightning, a vivid white, made us both jump. Moments after that, the first fat drops of rain spattered into the dust of the gulley.

'We've got to get out of the channel!' I shouted.

Khainet turned a panicking face towards me. 'It's too high.'

'If the gulley floods . . .'

But we didn't have a choice. We began to creep up the side of the gulley, searching for tiny handholds in the smooth rock. Even in spite of her recent illness, Khainet made better progress than I did: younger, and with a stronger grip, she had an advantage. But it was hard going for both of us. The rain was sliding down in torrents and apart from the little handholds and juts, the rock was becoming slippery. Khainet stopped, clinging to the cliff, and squinted back to see if she could give me any help, but I urged her on.

'Don't stop! I'll be right behind you.' This was not true – I was several feet below her – but I could hear the noise I'd feared so much: a steady, thundering roar above the sound of the rain. A flood was coming down the gulley.

'Hunan!' The panicked look was back on Khainet's face and I was sure it was on mine, too.

'Keep climbing!'

'Hunan, I can hear something!'

I didn't answer her. The boiling roar was coming closer and I didn't want to spend any spare energy on speech. I struggled upward, following the route that Khainet had taken. But I was too slow and too late. I caught a glimpse of a white race of spray as the flood rounded the bend of the gulley and then it hit. It knocked the breath out of me and swept me away. I had one last image of Khainet's screaming face and then I was whirled back down the gulley, as though I was of no more consequence than one of the little black seeds.

TWENTY-SEVEN

Planet: Muspell (Vali)

'You,' Glyn Apt said, 'are becoming a nuisance.'

'Sorry. Shouldn't have taken me prisoner, should you? Since I'm proving such a trial.' I sat down. Eld had already been taken out.

Glyn Apt gave me a baleful look and gestured to the Morrighanu who were flocking in behind her. These were younger women, not the goat-girls, with a fanatical fire in their eyes, and I could see the glisten and glitter of weapon enhancements through the skin of their hands and forearms. Birds played in a constant fluttering flock about their sleek heads.

They said nothing, only motioned for me to leave the cell and accompany them. Glyn Apt fell in behind, probably to keep an eye on me. We went down a strange labyrinth of passageways: nothing like the black-fern corridors, or the functional buildings of the vitki that I'd seen in Hetla. This place was like some ancient broch on Earth, dating from the earliest days of human history. It had been cut out of the turf, rough walls still showing an edge of withered grass, and there was a strong earthy smell to the place that I had not noticed on the previous evening. It suggested that the place where I had been brought in, and the cell itself, were some kind of front structure, leading underground, but I could not be sure. Eventually we came to a different kind of room, a stone chamber that I recognized from the tombs that dotted the islands of the Reach. Our ancestors had built them, during the less civilized time of Muspell's history when the culture had started looking back to the ancient ways of Earth. It hadn't lasted, but the tombs remained. This place was, perhaps, two thousand years old or more. It stank of death. I felt the seith flinch around me, curling inward to provide a protective sheath about my body. At the far end of the chamber was a low stone table. Glyn Apt sat down at it and started accessing a very anachronistic data display.

'Where are we?' I asked. Glyn Apt ignored me, head bent over the messages scrolling across the stone surface of the table. The air was thick with birds and the data stream was beginning to make me feel claustrophobic.

'Bring her a stool,' Glyn Apt said, without looking up. One of the Morrighanu hastened out, to return minutes later with a small stone bench. I took a seat before the table. Glyn Apt looked up and treated me to a long stare.

'You and Thorn Eld. What an unlikely pair you make.'

'I'm sure.'

'How exactly *did* you arrange your escape from the Rock?'

I decided to tell the truth. More or less. 'I didn't. It was the selk's idea. They took me to Eld.'

'The selk took you?' Glyn Apt looked blankly confused and I couldn't blame her. 'Why?'

'On Eld's instructions. Because of the woman known as Skinning Knife.'

I scored a direct hit with that. I could see it in her face. 'You know about her?'

'I know a lot less than you do, probably.' I didn't wait for her to drag it out of me, this time. I simply told her.

'. . . and so Eld and I are in search of her.'

Glyn Apt's stare deepened. 'You know only what Eld's told you, then? Surely *you* don't trust a vitki?'

I was on the verge of saying, 'I trust this one,' and then realized that it would make me sound like an idiot. Indeed, in thinking it, I *was* an idiot. I should not have trusted Eld any more than I trusted the Morrighanu themselves.

'No,' I said. 'But I trust him more than I trust you.'

'You think Skadi killed your leader?'

'Yes. Don't you? I think you believe the same, Glyn Apt. I think you believed that back on the Rock. Was it the Skald you wanted? Or were you after Skadi?'

Glyn Apt smiled. 'You're quite a one for speculations, Vali. Perhaps you'd prefer to share them with my commanding officer?'

Rhi Glyn Apt's CO arrived towards the end of that afternoon, and when they led me from the cell and back into the interrogation chamber, I realized how wrong I had been to characterize Glyn Apt as being technologically enhanced. Glyn Apt's commander bristled with machinery. I could see it gliding beneath the skin of her face and hands, always moving, shifting so that the very bones over which it lay seemed to move also, reconfiguring her angular features to such an extent that it was difficult to look at her. She wore the black body-armour of the Morrighanu, little more than a sleek toughened slickskin which would, I knew from experience, prove hard as steel. The inlaid birds had been holographically set, so that they glided across her shoulders in endless flight, and in addition to this vanity, her hair had been replaced by dark pinions. Her eyes were the silver orbs that I remembered from the valkyrie and the birds that swarmed around her head were both black and white, and closer to the vitki ravens than the birds of Rhi Glyn Apt and the others. She was not introduced to me by name and indeed, she was so far from human that I wondered whether she even had one.

'You,' she said to me, with so vitriolic a hate that I took a step back and cannoned into Eld, who was being brought back into the room. The remark had been addressed to him.

'Commander,' Eld said. 'I thought we'd run into one another again.'

'The secret stealer.' Her voice had a curiously metallic timbre beneath its harshness. 'The vitki Thorn Eld. You'll be a useful bargaining chip.'

Eld laughed. 'I doubt it. I'm probably as expendable as everyone else these days. The vitki have their minds on other things.'

'Things that we were promised.'

'What, like those rich lands of the Reach? You were never promised that, Commander. You asked for too much.'

'Not more than is rightfully ours.'

'There's some contention about that. You wanted everything, as I recall, behaved as though it was no more than your due. Morvern lives in the past. It's time to stop fighting old battles.'

'There is no such thing,' the Morrighanu commander said, 'as an old battle.' She stared at Eld for a moment, then turned abruptly to Glyn Apt. 'You said they claim to be pursuing one known to us.'

'One of them has a right to do so.' *That* was a surprise to me. I'd had no idea that Glyn Apt might be predisposed to fight my corner, but perhaps I'd been wrong.

But the commander clearly didn't think much of Glyn Apt's moral opinions. 'Take them outside. Shoot them, now that we have all the information we are likely to get.'

'Commander—' Glyn Apt cried.

'I don't want passengers, Glyn Apt.'

'But—'

Eld and I exchanged glances, but there was nothing we could do. I could feel Eld tense up, waiting for his moment. The commander made a quick gesture. 'Outside. Do it now.'

But then there was a rushing in the air, as though the walls had fallen away, and something was among us. I glimpsed a white face and hollow gaze, the flicker of talons. Suddenly, a Morrighanu lay twitching in spasm on the floor and the commander was rushing forward, talons bared.

'Come on,' Eld said. He broke away from the paralysed guard and seized me by the arm. With Glyn Apt, we raced down the passages.

'The exit's this way,' Glyn Apt shouted while elbowing her way past me, sprinting down the turf passage to a glimmer of daylight. We came out on top of a mound, like one of the barrows that one found in very primitive parts of the Reach. Anguish blasted up from below, shrivelling the seith like an uprush of heat.

Glyn Apt jumped down from the barrow and raced into the trees. Eld and I, slipping a little on icy ground, followed. By the time we stopped running, it was almost dark.

The place to which Glyn Apt had brought us was another broch, a stone ruin rising up through the trees like a broken tooth. It was squat, no more than fifteen feet in height, and empty. A trackway led past it, the snow gleaming beneath the moon's growing light. As we stepped into the broch I felt a shiver at the edges of the seith, as though someone had drawn a finger down my spine.

'Why here?' Eld asked, glancing uneasily around him. 'I think this is too exposed.'

'You'd prefer the woods?' Glyn Apt replied. 'This isn't Hetla, you know. This is Morvern's heart and the woods are full of beasts. But they won't come anywhere near human habitation and this is close enough to that. Those who built it made sure that it had its own protection. You can feel it, Skald girl, can't you? And so can you, vitki.'

'I can feel it,' I said. A strange sensation of *encasement, security, enclosure*, as though we had been sealed off from the outside world.

'It won't hide us from Skinning Knife, though,' Eld said.

'That thing was her?' Even in the faint light, I saw the flash of panic in Glyn Apt's eyes. She stood, chafing her hands. She had not had time to snatch up a coat and the slickskin armour did not seem to be keeping her warm. I reached out with the seith and confirmed her panic.

'Leave me alone,' Glyn Apt said, glaring at me.

'Sorry.' I couldn't sound all that sincere. I knew what it was like to have people poking and prodding at me. Glyn Apt took a fistful of her hair, which had come loose, and knotted it out of the way.

Suddenly Eld's head snapped up. 'Someone's coming.'

I could hear a curious hissing noise, nothing like that made by a wing.

'Down!' Glyn Apt dragged me back against the wall.

A light appeared through the trees. As we watched through a crack in the ruin's wall, I heard the skittering of hooves on packed snow and moments later a sled glided past. It was a long, lightweight thing, drawn by a team of creatures that resembled large goats: I saw their black curled coats, their slitted yellow eyes, the spiralling horns. On the sled crouched three Morrighanu, huddled under cloaks and clutching bolt-rifles. As they neared the ruin, the goats tried to pull back, tossing their heads in panic, but the woman at the front of the sled whipped them on. A minute later and the sled whisked out of sight.

'They're not looking for us,' Eld said.

'No. They are fleeing. But the question is, is there anything in pursuit?'

'Look,' Eld said. 'There's no point in panicking. If Skinning Knife wants us, believe me, she will find us.'

'Should you call your headquarters?' I said to Glyn Apt. 'Find out what's going on?' I almost said: *if there's anyone still alive*.

'What do you think I've been doing?' the Morrighanu retorted. 'Ever since we were forced to flee, I have been attempting to contact them, on the concealed channel. There is nothing but static. My birds can't get through.'

'All right,' Eld said, wearily. 'We may as well try to get some rest. Vali and I will sit watch.'

'I should prefer it if we took double shifts,' Glyn Apt said. 'I do not require sleep at the moment.'

'I don't want to have to watch out for Skinning Knife, wild animals and you,' I said.

Eld reached out and touched the Morrighanu lightly on the arm. I heard a faint hiss. A fleeting glimpse of surprise crossed Glyn Apt's face.

'Neither do I,' Eld said, as the Morrighanu slumped forward. We put her against the wall, and I searched her as we did so. There was a serviceable knife attached to her belt, and I took it, making sure that she carried no other weapons. Unfortunately, she did not. The haste with which we had left the first broch had led to that. And only then did I sleep.

When I woke, Glyn Apt was still lying sprawled against the wall of the ruin, quite still. Whatever Eld had dosed her with must have been powerful, unless he had repeated the dose when I'd been sleeping. I rolled over and stood up, with the stiff ache of cold in my bones. There was no sign of Eld, but when I walked cautiously to the edge of the ruin, I saw that the goat sled was back. Thorn was talking to the Morrighanu who rode it. The goats stamped in the early morning cold, their cloven hooves making patterns on the frosty ground. A crimson sun was rising up through the trees, dispelling the mist.

'Eld?' I said. I walked out to join him and the Morrighanu.

'Vali, there you are. My associate,' he said to the Morrighanu who was standing on the runners of the sled. She looked at me curiously and I found myself staring back. She, and the other two women on the sled, looked like the goat women I had seen before. Each had a cloud of fleecy black hair, bound back with leather thongs, and yellow eyes with a horizontal pupil. Their faces were long and narrow. I did not like to think about any possible genetic connections, and I had to work hard to stop my gaze from straying back and forth between the women and the goats. Eld gave no sign that he saw this confusion.

'These women are on their way back to the broch,' he said.

'Is that wise?'

'We must find out what has happened to our sisters,' one of the goat women said.

'By finding out, you may die,' Eld remarked.

'The shadow-woman has left,' one of the women said, in a surprisingly deep, resonant voice.

'How do you know that?'

'Because there is one survivor, the daughter of one of the warriors. She hid in a thorn thicket. She saw the attacker, the shadow-woman, leave. She said that the shadow-woman was covered in blood and licking her lips. She stepped into the air and disappeared. The child remained hidden, not daring to go back in. I have spoken with her this morning by bird; she is still there.'

Poor girl, I thought. What a thing to witness, knowing that your mother had been inside. I remembered virtual-Idhunn: had the real-life correlate, daughter of a Morrighanu, experienced anything like this? I found myself missing Idhunn all over again.

'Did she say whether the shadow-woman was carrying anything?'

'She did not.'

Eld drew me aside. 'It would be useful to go back with them.'

'Useful or suicidal?'

'They wouldn't be returning unless they were reasonably certain that the danger had passed,' Eld said, but he did not look sure.

'Are you certain? These Morrighanu seem as crazy as the vitki to me.'

'Point taken,' Eld remarked, rather sourly. 'But as I have said on several occasions of late, if Skadi wanted to find us, she appears able to do so with ease. There is still a rather large issue as to who is pursuing whom.' He paused. 'And I must admit, I'm rather curious to see exactly what she's done.'

'You knocked me out!' This came from Glyn Apt, white-lipped and furious, staggering from the ruin.

Eld surveyed her coldly. 'Of course I did. What did you expect?'

She looked at me. 'You have my knife. Give it back.'

'Make me.'

'Sister!' One of the Morrighanu on the sledge stepped forward and gripped Glyn Apt by the arm. 'You're alive.'

'I am alive because I ran.'

The goat-eyes flickered and fell. 'As did we.'

'There's no shame in that,' I said, 'given what you were facing.'

'There is always shame,' Glyn Apt said.

'We are going back.' The Morrighanu crouched at the front of the sledge raised her head for the first time and spoke.

'Of course,' Glyn Apt said. 'We have no choice.'

'Vali?' Eld was looking at me carefully.

'All right,' I agreed. 'We'll go back.'

TWENTY-EIGHT

PLANET: NHEM (HUNAN)

I opened my eyes to see a circle of sky: hot and blue-green. The air smelled of steam and for a moment I thought I was back in the bell tower after a night of rain. Then I remembered, with a rush of dismay. But at least I was still alive; I didn't know whether to be pleased about that or not. I felt clammy and over-warm, and there was a bursting pain in my ankle. Groggily, I raised myself up. I was lying on a little mud beach. Water lapped on its rim and all around rose ochre rock walls. Across the water, I could see a narrow opening, a cave. The flood must have washed me through. There was water at least, but no way out unless I climbed or swam. I was very thirsty, but the water was too muddy to drink. I pulled myself further up onto the beach into a rim of shade, thinking that I was lucky – at least, in the short term – not to have been dashed against the city wall, or washed out into the poisonous sea.

I don't know how long I lay there. I remember opening my eyes at one point and discovering that the circle of sky above me had turned black and was filled with stars. I stared at it until I fell into it, and when I looked up again, it was washed with a faint pink light like the inside of a shell.

Something was buzzing. Above my head, I saw a large insect, a thing with a short, bulbous body and whirring wings. I swatted at it, thinking it was about to attack me. I'd never seen anything like it before, but I remembered the swarms of stinging flies that used to come in the hottest days in the colony, how much their bite hurt. I still had pinpoint scars on both forearms from those bites and so I batted feebly at the insect. It did not go away. Instead, it grew much larger, coming down through the mouth of the pothole in which I was lying, until I could see the black bristles and the bulging eyes and the flickering wings.

It landed unsteadily on the little beach, tilted at an angle that looked dangerous to me, and someone leaped out. They wore tight clothes, as brown as earth, and a shiny helmet like a beetle's wing. The helmet was lifted off, and to my surprise revealed Mayest. But Mayest was dead, I reminded myself, and Khainet had killed her, or so I had thought. I struggled to sit up, to drag myself away, but the figure was already striding over to me, saying, 'Don't move!' She knelt by my side. It was not Mayest, I told myself. It could not be. Mayest had had three sisters; perhaps it was one of those, or yet another version of the northerner. There was no sign of any weapon. I peered at her and I could not have told that she was not Mayest herself.

'Who are you? How did you find me?'

'I am Ettia. I've been sent to find you. We have a way of tracking. You're hurt,' she said.

'My ankle . . .'

'It's not broken. I think you've just sprained it.' A sharp look. 'Dehydration, too. You need water.'

After the flash flood, that struck me as very funny. I started to laugh and couldn't stop. I wheezed myself into weakness and Mayest's double hauled me upright so that I was leaning on her shoulder. 'You'll be fine,' she assured me, and the words had a hollow ring. I did not know where she was planning to take me, only that nowhere was good for me now. I didn't know whether or not to tell her about Khainet. If I kept quiet, there was a chance that Khainet might get away – but maybe she was already dead, swept away by the flood that had with such cruel mercy spared me. Yet she was Mayest's killer, and if I told them that she had fled with me and they found her – I didn't know what to do and that made me weaker than the pain and thirst. I sagged in my rescuer's grip and Ettia had to shove me through the door of the flying machine. When I was securely fastened on a little bench, and the flying machine was lurching up from the pothole, I glanced up and saw that my questions were answered. Khainet was strapped to the opposite bench. Her scarred hands were tied, and her red-rimmed eyes were burning above a gag that looked more like a cage. She would not meet my gaze.

The machine flew on, veering over the red-and-ochre of the plateau. My eyes stung with the wind but I could still tell that we were flying north, and soon the green domes of Iznar were hanging on the horizon's edge.

*

I could not believe that we were heading for Iznar. That would mean that Mayest's group were in league with the men, and I just could not believe that they would allow women to work alongside them; if anything that Mayest had told me had been true. But as the green domes grew larger against the mountain shadow, everything came rushing back, swift as flash flood: childhood, Father and House Father, the long stupid years, the woman falling, falling onto the baking flagstones, my children. The root cellar and First Joy, lying still and bloody like someone who had crashed down from a great height.

The sudden darkness was hot and stifling, closing down upon me – but then the machine turned and dipped, causing the patchwork farmland to swim up. Part of me still could not believe that I was flying; it didn't seem possible for women to fly, only to fall. Iznar was behind us now and I was filled with thankfulness. I looked across at Khainet and saw that she had closed her eyes. I could not blame her; I didn't want to look at those green domes any longer than I had to.

I spoke to Ettia. 'Where are we going?'

'Not Iznar. I'm sorry, I should have told you. To the mountains.'

'Aren't you afraid, flying so close to the city?'

'Things have changed. They'll see me as an enemy, true, but they'll think I'm from one of the mountain militias.'

I saw a quick, cold grin appear under the rim of the helmet. 'This is one of their craft, after all. We captured it last year, run it on rock oil.'

'And Iznar won't . . . respond?'

'As I said, things have changed. The Hierolath is dead; all the men are fighting and bickering like a bag full of efreets. We're not so . . . united ourselves, but the more fragmented they become, the stronger we grow. They might want to shoot down an enemy craft, but ammunition is becoming more scarce. They won't attack unless I pose a direct threat.' Again that grin. 'All the better for us.'

'You said you were taking us to the mountains. Does that mean to the—' I stumbled over the word, 'the laboratories?'

I suppose I meant to trap her, but she just said, 'Yes. To the Stronghold. Don't entertain thoughts of escaping from it, by the way. You won't be able to.'

Minutes later, I understood what she meant.

TWENTY-NINE

Planet: Muspell (Vali)

After seeing Idhunn's body and the man we'd found in the stream, I had a pretty good idea what we would find back at the stronghold of the Morrighanu, and I lived it in full dismayed anticipation during our journey back from the ruin. I didn't grieve for Glyn Apt's commander, who had been all too ready to see me dead, but it struck me that I'd seen too much gore and horror these last few years. Maybe I should have chosen a quieter profession. I had only myself to blame.

The memories of death seemed a strange, unwholesome contrast with the eerie forest; the grey trees and glittering frost, the burning sun floating above the branches and the air scented with cold. The only sound was the hissing of the sled runners along the track and the swift patter of the goats' feet. I could not help thinking of the ripped red ruin awaiting us.

As if she had read my thoughts, Glyn Apt murmured from where she sat behind me on the sled, 'The Red War Raven.'

'What did you say?'

But it was Eld who replied. 'She is their patron, a goddess from Earth, from very ancient times. She was the deity of battle.'

'How appropriate.'

'Not to mention the Birds of Rhiannon,' Eld continued. 'Like the hugin and munin of the vitki.'

'You take a lot from myth,' I said.

'What else is there, at the end of the day? You have to make meaning in this world and we kept our heritage. The vitki and the Morrighanu alike are good at that. Don't the Skald do the same thing? Aren't you known as a witch clan?'

'Perhaps.' It was my turn to be defensive. 'It depends who you talk to.'

Glyn Apt's blue eyes glinted. 'You in the Skald, do you believe in gods?'

'We believe in the forces of nature, but we don't deify them.' I was quite happy to engage in a theological debate, given what I believed to be waiting for us. 'However, we believe that the forces known as gods may, over time, accumulate a kind of separate existence in the minds of generations of humans.'

'A weak answer,' one of the Morrighanu said from the front of the sled, in her deep voice. 'Gods exist or they do not.'

I saw Eld smile. 'You believe, then?'

There was a fanatical glint in the goat-eyes. 'The goddess walks Morvern in many guises. How can one not believe?' But as the woman spoke, I was watching Glyn Apt's face and I did not think that she looked as certain as her colleague. Or perhaps it was just the dataflow, weaker now. I wondered whether she needed to be in range of a particular signal. Her birds still occasionally flickered about her head, but their white wings were as translucent as ghosts.

'And this . . . assailant, from whom you fled. Is she a facet of the goddess, perhaps?'

'Perhaps.' The woman's face was sombre.

'You really believe that?' I was genuinely curious.

'Why should it matter to you what I believe?' the Morrighanu said impatiently. It was a fair enough point. But now we were almost at the broch. The Morrighanu who held the reins slowed the goats down to a silent, stealthy walk. At the end of the track we halted, leaving the sled concealed behind an outcrop of rock. The three Morrighanu swarmed upward, vanishing with alarming speed up the rock face. Glyn Apt shouldered her way past me and sidled to look into the clearing that housed the broch. I followed, peering past her. All was quiet. The entrance to the broch stood open, outlined with frost. A faint mist hung in the air before it, fragile as a veil, and it struck me that this was indeed so, that the mist represented the veil said in legend to hang between the worlds, and that those within the broch were already in the afterlife of our ancestors and could be glimpsed there, if only we had the courage to step into the clearing.

Moments later the silence was split by a shriek. Glyn Apt jerked back, nearly hitting me in the face, but the noise was soon explained when one of the Morrighanu descended the rock face at speed, carrying a small form. The girl who had hidden in the thorn thicket – perhaps eight or nine years old, face shining white with terror, mouth agape, eyes staring at nothing. Then, to my ashamed relief, she was out of sight as the Morrighanu carried her to the sledge. I looked back to find Glyn Apt gone. She and the remaining two goat-women were sprinting across the clearing and into the broch. Instinctively, and stupidly, I started after her but Eld drew me back.

'Look,' he said. 'You don't owe them any loyalty, do you, just because they're women? They were quite willing to serve both of us up on a platter at a banquet of war yesterday. If Skadi's still in there, better the Morrighanu find her than we do.'

'This is very true,' I agreed. 'So, we wait?'

'And see what comes out. If anything.'

But the only thing that came out of the broch was, to my relief, Glyn Apt herself. She motioned to us to approach. 'It's clear.'

'How bad is it?' Eld asked as we neared the entrance to the broch. Glyn Apt's pale face was composed.

'Come and see for yourselves, vitki, Skald.'

We followed her down the turf passage. My senses were flinched, waiting for horror: the stench of blood and torn flesh, the sights of bodies snatched wantonly apart. But in the command chamber, and the cells, and the interrogation chamber beyond it, there was nothing to be seen. The place was clean, empty and quiet, as though everyone who had been there on the previous day, the whole humming hive, had simply packed up and gone.

'Where are they all?' Glyn Apt whispered. Her eyes were

wide. But now it was Eld's turn to grow pale and lean back shakily against the wall.

'Vali,' he said, and it was then that I unfurled my senses, reached out with the seith and felt what he felt.

It was pure destruction, sheer violence, as though it was still going on around us, an unceasing pageant of horror. It was all sensation, unaccompanied by imagery, running down my nerves and neurons, filling me with the knowledge that I was being slaughtered and also with a cold, alien joy in the slaughter itself. Skinning Knife was in my head, all at once, overwhelming, and with a great effort I shut the seith off. The psychic shrieking stopped. I found that I had fallen to my knees and that my hands were clamped over my ears.

'So it was with me,' Glyn Apt said, 'when we stepped in here earlier.' She reached down a hand and pulled me up.

'She's trying to blind us,' Eld said, 'so that we're limited to the physical senses, to technology. I don't know about you, but I don't feel that either is likely to get us very far.'

'Don't worry,' I told him. 'I'm used to being blind.'

Together with the Morrighanu, we made a thorough search of the broch, but found nothing. One of the women, whose names I still did not know despite repeated requests, went back to speak with the traumatized child and learned that she had run out in the first minutes of the attack. She could not say what she had seen, but the Morrighanu felt it from her, and it had been killing, sure enough.

'And yet there is no sign of anything,' Eld said in frustration. 'No blood, no bones. Nothing.'

'Well, she can't have conducted her slaughter and then spent the rest of the night mopping the floor. She left Idhunn's body, after all. And that corpse we found. There must be DNA traces, at least.'

'I've done multiple scans. I can't find any physical evidence at all, apart from the usual – shed skin cells and hair. But there's no trace of blood. This is impossible.'

It struck me now that the leaving of Idhunn's body and the other man's might have been intentional, rather than the result of disturbed flight. A calling sign, a warning. Whereas maybe this had been business as usual.

'I can hear something,' Glyn Apt said suddenly.

We listened, but all I was aware of was silence. I didn't dare use the seith again, and open myself up to that beyond-sense shrieking. Eld, too, was looking at the Morrighanu strangely.

'What can you hear?'

'I don't know.' Glyn Apt frowned. But I realized she was right. It was not so much that I could hear something, however, as feel it. It seemed to be travelling up through the floor and down through the walls at the same time, and it made me first queasy, then nauseous. Eld and the Morrighanu were glancing around them in alarm.

'Is it an earthquake?' Eld asked.

'Not here, surely. We've never—' Glyn Apt shook her head furiously, like someone who has wasps in her hair. 'We have to get out. Now.'

And once more we fled from the broch, coming out into the silent morning. But the tremor, or whatever it was, that had so displaced us inside the broch was no longer in evidence in the clearing. Here, all was peaceful. When we had reached the shelter of the rocks, we looked back. But the broch had gone.

'That's impossible,' Glyn Apt echoed. The rocks extended down to the floor of the clearing in an unbroken seam. There was no sign of the broch.

'Where is it?' Glyn Apt said, raw-voiced. 'Where has it gone?'

Someone, somewhere, must be having a good laugh at our expense, I thought. We searched the clearing, but there was no sign that anything of human construction had ever been there. Glyn Apt stood to one side, speaking rapidly and anxiously into a hand-held communicator. The private channel had, she confessed, been linked in with the broch, and now that, too, was gone.

'There is nothing but static.' Glyn Apt sat glumly down on a nearby rock.

'But you can get through on the hand-held?'

'Yes. High command is sending a wing.'

'Not for us, it isn't,' Eld said.

Glyn Apt was staring at me absently and I knew what she was thinking. I crouched down in front of her and looked up into her pale, pouchy face. With the dataflow gone, she seemed to have aged overnight and I could not say that I was surprised.

'I have no intention of becoming a prisoner again, Glyn

Apt. If we are to go with you, we work together, and this is to be made clear to your high command.' What was left of it.

'They will not accept you,' Glyn Apt stated, very cold. 'You are Skald. An enemy.'

'This is not a time to start making parochial distinctions,' Eld said. 'She is working with me, and I am vitki. Do you not think we should be thinking more widely, about a common enemy?'

'Parochial?' Glyn Apt spat. 'You expect me to set aside a thousand years of hate, against all policy of my high command?'

'Yet you defended me against your own commander,' I said. 'What was all that about?'

'I was prepared to defend you,' Glyn Apt said, tight-lipped. 'You are a woman, with reason for vengeance. But I would have let her kill the vitki.'

'That's not a reason. Glyn Apt, if I need to do so, I will contact the high command of both vitki and valkyrie and ask them to put pressure on your organization in this matter.'

'You think they'll respond?' Glyn Apt said. 'I've had time to do a little more research into this quest of yours. It isn't even approved by your own command, is it? This foreign enemy was the only person you could talk into accompanying you. And I know that you have been outcast from the vitki ranks as a result of your vendetta against the project of Skinning Knife.'

'Eld? Is that true?' I said into the sudden silence.

'Yes, it's true,' he answered after a moment. 'But you

should know that I believed that Skadi killed Idhunn. I don't think you have much doubt about that yourself, do you?'

I gave a slight nod. I didn't want Glyn Apt to know that I'd actually spoken with Idhunn, or what was left of her in the Morrighanu information system. I hadn't had time to investigate her coal of information, either, and that frustrated me. So what, then, was Eld's story?

Both Glyn Apt and Eld were on their feet now, facing one another. I did not fancy Glyn Apt's chances against the vitki. I moved so that I was an equal distance from both of them.

'Glyn Apt,' Eld demanded, 'be reasonable. Whatever you think of me, whatever denial you might be engaged in, at least let me talk to what's left of your high command.'

'They will not listen to you,' Glyn Apt said, but I had already made my choice. I had the Morrighanu on her knees with her own knife at her throat before anyone else could move.

'Give him the hand-held. Put him through, or I'll kill you.'

After a moment, Glyn Apt complied, as I watched her hands carefully. Eld took the communicator aside and spoke into it, out of earshot. I gripped Glyn Apt, keeping the knife steady. The other women watched me, with wary goat-eyes.

After a few minutes of conversation, Eld came back to our tense little group and held the communicator to Glyn Apt's ear. She listened, with every evidence of distaste. At last she said, 'Very well, then. It seems you've convinced someone, at least. We are all to go back to High Command, and discuss the situation.'

'Good,' Eld said. 'Vali, you can let her go now.'

I did so, pushing the Morrighanu so that she sprawled across the still-frosty ground. It gave me a little satisfaction, at that. She huddled together with the other women, speaking in low, fluid voices, occasionally casting unreadable glances in the direction of Eld and myself. A short time after that, the silver-and-black wing blasted down out of the sky.

Whatever my feelings about the Morrighanu, it was good to be out of the clearing and away from the vanished broch. Glyn Apt's colleagues remained below. I saw the little figure of the goat sledge, tiny as a toy, retreating through the forest below and then it was gone.

The sense of the broch still lingered around me and inside my head, as though the edges of the seith had been withered and blasted by fire. When Glyn Apt had stalked off to speak to the pilot of the wing, I put aside what remained of my Skald pride and spoke of this to Eld, who just gave a grim nod.

'I don't know what we're doing here, Eld. We seem to be thrashing about in utter confusion, whilst our enemy walks in and out as she pleases and leaves havoc in her wake.'

'Perhaps that's the point. Weaken us with a sense of our own powerlessness until she chooses to strike. She seems to like to play.'

'Well, it's working.' I stared out of the porthole of the wing as we swept low over the forest: a grey-and-white waste, touched with columns of flame. I could almost smell the burning. Spring, it seemed, was coming fast, in fire.

Skinning Knife had saved our lives. A few moments later, we'd have been shot. It could not be coincidence that she'd arrived when she did. Would she have killed us too, if we hadn't escaped? There was a game being played; I could feel pieces of puzzle and I didn't understand them. I wasn't ready to share these speculations with Eld, but he was watching me, clearly wondering what I was thinking. So I said, 'Which is worse, Eld? Something that kills for the love of it, like some beasts do, or something that schemes and plans and wants to see what will happen?'

'Assuming they're even separate. It's a mistake to think that hot and cold cannot exist in the same being – a passion for pain combined with clinical precision. I've seen that in Skadi, Vali. So have you.'

At that point, Glyn Apt returned, looking even more sour than usual.

'We'll soon be making the descent to High Command,' Glyn Apt said. 'The pilot is expecting turbulence. You'd be advised to strap yourselves in.' She looked as though she would much rather not have told us that part.

Coming down to the High Command was not a journey I like to remember. The wing rocked, buffeted by the winds that tore through the gaps in the mountain wall. I tried the map implant, but could not determine whether this was the wall of rock down which Eld and I had descended only a few days ago. Like all the terrain in Darkland, it was black and glassy: I looked out of the porthole of the wing to see a snaggled line of teeth, cresting up from the snow below like the spine of a dragon. Shortly after that, a blizzard whirled up and the desolate scene disappeared as completely as the broch, behind a wall of white. The wing hung for a long time, riding the wind, veering from side to side as though we rode the waves. Eventually the pilot must have got clearance or spotted a gap, because the wing surged forward and the tumult outside was abruptly curtailed by darkness.

'Is this it?' I said, into the quiet. For all I knew, we'd suddenly died.

'It is.' Glyn Apt released the door catch and the door fell open into a blast of air from the stabilizer jets. We followed her out into a hangar, carved from the rock of the mountain.

'They're waiting for us now,' Glyn Apt explained. Her manner had changed: she seemed nervous, almost eager. I wondered whether she had experienced a change of heart in bringing us here, or whether she was planning some further trap.

She led us along a narrow passage and through a set of doors, into a room that immediately reminded me of the council chamber of the Skald. It had the same high-arched roof, spanned by ribs of stone, and even a round table; and it felt as though it had been carved in very ancient days, perhaps when the ancestors of the Darklanders had first come here. The room was, like the Morrighanu themselves, familiar, and therefore disturbing in its familiarity.

Around the table sat a number of people, perhaps twenty

in all. It was impossible not to notice the ebb and flow of tension in the room, twinging across the edges of the seith, and when I studied those who were seated there, I understood why. They were not all Morrighanu. At least a third of them were men, and therefore presumably vitki, and three were clearly valkyrie, as chilly as their vitki counterparts. Their blank silver stares rested upon me as I followed Glyn Apt through the door, lingered without interest, until they fastened their gazes upon Eld and did not let go. Eld showed no sign that anything unusual had occurred. With Glyn Apt escorting us, we took two seats on the farthest side of the room. Thorn was the first to speak.

'Am I to take it, Heldur, that you've actually decided you have something to say to me after all?' He addressed a man sitting opposite us: elderly, perhaps in his late seventies, with a shaven head and the rapacious face of a gannet.

'It seems you may not have been entirely mistaken in your conclusions, Eld. The rescindment of your position still stands, however, until we have additional evidence.' I had been expecting a harsh caw of a voice, but the man spoke like an academic, in a thin, reedy tone. A single feather fluttered down from the ceiling and he caught it in his palm, closing a wrinkled fist over it. When he opened his hand once more, the feather had gone. 'Ah,' he said. 'I see word has finally come.'

'It makes no difference,' one of the other councillor women said. She, too, was old: completely bald, with dead black eyes. 'Our weapon is gone. What do you have to say about that?'

'I have nothing to say,' the old vitki answered, and added, 'Madam, I think you may mistake me for someone who cares.'

At once the Morrighanu were on their feet, but the elderly woman waved them impatiently down again. 'Sit. You cannot expect sympathy. I would not extend it, were the circumstances reversed – oh, I was forgetting. Of course, they have been so.'

'Indeed,' the old vitki said. 'Our laboratory.'

Glyn Apt's mouth quirked in a humourless smile. 'At least the vanishing of our little broch did not take half the forest with it.' *Same phenomenon?* I wondered.

'And so,' the old vitki continued, turning to Glyn Apt, 'you were the one who followed the quarry to the Rock, were you not?' I sat up a little straighter at that. Had the quarry been myself? Or Skinning Knife?

'That is so,' Glyn Apt said.

'And found another prize instead,' the vitki murmured. His gaze passed over me to Eld, as if I was not only of no consequence, but had not even been seen. If that was the way they planned to treat an enemy agent, I thought, it was fine by me. I was still hoping to hear something about the progress of the war.

The valkyrie stared blankly ahead, as ever. The Morrighanu continued to look fierce and angry. I decided that I had little useful to contribute. Eld had brought me here; he could handle the difficult questions. But his next comment surprised me.

'So,' he said. 'What else has vanished?'

'It is not "what else",' the old vitki said, 'but "who". People are vanishing.'

'People are being killed. By the girl you championed.'

The old vitki ignored Eld's remark. I realized, with a sick sense of dismay, that the old man was now staring directly at me, and saw me all too well.

'Skald girl,' he now said, soft-voiced. 'You know, do you not? You spoke with the avatar of your leader?'

'I have no idea what you're talking about.' My voice seemed to ring out very loudly in this tall stone room, and echo.

'Don't you? The woman who called herself Idhunn, who years ago belonged to the Morrighanu, whose mother went to another world and stole someone away?'

'What are you talking about? Which other world?'

'A world named Mondhile. A place you know as well as anyone here.'

I kept silent. Frey's ripped spirit seemed to hover about the chamber, as suddenly as if summoned.

One of the valkyries finally opened her mouth. She spoke hollowly, as if from the bottom of a well. 'She knows it. She killed your kinsman there.'

I started to say something, but Eld put out a hand. The valkyrie continued, 'And was it not the Skald who ordered us to be sent to the cliffs of glass, who exiled us, prohibited our return so that we had to eke out an existence on the glacier and in the forest?'

One of the vitki gave a harsh laugh and said, 'Don't you think we ought to be thanking them for that?'

'Never mind what the Morrighanu girl is doing. If she wants to kill, then let her. She will only weed out the weak. Is not our war against the Skald itself?' the valkyrie said. Her silver eyes turned to me, and again it was as though she did not see me, but was looking through me. I remembered an old story of the Reach: that a dog with silver eyes can see the wind. I wondered what she was really looking at. But above all this was the thought: the Skald exiled the vitki, and those who became the valkyrie. Had the original valkyrie, perhaps, even been members of the Skald itself? It was an extremely disquieting thought, that our own might have turned against themselves and been sent away. But Idhunn too had said as much, when I spoke with her avatar. And what happens once, can happen again: the tritest lesson of history.

'Did you know this?' Eld asked.

'No, and I do not know whether it is true.'

The valkyrie stood, bristling. 'Of course it is true. Every child knows it. We were exiled by witches.'

'What is taught is not always what is true. I'd have thought you would have known that, living here.'

'This is pointless,' one of the other vitki said. 'Glyn Apt has looked into her head. We know what she knows of Mondhile. That is the matter at hand; everything else is irrelevant.'

'Trial by combat,' the valkyrie declared. She either wasn't listening to the vitki or didn't care: she had her own agenda.

'She's my associate,' Eld said. 'I won't allow that.'

'I should like to see you stop me,' the valkyrie replied.

She put her head on one side, regarding me coldly, like a hawk. 'Shall we test it, you against me? The soft path against the path of iron?'

'Look,' Eld said wearily. 'Internecine squabbling is all very well, but it won't get us anywhere.'

The old vitki was staring at Eld, with sparkling malice. 'When we last spoke, you suggested that the war has been a mistake. Because that could be construed as treason, you know.'

'I did not speak of the war, as you should remember,' said Eld. 'I spoke of common cause with the Reach over this Morrighanu woman. Nations may have such, even when they are at loggerheads. It is simplistic to think otherwise.'

'Are you calling me a fool?' the old man asked, as if he was hoping that the answer would be 'yes', but Eld merely smiled and did not answer. 'But still,' the old vitki went on, 'the woman from the Skald will be permitted to stay, at least, for a while, before the expedition sets off.'

'Expedition?' Eld asked, neutrally.

'The Skald girl has experience of Mondhile.' The vitki looked at me, with seeming blandness.

'What?' I said. 'You want me to go back to Mondhile? Why?'

Back to what passed for the graves of Frey and Gemaley, and a feral people.

'Not alone. Eld will go with you. And Glyn Apt.'

None of us, I thought, could look very pleased at the prospect of *that*.

*

We left the next morning, on a little Morrighanu space craft. Muspell does not have a large space fleet; the war at present was confined to planet-side, apart from a few skirmishes. Eld and I were confined separately – I don't know what they thought we might try, but seizure of the ship was probably in their minds. My cell had a portal screen and I was able to watch my world fall away, serene and clouded, the northern seas already more free of ice than they had been when I came back home, with spring on the way and war in its wake.

When Muspell was no more than a marbled sphere, the door opened and Glyn Apt came in.

'Mondhile,' she said.

I gave her a hostile glare. 'You know everything I know.' But there was that coal of information that Idhunn had given me, information that was buried so deeply it would be difficult to access . . . I tried to keep the unease from my face.

'No,' Glyn Apt replied. 'In fact, I don't.' The data began to run across her face with increased density and speed, until her features became obscured behind its moving blur. 'When you went there, in search of your faithless Frey, what did you know about it?'

'All I know came from a report that had been sent into space a generation ago, broadcast but incomplete. An anthropologist, who went to Mondhile with a Gaian religious mission and never made it off-planet.'

'And people who enter a state called the bloodmind. You mentioned that, during interrogation. Interesting.'

'Yes, a fascinating spectacle, seeing humans and animals tear one another to pieces. Made my week.'

'I would have liked to have seen that,' Glyn Apt said, as though agreeing.

'I'm sure you'd have been right at home.' Perhaps that was unfair, but I didn't care. I looked out of the viewport. Muspell was invisible now against the starfield, Grainne still hot and yellow-gold. I stared at my sun until it faded. Glyn Apt, meanwhile, was staring at me: I could feel her gaze on the edges of the seith, wrinkling it like fire.

'You're going back,' she said. I couldn't tell what she meant.

'I've no choice,' I retorted.

'Yet you're going.'

'Obviously.'

'I have never been,' Glyn Apt admitted, sitting companionably down on the edge of the bed. I didn't see her as being one for girlish chats. The dataflow had stopped now, apart from the occasional tick of information, and without it, she again looked older, more human. I wondered what her history was, what it had been like for her as a part of the Morrighanu.

And it seemed a banal thing for her to say. 'Of course you've never been. It was virtually uncharted until Frey got his hands on that anthropologist's report.'

'Is that what he told you?' she asked.

'Well . . . not in so many words. It's what we surmised.'

'The original data on Mondhile were held by the Morrighanu. One of our ships picked up the transmission. We first went there fifty years ago.'

'The *Morrighanu* went there? Why?'

'The original intention was to set up a colony. We were persecuted at the time – vitki and our kind do not always get along – and we wanted another option. We looked at Nhem, and did not like what we saw: at the time, the vitki were in contact with the then-Hierolath. We did not like the idea that what had been done to the women of Nhem might be done to ourselves. So we looked at other worlds.'

'Did you set up a colony on Mondhile?'

'No. The people there communicated with us, as they had not done with the Gaians, but they were clans, at war with one another, and there was no land for us to take. It was clear that the scouting party would be killed unless they left, but in any case they had seen enough for a colony to be unnecessary.'

For once, I was ahead of her. 'They witnessed the bloodmind.'

Glyn Apt nodded. 'They saw women fighting alongside the men – warriors known as feir, who had lost conscious awareness and the power of speech for much of the time, who were in essence feral. Human animals. The condition was partly genetic, and partly tied into ancient technology that runs under the earth of Mondhile, and affects behaviour. Technology that could be replicated, and genes that could be altered.'

'So it wasn't all Frey's plan,' I said. 'He stole your ideas.'

'We took what we needed to protect our own,' Glyn Apt said, bristling, 'and Frey took that for the same reasons. But his understanding was incomplete, and that's why he went to Mondhile, to find out for himself.'

'And Nhem? Why did he go to Nhem?'

'After what we had seen on Nhem, we sold information to the women of the Nhemish resistance. We hoped they could breed it into the next generation of Nhemish women: release it as a mutagenic virus so that when the women reached puberty, they would turn on the males.'

'It's that precise? Wouldn't they turn on one another?'

'Maybe. I doubt if it can be made that precise, to be honest. But you saw what Nhem is like. Any chance of destabilizing the existing order, they take.'

'It can't have worked – or hasn't it had time? When did you sell it to them?'

'Several decades ago. And no, it has not had time to work yet. They are still experimenting with it; it was never properly implemented. You've met one of the results.'

I could not think who she meant at first, and then I realized. Something flared deep inside my mind. Idhunn's coal of information? 'Skinning Knife?'

'Skadi was created and born on Nhem, one of the first products of the breeding program. Her mother is Mondhaith – they bred her, and another girl, pathogenetically.'

'What happened to the other girl?'

'She's still on Nhem. There's a situation developing. But I haven't had recent word.'

'How did Skinning Knife get from Nhem?'

'The resistance camp was attacked. Skadi was rescued, but the sister was taken. Skadi was sent to the Morrighanu, for training. I suspect that in any case she was more than the Nhemish resistance could handle – perhaps she had already killed, I don't know, and they realized that they had created a monster, not a saviour. She broke away from her foster mothers, who were one of the extreme sects, lived wild for a time, then was picked up by the vitki. She has had a violent, confused history on Muspell.'

'So why are we going to Mondhile?'

'To find Skinning Knife's closest living relative,' Glyn Apt said.

THIRTY

Planet: Mondhile (Vali)

Strange, to be returning. After all, I had left Mondhile only a short time before, and I'd thought never to go back again. A beautiful, savage world: one where I had made friends, and enemies. But the enemies were dead now, and there was no reason to be afraid. Perhaps I should seek out Ruan – but something else in me told me to leave him to his life, trouble him no further. I no longer had his sister's bow: it was back at the Rock, or maybe taken by a Morrighanu as a keepsake. That was appropriate, in a way. I could see why the Morrighanu had sought out Mondhile; they were two of a sort – wild, aggressive, preferring remote places. And perhaps that was true of me, too.

Skinning Knife: an intended nemesis of Nhem. Given what they'd done, the ruling classes of Nhem deserved everything they'd got. I wondered once more about the aftermath of the Hierolath's death: had it really had any effect, made any appreciable difference? The women of the Nhemish resistance, desperately grasping at straws of solutions. But it explained why Frey had come with me to Nhem: he'd been looking for clues to Skinning Knife. Maybe he'd known her: was she the link between myself and Gemaley?

Lost girls, all with warrior talents, and some missing part of Frey that made him want to be their mentor, their controller? He was dead; I could not ask him, and found that I had no real wish to do so.

The door whisked open then, and Eld was standing on the threshold.

'They've decided to give us a freer rein now we're out in space.'

'Glyn Apt told me why we're heading for Mondhile.'

'Yes, she had a word with me, too. This is a fast ship; we'll be there in a couple of days. She wanted to know whether you wanted to be put out for the duration.'

'I'd rather use the seith,' I said. *Or rather, what's left of it.*

'As you wish.' Eld withdrew. I lay back on the bed – alone at last – and sank into as much of a trance state as I could muster. Later, it became sleep, an uneasy, unsettled state that eventually turned to deep unconsciousness, mercifully without dreams. When Glyn Apt once more came to wake me, it was to tell me that we had reached Mondhile.

It looked as it had the last time: a dark world, mottled with crimson that I now knew to be the red leaves of satinspine coming into their spring promise. The immense peaks of arctic mountains split the pole, running down in ridges across the northern continent. As the Morrighanu ship twisted downward, I recognized the glaciated wall of the mountains known as the Otrade, or Snakeback, ghost-white in the sunlight against that oddly green sky. The ship came in fast and low, turning over great river estuaries, the skeins of islands visible along the coast. We were heading inland, towards the mountains. I glimpsed roofs and turrets: settlements few and far between. Despite its clan system, Mondhile was not designed for co-operation. I dreaded seeing Gemaley's ruined tower rising from one of the crags, but I thought – or hoped – that we were too far north. I was certain that I recognized some of the lakes, however, strung among the mountains like beads. But then we were coming in over a black expanse, a high plateau at the edge of the Otrade, marked with patches of white that I was unable to identify. Some kind of vegetation? Ice? We were coming down, the ship hissing as the stabilizer jets came on.

'What's this place?' I shouted to Glyn Apt, over the landing roar.

'It's a moor. I don't know what it's called. It's where the original team landed; there's supposed to be an old base here.'

A sudden silence. We had stopped.

'Well,' said Thorn Eld. 'This is going to be interesting.'

Early evening, Mondhile. Glyn Apt and the Morrighanu crew busied themselves with tests and readings, which from my point of view had all the character of oracular divination. Morrighanu technical speak was encoded, with talk of runes and signs. If Eld understood it, he gave no indication of doing so. We were allowed to go for a walk, as long as we didn't pass from sight of the ship.

'We're tagged, anyway,' Eld said. He held out a hand and I saw a thin red line on the skin at the back of his wrist. 'You've got one, too.'

When I rolled back my sleeve, I saw that this was the case. So that's why my wrist had been aching. Yet another invasion. Eld was looking at the scars of my adolescent cuts, again without gloating or any visible pity. After a moment he said, 'Do you have any idea when it gets dark?'

'This is quite far north, and it's spring.' It had been early spring when I arrived on Mondhile, with the buds just coming out, but judging from the red trees I had seen on the way in, spring came quickly here. Perhaps it was a short summer; that made sense. Despite everything that had happened to me here – everything that I had done, too – I still felt strangely at home in this northern place, the quiet, bleak expanse of the moor suiting my sombre mood.

'Glyn Apt said the person we've come to see was a relative of Skinning Knife. How are we going to find them?'

'She's a woman. Glyn Apt has some plan involving scanning for genetic markers,' Eld replied. He seemed ill at ease all of a sudden, at variance with the usual vitki calm, emotions held in severe check. 'It's a speciality of the Morrighanu.'

'So why didn't they just trace Skadi in Morvern?'

'They did. Tracing her is one thing. Catching her, once she's gone rogue, is another: Skadi can evade capture – you've seen how she can come and go in an eye-blink. And

Glyn Apt hinted that there was another problem, as well, that Skadi has a way of evading the detection mechanisms. Didn't Frey change the appearance of his DNA? That's part of why they want this woman. She's Mondhaith. She's more evenly matched with Skadi than even the most enhanced Morrighanu and she might know things which will help catch her.'

'But is she here?' I looked out across the empty expanse of the moor: black earth, low shrubs whose leaves were indigo and dark green. 'How do they know?'

'We are here because she is,' Eld said patiently. 'We followed her in.'

Suddenly the evening chill seemed sharper, the moor's expanse threatening rather than familiar. I thought of those bones, rattling in a forest cottage, of the man lying face down in an icy stream, bleeding out into rosy snowmelt. I remembered a people who turn feral in the blink of an eye.

'She's here?' I asked. The seith rippled at the edges, as though I might conjure her up.

'So they tell me.' Eld looked no happier than I did.

'What if it runs in the family?' I said, and started to laugh. That was, after all, the whole point.

'I think we should go back to the ship,' was Eld's only comment.

It was growing dark, in any case; twilight creeping over the silent land like a lid coming down, casting the bushes into blue shadow. The lights of the Morrighanu ship looked almost welcoming.

'Did you see anything out there?' Glyn Apt questioned us. 'Sense anything?'

'No.' Neither Eld nor I wanted to tell her that we'd managed to spook ourselves very effectively without external help. But Glyn Apt herself did not look happy, and there were the signs of weariness underneath the dataflow. Her pouchy eyes were red-rimmed.

'All right. Vali, you know this place better than I. What kind of night predators do you get?'

'Well, there are visen. They're eyeless; they hunt by smell. Something called altru, which I didn't see, but which everyone was afraid of. The creatures they ride – mur – are wild, too. There seemed to be quite a lot of things, now you mention it.'

Glyn Apt nodded as though she'd expected this. 'We stay in the ship. No one goes out until dawn, and then we do a scan first. We've just done one, by the way. There's nothing within a quarter of a mile.'

I had no problem with that and neither, from the look on his face, did Eld.

Morning. The seith told me that, and more reliably, so did the dawn light showing through the viewport. Mornings on Mondhile, not many of them, a few days, but always that same quality of light, impossible to define, peculiar to every planet. Mondhile's was redder than most, perhaps, the huge crimson sun rising over the reach of the moor.

The curving cell door was unlocked. I stepped into the

corridor and found light streaming in, and fresh air overriding the antiseptic no-smell of the ship. A single feather drifted down from the ceiling and I was back in the Rock, watching that single betraying piece of information as it descended.

Glyn Apt crouched in the open doorway, face pasty in the dawn light. Her skin was entirely free of the dataflow and she was quite still.

'Glyn Apt?' I said and then, when she did not respond, 'Commander?'

No reply. But by that time, I'd heard it for myself. There was a battle out on the moor.

I ran to the door and looked over the top of Glyn Apt's head. There must have been a hundred or so: warriors on foot, or mounted on the terrifying fanged beasts that the Mondhaith called mur, halfway between horse and wolf with snaking necks and knowing scarlet eyes. The warriors wore leather armour, like Ruan's, and they carried bows and swords – intricate, well-crafted weapons stained as red as the sun, or a beast's eye. The front line was almost all female, perhaps the feir warriors that Glyn Apt had mentioned. They were naked to the waist. Some of them had missing breasts, the skin stretched and shiny with scar tissue. Their hair was matted with what looked like black-and-white lime, and they were heavily tattooed. They reminded me of my Viking ancestors. They looked like lunatics, with their long teeth and claws. I remembered Gemaley and something in me wanted to shrink back into the ship and lock the cell door behind me. Something else in me, however, did not.

It was easy to sense the bloodmind. It washed against the edges of the seith like a hot red tide, lapping warm as sunlight, pulling me into the fray. I'd have joined them, I think, if the spear hadn't come out of nowhere.

Glyn Apt cried out as it shot over her head. I had a split *so-this-is-it* second to react and know, and then the spear hit me in the gut. The impact should have knocked me backwards – it should have killed me – but instead there was no pain, only a spreading heat, and the spear had gone straight through me. I looked down in wondering shock. No blood. No wound. Nothing.

Glyn Apt was staring at me as though I'd grown another head.

'*What did you do?*'

I'd have loved to have pretended that it was some arcane Skald ability, just to carry on seeing the Morrighanu commander looking so panicked. But I hadn't the faintest idea what I'd done, or whether I'd even done anything.

'It's not real,' Eld commented. He sauntered around the edge of the battle as though out for a morning stroll.

'Then what is it?' I looked out across the battleground. It seemed real. It even smelled real, blood and earth and shit.

'Don't know,' Eld said.

'What were you *doing* out there?' I was surprised to find how angry I felt.

'Glyn Apt opened the door and we saw it. There was nothing on the monitors – according to the scanners, the moor's deserted. Then I saw an arrow go through the ship and I thought it was worth a closer look.' As Eld spoke, a raven soared down from the sky, perched on his shoulder for a moment, then disappeared. Eld gestured to the place where it had been.

'Recordings. Information. I think that's what this is.'

'A recording? Broadcast by whom? They're not that advanced. These people regard wheels as a luxury.'

Eld shook his head. 'Again, I don't know. I was hoping the commander here could shed some light on the subject.'

Glyn Apt looked uneasy. 'It might be a Morrighanu device. It might not. There's all sorts of tech buried in the earth of this planet, all kinds of data transfer devices. The moats around the towns, the energy lines – it's all a hangover from the ancient colony days. Don't ask me how it works.'

'And Skinning Knife's relative?' I looked again and the battle was gone. The moor was untroubled under the morning sun, mist burning off the black earth like steam. The air smelled of herbs and frost.

'Out there,' Glyn Apt said. 'Out there somewhere. And today is the day that we will find her.'

The search party consisted of Glyn Apt, Eld and myself, armed with Morrighanu weaponry and the DNA scanner. The scanner was a strange thing: I'd expected a metal box, like a tabula, but this was organic, a lumpy thing like a bundle of lichen or moss, with filaments trailing from it. It did not look like any tech to be found on Muspell, but then, I knew little of Morrighanu devices. I wondered whether it might be vitki, but from the curious way that Eld eyed it, perhaps not.

At least Glyn Apt had unbent sufficiently to endow us with weapons. But under present circumstances, she had no reason to suppose that we were not to be trusted. We'd come here on a Morrighanu ship, after all; we had nowhere to run to on Mondhile, no means of contacting Muspell to ask for someone to come and rescue us. Even if Eld possessed any means of communication, I wasn't sure that the vitki would bother to rescue him, given the war situation back home and his exchanges with the old man. We were entirely dependent on the Morrighanu, and I wasn't even sure that they were the enemy, in any case. I suppose I wanted to see them as a kind of Skald, because they were women, and warriors, just as we were. Perhaps something in me had learned to see the Skald as hypocritical, too, because it claimed to love peace, and yet used assassins such as myself, whereas the Morrighanu had no such pretences. But to me, the Morrighanu seemed too reliant on technology; Glyn Apt's constant dataflow was rendering her more inhuman and, at the same time, making her more vulnerable than the more basic practices of the Skald would. If the dataflow failed, how would Glyn Apt fare then? On Nhem, I'd worried about becoming too reliant on the map implant, and there had been times when technology had let me down in a way that an understanding of the land, of wind and light and shadow, of footprints in the soil and the direction of the flight of birds, never would. Maybe that was why I felt a certain kinship with the Mondhaith.

And Skinning Knife's relative, whom we were now setting out to find . . . Would I find the same kinship, the same connection, with her that I'd found with Ruan? Or was she – more likely, I thought gloomily – another Gemaley, fierce and mad, a born killer? Seeing what Skadi had achieved I was beginning to doubt that she'd be anything but the latter. And what about this supposed sister on Nhem?

Both Glyn Apt and Eld were silent as we made our way across the moor. Glyn Apt was, I thought, intent upon the information that was coming from the DNA device. The dataflow across her skin had changed character: I still couldn't interpret it, but it seemed denser, packed with odd flickering images. Once I glanced at the Morrighanu and saw that another face had become fleetingly transposed across her own – Mondhaith, with white-on-white eyes and a fanged snarl. I must have flinched back, because Glyn Apt gave me a chilly look and asked what was the matter.

'What are you seeing, Glyn Apt?' Eld said, once I'd explained. It was a moment before she answered, then she said, 'That battle we saw. It's as though this moor is haunted. I can see people – and more than that, I can *feel* them. It's as though their lives and their concerns have become packed into a fraction of a second, and downloaded into my mind. DNA alone would not account for that.'

No surprise if the moor *was* haunted, I thought. Such a dark, stark place: the black bushes and blacker soil, line upon line of it, undulating towards the mountains. Thunderheads were building up, hiding the glaciated summits in their anvil mass, and I could smell a storm on the wind as it lifted the hair at my neck, making my scars and the socket of my eye ache and twitch as if electric. I shook off the sudden prickle at my nape and said, 'Mondhile's people may not have much in the way of technology, but their world does, as you yourself said. The old energy lines, the network set up by the original colonists . . . Who knows what that's become? Or what kind of information might be conveyed through it?'

'That's a good point,' Eld said. 'We've no idea what kind of tech was really installed here, first off.'

'They weren't like Gaians,' Glyn Apt explained. She tapped the tip of her gun impatiently against her boot. 'They didn't believe in manicuring planets, any more than we do. They thought you should fit the inhabitants to the world. That's why so many of the lifeforms here are genetically engineered.'

'Not so different to the vitki,' I remarked. 'Or *your* lot,' – this was to Glyn Apt.

Eld snorted. 'That didn't have an ecological basis. My ancestors just wanted to experiment.'

'*We* had purpose.' Glyn Apt spoke coldly.

I thought of the selk, and of Skinning Knife. The Morrighanu had purported to want to help the women of Nhem, but was that really true? A tangled web of motivations and agendas, it seemed to me. But I wasn't all that different, and neither was the Skald.

'Look,' Eld said, sharply. We followed the direction of his pointing finger, to an outcrop of rock. Three people were standing on it: two women and a man. They were Mondhaith. The seith prickled around me but even if it hadn't, their long limed hair and tattooed faces would have shown me that they were feir warriors – that and the long bows they carried. They were upwind of me and I could smell them, too: a sharp, animal astringency. One of them raised her bow.

'More hallucinations?' Eld started to say, but before he could finish I'd grasped him by the arm and dragged him down into the scrub. An arrow hissed over my head and buried itself in the black earth. Glyn Apt's weapon was up and firing; a bolt sending warning splinters from the rocky outcrop. The feir vanished as swiftly as they had come, melting down into the moor. The arrow remained, quivering.

'I couldn't feel them,' Eld said. He looked most put out; I suppose the episode had offended his vitki pride.

'Neither could I,' I said. 'I'm just not taking any chances.'

'They showed up on the dataflow,' Glyn Apt said. She was checking her weapon. 'That's how I knew they weren't a hallucination.'

'I don't suppose this person we've come to find was among them?'

'No. Besides, they were too young. This woman is old. But she came this way. There are traces of her here, and recent ones, too.'

We went on. But I did not think we had seen the last of the feir, and we were right. All of us remained wary, but Glyn Apt needed to concentrate on the business of tracking our quarry and so the burden of look-outs fell to Eld and me. No one said much. The bleakness of the moor was starting to have its effect on me: the silence, broken only by an occasional bird rocketing up from the scrub, the long distances ending in the mountain wall, shimmering with cold . . . Perhaps if I had been a different kind of person it might have depressed me, but as it was, the harshness of this place lifted my spirits. Unlike Morvern, there was no human heaviness hanging over it, despite the still-present threat of the feir and what I knew of the Mondhaith. The land felt untouched, untainted, even though I was aware of some of what the early colonists had done.

We were at the very edges of the moor now and had been walking all day, with only a break for a ration pack. Glyn Apt seemed to have withdrawn even further into herself; Eld appeared merely sombre. I wondered what Glyn Apt would decide to do if we didn't find our quarry: camp out, or ask the ship to fly over? But that would depend on the suitability of the terrain to provide a landing place, and on whether the Morrighanu wanted to risk scaring away our target, if she was indeed so near. But the sun was sinking down into a red mist at the horizon and I did not like the idea of camping out all night. We'd seen three of the feir, but what if there were more? They'd made their intentions plain enough. I hoped Glyn Apt's weapon had given them second thoughts, but then thought wasn't the feir's strong point. Remembering the people under the bloodmind in Ruan's town, it seemed to be a state that consumed normal caution like brushfire. And for all I knew, there were enough of them for a few to be expendable . . .

We walked on. The sun fell, its lower rim touching the horizon and smearing out into a crimson pool. I had expected the feir to come after the true darkness fell, but they were upon us just as the moor sank into a hazy grey twilight, swarming out of the shadows like moths and all the more frightening for their silence. There were perhaps a dozen of them. Eld killed two of them immediately, bolts striking easily through their leather harnesses and into the sinew and bone beneath. One was a man, one a woman, but they died as silently as they had attacked, teeth bared, seeming almost not to notice as their spirits fled. Perhaps those spirits had already gone on ahead, fleeing the animal flesh. I killed another, a woman, and saw in her face the echoes and traces of Gemaley, whom I had not been able to kill. I don't believe in scapegoats, but maybe the world does, providing me with someone on whom to take out my rage and hate. But I'd never met this woman before and she died quickly. It did not make me feel better.

Beside me, Glyn Apt gave a sharp exclamation. One of the arrows had nicked her throat. Blood spilled through the data stream and I saw the data rearrange itself around it, flowing over the red thread. The Morrighanu cursed and swatted at her throat, but it wasn't a deep wound and in moments the one who had shot her was dead.

And then the feir stopped. They had been rushing towards us; now they halted in their tracks and turned. The wildness in their faces was replaced by a peaceful blankness. I saw the berserker rage of the bloodmind drain out of them, the light of consciousness come back behind their eyes. And that light was filled with fear. They melted away into the rocks, still moving, without a sound.

Cautiously Eld stood, ignoring Glyn Apt's warning hiss.

'Who are you?' he breathed. I stood in turn, and saw through the gathering dusk that we were no longer alone. Someone was walking where the feir had been.

At first I thought it would be another of the Mondhaith – who else would it be, after all? – but then I saw that it wasn't human even to the extent that they were. It was tall, dressed in robes that looked as though they had been woven out of grass, or moss, and its face was elongated into a long muzzle. The eyes were red, like a mur's eyes. It reminded me of those ancient gods of Earth, part human and part animal, but the feral quality of the mur, that predatory ferocity kept in difficult check, was missing. When I sensed it with the seith, it reminded me of the selk: something sad and wrong, that should not be. The tabula hummed as it spoke, feeding information into my map implant that told me it was speaking in Khalti, the local Mondhaith tongue.

'You are the women from outside the world. Why have you come back? You told us that you could do nothing for us,' she addressed Glyn Apt.

Beside me, the Morrighanu's face was wary. She dabbed absently at the blood on her neck and then she said, 'I don't know who you think we are. I suppose you saw the ship, back there upon the moor. It is not the same ship that first came here, and we are not the same people.'

The being radiated uncertainty. It continued, 'You came here last three hundred moons ago – the small moon's turn. When we were young.' From the use of the pronoun, I couldn't tell whether it was referring to itself in the plural, or others like itself. 'We told you how we had been driven away by the settled people. You said that you had made us, beneath the earth, and when we asked you to take us with you, you refused. You said that we must stay here.'

'It was not I who told you these things,' Glyn Apt said harshly. Guilt? I didn't know whether the Morrighanu even entertained such a concept.

'But you are of the same people,' the being said.

'Yes.'

'How did you control the feir warriors?' Eld interrupted.

'I did not. They are afraid of us. They think we are from hell.'

I nudged Glyn Apt. 'Do you know who or what that person is?' I whispered.

'An earlier experiment,' the Morrighanu said. She spoke very low, but the being heard her.

'You made us, and you left us,' it said. It sounded like the selk, too, remote and sorrowful, with no real anger at what had been done, but only bewilderment.

'A child was taken from here, many years ago,' Glyn Apt said. 'We're looking for a woman who is of her family. We believe she is here, on this moor, now. She would be old. Have you seen her?'

'I have seen her,' the being replied. 'I saw her when she was a child, with the child who was taken, and again, years later when she was grown.' Eld glanced at me at that, and I could see why. How old was this being? 'She is here now, and has been with us for moons in the still place, but perhaps she is dead. She was ill when she walked the moor and that was in the winter.'

'We need to find her,' Glyn Apt said. 'Can you help us? What is the still place?'

The being looked at her. 'Why should I help you?' it asked.

'You spoke of the settled people, who drove you from the towns. And the feir, who are afraid of you. The daughter of the child who was taken was an experiment that succeeded on one level – she has many abilities – but failed on another, because she is mad. I would ask you if you wish to see more people hurt by this project, which I grant you, has been misguided from start to finish.'

The being looked at her. 'It is too late,' it said. 'I do not care.' And then it was gone, between one blink of an eye and another, into the twilight land.

Glyn Apt summoned the ship after that. None of us wanted to be alone with the feir, and though no one said so, I could not help wondering if it was the being itself that made us more afraid.

I slept in the same small cabin and now it felt like sanctuary rather than cell. But I dreamed that I woke, and went to the door of the ship, and looked out. The moor had gone, and in its place was a sea, heaving and dark and cold, a sea of Muspell rather than Mondhile. A selk was coming through the water, arrowing and sleek, and it spoke to me. It said, 'Our kin is right. It is too late. No one cares for us and so we, in turn, have ceased to care.' Before I could ask it any questions, it was gone beneath the waves and then the sea was gone, too, with nothing more than ice between my feet and the distant horizon.

In the morning I asked Glyn Apt if she knew of any more experiments. The selk had disturbed me; the being on the moor had disturbed me more. Three very different worlds and yet with threads all in common: the Mondhaith themselves, engineered long ago, if reports were to be believed, to fit their environment. Crossed with predators, perhaps the ancestors of the mur. I remembered the glint of a wicked intelligence within a blood-red eye. Sentient beasts and unsentient humans; the legacy of a common heritage that said *why not?* Why should we all be one manner of thing, one species? Mixing and matching, splicing and shaping . . . And what was intelligence, after all, but an accident of humankind?

I found such philosophical questions difficult. Ultimately, Glyn Apt and I were the same, I thought, and so perhaps was Skinning Knife herself. Just give us something to kill.

And as if on cue, Glyn Apt came in then, to tell me that her team had found the traces of Skadi's relative.

She was underground. We thought at first that she must have gone there to die. The signal trace came from beneath a ridge of rock at the heart of the moor; a high spine of bare granite-like substance. The Morrighanu and I brushed aside scrub and eventually we found the entrance to a cavern. Both of us paused at that point.

'She might be injured,' Glyn Apt said. 'On top of that, there's the feir and that thing we spoke with. I don't like the idea of meeting any of them down there in the dark. And I don't know what it meant by "the still place".'

I agreed. With Eld keeping watch at the entrance, the Morrighanu and I switched on a torch and made our way down into the cavern.

It was Morrighanu technology. I knew that from the glimpses I got of Glyn Apt's face noting the curvature of walls and ceilings, and flickering with recognition at the runic inscriptions carved into the doorways. The dataflow was busy, numbers and letters tumbling over her skin in the reflected light from the torch, presumably transmitting data back to the ship. At last she said softly, 'It's hard to know how far this was authorized.'

I stared at her. 'You think it wasn't?'

The Morrighanu shrugged. 'Hard to say. We're an organization of sects, whatever people like to pretend. We're as divided as the vitki.'

Or the Skald, I thought but did not say. 'Could a rogue sect have set up something like this? Maybe they wanted to establish a stronghold, even if a colony was out of the question.'

'This?' Glyn Apt waved a hand. 'This is just a cave, nanolined with blast-film. It's nothing special. But what's in it might be. And here on this little world, well away from Muspell, well away from the main star stations, where no one will ever find it . . . what were they trying so hard to hide, I wonder?'

'Their genetic project,' I ventured. 'To keep it out of the reach of the vitki?'

'Or out of the reach of their sisters,' Glyn Apt said, and marched on behind the beam of the torch.

As we went, I saw what she had meant by the blast-film shell. Further into the cavern, the walls crawled with technology, sheets of data sliding endlessly across the film like the data display across Glyn Apt's skin. And I was able to interpret none of it.

Neither, from her uneasy glances, was the Morrighanu commander. 'I can't believe this is still running,' she said.

'What's powering it? Is it solar?'

'I have no idea.'

'And is it actually doing anything?'

'I don't know.' But at that point, Glyn Apt leaped back and cannoned into me. We both fell against the wall and I felt, rather than saw, the data stream pause and glide across my own skin, like a swarm of insects.

'Glyn Apt, what—'

'Sorry.' As far as I could remember, it was the first time that the Morrighanu had offered a word of apology, however perfunctory. 'I thought it was real.'

I looked over her shoulder and saw an image, a holographic rotation: the being we had met, or something very similar, changing from child to adult, withering and dying, an infant once more.

'A display,' I said. 'What they were trying to achieve?'

'Perhaps they kept it as a warning,' Glyn Apt murmured. 'They hoped to come back, knew that the feir were afraid, held the image in place to prevent anyone from coming in here.'

A nasty thought struck me. 'Unless the reason the feir are so afraid is because this image has another function.' I could see Glyn Apt taking this on board.

'Very well,' she said. 'Let's see.' Taking a knife from her belt, she threw it towards the image, into the shimmering field that surrounded it. I think we were both expecting something dramatic to happen, but instead the weapon simply clattered to the floor and the image continued to rotate in unceasing transformation.

'It won't hurt you,' someone said from beyond the next doorway. The tabula hummed in translation and I saw the animal-faced being, or another very like it. 'There is nothing here that can hurt . . . no longer.'

'No longer?' Glyn Apt echoed.

'Feir came, and feir died. I and my siblings came and went as we pleased, the place is safe for us. But others – no. It is the one place where we can be safe.'

'So if the feir died,' Glyn Apt said, weighing consequences, 'how is it that Vali and myself are still standing here?'

'Things changed here, over the years. The weapon that was is a weapon no longer. One by one, things have stopped working – the machine that fed us as children has been silent for many years; the heat has failed also.'

So Glyn Apt had not been entirely correct. The Morrighanu outpost was powering down, bit by bit. Perhaps the display did not take up a great deal of power, and so had remained. But I still did not like this talk of weapons.

'She's here,' Glyn Apt said, getting back to the matter in hand. 'The woman, the relative of the child who was taken.'

'Yes, she is here, in the still place. She is ill, on the verge of death. We cannot help her. You might.'

I turned to Glyn Apt. 'You're carrying a med kit, aren't you?'

'Yes, but since we don't know what's wrong with her . . .'

'Then best find out.'

Curiosity was burning me as we stepped through the doorway, and in its wake came memories and fear. It wasn't a rational thing, for I knew this woman was old and ill, but when was the legacy of the past ever rational?

We walked up to what was evidently some kind of stasis chamber. It hummed faintly, and I could see the gleam and glisten of a life-support web. Lucky for her that this hadn't powered down, too.

And what came over me when I set eyes on her was simply and only pity.

Clearly, she had once been a tall, strong woman. Even curled as she was about herself, the ropy muscle and taut sinew was still visible in her bared arms. Her flesh had shrunk back from the bones of her face, but you could still see the beauty that had been in it, the fierce cold kind of beauty that seemed commonplace on Mondhile, looks to match the landscape. Her eyes were fanned with lines: she had more humour than Gemaley, then, but a sense of humour had not been Gemaley's strong point, and if Skadi had one, then it was twisted in the extreme.

Her eyes were closed. Her death hung about her face; visible as a shadow. It would not, I thought, be long. Glyn Apt went to her side and unstrapped the med kit.

'Can you tell what's wrong with her?'

'It's pneumonia, or a version of it. I don't need the med kit to tell me that. Easy enough to cure.'

'Many of the settled people die of it,' the animal-faced being said, and again it sounded sad. I couldn't blame it. The Morrighanu must have inadvertently shown it so much, and given it nothing: confining it and its kind to the margins of its own world, just as the selk had been marginalized. And there wasn't much we could do about it: if we took it to Muspell, how would it survive? I didn't even know how many of its kind the Morrighanu had created. Muspell was swinging into war and Morvern was an unkind land even for its own.

Glyn Apt had sat down on the side of the bed, a bolder move than I would have been inclined to make. True, Skadi's relative was old and dying, but she still had sharp teeth and sharp claws, and I'd have put good odds on her having been a warrior. If she came round and discovered an alien bending over her – but Glyn Apt did not hesitate.

'Help me with this,' she said. I put aside my misgivings and came over, to roll the woman's sleeve above the elbow and insert a biochip. Glyn Apt muttered a diagnosis into the tabula and after a moment, the chip gleamed beneath the woman's skin. 'We'll leave it to do its work,' Glyn Apt said. Together, we retreated to the far end of the room, where the animal-faced being stood.

The story of that day and that night? We watched and waited. Eld came down to join us, saying that the ship was once again nearby. We debated whether to move the old woman to the life-support pod on the ship, and decided against it. At least we knew she was compatible with the 'still place' beneath the moor. She moaned and muttered in her sleep, but the tabula made no sense of it and it seemed she was too far gone to remember her own language. Glyn Apt, the data stream stilled, stared at her as if willing her back into life and Eld was for the main part silent, lost in his own thoughts.

I slept. Towards dawn, I woke, to find the old woman sitting up and watching me. Glyn Apt and Eld were still asleep and there was no sign of the animal-faced being.

We spoke. And I learned a little about Sedra ai Kharn, who had come out into the world to die.

THIRTY-ONE

Planet: Mondhile (Sedra)

I'd been held prisoner before. Once – a long time after the skirmish on Moon Moor – the warband had run foul of a clan group in Esker Forest. It was a very different type of terrain – ger-wood rather than satinspine, all brown fronds and narcotic pitcher plants – and we'd simply walked into a trap. Next thing I'd known, I was dangling upside down from a branch with roars of derisive laughter echoing in my ears. The enemy clan had let me dangle for a while longer, then cut me down and caught me in a net. Trussed up like a bird for the table, I'd been carried into some local stronghold and locked in the cellar. After that it was the usual story: threats, a bit of half-hearted torture, offers of a ransom, a boring couple of days cooling my heels in the dark, overpowering the jailer, disguise, flight – that sort of thing. It made a good story for a few weeks afterwards and then other things had happened and I'd forgotten about it.

Now, I was a prisoner again and it all came back to me. The worst thing about it was the tedium, that and not knowing who had got hold of me. If it was a rival clan – and I knew of none in the vicinity of Moon Moor or the immediate mountains, which suggested that they'd taken me some distance away – then they'd get little enough out of my family in the way of a ransom. After all, I'd packed myself off to die, so there was no point in expecting the clan to want me back again. My relative Rhane might agree to it as a point of honour, but why bother? Might as well let them kill me and save myself the trouble. It was unlikely to be the fever that carried me off: I was already feeling better. I drifted in and out of dreams, maybe my own illusions, maybe someone else's. I know it went on for a long time – I felt the moons turn and spin in the sky, over and over again.

And if it was the half-humans who had taken me? Well, that was just an unknown quantity. Anyway, whoever it was had me where they wanted me. I was securely bound, and though whenever I came into semi-consciousness I strained and struggled, the bonds did not give even a fraction. It might have been different years ago, when I was young – maybe; but not now, old and weakened by the fever. I should have died with the warband, I thought. This was just embarrassing.

And at last I woke, and felt better. I sat up and found myself looking at a ghost. There was suddenly a lot of light – too bright, dazzling. I shut my eyes and turned my head to get away from it. The light was dimmed.

'Is that better?' someone said, in recognizable Khalti, but with an accent. Her words hummed, like a flight of insects. Slowly, my vision cleared. The ghost was a woman, quite young. She was insubstantial, as all ghosts are. So, I really had died, then.

'I'm dead,' I replied. I felt quite pleased, despite the bonds. I'd really done it, got it over with, and now I would go on. But there was still the same question: if I was really dead, why did I feel so creaky and old? Maybe my spirit remembered its body and once that memory faded, I'd feel better.

'No,' the ghost said, patiently. 'You're as alive as I am.' Well, *that* made a lot of sense. I could see her more clearly now: the light kept adjusting itself. She wore the kind of leather armour that you find to the north, in Harrapath, but much better made, almost without joins. Better humour her, I thought. I was disappointed that it was not the warrior with the ruined jaw who had come to me, but at least this girl looked as though she'd seen action: her face was badly scarred and one eye was puckered up. I approved. I looked forward to hearing her story.

'Who were you? What was your name?'

'My name is Vali. I am from a place called the Reach, on a world called Muspell. You won't have heard of it.'

'It doesn't mean anything to me.' Must have been from a lot further north, then.

'And your name?'

'Sedra. From the Racewater clan, the ai Kharn, of Ulleet.'

'Were you lost? Or travelling?'

'Neither. I went out to die; it was my time.'

'To die?' The ghost – Vali – sounded horrified.

'I told you, it was my time. The signs said it and if I'd waited another winter, I would have burdened the clan.'

'A hard thing,' Vali said. I felt her touch my hand and her skin was surprisingly warm.

'Why? It's a perfectly normal thing to do.'

'Sedra, if I release you, do you promise not to hurt me? Do you give me your word?'

'Of course,' I said. A word is just a word, not a deed. Vali was a foolish, trusting ghost. I'd be on her as soon as the bonds were off. But then she showed me that she was less foolish than I'd assumed and my respect for her rose.

'I have a weapon,' she warned. 'It'll be trained on you.'

That made me much less likely to attack her, but not for the reason she might have thought.

'I won't try anything,' I said, and a moment later, I felt the bonds twitch and then they were gone. I was free. I sat up.

I was in a long, low stone chamber that looked as though it had been hacked out of the rock. And I'd been wrong about being taken a long distance. I recognized the stone as the kind that lay under Moon Moor: a crumbly, dusty rock. Here, in this chamber, it had been smoothed into an arched ceiling. It looked old and I wondered if it had been one of the storage places that the ancient families used. I knew I was right that no one lived near Moon Moor these days, but in older times there had been houses in the surrounding forests: I'd seen the ruins during my time with the warband. And of course, there was the place under the ridge, if I hadn't imagined the whole thing.

Didn't look like Eresthahan, though. And I probably wasn't dead. I didn't smell like it, anyway.

'Is there water?' I asked. 'I need to wash.'

Vali was sitting on a kind of fabric chair, a flimsy thing. She was holding something little that caught the light. It did not look much like a weapon to me, but who knew what kind of things ghosts might have?

'Of course,' she said. Still holding the weapon, she gestured me towards a smaller chamber, also hacked out of the rock, with a pitcher of water in it. She withdrew while I stripped off my clothes and washed and I examined the little chamber closely, but there was no way out of it. The light came from a metal strip in the ceiling, like nothing I had seen before.

'I've got spare clothes if you want them,' Vali called. I hesitated. These were my death clothes, but on the other hand I'd been living in them for the past who-knew-how-long.

'Give me what you have,' I told her, and she threw through a tunic and trousers. I'd keep my old cloak: that showed enough willing to the dead, I thought. I dressed and went back out.

'So,' I said. I might be slow on the uptake, but I wanted to make sure. 'This isn't Eresthahan. I'm not dead.'

And neither was the ghost. She'd done something while I was washing, something that made her very real. I could feel her connection to the world now; she was earthed.

'You're real,' I said.

'What you sense in me is something called the seith. It's a kind of . . . well, never mind. Yes, I am real. But I'm not from here.'

'You told me. Another world.' That was as may be. I thought of the moons, the sparks that could sometimes be seen travelling across them, the cities that were said to lie in peaceful ruin on their surfaces; and the stories about folk from other planets. I'd never really believed, even so. Ghosts were real, everyone knew that. But people from the stars? Even so, I'd lived long enough to realize that I didn't know everything.

'I want to talk to you about your world,' Vali-the-ghost said. 'I've been here before, you see. I know a little about it, about how you live your lives.' She paused. 'And I want to talk to you about a relative of yours.'

I stared at her blankly. 'A relative?'

'I know this is surprising,' Vali continued, 'but I have good reason for asking. We've done . . . some tests. The relative in question was your sister. You probably don't remember her.'

'Oh yes I do,' I said. I felt as though my life had come full circle: from my sister, and back to her again. 'It's true that we don't remember much about our childhoods, but I remember her. On Moon Moor.'

'That's here, isn't it? The big stretch of scrub – I don't know the name for the plants.'

'The black moorland that smells of spice, yes. We lived here when we were children, in burrows. Then, one night, she was taken away by spirits.' I told Vali the story. When I'd finished, she was frowning.

'Sedra. What if I told you that your sister did not die?

That she was abducted, by people from another planet, a world called Muspell? Taken in order to be . . . understood.'

'Understood? How?'

'Your people are not like other humans. As children, you don't possess self-awareness. That only happens in adolescence, when you go back to your birthplace and your consciousness is triggered by a network of ancient technology.'

'Tech—' I did not recognize the word.

'Machines,' Vali said, but I didn't understand that either.

'I don't know what you're talking about.'

Vali sighed. 'All right. I'll try to explain it a bit better. The women of a world called Nhem were changed by the men of their society. They were bred to be like animals, without self-awareness – like you are in the bloodmind, but without the violent instincts. Those women of Nhem were helped by women from my world, the Morrighanu, who tried to find an answer to their plight. They came across records relating to Mondhile and they thought there might be an answer here, because of the bloodmind. They thought if they studied it, they could understand better what the men of Nhem had done and then they could reverse it. There is a species on my world, the selk, who also undergo a similar process, but they were too far from human to provide any real answers at that point. So the Morrighanu came here and they found a Mondhaith child and took her away, back to Nhem. Your sister never became properly self-aware.'

'Is she dead?'

'Yes. I'm sorry.'

I bowed my head, but only for a moment. At least I'd be seeing her soon.

'You ought to know that she had a child. A daughter.'

'A daughter?' I smiled. 'I'd like to meet her.'

'Well,' Vali said and she did not look so happy. 'I'm not so sure that you would.'

I stood on Moon Moor, looking out across the black heath. The lowest horn of Embar was touching the line of the horizon and Elowen was already up, trailed by its attendant star, the Hunter. The lowest moon was washed with rose light, the last of the day's sun. Vali-the-ghost came to stand by me as I stared at the sunset.

'This is a beautiful world, this Mondhile of yours.'

'You said you'd been here before.' I still found it difficult to accept that she was from another planet, even though I had now met some of her companions. It was easier to see her as coming from another clan. 'Where did you go?'

'It was south of here, but not far south. Still cold. Those mountains look a little familiar. I consulted my— I looked at a map I have, and I think this is the northern end of them, seen from the other side. Thick forests . . . a tree with black bark and red leaves.'

'I know where you mean. Do you know people there?'

'I met a . . . family. They lived on a black line of energy.' She was looking at me sidelong, staring at me to see how I might take this.

'A black line? You'd have done better to avoid them, then.'

Vali gave a short laugh like a bark. 'You can say that again. They were wild – at least, one of them was. A killer.'

'People who live in such places enjoy killing,' I said. 'For no good reason. They'll go to war, but not with any goal in mind, or to protect their lands or clan. They like to see shed blood. What happened to that family you met?'

'The girl – the killer – she died. A young man whom she'd taken prisoner killed her.'

I approved. 'Good.'

She laughed again. 'You're a violent people, you Mondhaith.' She did not sound as though we disappointed her.

'I suppose so.' I'd never really thought of it like that before.

I still did not know what to make of that story. Vali had told me more of it and I had spent most of the day turning it over in my mind, trying to see how I felt about it. My sister, stolen away to another world. Her child, bred from her without a man (and where was the fun in that?), and trained to be a warrior. And not any warrior, but a kind of ultimate killer. That was a strange idea: we all do the best we can and some of us are better than others, but there is no need to think that any one person could or should be better than *everyone* else. It did not seem realistic to me. I liked to think of my sister's child, a daughter, alive and well and with such skills, but I wasn't sure about the use to which she was putting them. It sounded too much like the people who lived on the black line to me. But perhaps my niece had some goal in mind that Vali-the-ghost did not understand, or had misunderstood. After all, she'd said that she wasn't like us. With a great effort, I tried to imagine how it must be for my niece, raised in a place that could not understand her. It must be like someone from the inner lands, who is snatched by island raiders and put to work on a ship. All at sea, not understanding anything properly.

'Tell me about your place,' I said to Vali. 'What is it like? Is it like the moon, or like here?'

And so she told me. Her story took us into the night and halfway through we went back down the hidden steps to the old store, to avoid the biting moths and the creeping frost. The ghost had brought some kind of liquor with her, a fiery stuff, almost as good as the one that my own clan made. Then, after many stories and when the bottle was half down, she told me that if I really wanted to see what her world was like, I should come and see for myself.

And this is what I did. Perhaps it hadn't been my destiny to die out here after all.

When I saw the thing that was to take me to my niece, however, I nearly told Vali to forget the whole idea; I'd stay where I was and end my days on Moon Moor. I'd like to say that I was brave, and happy to travel above the surface of the world with no more care than if I set foot on a ship bound for an island in sight. But the truth was that it horrified me. The thing in which we were to travel looked like the insect that had carried my sister away: multi-legged, with a humming body and a strange smell. Vali told me that it was a Morrighanu ship, and she told me, too, a little about the Morrighanu's counterparts, the vitki and valkyrie. They did not worry me. I'd met people like them in the warrior clans, the feir who live too close to animals and mimic their ways in war; and in the south, the clever people in the political assemblies who are as bad, but in a different way. Perhaps, from what Vali said, I might have something to fear from the vitki, but I was dead already, or may as well have been. And from the sound of it, I thought with an odd burst of pride, it seemed that they had something to fear from me, or at least from my niece.

In the end it was curiosity as much as anything that made me step through the door of the insect, and allow Vali to bind my hands to the arms of my chair. Had she not done so herself, there was no way I would have allowed this, death-seeking or no death-seeking. The insect responded to the speech of the warrior Glyn Apt; she did not need her hands. It was most obedient. Vali said that they could give me medicine which would make me unconscious, but I wasn't having any of that, either . . . until the plunge and roar as Moon Moor fell away beneath me, perhaps forever, and the mountains spun up and then down until they were as small as patterns in the snow and I saw my world as a ball. I did not beg her for the medicine then, but I did say through gritted teeth that it might be easier for her if I slept, and did not pester her with questions when she was busy. To her credit, Vali did not smile, but touched something cold and then hot to the bare skin of my wrist, and that was that. When I next woke up, we were flying through night.

I lost all track of time and it was dreadful to be away from the surface of the world and the sense and pressure of metal and water beneath my feet. I did not know which way was up and my blood sang in my head so that my sight grew dark and then bright and then dark again. Vali gave me something for that, too – she was quite the satahrach in her way, though so young. I did not entirely like what I heard about her world – although her own home seemed to be well run, and people lived in a normal enough way, even though they were at war. But I was used to war and it sounded interesting, if nothing else. I was pleased when she told me that her home of Muspell was not far away now.

We had time to talk, on the way to it. She struck me as an honourable woman, a warrior, though her childhood had been very strange and some cruel things had happened to her. She told me, with an air of one confessing a terrible thing, that her brother had slept with her. I did not at first see why she was so ashamed, but then I realized that she had been very young, and it had been rape. I told her it was an honour breach, and she should track him down and make him pay. Then she had been seduced by a man who had betrayed her trust, and been raped twice more, once by an old man who ruled some city, and then by the girl of my world. The last two were dead and I told her that it was clear that she was learning. But she must look for patterns, I said also, and see why such things kept occurring, for clearly she was seeking them out. She should not see herself as foolish – many folk will rape and torture if they have the chance, and they are the ones at fault. But they are best avoided, all the same. Vali-the-ghost looked startled when I said this and told me that their satahrachs said the same thing. *Of course,* I replied. It was obvious. She was quiet after that, for a long while, and I suppose she was thinking about it. It's often the case that we can't see as far as our noses, however wise we might be in the ways of others, and there's no shame in that.

Shortly after this conversation, a glowing sphere appeared in the window of the insect and Vali told me that we had reached Muspell.

I had been afraid that we would go to a big town. I don't like towns: there are, obviously, too many people in them, all living side by side like ghats in a hive. Vali said that she was not fond of towns either, and in any case we would not be going to one if she could possibly help it. From the window of the craft, I saw that she did not lie. I caught a glimpse of one settlement, bigger than any I had ever visited or had heard of, with huge buildings like stone slabs around a wide bay. Its name was Hetla, so Vali told me, and we flew over it.

Soon, the ship was flying above trees and forest. I could feel the pull and tug of the world beneath me and it was not my own place, but it was earth and stone and metal and therefore was real. The trees were different to those of my north: grey and fleecy, with smoke drifting up from them, and there were scars in the forest, great crumbling swathes which looked as though they had been made by fire. Then the craft was falling, twisting over the grey trees and sailing over them to the face of a mountain wall. I thought that we were going to hit it but I would not close my eyes, and then a gap opened in the stone and we were through. The craft stopped and it was strange no longer to be moving.

'We're here,' Vali explained.

She unstrapped me from the bonds and helped me as I stepped stiffly down from the craft. The stiffness earned me a sharp look.

'We can give you something for that, if you want,' Vali said. 'Medicine. It'll make it easier for you.'

'I'll think about it,' I told her. I was tempted and annoyed at the same time. I wanted to get outside, out of the chamber in which the ship now sat, to smell this different air.

Vali obliged me. Together, we walked to the mouth of the cave. It was close to twilight and I was surprised that this world had the same kind of time: I don't know what I expected. But there was a smear of sun above the trees, and the air was cold and fresh after the stuffiness of the craft. The rock on which we stood was metal-rich, but I could not tell what kind it might be, only that it streaked the mountain wall with veins that were as thick as rivers.

'This place is called Morvern,' Vali said. 'And that is Sull Forest.'

'People live here,' I observed. I could feel them – knots and pockets of life in the wasteland before us. This was a sullen landscape, the kind beloved by warrior clans. It reminded me of the forests around Moon Moor. I thought of my niece, and smiled.

'Yes, they do,' Vali said.

'And they are your enemies.'

'They are not my friends, that's for sure.' The sun was a dying gleam as she added, 'Come with me, Sedra. Come and meet the hunting party.'

THIRTY-TWO

PLANET: NHEM (HUNAN)

They had carved the stronghold out of the rock. Mayest's double, Ettia, told me that in the beginning it was done with fingernails, with chunks of rock and sticks taken from the shrubs which surrounded the cavern system. Then, when outworld help had come, it was done with machines, which were, to the folk of other worlds, primitive enough. I tried to tell myself that we had done well enough with the colony, for we'd had no such help, but looking at the gleaming surfaces around me, I was not so sure. What had we really achieved, after all, except camp out in the ruins of someone else's city?

I asked Ettia about the goddesses in our bell tower, but she had never heard of them and did not know who the city builders had been. To my amazement, she told me that the people of Nhem had originally come from other worlds and that Nhem was not known to have had any native folk, so perhaps the city was itself built as an outpost by people from somewhere else. Ultimately, Ettia did not know and did not seem greatly curious, although she spoke with interest enough about the colony and what we had done there.

And then she took me to the growing tanks.

It had never even occurred to me that such things were possible. I stared numbly at the creatures within, the women. All of them were human, or so I suppose. But some of them had fingers that were too long, with claws, and there were long sharp teeth in the round faces of children. As I peered into the murky waters of a tank, the eyes of the child within snapped open, to stare back at me, and they were hungry. I stepped back. Ettia was looking at me too, without expression.

'They're alive,' I said.

'I told you. They're being grown.'

'And Khainet – she came from one of these tanks?'

'Khainet and her sister.'

'You grew them together?'

'No. Khainet comes from further down the line. She was a later model. An improvement. Psychologically, at least.'

'Women warriors,' I said. It tasted strange on the tongue, like poison.

'Weapons won't be enough. The *will* won't be enough. Our enemies have both, as well. We have to have elite troops, born killers.'

'Isn't there another way?'

'What would you suggest?' Ettia's face was curious, but only slightly. She had already made up her mind, I could see, and was listening to me just to be polite.

'Do as we did. Go somewhere else. Try to forget the anger we feel, mould it into something else. Use it as compost, to grow.' I thought of the root cellar. Had I grown from that bloody compost?

Ettia nodded, but absently. 'Perhaps. One day, it will be possible, I'm sure. But for now, we're too far down another path.' Then she looked at me more closely, as if seeing me for the first time. 'Don't you want the men dead, Hunan? For what they did to you?'

I thought about this. I thought again about the root cellar, the cool damp dark, and my son's body flying backwards to hit the wall, crumpling, lying still. Had I wanted him dead then? I did not know. I had reacted because the bird had startled me, hadn't I? Surely I had not attacked him simply because he had been there, because House Father had struck me the night before and the memory was as vivid as a bruise in my cattle-mind? I had run because I had been afraid, hadn't I? I had not used the tools on the wall of the root cellar to dig down beneath the stored roots, finding earth, scraping out a grave, piling the small body in it, covering it over again . . . I had not done that.

'Maybe I want them dead,' I said. 'But most of all, I want them gone.'

Later, they took me to see Khainet. They had put her in a holding cell, deep in the mountain, and I could see that they were afraid of her. Her eyes, as she looked at me, flickered between appeal and defiance.

'I'll leave you two alone,' Ettia said. 'But the conversation will be recorded, and please don't bother trying to open the door. You won't be able to.'

Then she went away.

'They say they made me,' Khainet said. 'Created me. But I don't remember.'

'It's all right, Khainet.' But it was not. I hadn't been able to save any of my children and I couldn't save Khainet, either.

'I didn't mean to kill her,' Khainet continued, after a long silence. 'It was an accident. She said she wanted my blood. Just a little, she said, but I didn't believe her. I thought she wanted me dead. She came towards me with a needle. She tried to take my arm and I thought she was trying to poison me. They did that in the house of use. They'd prick me in the arm and everything would go black and I'd feel sick when I woke up. So I knocked her backwards.' She hesitated. 'You and Seliye told me once in the colony that we should not want to kill, that it would make us like the men and we should try to be as different as possible. I'm not like that. Are you disappointed in me?'

The sound that First Joy's body made as he hit the wall. And then the silence.

'No,' I said with an effort. 'I'm not disappointed. I wish things had been different, that's all.'

'They say we are to go to another world,' Khainet said. My head went up at that: I thought she meant that Ettia had threatened to kill us. But then she added, 'The place where that woman who killed the Hierolath comes from.'

'Why?'

'To help find my sister.'

Ettia came back into the room, then, and I asked her if it was true. She said it was. We would leave in the morning. Others wanted to meet Khainet. But when I asked her why, she would not tell me.

THIRTY-THREE

PLANET: MUSPELL (VALI)

It was now some days later. When we'd returned from Mondhile, Eld and I had discovered that the Morrighanu had asked for Skinning Knife's sister to be brought from Nhem, and she had come to Muspell in the company of another woman named Hunan. I assumed they would be as cattle-like as the other women of Nhem, but to my surprise Hunan seemed as self-aware as anyone else, although it was clear that she'd had little experience of technology. We taught both her and Sedra how to work the ration units and the light switches, the taps and flushes. Sedra seemed to enjoy this: she stood turning the lights on and off for about ten minutes before Glyn Apt told her to stop, but Hunan seemed bewildered by it all. She was typically Nhemish in appearance, at least from my limited knowledge of that world: a small dark-skinned woman, with long hair of which she was clearly proud. She told me a little about her home, the ruined city they called Edge, and I was amazed she'd survived there for so long. She had a certain authority, but it was clear that something was troubling her. I didn't need the seith to tell me that, and I did not think it was related simply to being whisked through space. But I did not want to press her.

I watched Skinning Knife's sister closely as she sat in the holding cell. *Khainet*. She'd killed, so Glyn Apt had told me, but I did not yet know the circumstances, despite pestering the Morrighanu. Apart from that knowledge, there was nothing to suggest a killer. She seemed listless, but perhaps she'd been drugged. I could see it in Sedra, that same quality that the dead Gemaley had possessed: a dangerous, feral stillness. Sedra made no secret of the delight that she took in the chase and the kill, and why should she? On Mondhile it was normal. But Sedra had something that made her different to Skinning Knife, and to Gemaley: she was sane.

I wasn't sure whether the same could be said of Khainet. She did not look like Hunan. But Khainet's resemblance to the angular, pale-skinned Skinning Knife was there and it made me chilly to look at her. I wondered how she felt about her sister: Khainet and Skadi might have been raised in a tank, their mother a captive alien, but whatever might have been done to them, the women of Nhem – and Mondhile – still seemed to have feelings about their families. Did Khainet think about her sister – just as Sedra had – worry about her, long to meet her? I hoped that the last wasn't the case. Those same sentiments were unlikely to be shared by Skinning Knife, from what I'd seen.

Khainet couldn't see me looking in through the one-way glass of the holding cell, but occasionally she raised her head and glanced up, as if she suspected that she was being watched. At length, Eld came to join me and we watched her together. I should not have been surprised to learn that the same kinds of thought were going through his mind. At last he said, 'She looks a little like . . .' – confirming my suspicions. As if she had heard, Khainet turned her face to the wall.

'The other one is still in interrogation,' Eld told me. 'Hunan.'

'I hope they're treating her properly. She's been through a lot and she isn't young.'

'They know that,' Eld said. 'Don't worry. The Morrighanu respect women who survive things. Glyn Apt didn't think she'd survive a mind 'ride. She might seem fairly integrated, but she isn't.'

'Glad to hear that.' I didn't think they'd shown much respect to me, but then again, I was an enemy.

'She's hiding something, though.'

'How do you know?'

He shrugged. 'I've spent a lot of time interrogating people. I don't know what it is, but it's bad. I can almost smell it on her.' A black wing flickered momentarily around his head.

'She helped Khainet escape,' I said, not really believing my own protest. I'd sensed it on her, too. 'Maybe it's no more than that. She felt guilty about the woman Khainet killed, she told me that.'

'I think there's more,' Eld said. 'But the Morrighanu will get it out of her, eventually. They want to know why. And so do I.'

I looked at him, puzzled. '"Why"?'

'Why some women break out of the genetic conditioning. Why those women, and not others? There weren't many, you know. Hunan says a few hundred in her colony, more who didn't survive the journey south. The women's resistance took in some of the refugees but then they started sending them south to Hunan's colony instead, using information transferred by birds that the Morrighanu gave them – the resistance colony was too close to Iznar, and they'd run out of room.' He paused. 'A few hundred only, out of a population of nearly five million.'

'Did they target, or did the birds just get drawn to particular individuals, I wonder? As for the numbers, even five million isn't large. I hadn't realized the population of Nhem was so small.'

Eld's lip curled. 'They're self-limiting. In the beginning of Nhem, the elders said that medicine and science were the work of a devil, so half of them died of disease. Then all that changed and they embraced technology wholesale, but that meant they could wage more effective war and so another chunk of the population got wiped out. Their numbers have been climbing slowly over the last century or so, in spite of the recent civil conflicts.'

'Glad I was born on Muspell,' I said.

Eld laughed. 'Glad you were born in the Reach, you mean. You must miss the Skald, your women's councils, all that support.'

I thought of some of the back-biting that took place in the Skald. 'Yes. The support.' I wondered how Hunan had found life in her colony of women, whether it was really surviving, or collapsing beneath the weight of internecine strife. If we had the power, would we be any better than the men of Nhem? I liked to think so, but comforting thoughts aren't the same thing as reality. And if the Morrighanu and the valkyrie were anything to go by . . .

The door opened then and Hunan came in with one of the goat-eyed guards. She looked exhausted, but not afraid, and that made me think that Eld might have been right after all.

'Is Khainet well?' she asked me.

'See for yourself.' The young woman was sleeping, or feigning sleep. Hunan frowned.

'How long are you going to keep her locked up like that?' The tabula hummed and clicked beneath her words, and she seemed to stutter, as though speaking erratically. I wondered what language she had learned to speak in her isolated home. The Mondhaith gained language quickly, according to Sedra, once they recrossed the moats of their settlements and their conscious awareness clicked in. Was it the same for these women? It seemed odd to me that language could work like a switch.

'Until we're sure that she's no longer a threat to anyone,' Eld told her.

Hunan turned on me as if Eld did not exist, and I realized that for her it was too much to challenge a man. After her upbringing, I could not blame her. 'How can you see her as a threat? You, in this great fortress, with all these warrior women?'

'She's already killed someone,' Eld explained. 'That makes her dangerous.'

'These others have killed,' Hunan continued. *'You've* killed, and the old woman – Sedra. She enjoys it – she told me so herself.'

'True. But Sedra comes from a society where such things are normal and she knows that here, they are not. I don't think Sedra kills without a reason. And those same wild genes are in Khainet, but she doesn't seem to have the same restraint.'

Hunan stared at him. 'Do you think she's not sane?'

'I don't know. Do you?'

'I'm not even sure what "sane" means.'

And it was into the ensuring silence that a voice crackled over the receiver, to say that Skinning Knife had been located.

It was in the heart of Morvern, almost the geographical centre of Sull Forest, that traces of Skadi were found. I wondered whether there was any significance in this. It was impossible to know what was going through Skadi's head, child of three worlds that she was, and mad besides. Small wonder that she was mad: torn between the conflicting heritages of Mondhile and Darkland and Nhem.

They'd tracked her down in the usual way.

She'd killed.

By the time we got there – Sedra and myself, Eld and Hunan, and the Morrighanu hunting party – she had long gone, but the traces of her remained outside the little cottage. Sedra scented the air like a hound.

'She smells like my sister.' I thought there was a trace of satisfaction in that remark.

'Can you track her by scent?' Eld asked, sharply.

'No,' the Mondhaith woman said. 'At least, I might be able to do so for a short distance. But if she is as good as you say, she will be able to hide her scent. And depending on how far she is Mondhaith, she will be able to disguise her scent by means of her will.'

Eld looked as impressed as I felt at that, I am sure.

As we'd discussed, it wasn't so much a question of finding Skadi, as taking her alive, and that, the commander said, was why we needed Sedra. Someone who knew how Skadi thought, who could predict what she might do. But I wondered, too, whether Sedra might serve another purpose for the Morrighanu: a new source of Mondhaith genes, perhaps?

The person who had alerted the Morrighanu to Skadi's presence was local, a woodsman. He seemed sharp enough: he'd gone to the cottage earlier that afternoon to borrow a tool, heard no one there, and had looked through the window. When he had seen what was inside, he backed away, did not go in, touched nothing, and contacted the Morrighanu. Now he stood at the edges of the clearing, staring at Sedra.

'Vali, Sedra,' Eld said. 'Come with me.'

Inside, it was surprisingly neat, despite the blood. Skadi had not run amok, it seemed. The butchery of the occupants

– an elderly man and his wife – had been done with her usual precision: spines filleted and hung from the rafters, along with an arrangement of bones. There was no sign of a struggle; no doubt the pair had gone to their deaths convinced that it was the right thing to do.

'She is a dreamcaller,' Sedra said. Her accented voice sounded startlingly loud in the blood-stained silence.

'What's that?' Eld asked. But I thought I knew.

'Like the feir,' I said.

'Like some of the feir,' Sedra corrected me. 'Someone who can lure other people to their deaths, make them see what isn't real.'

'How do they do that?'

'It's a gift. And sometimes they use a dust to enhance it.'

'Narcotics,' Eld said.

'She wouldn't have known about that, from Mondhile, though. Would she?' Unless she had been there, the thought struck me. Or unless she'd simply discovered her ability by trial and error. The feir, and battles that weren't real. Experiments in Sull. The disappearing laboratory. The broch, with Skadi arriving so conveniently soon, and no trace of real destruction apart from that psychic imprint.

Eld said, 'You thought that Mondhile was a little-known backwater world. That the only thing known about it was an incomplete anthropologist's report. Yet Frey Gundersson knew more about it than you did, it seems, and so did the people who brought Sedra's sister to Nhem.'

I looked around the cottage. A neat, clean place, now

defiled by death. The bones had been hung in patterns: from certain angles, some of them made the same shapes.

'Sedra,' I said. 'What *is* this?'

'It's like a hunting lodge.' She sounded matter-of-fact. 'We display the bones of the kill.'

'In patterns, yes? What do they mean?'

The old woman looked taken aback, as though the question of meaning had never occurred to her. 'There is no meaning. The patterns are ancient, ritualized.' She thought about it. 'Maybe they had a meaning once, but not any more. And they are not like these. These are new, as though someone has made them up.'

'What's bred in the bone,' Eld said softly.

'So Skadi is behaving like a Mondhaith person,' I said, 'but out of context.'

'That can't be the case, though. Cultural factors aren't carried genetically.'

'Maybe it isn't a cultural factor, though. Perhaps it's something innate. Like birds that dance to attract a mate, or make bowers of leaves and flowers.'

Eld's eyebrows rose. 'You think Skinning Knife's looking for a mate?'

'What should she want with one of those?' Sedra said with scorn. 'She already has all she needs.'

'Maybe not, but I think she's acting out aspects of Mondhaith behaviour without understanding what she's doing. Because she does them imperfectly, in a place where they have no real meaning.' I gestured to the human wreckage around us. 'Like this. She hunts, she kills, she *arranges*.' I shivered as I spoke. It reminded me of Gemaley, of her taloned fingers inside me, of the burnlight in her eyes as she took pleasure in my hurt. Was Sedra like that? I'd said she was sane, but how sane were any of them, by our standards? Could you even apply those standards? Maybe Hunan had been right when she'd said that she didn't know what sane meant. But we did not have time for a sociological debate.

'One thing's for sure. We have to find her,' Eld murmured. He gave me a sharp look. 'Can I have a word with you outside?'

Leaving Sedra among the bones, we stepped into thin sunlight and fresh air.

'I'll be honest with you,' Eld said. In my experience, whenever someone said that to me, they were about to tell me a lie. 'Let me play devil's advocate. I dragged you up here, after all. If it wasn't for the fact that she'd tried to kill you, and that she killed Idhunn, if it was up to you – would you be inclined to just let her get on with it?'

'What?' I thought of the two ruined corpses in the cottage behind us, old people, Darklanders maybe, but ones who had never done me any harm. For all I knew, they'd been a pair of retired state torturers, but chances are they were just ordinary people, getting by in this harsh wild land as best they could.

'Morvern is full of ghouls, Vali. We've met some of them. The deaths for which Skadi has been responsible are relatively few. There are things up here that have cut a swathe through the north – one more wouldn't make a lot of difference.'

'You said you were playing devil's advocate. There has to be a reason why you decided to go after her and why you involved me. You involved me because I'd been to Mondhile. I think you see her as a key,' I said. 'Frey saw the Mondhaith – saw Gemaley—' it was hard to say their names – 'as a key.' Why else were the Morrighanu so keen to capture Skadi alive, rather than simply killing her from a distance?

I could see from his face that I was right. 'Of course. It's been there in all our conversations. A key to consciousness. The trip switch, somewhere in her genes. But what makes her special, Vali? Why couldn't Frey have just concentrated on the selk? We have enough of them captive, after all.'

'I don't know. The selk are a very long way from human, remember. They're animals, ones that got engineered to have seasonal consciousness. Maybe they are a key, but Frey couldn't find it in them and neither can the vitki who are working on them now. The Mondhaith are closer to human and the Nhemish women *are* human. Skadi is engineered Mondhaith. Somehow, the key is in that engineering.' All these beings, with a single thread in common and one thing that would differentiate them. 'Eld, listen. The Nhemish women don't control their sentience or its lack. They're like cattle, and then sometimes the switch gets tripped by tech that came from the Morrighanu and they become conscious beings. The Mondhaith are like another type of animal. When they're children, they're wild and feral – wolf kids, if you like. They go back to their homes and something – some piece of ancient tech perhaps

– trips them into sentience.' Had the Morrighanu learned something on Mondhile, something they'd used to create their birds? 'Then they revert, during the masques or during battle, or if they're cornered or angered, according to Sedra. But they can't control it either – at least, not to any significant degree.' I remembered that town full of people, their sudden brutal transformation. When you come face to face with a person, and there's no one looking back at you out of their eyes, that's a shocking thing. 'Frey thought he could control it but I think he was deluding himself. He thought I could control it, too – enter the animal mind, during what was supposed to be my ingsgaldir.' My hand crept up at that point, to touch my scarred face. 'But I can't either. The selk can't – it's a seasonal thing with them. What if Skinning Knife is the anomaly? The one who can control it, trip her own switch? The Morrighanu can't fully understand the technology that they've got, otherwise they'd have done a better job.'

Eld was watching me narrowly. 'But why should she want to?' Then he answered his own question. 'Because she's fundamentally mad.'

'Or fundamentally sane, but running on different programming. You could make a case for the whole of Mondhile being psychotic, but I think that's too simplistic an explanation.'

Eld glanced around at the quiet forest. A light mist had crept in, and was hanging among the grey trees like a banner. 'The forensic team's waiting. Get Sedra, ask her what she thinks, and then we'll get out of here.'

I was only too ready to leave. But when I stepped back through that charnel door, to find the Mondhaith warrior and tell her it was time to go, I found the cottage was once more occupied only by the dead.

THIRTY-FOUR

Planet: Muspell (Sedra)

Vali was right, and that pleased me. I liked to think that she was beginning to understand us a little. And I thought with affection of my unknown niece who, feeling the need for a display of her abilities, had arranged this hunting lodge. A pity she'd chosen people for it, rather than beasts, but the basic principles were there. When we met, and got to know one another, I would teach her better – but then I told myself I was being foolish. Surely they would kill her for this. My sister's child did not fit in this world; she and I did not belong.

They had not killed her before now because she was valuable to them: something to study. I had been brought here to help capture her, not kill; with the machines they had, it surely would have been easy enough to track her down. But that could not last, I thought. They might indeed study her for a time, and I might be able to teach them a little about her, but after that she would be put to death. I did not blame them for this, as I stood in the meaty stink of someone else's blood. Mondhile is a wide world, and an empty one. There's plenty of room for those who don't belong to wander its spaces, but in spite of these northern forests, this world was too little to contain a liability such as my niece.

No, they would have to kill her and I would have to help them.

I did not feel the same way about the other girl, the one named Khainet. She was not Mondhaith; I could tell that from the first moments of our meeting. She looked a little like my sister maybe, the faintest traces were there, and yet it wasn't enough. When I looked at her I felt no kinship, no connection, and I did not know why this should be.

As I was standing there, thinking this through, there was a sound in the rafters. I looked up, and saw an eye. It was yellow and cold, and after a moment it silently withdrew. I was curious to see what it was – an animal? A bird that had got in? – and so, being careful not to disturb blood or bone, I drew a chair across the room and stood on it, to have a closer look.

The rafters opened out into a wide roof space, easily accessible from below. Now that I was up here, I could see a folding ladder tucked up against the ceiling, able to be drawn down and climbed. I didn't bother with this, but grasped the rafter and, with some difficulty, hauled myself into the roof space.

Standing here, I found that it was quiet and hot. The warmth of the stove had risen to fill the ceiling space. A skylight in the roof was open and there before it on the stripped boards I saw a single droplet of blood. There was no sign of the bird, or whatever it was, but the open skylight was letting in a cool draught of fresh air. I took a breath and walked over. At first I thought that the animal was some kind of scavenger that had got in to have a taste of what lay inside, but then it occurred to me that this might be how my niece had left the premises. I looked up at the skylight and there she was – not the sight of her, for the sloping roof was dusted with snow and bare of footprints or tracks, but the scent. I could smell her. She smelled like my sister, impossible to describe or define, entirely individual and herself. It made my eyes burn for a moment and the snowy roof blurred. My sister was dead, I told myself, and I had her child to find.

The forest grew very close to the house here and I knew how she had left – straight through the treetops. Her scent hung in the air like a promise: she was not long gone. I meant to call to Eld and Vali. I meant to tell them where I was going, but I could not see them down below and the trace of her scent was fading. So I went after it, through the skylight and into the branches.

I climbed down one of the long ashy trunks, holding my breath. I could hear the tree singing to itself, the sap snaking through trunk and branches, driven deep and sluggish by the winter cold but starting at last to stir.

Among the trees, it was as though the clearing and the cottage had never existed. The faint sounds of Eld's and Vali's voices, and the humming of their vehicle, were abruptly cut off, as though they had been swallowed. I felt immediately more at home, away from people, in the company of the world and one of my own kind. Almost. I could still smell her but the scent was fading fast, more quickly than it should have done, and that confirmed to me that she had other talents besides the summoning of dreams. But so did I. I masked my own scent just in case, reaching inward, making adjustments. I had not told Vali that I could do this. Some knowledge you do *not* share. You do not know how it might be used against you. Vali was not my enemy, but I did not think of her as my friend either. She was my ally, and allegiances can change.

There was a little patch where the scent seemed to be concentrated – I looked down. There was a single drop of blood lying on the snow, staining it pink and only just starting to sink in. She had been hurt, somehow. She was bleeding – unless it was her time to bleed, but Vali had mentioned that the women here did something to prevent that. Perhaps my niece had chosen a more natural way – but I went down on one knee and smelled the blood. From a vein, not from the womb. It smelled thinner, less rich.

I found it hard to believe that one of her victims had managed to wound her. Vali had said that she moved with speed and stealth, and they had been old. Perhaps she had cut herself on something; snagged skin on the rough rafters. But that seemed clumsy and I didn't think she was like that – then again, maybe I was idealizing her, my dead sister's child, my sister grown and come again. Old and foolish, now I should start thinking more like the warrior I had been and less like a doting aunt.

And that meant that the blood might be deliberate. A lure.

THIRTY-FIVE

Planet: Muspell (Vali)

A flicker of movement, a beat of wings. Glyn Apt's head jerked up.

'Something's in the woods.'

We ran, weapons up, senses screaming. Within minutes, we were surrounded by the great trees, the soft grey mass of their leaves concealing the sky. I had never been anywhere so oppressive, not even on the little pod that had first taken me to Mondhile.

We pressed on through the cloudy leaves, churning snow beneath our boots, leaving tracks that were so obvious I was sure that someone would not be far behind. Yet no one came. It was as though the world, the galaxy, had contracted down to this forest, that the only light there was came filtered through this soft grey foliage, that the only air was filled with snow and cold and silence. Glyn Apt and the Morrighanu moved like ghosts through the trees.

It was a shock when the trees thinned out to reveal a river lying between narrow banks and frozen solid. It gleamed in the faint light, like metal. Along its banks were tall thin plants, each with a fuzzy woollen head. They were frozen, too, tassels of ice. One of the goat-eyed Morrighanu started to run towards the river and just as I was about to call her back, Skadi dropped from the trees.

She might have looked ordinary, standing still: tall and angular and pale-haired, dressed in shadow grey. One moment she seemed naked, the next, not. I could not tell what she was wearing. She was smiling, and in that smile I could see Sedra: it was more like an animal's grin.

'Well, now,' she said, and her voice wasn't at all human, though I can't say how. She sounded like an animal, taught to speak. Then her face grew still and remote, as though she was listening for something that I could not hear. She reached out her hand and beckoned to one of the goat-eyed Morrighanu.

'No,' I said, 'don't,' but it was as though my words had been swallowed by the cold. I tried to speak again and couldn't: she had locked my lips together, some bleak and bloody piece of magic, I could not help but think. The goat-girl tottered forward.

'Sister,' Skadi said, when the Morrighanu was within reach, and then she gave a casual swipe and the goat-girl fell. She did not make a sound. The blood from her throat fountained out over the snow and was taken by it, absorbed quickly as though the cold was drinking it in. I stood stone still, sealed into the world. Skinning Knife was standing in front of me, all at once; I had not even seen her move.

THIRTY-SIX

Planet: Muspell (Sedra)

I saw Vali standing stone still by the frozen curve of the river and the person before her could only be my niece. I started to run, stumbling through the snow. When I was young, I could run like the wind, but now I moved like an old animal, stiffly, joints creaking. This dying business suddenly seemed appealing all over again.

I thought Vali would be dead before I could reach her, but I was wrong. As soon as she saw me, my niece made no move. She looked like me: light to my dark. She looked like my sister, if my sister had grown into a woman – as indeed she had, I reminded myself, but not on Mondhile. She wore the local armour and her hair was braided, very complicated, but other than that she was visibly Mondhaith. She was using illusion to shift her appearance, but I could see through it to what she was.

And she was feir. I would have been proud of her, except for that. I'd already seen that she loved killing. What I hadn't realized before now was that she lived for it. I could see the feir light in her eyes. I could almost taste the blood on her tongue.

As I came towards her, she looked lost, but only for a

moment. The feir light faded from her gaze. She said – in the local dialect, for I heard the box humming at her belt – 'Who are you?'

'I am your aunt,' I said. 'You are my sister's child.'

'You look like my mother,' she whispered. I think Vali would have started to back away then, but I motioned to her to keep still. It's difficult for us to see prey sometimes, unless they are moving, but she was not to know that. I laughed. 'More like her than I used to do. I had black hair – it's grey now, as you can see. But she was always as pale as a moon.'

'You are from her homeworld,' she said. 'From Mondhile.' It sounded strange, in that odd accent, and strange, too, to hear the longing in her voice.

'Have you never been?' I asked, but I knew she had not. 'No? Then come back with me, niece.'

Now it was her turn to laugh. 'You think they'd let me? They don't like what I do.'

Neither did I, but she'd fit Mondhile better, at least. Vali's face was grey with fear and shock and something was nagging at me: I could smell fresh blood and when I moved a little, I saw that someone was lying in a huddled mass further down the slope, towards the river. My niece had killed again. Well, so there was that.

'I'll talk to them—' I said, but at that moment a bolt of something hurting-bright shot over my shoulder and hissed into the snow. My niece was gone, upward, I thought, into the trees. She had that feir swiftness. I'd thrown myself flat into the snowbank and when I scrambled up, Vali and Glyn Apt were running down the slope.

'Where did she go?' Vali gasped. She seized my arm.

'She is feir,' I said. 'And she is a dreamcaller.' *And she is my sister, come again*. But I did not think Vali would want to hear that.

They asked a lot of questions. Vali was present, but she said little. She leaned against the wall with her scarred face in shadow and I could tell she was thinking hard. The vitki Eld was patient; Glyn Apt demanded answers. I sympathized. Smooth, political Eld was not my kind, but I liked the Morrighanu commander well enough. She relied too much on machines, as these people did, but it might have been possible to train her out of that, given time.

They wanted to know about the feir, about dreamcalling. I told them all I knew: that the feir were closer to animals than humans, that they preferred to spend their lives in the bloodmind, without too much conscious thought. They had a degree of control over it, whereas most of us do not.

'Perhaps it's because we fear it,' I said. 'And they do not, so because they embrace what they are, it comes more readily to their hand.' I thought Glyn Apt understood that very well.

'What about dreamcallers?' she said.

'They bend reality to their will. They make us see what is not real, or make us fail to see things even when they are not there.'

Vali and Glyn Apt exchanged glances. 'The moor. And the broch,' Vali murmured.

Eld shifted, clearly restless. 'But the machine readouts were negative.'

'Maybe she made us see them as negative,' Vali was trying to explain.

'I'm not prepared to attribute that degree of power to a savage,' Eld said.

'But she's not a savage, is she? She's got Mondhaith abilities and Morrighanu tech, never mind what she might have picked up from the valkyrie. That's a powerful combination. Assuming,' Vali shifted awkwardly, 'that she did not come in the company of your Commanding Officer. What if they wanted to see if she really could fool vitki and Skald, as perhaps she'd claimed?'

'We know she could,' Eld said quietly.

'But maybe she wasn't believed. Maybe they wanted to see for themselves what she could do. And then maybe she turned on them. Or again, perhaps she didn't.'

Eld looked doubtful and I saw that my niece had already achieved one of the first ambitions of the dreamcaller: confusion and paranoia. I said as much. There was a short silence.

'We've scanned the area,' Glyn Apt said. 'There's no trace of her and after what happened earlier I feel this means nothing.'

Vali shifted position against the wall. 'What happened to the body of the Morrighanu she killed?'

'We brought it back. It's in the morgue. It's been autopsied,' Glyn Apt replied.

Vali looked faintly disgusted, though I did not understand

why. 'You speak as though she's no more than a piece of meat.'

Her disgust was mirrored by Glyn Apt. 'You are a killer yourself, Vali. Why should you care?'

'Because she wasn't one of my targets, that's why. And speaking of pieces of meat, what have you done with Khainet? Is she still in the cell?'

'Yes, and will remain so until we've finished the tests.'

'How long will that take? And what about Hunan?'

'What about her?'

'She's old and she cares about Khainet as a daughter. She wants to know what's happening. She asked me.'

As a daughter? I thought. These women seemed to care about their children as we did about our siblings.

'Is anyone looking after her?' Vali demanded.

'No. We thought she would prefer to be left alone.'

'Did anyone actually ask her?'

Glyn Apt looked surprised. 'I didn't think it was necessary.'

Vali sighed. 'Very well. I'll talk to her later.'

'Odd though it may seem,' Eld remarked, 'we are still on track. Abred is thirty miles further north of the broch, and that in turn is fifteen miles north of where Vali and I found the corpse in the stream. Follow that line through, and it leads to the wastes around Therm.'

My niece was like myself, I suddenly thought. She was heading for a place to die, too, just as I had been.

Glyn Apt sat back in her seat. 'Well, then. I should like to be waiting for her, when she reaches Therm.'

'Hard going by air or sea,' Eld said.

'Why?' That was Vali.

'Remember when you arrived? The land up there – if one can call it that – is like that. All ice and shallow channels. You could get to Therm with an icebreaker but it would be a long, hard slog. Wings are quicker but there's nowhere to land, the ground is too unstable. You'd need a small canoe.'

'I want to go with you,' I said.

Glyn Apt looked at me. 'That's why you're here. You know how she thinks.'

Feir, and dreamcaller with it. I was beginning to understand, it seemed to me. 'I know that,' I said. But what I did not say was whether, if it came to it, I would allow them to kill her.

THIRTY-SEVEN

Planet: Muspell (Vali)

Before we left, I spoke to Hunan and she was glad of the chance to talk. The Morrighanu and Mondhaith might wall up their feelings, but Hunan did not. Maybe having been denied speech for so long, she wanted to make the most of it. But there was still something she was holding back and I did not know what it was.

'She's like my daughters,' she said, after a while. 'She doesn't look like them, but she reminds me of them.'

'What happened to your daughters?' Knowing what I knew of Nhem, that could be nothing good.

'I don't know. Maybe they lived, maybe they were put to death because of what I did.'

'Is there any way you could find out?'

'No. They don't record the deaths of women.' She paused. 'All of Edge – I hoped with every one that came, that she might be one of my daughters. Perhaps they're even there, and I just don't know it. Khainet – she's not human, is she? I saw her sister, Glyn Apt showed me the recording. But,' she frowned, 'Khainet spoke of her sister – she remembered her, and their mother. She said her sister tried to protect her, when the men raided the laboratory.'

'Maybe so. But I think she's changed since then.'

'Maybe the raid was the start of her madness,' Hunan said, but she did not sound sure. Then she added, 'Sedra frightens me.'

'Sedra is . . . more alien than you or I. She has a different way of doing things.'

'You're going after Khainet's sister now?'

'Yes.'

'I've asked Glyn Apt to get us a passage back to Edge. I don't know whether she'll agree. I don't think they'll let Khainet go.'

'The Morrighanu have ships of their own. Nhem doesn't have the technology to protect its airspace, not now the Hierolath's gone. The place is in chaos, apparently.' I did not want to mention the tests on Khainet, and I thought Hunan was right. Khainet had been brought here as an experimental spare, I was certain, a backup if Skadi died.

'I saw Iznar. It had been bombed.'

I felt uncomfortable. 'I seem to have set the stage for a civil war.'

'It would have happened sooner or later anyway,' Hunan said wearily.

'I'd be glad for your sake if you arranged passage home,' I told her.

'I don't know what I'd find in Tesk,' she said. 'Everything's changed. I'd have to tell them what I've seen and they know about the women's resistance, now.'

I smiled. 'You're connected with women who could help you.'

'I'm not sure if that's a good thing. There are . . . things I have to face.'

I waited, but she did not say anything more and shortly after that a raven came and told me that I would be going to Therm.

The wing landed us on the deck of the same warship that had taken the Rock. It seemed strange to see it after so short a time, but when I asked Glyn Apt about the Rock, and about the war, she only smiled and said that it was going well. That meant: not well for the Reach, then, and my heart sank. I didn't know whether the presence of the warship in Morvern waters meant that the Rock had been secured, or whether the Reach had repulsed the invasion. And since no one would tell me, I decided to find out.

Midnight. I was allowed a certain freedom on the warship, carefully curtailed from venturing into any restricted areas. The Morrighanu ship reminded me of their spacecraft: data streaming over walls and floor so that the interior of the ship seemed to be running with water. It made me feel cold. The air was filled with shadowy birds, so that standing inside the ship was like being outside on some glassy wet sea crag, the sky hidden by the beat of wings. From the deck, the wasteland of the northern sea stretched to the horizon, still rimmed by the hidden sun at these late spring latitudes, the heavens shimmering with arctic light. The breaking ice floes reflected that light, casting back against the watery sides of the warship, which ploughed through the thin edges of the ice like a footstep on frost. Later on, when we reached the thicker floes, it would be a different story.

At length, Therm became visible: a gleaming cone rising above the icefield. It was clear that it was huge, but from this distance it seemed insubstantial, a volcano's ghost. I looked at it under the flickering curtain of light and thought of Mondhile and a woman who belonged nowhere.

No one was watching. I had been given my own small corner of a dorm, but I felt that I'd be more unobtrusive here on the deck, and the bleak silence – broken only by the distant hum of the warship's engines and the churn of the waves against the hull – suited my mood. I ducked behind a stanchion. A pair of Morrighanu walked past, faces silvered in the moonlight. One of them spoke a word and a feather fell to the deck, to disappear. Then they were gone and there was only myself and the icefield and the seith.

I did what I had done before, went where I had gone earlier: diving inward into a place that was, I realized, as cold and dark and bleak as the northern sea. I did not want to look at what I had become. I swept through it, seeking warmth. Down through clouds of ash, billowing blackness, down past something that snapped at me with razor teeth and spoke in a man's voice. I had buried it deep enough, after all, like some treasure that only the gods could find. Not even Glyn Apt could reach this, I thought with chilly satisfaction, not even dead, torn Frey.

And there it was. It glowed hot and red and gold: the coal that Idhunn had given me, carried in a bird's beak. I tried to grasp it but I couldn't: it swerved away from me and fell into darkness. But the bird itself was back; I felt its cold feathers brush against my skin, a drift of information. I had the key and I used it to slide under the gateways of the Morrighanu information network and into the system.

The Reach. Still at war, but not going as badly as I'd feared. Lots of vitki propaganda, labelled as such and kept separate from the real reports, the propaganda obviously destined for the masses of Hetla and the more southerly cities. Something about the selk, which I tried to grasp, but which whisked away from me like an eel in a river. Tiree had come under heavy fire, but was resisting, and the navies of the Reach had sent one of those massive war-wings to the bottom of the sea.

And then my goal: glimpsed as though it was reality, a report that contained an image of the Rock against a clear spring sky.

The Morrighanu had left a garrison at the Rock when the warship had been recalled to Morvern. That garrison was still there, but the Rock was intact.

Once I knew that the Rock still stood, that – assuming the rest of the war didn't see it destroyed – I still had a home to go to, I felt a burst of light emanating out from that piece of information, dispelling a little of the cold and dark. Lighter than I had been since the Rock was taken, I called the white-winged bird back to me, folded it safely into the depths of my head, and sought my bed. I slept for perhaps three hours before Eld's raven came to me once more, to tell me that it was dawn and the warship had travelled as far as it could.

THIRTY-EIGHT

PLANET: MUSPELL (HUNAN)

When the guard woman came for me, she told me that Khainet was 'unsettled'. I did not know exactly what she meant by this: whether Khainet was ill, or simply unhappy. Small wonder if it was the last. They were so cold, these women, as cold as their country. The chill sank through to my bones; I did not think that I would ever be warm again. I asked them for a heating device, but the guard at my door told me that the room was as hot as it could get. She brought me a blanket, made from some unfamiliar fleecy stuff, nothing like the thin insect-weave blankets that we had in the colony.

I missed Edge. I missed the heat and the light. I even missed the shrieking of the efreets towards twilight, and the space: the views across the city and the sea. Here it was like living in an animal's burrow, or a root cellar. I kept thinking that I heard a voice, crying out in pain, but there was never anything there.

I thought that Khainet would surely feel the same way, but when I had last spoken to her, she said that she liked it here.

'How can you like it?' I asked, amazed. 'They have put

you in a cage. They do tests on you – you told me so yourself.'

But Khainet just shrugged. 'It's better than the house of use, or the men's city,' she said. 'They are all women here. They have weapons and they know how to use them. They fight. My sister fought. She's here, they told me that. I want to see her, but they won't let me.'

'They are all women in Tesk,' I said. 'And in the mountains where you were born.' *Made, or born?* I still did not understand.

But she said, 'In Edge and in the mountains, they are afraid the men will come. Here, they have no such fear. They despise men, one of them told me so. They use them for sport as the men of Iznar use us. They belong to no one.'

'They are warriors,' I said. 'Is that what you want for yourself?' The weapons carried by the Morrighanu frightened me, and so did the ease with which they could deliberately kill. Killing should be a hard thing, or so it seemed to me, but then I'd done it easily enough, hadn't I?

'Why shouldn't I?' Khainet demanded, fiercely. 'If I'd had a gun, when the men came, I could have killed them. If we had weapons in Tesk, we could hold them off if they came. At the least, we could kill one another, rather than go back.'

I wanted to tell her that the answer did not lie in what weapons we might have, but the truth was that I did not know. I had never known. The reason we had no weapons was because we did not have the ability to make them and so it was not our choice. If we had a choice, what would we do?

And now the guard was telling me that Khainet was 'unsettled'.

I heard the noise before I saw her. Her voice carried down the corridor, high and shrieking, without words. I shook off the guard's hand and ran, as quickly as I could. But the guard caught me and dragged me back. Someone came swiftly out of a door, with two other Morrighanu, and the door was slammed behind her.

'Why is she here?' a woman said, frowning at me. At first I thought she was as old as I: her head almost completely bald, apart from a few wisps of white hair. But her face was a young woman's, with ancient eyes set in stretched skin. She looked as though her face had been taken apart and then put back together again; there was something not right about it.

'Commander Glyn Apt's lieutenant asked for her to be brought. It was thought she might calm the prisoner down.'

'Oh, I don't think so,' the old woman went on. 'I think it's already too late for that.'

'What do you mean?' I said. 'Let me see her!'

The old woman shrugged. 'Very well. If you want to.'

The shrieking had stopped now, and in its place was a waiting silence. I went to the door and looked through the grille. Khainet was there, crouched in a corner of the room. Her long hair had come loose and it was all over the place as though she'd been running her hands through it. She was chewing a strand of it, and she looked up and her gaze met mine.

There was no one there, no recognition. Her gaze slid

away from me, roving over the room. She looked like a trapped animal. As I watched, she opened her mouth and howled. I thought of her mother, kept in a cage. I thought of her sister, of Skinning Knife.

'Yes,' the old woman said at my shoulder. Her eyes sparkled with something: I would have said malice, except that there was no real enjoyment in it. She seemed even less human at that point than the girl in the locked room. 'You see it, don't you? She has gone to join her family.'

I turned on her. 'What did you do to her?'

'Why, no more than give her back her heritage. Flicked a switch, you might say. A pity. She doesn't have the strength to carry it. It seems we can turn her on but not off. But maybe she'll come out of it of her own accord.' A pause. 'She asked about her sister, when we took her to the lab, wanted to know if she could meet her. And now she has. In a way.'

'What you people do,' I managed to say through my fury, 'it's monstrous. You play with other people's lives.'

'That's true,' the old woman said, 'and if we hadn't, you would not be standing here as a thinking thing, would you? You would still be an un-named sheep, serving a man in Iznar.' She raised a hand and a bird grew out of her fingers, white as fine sand. She threw it into the air and it flew down the corridor and away. I was taken back to my cell after that. I did not see Khainet again, and they would not talk to me about her, even though I asked each time the guard came by.

THIRTY-NINE

Planet: Muspell (Vali)

Sedra met me on the deck, chafing gloveless hands against the early morning cold. Glyn Apt had offered her a pair of gloves but she said it made you soft. I didn't feel like competing; I was bundled up in a slickskin over a woollen fisherman's jersey. Sometimes you don't need high tech, true enough.

'This is a good land,' Sedra said.

I smiled. 'There's nothing here.'

'That's what I mean. You have too many settlements on this world. I've been looking at maps.'

'It's sparsely populated in comparison to most.' I stared out over Therm. The volcano's peak was pallid in the dawn light. Loki's ragged face hung over its shoulder, the moon seeming closer than it should. There was a last drift of electric glow across the icefield, casting shadowy reflections, and then the red sun was coming up once more.

'Today we go to Therm,' Sedra said.

'Or as close as we can get. We're going by boat. Do you think you—'

'I'll make it,' She interrupted. Then her head went up. 'There's life here.'

'Life? Well, this ship has a large crew . . .' But then I saw what she meant, the first few heads bobbing in the water. The selk had found us.

Sedra was curious, and, I think, charmed. She wanted to talk to the selk, but I asked her to hold back. I persuaded Glyn Apt to bring me a wire and I slid down it, to hover over the oily churn of the sea.

'Are you who I spoke with before?' I called. 'Are you the ones who helped me?'

They came closer, sinewing through the icy water. But it was with an animal's curiosity. There was no flicker in their eyes, only the spark of light from the red sun. It was spring now and their sentience had fled with the winter. There was no sense to be got out of them: the chasm had opened up once more. I signalled to Glyn Apt to draw me up on the wire and found Eld waiting on the deck.

'I thought it was probably too late in the year, that they'd changed and lost their sentience,' he said. 'Pity. They know the waters. They might have been able to help.'

'They might have seen it as nothing more than a human affair,' Glyn Apt said. 'And even so, they aided Vali before because they thought she might help them. But if they had their awareness now, they would see that she is in no position to do so.'

That made me wonder how the captive selk were faring, in the tanks beyond Hetla.

'They are like us, those water creatures,' Sedra said. She'd been paying close attention. 'Like my people.'

'But not so fierce,' I said, teasing.

Sedra grinned. 'How do you know what they get up to when the humans' backs are turned?'

True, I thought. I had no way of knowing what their lives were really like.

Glyn Apt had arranged for two canoes: one for Eld and myself, and the other for herself and Sedra. Interesting that she'd trust an almost-alien warrior over one of her own countrymen, but I couldn't be surprised. Then it was back down the wire for all of us. I was worried about Sedra – it was only a few days, after all, since she'd been at death's door – but I needn't have been. The situation seemed to be giving her a new lease of life. She went fast down the wire and slid into the canoe. Glyn Apt and Eld took the front oars; the canoes had a form of wing power, but it wasn't enough for these narrow channels. Manual dexterity was necessary.

I looked back once, to see the warship swinging around on the morning tide. I wondered if I'd see it again. Ever since the fenris attack, something in me believed that I would die out on the ice: the place I found the most beautiful, and feared the most. Had Sedra felt the same about the moor? I wanted to ask her, but the canoes were pulling too far apart.

Eld and I fell into a rowing rhythm, almost hypnotic. The morning wore on. Soon, the spring sun was casting brilliance across the icefield and I had to turn the goggles up to maximum to shut out the glare. Even so, it made for slow going. Sometimes the cone of Therm seemed very distant, at other times, disconcertingly close. I couldn't seem to get a grip on its location, although when I checked the map implant, the volcano lay in a steadily decreasing handful of miles to the north-west. Wings fluttered around Eld's head and a moment later, the vitki's voice said through the map implant: 'We should reach the edge of Therm's glacier in another three hours.'

Close, then. And would she be waiting for us? Could she see us coming, two little dots snaking through the maze of channels that ran between the floes? Did she have plans? I'd long since ceased to think of her as any kind of human, I realized. Perhaps, remembering that glimpse of her in her woodland lodge outside Hetla, polishing the skull in her lap, I never really had. She was like Gemaley, her distant kin, assuming fairy-story proportions in my head, the wicked witch in her castle of ice, the spirit-woman with the skinning knife. That castle wasn't very far away now, just a part of my own world, and she was one woman against four trained fighters. But I thought of the dreamcallers, of the feir, and my heart leaped and poked in my chest.

Early afternoon, and the red sun was at its peak with the snow bloody across the icefield. Therm, too, was stained red and when, in a moment of cloud shadow, I turned the goggles down to see what it was really like, I saw that the whole of the western sky was a delicate pink, fading to a deeper crimson at the horizon's edge. It looked barely real, not like my world at all. Therm was huge, and now that we had come further I could confirm with my own sight that it was not one volcano at all, but part of the great arctic ring of fire. The peaks marched into the distance, to be lost against the rosy sky.

We halted at the edge of a slab of ice, sheltering under its lea just in case, to eat some of Glyn Apt's rations. The Morrighanu seemed to rely heavily on dried fish, which suited me. Sedra made no comment on the food: I suppose she was used to eating whatever she could forage. And this wasn't such a barren land after all. Down in the clear waters around the ice, I saw shoals of many different kinds of fish gliding through the green depths. The floes, breaking up as they were, seemed too fragile to support fenris and that improved my mood as well. By the time we set out again, I was almost cheerful.

Later in the afternoon, we reached the edges of the glacier of Therm. No mistaking the closeness of the volcano from here: it was immense, dominating the landscape. Now that we were so close to it, I could see how irregular it actually was, not really a simple inverted cone at all but a towering summit of shards and pinnacles of rock. I thought of that fairy-tale ice castle all over again. We left the canoes tethered to a spire and assessed our options.

According to Glyn Apt, who of all of us knew this land the best even though she had never been to Therm itself, the old volcano was riddled with caves.

'I don't know what kind of set-up she could have in there. Depends how much technology she's appropriated.'

'Or whether she's bothered with it,' Sedra said. There was an odd note in her voice, almost of pride, and I gave her a sharp look. Something about her tone worried me, but I told myself it was natural enough. Even given the nature of Skadi, she and Sedra were both Mondhaith – of sorts, at least

– and we were not. People clustered in packs. Especially when they weren't really human at all.

Between them, Glyn Apt and Eld made the decision that it was too late in the day to strike out across the glacier. There was perhaps a mile or so before the slopes of the volcano really began. Even though it would be late by the time we reached them, the arctic sun stayed only just below the horizon at this point in the year and we'd have enough light to travel by. But we were also tired and would need to rest, and Glyn Apt did not like the notion of being closer to Skadi's lair when we slept. She did not say, but I knew what she was thinking, that Skadi had managed to cast her hallucinatory lure over an entire garrison of Morrighanu warriors. We would need Sedra alert and awake.

So we made camp at the edge of the ice. Sedra and I would sleep for the first part of the evening. We held to the pretence that Skadi was more likely to attack at night, but I think it was just that this reflected our own vulnerabilities. After all, she'd never waited for darkness before. She didn't need to.

Sedra, as far as I could tell, fell asleep within minutes, but I lay wakeful. Glyn Apt and Eld occasionally conversed in low voices and once a grey bird shot out across the ice, flying low towards the water. When it reached the sea it split into two birds, black raven and white, and each flew off in a different direction. I assumed this indicated some kind of joint report and I felt an odd, faint sensation that I eventually identified as jealousy. I rolled over in my sleeping pack and looked at Sedra. The sky had darkened to green and the old woman's peaceful profile lay against the clear sky. She did not even seem to be breathing, but then I saw her breast stir. Her hawk face had smoothed a little in sleep; I could see the beautiful girl she had once been, saw, too, the resemblance to her niece. I'd rather not have noticed that. I closed my eyes, expecting the horror of being on the ice to overwhelm me.

And perhaps it did.

I thought I was dreaming. I remember falling asleep, and I think I recall Eld bending over me to tell me that it was up to Sedra and myself to keep watch. I even remember turning to Sedra and asking her whether Mondhile had the veils of light that were now sweeping across the northern sky. But that is all. The next thing I recall, I was out on the glacier.

I turned back, but there was no sign of the others, nor of our canoes. Therm still towered in the near distance, but the land looked different, somehow: grander, and even more icelocked. Looking out over the sea, there was less water, and the bergs clustered closer together, floating whales of ice. I could hear something singing and knew it was the selk. A great gladness rose in me and I went in search of them, stumbling out over the ice. It was hard going at first, but then it became easier until I was gliding across the thin covering of snow towards the shattering sweetness of the song. The sun had long since risen and the sky was again that hazy rose.

The snowstorm came up out of nowhere. One moment

the sky was perfectly clear, and then next, I was staggering through a full blizzard. Icy needles of snow hissed against my face but they did not hurt and I was not cold. I knew that this was a very bad thing, that it meant that I was close to death, but I could not bring myself to care. Anyway, I could see a light through the snow and that indicated safety. I went towards it and saw that instead of one light, there were two, shining in beacon brilliance through the falling whiteness. And even when I realized that they were not lights after all, but eyes, I still did not care and walked on. This is how it should have been that last time, the time of my ingsgaldir, I told myself. Either the fenris should have killed me or I should have killed it. Now, I'd have another chance.

It was very close now. I saw the round cat ears, tufted with fur, the long canine face and the glistening teeth. Its fur was banded black and white, shading into grey beneath. It had a bright, quick light in its golden gaze: it knew who I was and why I had come, and when I stopped a few feet away from it, I saw that it was not an animal at all, but a woman.

Skadi was no longer wearing her armour. She was dressed all in furs, with small neat boots and gloves made of something soft that I thought might be catskin. Her hair was loose and she was smiling, but the golden eyes were the same. I had not thought her eyes were golden.

'It was you,' I said. 'It was you, out on the ice that time. You tried to kill me.' But that beast was dead: it had been shot. They could not be the same and she shook her head.

'Not I. But not a beast, either. Someone you never knew. A vitki, brother of Frey Gundersson.'

'Frey had a brother?'

'I can't remember his name.' She looked dismissive. 'The purpose of your ingsgaldir wasn't to permit you to control animals, as Frey tried to convince you – more mind games. It was to see through illusions to what lies beneath. Yes, pack control is part of being a vitki, but only a part.' She came close to me. I could smell her and she was rank and musky. Woodsmoke clung to her like a pall. She leaned forward and kissed me on the forehead. Her lips were icy.

'Congratulations. You've passed. It's a good thing to achieve, before you die.'

And that's when I saw the blade.

The witch of the north, who pares you, frees you from your frail unnecessary flesh. The woman who, with her skinning knife, flays you and strips you down to the whistling bone, the hollows of your body, so that the north wind whips through. The woman who liberates your spirit, allowing it to wander the earth while she and her beasts feed on your discarded, rotting meat. That's who Skadi was. I'd been right. She wasn't human.

Everything slowed. The blade drifted down through the air like the arctic lights, floating towards my throat. I felt its breath before I felt its bite – but the bite never came. Years ago, the fenris had exploded in a burst of bone and brain, as my rescuer fired a bolt into its head. Now, it was as though the whole world exploded: the ice shattering, the sky breaking apart and the stars cascading down. It was only for a moment, as Sedra threw me backwards and my head hit an outcrop of icy rock. I heard Eld and Glyn Apt, shouting out, and I sat up.

I was still alive. So were Eld and Glyn Apt. But Sedra and Skadi were gone.

FORTY

PLANET: MUSPELL (SEDRA)

We watched them searching for us, from the vantage point of a nearby crag. They could not see us, of course, and my niece's magical birds made sure that we would not show up on any of their mechanical devices. I'd have gone down and reassured them, but I wanted to keep an eye on my niece.

Skadi was sulking. But she wasn't in the bloodmind that the feir warriors love so much; she was perfectly self-aware.

'What did you think you were doing?' I asked. 'Were you going to kill us all?'

'Maybe not you,' she muttered. 'But the rest – why not? They want to kill me.'

'Niece, you are a liability.'

'Why don't they just leave me *alone*?' She sounded like a young girl, newly returned from the world. 'That's how this started. I did what they told me to do, in Sull Forest. I killed who they told me to kill. I linked my mind to their machinery; I folded the forest.' That made me prick up my ears, but she went on, 'But then they began asking me questions – how did I kill so well? How is it that I can cast such illusions, when even the foremost vitki struggled to do so?'

'It's because of what you are,' I said.

'I know that *now*. But they didn't bother to tell me, so how was I to know?' She paused. '*Her* lover – the one called Frey – he understood me. He took me to a hunting range in Morvern, set me against the captives. I killed as many as I could find and he was very pleased. But then the vitki insisted that I came back and be tested.'

'I can see how you would not want that.' I looked at her. 'So what do you want, niece?'

She hesitated. 'My name is Skadi, not "niece".'

'A good name,' I said, though it seemed outlandish for this almost-Mondhaith girl to bear a foreign word, and it grated on me to be speaking to her through the medium of the box, that she did not understand her own tongue. 'What does it mean?'

'It means "Shadow". And you ask me what I want. I want to be myself, nothing more. To do what I am called to do.' She reached out and grasped me by the arm. It was a warrior's grip. 'And you can help me, can't you? You can show me what kind of thing I'm supposed to be.'

'Skadi, I am not even supposed to be here at all. I never thought I'd see another planet, another world. I went out into the wilds to die. This is like the afterlife for me.'

'Then that proves it, doesn't it?' she said eagerly. 'You can never have been intended to die. The spirits must have meant you to live – to come here and teach me.'

I didn't know what spirits she meant. I knew nothing about the beliefs of these people. But her grasp of my arm was so tight that it hurt. I heard myself say, 'Perhaps that's true.'

'You can show me how to control the illusions, to make them real – without the aid of the machines. How to wield the ability.'

I laughed. 'You seem to be able to do that quite well enough yourself.' But her words made me deeply uneasy. Make illusions real? I'd heard of a few folk doing that, stories from the very long-ago. No one could do it now. *I folded the forest*. Something told me not to betray my concerns, however. If she felt that it was a common trait of our people, maybe she'd be more wary of me.

'Tricks,' she said, almost spitting. 'Technology and trickery. I have enough stuff in *here*,' she tapped her forehead, 'to power a planet, it sometimes seems. I want it gone. It makes me weak. I know that what I do doesn't depend on it, or on their technology.'

I could understand that well enough. 'Very well,' I said. 'I'll teach you, if you wish to be taught. We'll start now. Do you see those three, your enemies?'

They were plainly visible a short distance across the icefield, huddled together over some piece of instrumentation. My niece made a sound in her throat like a growl. 'I see them.'

'Then watch and learn,' I told her. I cast an illusion of my own, calling upon the swirling blankness beneath the ice, the cold rush of the air, the whiteness of the snowscape. It was easy to work with such a canvas. So little colour, just pearl and pale against the pink backdrop of the sky. I drew the blankness up around the three who stood on the ice and blotted them from view. I saw Skadi's eyes widen as she half-realized what was happening. Then I reached out as if to reassure her and jabbed the pressure point below her jaw. Machines may not have let her down, but trust had. She crumpled to the ice but I caught hold of her and let her down as gently as I could. I estimated that she would be unconscious for a little while longer and I went down from the cairn of rock.

My niece could not see them and neither could they see me. I cast further illusions, working with the world and with the materials at my disposal. Once, I looked up to see the warrior of Moon Moor standing close by on an outcrop of ice and she grinned again when she saw me. My heart sang in me, for I thought I knew why she had come. But I also knew there was more that I had to do and then she faded, the bright snowlight cascading through her and blotting her from view. My death would be a while longer yet.

While Vali and the others chased shadows by the sea's edge, I made myself busy by taking one of the long folding sleds that had come with the canoes. There was some kind of engine attached, but I didn't bother with that; it was time to work with what I knew and understood. I looped the rope over my shoulder and dragged the sled back up to the cairn, where my niece lay unstirring. I must confess, I was glad to find her still there. I loaded her up onto the sled, anticipating difficulty, but she was quite light beneath all the skins and the sled glided smoothly on its long runners. I strapped Skadi down as best I could: the sled had clamps on either side, which suggested that it was intended for use in transporting prisoners. Then I located the sled's harness, secured it over my shoulders and over my breast, and set off across the glacier. It was hard. I was too old for this. The volcano towered in the distance and there was still much of the long day to go. There would be time, I thought, if only my own strength did not give out first. There would be time.

FORTY-ONE

PLANET: MUSPELL (VALI)

It didn't take us too long to work out what had happened. Skinning Knife had been distracted by Sedra and it was inconceivable, Glyn Apt said, that the old woman could have killed her. So Skadi must have taken Sedra away, spirited her into the white wilderness before us. Perhaps she intended to slaughter and display her aunt as a warning to us, or perhaps she wished to hold her as a hostage. If that were the case, Glyn Apt insisted, and Eld agreed, then we would undertake no negotiations save those that took us close to Skadi. Sedra was expendable. I did not like the idea, but I had to agree. Besides, I did not think Sedra considered herself indispensable – but that wasn't the point, at least if you were Skald and not vitki.

Shortly after that, we discovered that one of the sleds was missing, and that confirmed Glyn Apt's theory. We estimated that Skadi was maybe an hour ahead of us, and she knew the lie of the land better than we did, but the sled had made faint tracks in the ice and we followed them. We would halt when dusk fell, Glyn Apt decided. There might be other dangers beside Skinning Knife: night-hunting fenris, for instance.

'And maybe other things,' the Morrighanu added.

'What kind of "other things"?'

Glyn Apt looked uneasy, which was an achievement all by itself. 'They tell stories about Therm, even in Morvern.'

Eld laughed and Glyn Apt bristled. Eld said, 'They tell stories about Morvern, even in Hetla. About how everyone has two heads and keeps a pet troll.'

'You've seen Skinning Knife,' Glyn Apt retorted. 'Imagine what kinds of thing Morvern tells stories about.'

It was twilight by the time we reached the slopes of the volcano: that deep greenness of sky with the veils of light already starting to drift across it. After Skadi's attack, I'd increasingly begun to feel that this would be my last night on Muspell. It so nearly had been, and nothing we could do – technology, the seith – seemed able to protect me. With the aid of the Skald, I'd been able to develop techniques that on another planet – Nhem was one of them – could see me hanged for witchcraft, but Skadi made me look like a mere infant. I should have gone to her in that forest cottage, something whispered to me. I should have let her pare my soul from my flesh, strip me down to air and nothing. But then something else whispered to me that I'd fought Frey, who had called out the same kind of weakness in me, who had broken in through all the chinks and crevices in my armour. I'd fought Frey, and won. I wasn't a witch or a member of a super-race. I was just a woman with abilities, who had been trained in a particular way. And so was Skadi.

'I suggest we stop here,' Glyn Apt said, cutting the motor of the sled. We'd been running quietly, gliding along, but with the motor dead, the humming in my bones stopped and the world suddenly seemed a place of vast silence.

'It's as good as any,' Eld said. We were close to a long ridge of ice, with crevices that would provide shelter on three sides, if not from above. I agreed, but part of me wanted to go on, just get it over with. I held tightly to the memory of setting the visen pack on Frey, of realizing that he was finally, truly, dead. Aside from my brother, I reminded myself yet again, everyone who had ever hurt me was dead. Inductive logic was encouraging. But just because the sun has risen every day until now, it did not mean that it would rise tomorrow. At least, not for me.

With these dismal thoughts at the forefront of my mind, I helped the others set up a rudimentary camp. Glyn Apt was to take first watch, while Eld and I slept huddled against the side of the sled. Cold, discomfort and fear had served to exhaust me; I drifted off almost at once, watching the arctic lights. After what seemed like a few moments, but which turned out to have been a couple of hours, I was awoken by Eld.

'What is it?' I was immediately awake, nerves jangling.

'Glyn Apt's disappeared.'

Cursing, I got to my feet. 'You mean we've been sleeping unprotected?'

'I don't know about you,' Eld said, 'but I'm not unprotected even *when* I'm asleep.' Then he evidently thought better of the vitki sparring. 'Although with Madam Skadi, that seems largely irrelevant.'

'First Sedra and now Glyn Apt.'

'Glyn Apt might have gone off after her. I don't think the commander has much of a team spirit where non-Morrighanu are concerned.'

'Either way, she's likely to be dead,' I said. Eld gave me a close look.

'I know how you feel about Skadi. Believe me, I share it. But it's a weakness, Vali, and that's how she works. You've killed your enemies. You're still here.'

'Maybe so.' But I felt barely alive, in this freezing northern midnight. She had done her work, the mind's knife being the sharpest one of all.

We scouted around the camp and found traces. Glyn Apt's bootheel prints were rammed into the thin snow, marching with determination northward towards Therm. It looked as though Eld had been right, that the Morrighanu commander had decided to make the kill her own. Or sacrifice herself to save us? If she'd been Skald, or ourselves Morrighanu, I might even have considered it as a possibility.

After a brief consultation, Eld and I thought we'd be better off without the sled. We set off in Glyn Apt's tracks. It occurred to both of us that it might be a trap – Skinning Knife wearing someone else's boots – but the depth of the prints suggested someone of Glyn Apt's height and weight to me. Maybe that didn't mean as much as it might otherwise have done, but either way, the tracks could lead to Skadi and I found that I was anxious, now, for confrontation.

FORTY-TWO

Planet: Muspell (Sedra)

Of course my niece was angry when she woke to find herself up in the heights of Therm, in one of the lesser caves. She spat at me in chilly fury and I could see the bloodmind coming over her. Feir indeed, but I told her coldly that it was her first lesson.

'Kill me, then,' I said. 'Do you think I'm afraid? Then there'll be no one to teach you. Go to Mondhile alone and see how they treat you there. On our world, your kind are commonplace as insects and as easily swatted.'

She stood uncertainly in front of me and I saw the bloodmind start to ebb. She had more control over it than I'd thought and that was impressive.

'There's not just death,' she explained. 'There's pain.'

I had to laugh. 'I'm sure you're an expert. But do you really think I don't have control over my own death?' It wasn't true, but I couldn't let her know that. I stood to face her and let my lips draw back from my teeth. 'Do what you wish. Or choose to learn.'

She did not apologize, nor was I expecting her to, but she inclined her head and stepped back. 'Very well,' she said and her voice was a little more submissive. 'What do you choose to teach?'

'Survival, among other things. Endurance. You have these qualities already. What you do not have is patience.'

'They say patience is its own reward.'

'*Im*patience has got you noticed.'

That arrow struck home. She grimaced. 'That's true enough.'

I touched her shoulder and she did not flinch or draw away. A wild thing, I thought, nothing more than that. But the people among whom she'd been living did not understand. They were wild themselves, but they'd learned to hide it under masks and patches.

'But impatience,' I said, softly, 'will not necessarily get you killed.'

Now that I'd got her away from her hunters, however, I was becoming aware that I'd let myself in for a substantial problem. We could not stay here. They would kill Skadi and maybe they were right to do so. Even settlements on Mondhile often slew people, when it was clear that they were feir and not mehed, who merely wanted to wander the world, without killing. Yet on Mondhile, at least, she would have some kind of place. But that meant we had to get there. And in order to do so, we'd need a flying vehicle. My niece could pilot one, maybe, but first we'd have to steal it. Problems were piling upon problems. I voiced these thoughts to her.

Her eyes sparked. 'I should like to see Mondhile. Nhem

– a world of shit. Here – no place for me, though for a while I thought it was. When I learned of Mondhile, it sounded like a place of peasants and mad people.' She said this with no trace of irony. 'But then I met you.' She laid her hand on my hand for a moment and it was oddly affecting. 'We'll go south.' She was as excited as a girl newly returned from the world and I suppose I could not blame her. Her face shone. 'We'll steal a ship; it will be easy enough. They're all distracted by the war. We'll go to *our* world.' And I think it was only then that I realized how greatly she wanted to belong.

She slept after that. I think she was more tired than she cared to admit, for it was the sort of sleep that an animal sleeps: the sudden oblivion that follows furious activity. I watched her, as I had watched my sister while she slept in the hollows under the sky, or the burrows under the earth. I saw in her the woman that my sister had been and then the grief burst in me like a black bubble for that stolen girl, caged and used.

If Skadi's hunters came after us, I did not want to see them dead. But they were not my blood; my niece was. If they had to go, then I would see to it. And then we would go south.

Skadi had been sleeping for around an hour when I heard the noise. It was stealthy and small, the kind of sound that an animal makes when it hopes not to be overheard. As quietly as I could, I got to my feet and slipped outside.

It was still dark, but at these latitudes, that made little enough difference, and the moon was up. The cave lay behind a high pinnacle of rock. From most angles, it was well concealed: if I had not been expecting to find caverns, and if I hadn't been used to sounding out terrain, I might not have spotted it. Whoever now stood behind the pinnacle was looking for something, with deliberate, measured movements. Human, I was prepared to bet, and not animal.

I sent out hunting sense and someone was there to meet it. I felt as though I'd been slammed into a wall of ice. Breathless, I withdrew, but the person who stood there had recognized me and I knew them, too. The Morrighanu commander, Glyn Apt.

'Sedra!' Her voice had that whipcrack command but it didn't work on me. But next moment I realized she hadn't spoken out loud. It was the sense of my name that she'd transmitted, not the word itself.

I liked Glyn Apt well enough. I didn't want to see her dead. But nor did I want to fight my niece over her and if Skadi woke, that would be the end of the Morrighanu woman. I stepped out from behind the rock and tried to look frail and old and afraid. I clutched at Glyn Apt and she steadied me by the shoulders.

'*Where is she?*' So Glyn Apt was not able to sense Skadi, then.

'I don't know,' I quavered. 'She . . . she took one of the sleds. She strapped me to it. I don't know what she had planned for me.'

'But you got away?'

'I chewed through the bonds. All she bound me with was a leather strap. Maybe she thought she wouldn't need anything else.' I wrapped my arms around myself, shivering.

Must be careful not to overdo it, though. 'Commander, I am sorry. She took me by surprise.'

Glyn Apt gave a curt nod of the head. 'You're not to blame. We need to get you out of here.'

'Where are the others? Are they with you?'

'No. I chose to go my own way. I got tired of encumbrances. I followed the sled tracks to the foot of the glacier, then came up here. If your niece is not here, I will take you back down and then return.'

I looked at her and saw the arrogance in her, so deep that it was almost buried. But I knew what that was like; I'd been that way myself, when I was younger. It's a road to death, so much of the time. 'You go first,' I said. 'I'm not sure of my footing on this ice. I'll follow where you tread.' A flicker of the hunting sense: Skadi was still asleep. I caught the twitch and quiver of a bloody dream.

The Morrighanu should not have turned her back on me, but it would have made little difference. As we began to descend, I called up the dream of snow, sending the first soft flakes to touch Glyn Apt's face. She looked up, puzzled, at the clear sky, and I conjured blizzard, sending it whirling out of the starry night. Glyn Apt stumbled, throwing an arm in front of her face.

'Sedra!' she called. 'This – it's come out of nowhere! We have to find shelter.'

'You go on,' I replied. 'Don't wait for me!'

The Morrighanu turned. 'I can't even see you!'

But then I saw what she had not. We were standing on a path of ice that wound down the glacier. The edge of this geographical track was close, dropping several times the height of a man. To me, it was clear enough, but Glyn Apt, believing in the blizzard, could not see it.

'Wait!' I shouted. 'Stay there!' But it was too late. The Morrighanu took a flailing step from the path, and fell.

I rushed to the edge of the drop. Glyn Apt was already far down the slope, tumbling over and over. When she reached the bottom, she lay still. I sent out hunting sense and found that she was still alive, but unconscious. She would not remain alive for long, in this cold, and I had no way of reaching her. I had intended only to distract her, not cause her death, but there was nothing to be done. Cursing, I left her lying there in the cold light and made my way back to the cave.

FORTY-THREE

Planet: Muspell (Vali)

Eld and I only found her because of the white bird. It plummeted towards us out of the greying sky and landed on Eld's shoulder. I thought I heard it whispering, and then it was gone.

'Automatic distress signal,' Eld said, grim-faced.

'From Glyn Apt?'

'Yes. I don't know what's wrong. It's given me her location.' He held out a hand and tossed an invisible *something* into the sky. Moments later, a raven materialized and flapped slowly off to the north-west. Using the sled, we followed, for though it was still the glowing arctic dark, the raven itself seemed to gleam and Eld told me that this was a function of its climatic regulators. I turned inward, to find the white bird in my own head, that little stolen snippet of Morrighanu tech, wakeful and watching.

We reached Glyn Apt after about an hour. She lay in a fold of snow at the bottom of a ridge. At first I thought she was dead, for when we gently rolled her over, her eyes were open and staring. The data stream was still except for a single trickle of numbers, and when I put a hand close to her mouth, I felt no stirring of breath.

'She's gone, Eld,' I whispered, but he shook his head.

'There's no sign of vital damage. A fractured shin and wrist . . . a lot of bruising. Probably concussion. But she's still alive.' Wings flickered and I got the image of a heart, beating slow, slow, as if frozen. 'She's put herself into stasis.'

'The Morrighanu can do that?'

'Can't the Skald?'

'Sometimes. But it's a rare ability.'

Eld shrugged. 'It's useful. Morrighanu often meet with accidents.'

'How long will she stay like this?'

'As long as she needs to. Months, if necessary. Or so they like to boast. I suspect it's more a matter of weeks, or even days. And she'll need to be brought round by someone else: she can't bring herself out of it.'

'So what are we going to do with her?'

'Put her on the sled. Send her to the edge of the ice. It's a clear run.' For a moment I thought he was advocating that we send Glyn Apt to her death in truth, but then he added, 'I'll ask the raven to reprogramme her bird. It'll take itself back to the warship. They won't be able to land but they can send a copter with someone on the end of a line.'

'All right,' I said. It didn't seem right to leave her here and if something happened to Eld and myself, at least Glyn Apt would be in a more accessible location.

We strapped her with care onto the sled and Eld sent the co-ordinates. The sled moved away and I watched it go: a strange sight, seeing that long narrow form hiss away into the arctic dark with the Morrighanu's shrouded body on it.

It reminded me of a funeral barge, gliding through the frozen waste. A light morning mist was creeping over the ice and soon the sled was lost to view. As soon as it had vanished, I turned to Eld.

'I'm not going back. First Idhunn, then Sedra, now Glyn Apt.' The names were like a rosary, beads on a killing chain.

Eld just sounded weary. 'She's going to be difficult to take down. You know that.'

'You said it yourself. All my enemies are dead.'

Eld gave a slight smile. 'All except myself.'

'Are you my enemy then, Eld?'

'Do you know,' the vitki said, as if the thought had only just occurred to him – I was sure it had not. 'I really don't know.'

'I'll take that as reassurance.' I'd only had two hours' sleep but I was wide awake, and itching to get going. 'She's up there, Eld,' I said. I could see where Glyn Apt had rolled down the ridge, perhaps in an effort to get away. 'She has to be.'

'Well, then,' he suggested, 'let's go.'

It was a hard climb, up over ice as smooth and sheer as glass, and ragged rocks. I was glad of the Morrighanu armour, feeling it rush and shiver across my skin in an effort to anticipate the next move and protect me. Eld, despite being older and (I considered) less fit, stayed close behind. We used a gravitational axe and pitons to get up the ridge, moving cautiously as we drew close to the summit. I did not want to find Skinning Knife's booted heel stamping down on my fingers. But we crested the ridge without incident and found ourselves standing on a narrow ledge of ice. It curved upwards, towards a thin, twisted spire like ice candy.

And I could feel her now, like a prickling on the air. Just as I'd felt Gemaley, a predatory presence moving through Mondhile's woods, close to her black fairy-tale tower. It was the same kind of sensation, but bloodier, more eager. It made me swallow, hard.

'Eld,' I said, without knowing what prompted me to say it, 'Stay here.'

'I don't think so,' the vitki replied, mildly. 'I think you've proved whatever you have to prove. I know you work alone. So did I. So did Glyn Apt. Note the use of the past tense. You are not alone now.'

And I hadn't been alone when Ruan had helped me on Mondhile, but even so . . . 'I have to face her,' I said.

'No,' Eld answered patiently. '*We* have to kill her.'

She was coming closer. I felt the blade of her sliding through the air. I turned my back on Eld and stepped around that pinnacle of rock.

But it wasn't Skadi who stood there. It was Sedra.

She did not bother to pretend. She said, 'She's not for you. Leave her. I'll take her from your lands.'

I didn't have to ask where, but I said it anyway. 'To Mondhile?'

'If her mother had been left alone, that's where she'd be. With her clan. Not someone born in a tank and raised in a cage.'

Maybe she would have been like Sedra herself: fierce, yes, but not mad. More like me, or so I liked to think.

'Sedra, you'd never get her off-world. How do you plan to get her away from Therm? A hidden wing which in any case you wouldn't be able to fly? You've seen the warship waiting. They have detection technology, they'd be able to trace you.'

Sedra shook her head. 'She's like wood washed up by the sea, twisted and wrong. But I can make her into something new.'

'Are you so sure? She's a born killer.' That was Eld, at my shoulder. Sedra looked at him. 'This is a matter for women, Eld. You've no place in this.' She spoke gently enough and so did Eld.

'So what did you tell Glyn Apt?'

'She fell. I didn't mean to make her fall, but she did and it's done.'

'She's still alive,' I said.

'Good.' I thought she meant it. 'I don't wish any of you dead. Just gone.'

Whatever Eld might have felt, given another few minutes, she might have convinced me. So much death already, so much destruction. Maybe you grow out of wanting to eliminate everyone who's ever hurt you. Or maybe you don't.

But then Skadi woke.

This time, because Sedra was evidently doing something to hold it back, I could see the process of illusion at work. Like the Morrighanu, like the vitki, Skadi used her birds. A huge predatory gull, beak razor-sharp, drifted out over the snow. I could see the reams of data flowing through it, but there was something else, too, lying deep within: a kind of glowing seed. I looked up past it to see Skinning Knife standing on the ledge outside the cage.

It was really the first time I'd seen her without her weaponries of illusion and terror, but she did not look ordinary. Now that I could see her more closely, I saw that she was nothing like Gemaley: tall and thin, yes, with pale hair, but her face was more rounded, less angular and harsh, the mouth delicate and long, and her eyes were black hollows, not beast-gold, with a spark deep within. She did not have Gemaley's smiling delight in death, at least, not at this moment. Her face was grave and concerned, as though she was about to perform some unpleasant but necessary task. I had, however, no doubt as to what that task was to be.

The bird shed its wings, then its flesh, until there was something red and writhing coming towards us across the snowbank, and then nothing more than a flying cage of bone with that shining thing where its heart should be. Then the bone, too, was gone and the shining thing dropped to the snowbank. It hissed as it went in as though it was a real object, something hot. I saw a flash of numbers, and then Frey was standing in front of me: my dead lover, alive again, the golden eye gleaming but the grey eye gone, torn from a mass of ripped flesh. Frey grinned at me and whispered something that I could not hear. I felt a touch of the old weakness in me, but then I saw the numbers again and knew that Sedra was reining the illusion in. Frey wasn't real, and I knew it, and my own seith rippled out and shattered the image into fragments.

Skinning Knife jumped down from the ridge. It was a drop of some fifteen feet to the ledge of ice, but she landed lightly in a crouch. I felt the rush of heat as Eld raised his weapon and fired, but she was already on the move.

'Skadi!' Sedra cried. I brought the gun up. Skadi, who had been ten feet away a moment before, knocked it out of my hand. She lashed out, but once more Sedra came between us. I saw a long, bloody slash appear in the old woman's chest. She went down into the snow. Eld fired again and Skinning Knife shrieked, high and thin like a wounded seabird. She was once more on the top of the ridge and this time I followed, scrambling up the icy slope. She fled into the cave and I saw her roll as she hit the floor. But when I reached the place where she'd been, she wasn't there.

I looked around me. The cave was a narrow funnel, running up into the rock wall. A warm breath came from it. I looked up, but Skadi wasn't clinging to the ceiling. The funnel was the only way out, apart from the cave's entrance, and I didn't think she could have slipped past me. If I fired, there was the danger of ricochet. I shouldered the gun and drew the knife. Now that I knew she could be injured, it gave me confidence. It made her real.

Not liking the idea of encountering Skinning Knife in complete darkness, I decided to risk switching on the armour light. I went up the funnel of rock, sending out with the seith ahead of me, but I couldn't feel anything. It was as though I was walking through a thick fleece, a cloud made solid but invisible. The path was steep and narrow, winding up into the heart of Therm, and it was getting warmer. I didn't mind that, but I wondered just how hot it was likely to become. Therm was supposed to be dormant, but it would be just my luck if it decided not to be. I had to keep remembering to look up, and behind, but there was no sign of pursuit, or assistance from Eld. That worried me. I'd never liked the idea of turning my back on a vitki, and now here I was hoping for it.

No sign that anyone had ever been this way, but Skadi had been wounded. She'd been bleeding, but there wasn't a trace of blood in the breastlight from my slickskin and I couldn't smell anything, either. The rock floor of the passage was smooth, as if something burning had flowed down it and fused it into glass. And the air was growing colder again, which suggested that I was once more nearing the outside world.

Then I spotted it. A single drop of blood, crimson against the black glass floor. As I watched, it hissed into bloody steam. So she had been this way, after all. She did not need to cover her tracks: they were doing it for her. My spine prickled. There was the fleeting odour of burning blood, then a clear breath of air from further down the passage carried it away.

The passage ended in an arch that looked both ancient and man-made, though I hadn't heard of anyone living in Therm besides Skadi. I switched off the light as soon as I saw the faint greyness ahead. I did not want to step through unprepared. The seith was still being blanketed and that told me she was there.

I edged forwards, closer and closer to the archway. I could

see straight ahead now, to where dawn light was illuminating a long ledge. I couldn't see what lay over the lip, but it had to be the wall of Therm, either inside or out. When I reached the arch I hesitated for a moment then went through in a roll, coming up again to stand beyond the doorway but closer to the edge. The knife was in my hand and ready.

At least I'd found out what was on the other side of the ledge. It lay above the caldera of Therm, and though the great hollow of the volcano was dark, there was a dim firecoal glow far, far below and the air was filled with the reek of old soot: it was like standing in Hellheim's chimney.

Skadi was there. She was crouching on the other side of the ledge, some ten feet away from me. I could see her panting, like a wounded dog, but I couldn't hear anything. Her eyes were fixed on me, as blank and glassy as the rock. It looked as though they were holes in her skull. She had a hand pressed to her side and blood was seeping through her fingers.

I didn't want a discussion. Apparently, neither did she. She got to her feet and the seep of blood was no longer in evidence. Next moment, she was standing in front of me.

Panic, not competence, saved me. I was simply and sheerly so afraid of her that the seith came up in a great shielding rush and my feet took me backwards. Her eyes widened: I'd moved much faster than she'd learned to expect. I slammed back against the rock wall. She was there again and I was not. I was trying to keep close to the cliff face, away from the edge of the caldera, but it was hard. She drove me round and round in circles, but understanding was finally kicking in. I'd faced the feir before, on Mondhile. I could see what she was doing, see the illusions that she was trying to cast. Frey again, then the Hierolath, then Gemaley – she must have looked at the Morrighanu records. She knew who I feared and why. She tried to cast my brother, but my memories of him were distant ones now: I glimpsed a sullen youth, a man's body but a boy's cruel face and he was just a kid, I thought with contempt. Then it was Idhunn who was standing before me, or trying to: it was like seeing someone through a tank of water, too slow and shimmering to be real, but melting down all the same to a pool of blood and broken bone. It was this last that sparked the real anger in me. I rushed Skadi, feinted with the knife, and this time she was the one to pull back.

She lashed out. There was a blade along the side of her hand; I caught sight of the surgical instruments that were her fingers, scalpels gleaming under fingernails, cutting ridges across her knuckles. Her hands were red with blood but it was her own.

I thought: *if you can be wounded, you can be killed.*

The illusions were failing, now. Her grasp on me was fading and the realization of it showed in her face. I kicked out and felt her knee go out from under her. She went down and it filled me with a cold exultation, until I realized that it wasn't emotion at all: there was something trickling down my side. I looked down. One of the blades had penetrated the armour. There was a long gash down my flank and it wept red. It made me stupidly slow; next thing I knew, I was flat on my back, hammered down against the rock, and she was over me. The blade was coming down, flashing in the growing red light, and I struck upwards into her face. I tore her cheek into a bloody flap. She made no sound at all. There was a cold cut across my arm, ripping the armour open again, but it was just one more scar, I told myself. I'd cut my own arm, often and over, and I laughed. Enough is enough. She was expecting continued avoidance. I leaped, caught her round the neck, and we rolled to the edge. She fought frantically, kicking and clawing, but I'd stopped caring what damage she did. I slammed her head onto the rock, put my knee in her side and shoved. She went over but as she did so, she clutched my wrist. Her full falling weight pulled my shoulder out of its socket and I screamed. The blades of her hand ripped into my skin, grating on bone, slipping on blood. If it hadn't been for that, she might have held on. At the last, her face wasn't anybody's but her own, and it was bestial, feral, feir, not human at all.

'You are the weapon now,' the beast said. Then she added something and there was a gannet flying upwards, its razor beak aimed at my face. I jerked back and the movement pulled my wrist out of Skadi's grip. The gannet was gone, but my head felt filled with feathers and a sudden blinding pain. I felt stuffed and flooded with knowledge that I did not understand.

Through it, I glimpsed Skadi going down into the caldera, falling and twisting in silence. I did not see her reach her death. I was too busy attending to my hand, clutching and crouching over it, trying to strap it up before I bled to death.

If it hadn't been for Eld, I probably would have done. He was on the ledge a moment later.

'She's gone,' I said. 'Where were you?'

'Sedra,' he said. He knelt by my side and put his hand over mine, which hurt until the slickskin crept over it, joining us by a thin film. Then it separated, leaving me with a coating of flexible armour to stop the bleeding. It hurt like hell, but I wouldn't die from it. Whether I'd use my hand again was another matter.

'Sedra? She's dead?'

'Unfortunately, not. She went for me. She's quite the fighter.'

'I thought her niece had done for her.'

Eld grimaced. 'So did I.' He helped me up. 'Where is Skadi? Down there?'

'Yes.' I didn't feel like giving a blow-by-blow account and Eld seemed to understand this. I did not look back down into the caldera. I did not want to see anything looking back at me, some last dying dream. Eld helped me along the passage and I leaned on him without shame. I was feeling increasingly light-headed, but all I could sense of Eld was a kind of calm relief, and nothing more.

Once we got out into the icy morning, the cold made me feel better, more grounded. That went the moment I saw Sedra.

I hadn't expected so much blood. It stained the surrounding snow, which crunched pink under my boots. I knelt anyway. Her eyes were open. She whispered, 'You are alive. That means she is not.'

'I'm sorry,' I said, meaning it. 'But for you, not for her.'

'Was it quick?'

'Quick enough. She fell.'

Sedra's eyes closed for a moment. 'Quick enough, as you say.' She hesitated. 'There are other young women in my clan. Good hunters, good fighters. It was never meant to happen, that my niece should live.'

'Sedra, I—'

'And good enough for me. Not illness, some pain. But to be killed by a member of my clan – some think it's an honour. I just think it's family.' And she grinned, and before I could say anything like *goodbye*, she died.

I stood, looking down at her. Her face was white as the snow, in death. I regretted it, almost as much as Idhunn's death.

'If you wished,' Eld said, 'we could have her body shipped back to Mondhile.'

'It's a generous offer, Eld.' Surprisingly so, but I didn't say that. I wondered whether we should let the glacier take her, or whether she would prefer to be with her niece in death. 'I think perhaps we should. But there's a war on.'

'Well,' Eld said. 'You know my views about the war. We'll take her anyway.'

I slept next to her corpse on the sled, all the way back to the coast. In my own sick dream state, she was company, and she spoke to me. I can't remember what she told me, but she said that the day would come when I would recall it. My enemies were dead, she said. I did not need the knowledge now.

Then it was cold confusion for a while. When my head was clear again, I was staring up at the riveted black ceiling of the Morrighanu warship. I sat up. Glyn Apt sat across from me: they must have brought her round.

'We're heading for Morvern,' she explained. 'Eld tells me he'd mentioned going to Mondhile.'

'That depends on the war.'

'The weapon is with us now,' Glyn Apt said. She rose, but paused as she reached the door. 'Rest. We'll decide what to do with you once we reach Morvern.'

The weapon is with us, now.

I am the weapon.

I could feel it, a coal-glow deep within, like that coal that Idhunn's avatar had given me, making my head burst with hurt. Some kind of genetic switch, encoded information, compressed inside my head and ready for release – and with that, I thought I realized why Skadi had run. She wasn't the key, as everyone had thought; she was the key-bearer. *And now, I was.*

The white bird endlessly circled the coal. It wouldn't take much to strip it from me. They'd shown me that already.

We had returned to the Morrighanu High Command. I'd been awake for some time, but all of a sudden I became aware that the old vitki was sitting opposite me in the cell, staring at me out of sea-ice eyes.

'So, you've noticed at last,' he said. 'I expected you to do better than that. You killed my girl, after all.'

'Was she ever yours?'

He shrugged. 'She was our weapon. Now you are. I thought highly of Skadi, and she had many useful abilities which you don't possess, but it seems she was more expendable than I thought.'

'Doesn't bode well for me, does it?'

He grinned. 'No.'

'What about the other one? The sister?'

'Ah, the sister from Nhem. I'm afraid she's gone beyond hope. Couldn't hold it.' *Poor Khainet,* I thought. *And poor Hunan.*

'What are you planning to do? Mine my head again?'

'You're a weapon,' he said, rising. 'You're to be activated.'

And then he was gone. I didn't even see him go. Later, Thorn Eld came to see me.

There had been a council of war, Eld told me. But when I said that I knew what they had planned for me, his gaze slid away and I wondered whether whatever tenuous bond had been created between us was now effectively over. I hadn't expected that to last, either. I was surprised at how desolate it made me feel though. But I was used to desolation, and I was not defenceless. I had the seith, still. I had the white bird. And I was the weapon.

When the guards took me up on deck, I was expecting to see the coast of Morvern, not the Rock. But there it was, rising out of the churning spring tide, a black crag with the round towers of the fortress clustering around it. Now, three warships bearing the insignia of Darkland rode at anchor around it, and further south, I saw something huge rearing from the sea: one of the war-wings I'd seen in the yards of Hetla. For the only time in memory that I'd set eyes on the Rock, my heart sank.

Tiree was still under siege, Eld said. The Rock was the first place to have fallen, which I found plain embarrassing. But given Idhunn's apparent antecedents, it was ironic, too. They wanted to experiment with the weapon. They thought it would be interesting, to do so where we had begun. The Rock was a confined space, with a limited population against which the vitki high command had long held a grudge. The weapon would be copied and then released from my head, and the prisoners of the Skald would lose awareness, enter bloodmind. The fortress would be like that town on Mondhile, the corridors running red. Sedra would have considered this normal; I did not. Or perhaps it would be like Nhem, and they could simply walk in and slaughter the prisoners like the sheep they had become.

And perhaps it would not work at all, but I couldn't rely on that.

Eld and Glyn Apt had no say in matters now, even if they were predisposed to do so. Though it was still a Morrighanu ship, the ones who came to take me to the Rock were valkyrie: glacial women in white armour with hair like blonde glass.

One of them, however, was Morrighanu: Glyn Apt's CO, the woman I'd last seen in a broch in Morvern, who had ordered Eld and myself to be shot – the woman who had been slain by Skadi, or so I'd thought at the time. I looked closely, at first not believing, but she was the same. Recognition sparked in her eyes when she saw me. It confirmed that suspicion I'd had, that they had called on Skadi's powers of illusion, to see how far others – vitki, Morrighanu, Skald – could be fooled. And that raised the question of just when Skadi had gone absent without leave: Glyn Apt had clearly not been in on the plan, and neither had the goat-girls. Was that simply a matter of Morrighanu sectarianism? I tried to catch Glyn Apt's gaze when the commander walked in, but she was staring straight ahead and would not look at me.

They did not speak to me, but put me in restraints and led me down to a small waiting wing. We bounced across the sea to the foot of the fortress, to those sea steps which I had climbed so often before, but never as a prisoner. The damage done by the selk's sonics was still evident to someone who knew the fortress, although the hole had been patched.

There were no signs of any other prisoners: I assumed that the women of the Skald were being kept deep inside the Rock, where I'd been imprisoned under Glyn Apt's brief reign. With Eld and Glyn Apt following, I was taken up the spiral stairs to the lamp room. Although Idhunn's broken body was long gone I could still feel her lingering presence, a rueful ghost perhaps, or only my own imagination. But the lamp room looked the same as ever, with the great light turning to alert passing ships of the Rock's presence, in the ancient way. From here, the war-wing looked even larger, bristling with weaponry as it rode the tide against a reddening sky.

I'd expected torture, but the pain was quick. The old vitki simply reached out his hand and my vision was filled with raven's wings. There was a needle-hot twist inside my mind and I felt the weapon flee further in. The raven disappeared. The old vitki looked as sour as old milk as he said, 'It's not working. She's hanging on to it.' It seemed to me that Glyn Apt gave a trace of a smile. Eld looked merely thoughtful.

The old vitki was wrong. I was not hanging on to the weapon; it was hanging on to me. I could feel it twining around my neurons, becoming part of me, linked somehow with Idhunn's coal. And the weapon whispered and promised: *blood, blood and more blood*. It was pure predator and now I understood how Skadi must have felt, even worse, probably given that she was feir. Impossible to shut it out, even with the seith.

They could not get it out, so they locked me in the lamp room with it while they debated what to do. Maybe they hoped I'd tear myself to pieces and save them the trouble. But I remembered Mondhile. I remembered townspeople running through the streets, ready to kill whoever they found, fighting tooth and nail with a pack of wild animals. I remembered the light going out behind a woman's eyes as everything she was drained away into the sink of the blood-mind, and I thought again: *enough*. I could feel it in me, waiting and whispering. It was almost like a presence in my head: it might have been a kind of meme, an information virus, but it felt as though it had a personality, somehow.

I went to the thick glass window of the lamp room and rested my face against it. The glass was cold, frosted on the outside with a tracery of winter lace. I could break it, maybe, shatter it if I could tear one of the metal struts from the lamp casing. There was no way down, in safety. Skadi's falling form came before my mind's eye, twisting, turning towards her death. Maybe it was time for that, I thought, but as I leaned against the window, with the great cold sea swinging under the little moon and the ships cresting the swell, I heard something singing.

The selk were back. I could see them, gliding through the waves at the foot of the tower. Their sentience would be gone now; they were migrating up through these northern waters towards the poles, shoals of them, unaware of the danger posed by the war-wings of Darkland. But their singing was as sweet as ever as they navigated through the strait and it gave me an idea. If the weapon could turn humans into animal-consciousness, if the weapon was no more than a switch, then why not the reverse?

I still had a bird in my head. The bird was a piece of code, but I'd learned that it could be a little more than that, a carrier of information. I sat by the window, and sank into the seith, and listened to the song of the selk, and I wove it all together as best I could. The weapon was a glowing coal, fragments of DNA twisting like a falling girl, turning within the coal's gyre as I placed it into the bird's beak and sent it from me. The weapon tore things as it went out of my head; I felt something shift and warp inside my mind. There was a vision of tattered rags and filaments fluttering behind the bird as it shot away and I believed that I saw the coal go within it: shooting through the glass like a meteor and out over the open sea. I saw the coal fall into the shoal of selk, just as a single feather had fallen in the great hall below me, and caused this fortress, too, to fall. A ripple spread out from the place where the coal had gone, lighting up the sea and the heaving bodies inside it. For a moment I felt the group consciousness of the selk as it changed from animal dark to something that was close to human. I felt them realize; I felt them *know*.

I'd used the weapon. I didn't know what the result would be, but now all I could do was wait.

It was quiet up there in the lamp room. I could hear the slow engine that drove the lamp, a humming from somewhere deep in the fortress. I almost thought I heard Idhunn's voice, a whisper in the shadows, and I turned, just as all hell broke loose.

All the glass in the lamp room was blasted inward. If I hadn't been sitting on the floor by now, it would have taken my head off. The sound ripped through my mind, causing me to clap my hands to my ears. Down in the fortress, someone was screaming. It was barely audible in the waves of sound. I staggered to my feet and held tight to the sill in the rush of freezing air that billowed through the lamp room. Below, there was a black arrow in the sea, a mass that after a moment I identified as the shoal of selk. The sound grew and grew. The Hetla war-wing was swinging around, the arrow of the selk coming to meet it. I saw its guns start to charge and flare, sparks springing down the flanges, but then a cavernous hole tore open in the wing's side.

The sonic song of the selk, that once before had sent vitki down into the icy water . . .

The wing tried to rise, but the sea was already pouring in. I watched as the wing tilted, listed, and rolled. It went down in an immense shower of spray, hauling a vortex after it. The Morrighanu ships heaved in the aftermath, and the arrow of the shoal bunched itself together and shot through the sea. I expected them to attack the ships, but they were gone, down the strait in the direction of Portree.

Shortly after that, when my ears were still ringing, Glyn Apt came to tell me that the Morrighanu command had ordered its forces back to Morvern. Given that, the vitki could no longer sustain their assault on the Reach. They fought hard, but so, I understand, did we.

Within a week, the war was over; a ceasefire declared between the nations of Muspell. The Skald was reinstated by the Morrighanu, a graciousness for which it was thankful, but which it never quite forgave. Glyn Apt had already gone, home to whatever quarters she had in Morvern. Eld stayed behind on the Rock, declaring himself a political prisoner of the Skald. He was, he explained, in enough disgrace to make going home an uncomfortable option.

'My fellow Skald are looking a bit oddly at me,' I told him. We were talking through a force field wall but I didn't really expect him to try anything. He'd been given one of the more comfortable cells.

'Well, what do you expect? You keep running off with vitki, after all.'

I sighed. I'd already discussed the situation at length with Glyn Apt, before she went home. She'd given a faint hint that the Morrighanu might not be entirely unreceptive if I wanted to seek exile, but I wasn't sure whether that was what I wanted, either. I'd like to have found that I'd healed my wounds, come to terms with the past, forgiven and forgotten, all those things. But life isn't tidy like that. Eld and I . . . I didn't know where that was going. I thought of him as a friend and even that felt like a betrayal of myself, after Frey.

And Idhunn's coal still sat deep within my head and I could not grasp it to see what it might contain.

'Running off, indeed.' I nodded towards the security camera and there was a flutter of white wings. 'Eld?' The raven made it to the edge of the barrier before the white bird met it. Shades of grey are an inevitable result in monochrome circumstances. I strolled out of the cell complex and left Eld to mull things over.

At midnight, I waited on the sea steps. I thought at first that the information transfer had failed, but then there was a blur of shadow and Eld stepped out of it.

'That looks like a Morrighanu wing,' he said, nodding to the sleek little craft at the edge of the sea steps. 'I hope your cameras are off.'

'I took precautions.'

He only asked me where we were going once we'd set off, which I thought showed a certain style. I told him.

'And the ship, too, that takes us up from Morvern – that will be Morrighanu as well?'

'Glyn Apt is a conscientious person, despite her faults. She understands obligation.'

Eld gave a thoughtful nod. 'It's generous.' And I agreed.

FORTY-FOUR

Planet: Nhem (Hunan)

Strange, to see my own world as a ball from space. Strange, too, to see Iznar again as the resistance ship flew low over it and headed south. What had seemed like such a great city, such a place of horror and wonder, now looked shabby: the buildings low and clumsy. Even the green domes of the Hierolath's palace looked fragile, like eggshells, and smaller than I remembered. It had been a matter of days since I had left Nhem and it felt like years.

But Iznar was only a glimpse, quickly gone. After that, we were heading south across the Great Desert, the place where I had long ago expected to die, before I came through the pass in the mountains and saw the city lying before the soot-black sea. And here it was again: the spiky turret of the bell tower, the sand-coloured roofs, the crumbling walls.

I had been afraid, somehow, that they would be sorry to see me back. But Tare embraced me and wept, and said that they had not known what had become of Khainet and myself, that they thought we must have died, or that she had killed me.

'There was always something about her,' Tare said. 'Something strange,' – and the other women nodded in solemn agreement. Well, Tare was right, at that. And when I told them exactly what that something strange had been – a tale that took us deep into the night with the tallow lamps guttering down – there was a much longer silence.

The three others had not stayed in the city. They had taken Mayest's body back to wherever they came from: not by boat, this time, but in an airship like the one I had flown in. The other women of the colony did not blame Khainet for killing Mayest, though perhaps they should have done. Mayest was different, they said, and had condescended too much. No one had liked her. I remembered it differently. But this was not the time for either point. I knew that, and yet I could not argue the case too hard.

Since then, no one from the resistance had been back to the city, until the day that I arrived. I told them that this would almost certainly change. For the women who had flown down with me had told me that more women would be coming – across the mountains, across the sea – as the cities that the men had ruled gradually sank into civil dispute and a growing war. The resistance would keep sending out the birds, those strings of information that I now knew had been given to them by the Morrighanu, and slowly those birds would find homes in women of a certain genetic line.

And what then? Would we end up fighting the male-run cities, as the resistance planned to do? Would we make weapons and vehicles, learn to mine the mountains or buy technology from sympathetic outworlders? Would we free the cattle-women, the ones like ourselves? And if we did, what would we do with them? They were not us. They were different from us.

'They would work,' Seliye said, when I voiced this thought. 'They would work as we do.'

'They would be *useful*,' someone else said, and several of the women nodded in agreement. *Wives*, I thought. They would be wives, except that they would be the wives of women and not of men. How soon would it be before another set of hierarchies developed? How soon before the women decided that they were tired of being the low folk, that it was somebody else's turn? And what about the women from the resistance, used to names and words and tools and ships. What if they came here to live? How long before we became the under-women ourselves?

I left the women of Edge discussing crops and growing, and what it would be like with more hands to help with the work, and I walked back to the bell tower through the steaming early morning. Tare had offered me a bed for the night but I wanted silence. The streets were quiet but there were lamps burning in the houses and I knew that people would still be talking about the news.

Tare and Seliye treated me a little differently now that I had come back again. I was not the old Hunan, the Hunan whom they knew. I had seen things that they found hard to imagine, been to places they had never dreamed of. I had new ideas, ideas which had come from beyond Edge – beyond Nhem – and I thought I had seen a faint flicker of unease passing across their faces like cloud shadow, the same expression that they had worn with Mayest. I wondered when the whispering would begin, but then I told myself that it was just that I was tired.

The bell tower had not changed. It was still a little cooler than the street, still rustling with dust and the echoes of the cries of the efreets. The goddesses were still patiently waiting on the wall. I looked at their unhuman faces and wondered who they had really been. They looked like nothing that I had seen on my travels. Just some dead race: alien, gone. Then, as though a switch had been flicked in my own head, I saw their pointed faces and hinged hands in the long beaks and wings of the efreets, and the capes were not capes at all, but wings. Not gone, after all, just changed.

They flickered in the torchlight as though they were alive and it struck me then that Sedra and I had been closer than we knew. Both of us had gone out into the world to die, but each time the world had gathered us up and swept us back into the thick of things again. Maybe now it really was time for me to go, or growing close. But not quite, not today. I climbed the steps of the bell tower and when I reached the platform where Khainet and so many others had held their naming ceremonies, I paused and looked out across my city. Lamplight and starlight, a creamy smear in the sky that told me of the approaching dawn. There was a wind blowing down from the mountains, smelling of rain and change. I did not look any more, but went into my chamber, and closed the door behind me. The room smelled damp, of roots and earth. I shut my eyes and waited for what dreams might come.

EPILOGUE

We buried her on Moon Moor, in the crumbling black soil under a cairn of stones. There was no sign of any life, except the endless circling of the carrion birds overhead. I was sure there would be future battles on which they could feed. None of the feir came swarming out to cast their dreams, or to investigate the Morrighanu ship that rested on the scrub. But when I placed the last stone on Sedra's cairn, I looked up and I thought I saw someone standing on the ridge. It was close to twilight, and hard to see very well. She was wearing armour, and one hand rested on the swell of pregnancy. Half her face had been torn away, but she was smiling. There was someone standing behind her, but I caught only a glimpse and only for a moment. Then they were gone, and Eld and I stood on an empty moor, with a crescent moon rising in the east and a spring wind blowing.